D1246350

SOUL IN DARKNESS

NEW YORK TIMES AND USA TODAY BESTSELLING AUTHOR
WENDY HIGGINS

Published by
Wendy Higgins

Image licenses from: Shutterstock.com ©conrado "Romantic blonde beauty wearing white dress" and © belletatyana "Ancient Greek Apollo Temple in Side city, Turkey"
Graphic Design by: Jennifer Munswami © J.M Rising Horse Creations

BOOKS BY WENDY HIGGINS

YOUNG ADULT TITLES

Sweet Series from HarperTeen:
(upper YA Paranormal Romance)
Sweet Evil
Sweet Peril
Sweet Reckoning
Sweet Temptation

Eurona Duology from HarperTeen:
(upper YA Fantasy)
The Great Hunt
The Great Pursuit

Indie Published Standalone:
(upper YA Irish Urban Fantasy)
See Me

Standalone from HarperTeen
(YA Contemporary Romance)
Kiss Collector

ADULT TITLES

Indie Published Trilogy:
(Adult Urban Fantasy/Science Fiction Romance)
Unknown
Unrest
Undone

DEDICATION

To the guy in my creative writing class at George Mason University who told me everything I wrote was cliché—I still remember your expression as you looked down at my stories in front of you, trying to get a laugh out of the other literary writers, poking fun at the romance genre. Words have power, but sometimes insults become stepping stones. Without meaning to, you forced me to fight harder to elevate myself. The memory of you is a constant reminder to use my words to lift others, not tear them down.

So, thanks.

AUTHOR NOTE

I read many, many versions of the Cupid/Eros mythology, namely *The Golden Ass: Being the Metamorphoses of Lucius Apuleius*. Some of them were vastly different, with contradicting details. And many of the versions left me wanting, questioning, confused about a character's motives. I did what all authors have to do when they choose to write a retelling; I went with the details that felt right for my particular version of the tale, borrowing a little from here, a lot from there, and making up some things of my own. I hope you will forgive any wavering from your preferred account of the story.

Ultimately, the version I found most aligned with my vision used the Roman names, so I went with "Cupid" for the god of love versus the Greek form of "Eros."

I hope you enjoy the incredibly romantic mythology of Cupid and Princess Psyche (Sy-key/Sie-kee) as much as I do! Happy reading, friends.

"There is musick, even in the beauty and the silent note which Cupid strikes, far sweeter than the sound of an instrument."

~Thomas Browne

Prologue

The Third Daughter

On an island in the Aegean Sea during the Roman Empire, warm cypress winds blew across the cerulean Mediterranean, welcoming the isle's third royal daughter. Never had such a beautiful child been born. Her mother, the queen, and every nursemaid present gasped at the sight of the babe's perfectly formed face, lacking any of the usual misshapenness or wrinkles of newborns.

A sea breeze gusted through the arched windows as if even the lands sighed in awe. Full lips like pink blossoms. Chestnut waves of silken hair. Eyes round with golden flecks, surrounded by long, coal lashes.

Unlike the queen's first two daughters, this child had no bout of frenzied crying when she entered the world. She was quiet, almost contemplative as she stared with rapt attention at each woman who held her. The absolute peace of her arrival was like a breath of fragrant air. And so, the queen named her after the word for *breath* and *soul*.

Psyche. Like a whisper…*Syy-keyy*.

As with the births of their first two daughters, the king and queen of the isle brought gifts and sacrifices to the temple of Venus, goddess of love and beauty, to thank her for their child, imbued with aesthetic fortune. For years they had been barren, yet faithful to the gods, earning themselves the gift of three daughters. But prolonged times of blessing had a way of making the most grateful hearts take for granted that which they once held high. Soon, their attention was only for the child, growing more stunning with the passage of time, and Venus's role in their lives was forgotten.

All eyes and hearts on the island, royal or servant, belonged to Psyche. Even as a toddler, the youngest princess had a way of giving her full, unguarded attention to whomever she spoke, making them feel honored, even breathless. None could take their eyes from her. As she grew into a youth, word of her loveliness spread far and wide, bringing visitors to the island in hopes that they might catch a single glimpse of her famed beauty.

But what most saw as a holy fortune from the gods, gifted to this royal family, was not viewed as such by Psyche herself. For the third princess, physical perfection was not a talent or a blessing. Beauty was her curse.

PART ONE

PSYCHE

"She is a mortal danger to all men. She is beautiful without knowing it and possesses charms that she's not even aware of. She is like a trap set by nature—a sweet perfumed rose in whose petals Cupid lurks in ambush! Anyone who has seen her smile has known perfection. Venus in her shell was never so lovely…"

~Cyrano de Bergerac

CHAPTER ONE

FREEDOM SEEKING

I ESCAPED THE GUARDS AGAIN.

By now they knew all the places to look for me, and they'd no doubt find me soon. Still, I laughed as I sprinted to the side of the cliff, my stomach tightening in anticipation of the fall to come.

With a scream of exhilaration, I leapt, never stopping, and soared into the blue sky, legs kicking, gauzy skirts whipping, stomach swooping. The salted air pulled at my face as I flipped to dive downward. I sliced sharply through the surface, caught in the warm arms of the lagoon. Deep under water, my lungs constricted in a satisfying way as I kicked, making it to the top in time to inhale and wipe my eyes. I peered up as I bobbed on the water and laughed at the three worried faces above. The guards never dived after me. I supposed if I were floating, dead, or failed to resurface they would jump to my rescue, but it was always the same. Me smiling up. Them frowning down.

I enjoyed another minute of seclusion as they quickly scaled down the side of the rocky cliff and stood at the edge of the lapping water, muscled arms crossed, guarding me once again as I paddled on my back, the thin fabric of my dress swishing soundlessly around my body. Their frowns softened as they looked upon me.

"Why must you give us such a fright, Princess?" Boldar asked. He was one of the oldest royal guards, as old as Papa, the king of our isle, and he spoke to me with barely concealed adoration, exactly as he had since I was a young girl.

"For two minutes each week, I must have my freedom or I will perish."

All three men attempted to scowl at my dramatics but failed.

"You need but ask," Boldar said. "And we shall escort you anywhere your heart pleases."

"That's not nearly as fun," I said, running my hand along the water surrounding me. What my heart sought above all else was a chance to be alone in nature, and to be looked upon as an ordinary girl.

Well, I suppose "ordinary" was a lot to ask as a royal, but at the very least to be looked upon as my sisters were. Both were pleasing to the eye. People respected their talents—Dawn with her music and Miracle with her paintings—people conversed with them, speaking of literature, art and philosophy. If I attempted to speak of those things I got bizarre smiles and incoherent mumbling, eyes raking me from top to bottom. Even the women. I wasn't a person to them. I was an object. After seventeen years I should have been used to it; however, I wasn't. In every person I met, every new face, I sought the one who would finally lock eyes with me and see through to my soul within.

Until then, under the sky, in the ocean, among fields of wheat, with the animals, I was accepted, and I was alive.

I sucked in a breath at the feel of a nibble against my toe. Small, bright colored fish hesitantly approached, their toothless mouths touching my feet and legs with curiosity. I was careful not to kick out at their tickling touches, but I giggled furiously.

I truly did believe I'd perish without these outings. Craggy cliffs shielded this deep lagoon of crystalline waters. It was peaceful in its ominousness, closed in like a dangerous, well-kept secret.

When the guards raised their chins and nudged one another

about something they saw at the entrance of the shaded lagoon, I knew my friends had arrived.

I turned and smiled at the two dolphins, laughing as they circled me, sliding past and nudging me with their smooth noses. I always recognized the larger animal by the deep scar near its left eye.

"Hello beautiful and handsome. Lovely to see you, as always."

My older sister, Miracle, used to shriek and swim frantically to shore when the dolphins came to us. She loved to watch them from afar, but up close they frightened her with their wild power. Miracle was also too cautious to ever jump from the cliffs. Dawn, the middle child, was half as cautious, jumping when she felt the whim. As for sea life and other animals, she wasn't afraid, but neither was she outgoing. I think she wanted animals to like her, to come to her, but she found it hard to simply relax.

Dawn watched me with animals in the same way she watched me with men—too closely. Enviously. When it came to males, I did everything possible to quell her jealousies. I tried not to smile. I dressed modestly. I opted out of conversations. I swear, I attempted to be as boring as possible.

But no matter what I said or did, men stared at me with that same lost look on their faces. Mesmerized. Like I was a piece of art hanging in our castle to be gazed upon. I hated it. And I hated how my sister Dawn could never see how much I didn't want any of it. Miracle understood. Perhaps because she was older, so there was less competition between us. But I'd spent a good part of my life trying to make Dawn understand me, seeking her full acceptance, yet always falling short.

When it came to animals, however, I couldn't bring myself to downplay the connection for the sake of Dawn or anyone else. Wild beasts wouldn't understand my brush off. They accepted me wholly and paid no mind to my beauty. For that, I would forever reward them with my affections.

"How do you get them to come to you?" the youngest guard asked. He stared so intently he probably wouldn't have noticed if an army attacked from behind. "I've never once been approached by a sea creature."

"It helps not being a brute. The three of you probably swim with your swords on, grunting and splashing about."

They laughed, taking no offense.

One of the dolphins squeaked at me until I took him by his fin and he darted ahead. A peal of laughter gurgled from my mouth as water sprayed up and I held on tight, being pulled around the lagoon.

"Not too far!" Boldar shouted. "It's nearly time for dinner and your father is expecting guests!"

My heart sank at the reminder of Dawn's courtship dinner. I grumbled to my friends, "I have to go." Papa believed this was the match. A prince from the mainland with grape vines and olive trees as far as the eye could see. Even Miracle and her husband, Alesandro Christos, a prince from a land near Constantinople, would be visiting. And while I adored time with my sisters, I loathed large gatherings.

When we neared the shore, I kissed each dolphin and patted their backs before swimming until my feet could touch the bottom. I trudged onto the pebbled sand. At least I felt like I was trudging, but from the outright stares of the three guards, a symphony had erupted overhead with me swaying toward them in a sensual dance. I crossed my arms over my chest, causing Boldar to blink and then smack the other two with the backs of his hands.

The men ripped their eyes from my body and cleared their throats, motioning me ahead of them. I squeezed out my long hair as I walked and flapped the fabric around my hips, trying not to let it stick to my backside. They'd seen me soaking wet countless times, yet the shock never seemed to lessen, especially since I'd entered my seventeenth year.

I breathed deeply of the fragrant flowering bushes that grew wild along the path, trying to clear my head. On one side was the hill where our fortified lands stood, enveloped in a wall of earthworks overlooking the cliffs. Within those walls was our castle of stone and the town market with the homes of our wealthiest merchants. On the other side of the path, guarded by thick brush, was a sheer drop to the sea—vibrant in the spring sunshine, glistening in bright shades of blues and greens. No person could be called beautiful in comparison to what the gods made and oversaw.

Up ahead on the worn path, the deep braying of hounds broke out. I smiled as Olive and Berry charged down the trail on long legs, tails wagging as they approached me for scratches behind the ears. They licked sea water from my arms, sniffing me all over as I walked.

In twenty paces, we would take a heavily guarded side door that tunneled beneath the castle and into our royal lands. Never could I walk the entire path to the open beaches and fields. Never could I ride a horse through the isle's countryside, stopping to pick wild apricots and figs hanging heavily on trees, waving to commoners the way my sisters or parents could. Even flanked by guards, my presence always caused a disturbance.

Someday things would be different for me. Once Dawn was married it would be my turn. I would have a prince of my own and a home with more freedom. Once I was married, men would be forced to see me as a wife, a woman of value, not a maiden for their ogling. Someday.

CHAPTER TWO

PRINCE OF SOMEWHERE

BEING LATE TO DINNER WAS THE WORST THING I COULD have done. I'd rather have been seated when everyone arrived, but alas, my grand entrance caused every eye in the room to lock onto me, even in layers of cream fabric up to my neck.

"I apologize for my delay." I gave a small curtsy before glancing across the faces. Next to Dawn sat a slightly balding prince, his fine blue toga wrapped with a belt of gold to match the gold ringlet over his head. He stared openly, lips parted. When Dawn glanced from him to me, and back to him, I quickly looked away.

And there was Miracle, beaming next to her husband. She kept her curls short in the Roman style and swirled across her head with gold leaf pins.

I knew I should wait for introductions, but I couldn't help myself. I ran to her, hugging her and laughing as she kissed my cheek.

"So good to see you, Sister," I said.

"And you. Were you swimming in the lagoon again?"

I smiled, then glanced over when I heard Papa clear his throat. I knew my lateness bothered him, but when he looked upon me, all traces of anger evaporated into fatherly adoration.

"Prince Drusus, this is our third daughter, Dawn's younger sister. Psyche."

I gave the barest of glances toward our guest prince. "How do you do?"

"*Psyche.*" My eyes darted to him once more, a shiver of apprehension rippling across my skin at the way he said my name. His brown eyes bore into me. "The rumors have not been exaggerated."

I peeked at Dawn, whose jaw had locked as she stared down at her plate. Papa and Mother, oblivious as always to the discomfort, both laughed with pride and took one another's hand on the table top.

"Yes, well," I said, swishing into my seat beside Mother. "Have you had the honor of hearing Dawn sing yet? Her voice is heavenly. I couldn't carry a tune if you placed it in a basket for me." That last bit was all truth, though my lack of ability didn't stop me from singing. I actually loved when my sisters teased me about it. Everyone around the table chuckled.

Dawn finally lifted her eyes, and we shared a small smile. I still felt her prince's eyes on me and couldn't help being irked as my sister sat there, radiant in peach silk, her cheeks rosy, hair painstakingly curled into ringlets and pinned up.

"You're a bloom this eve," I told her before eyeing Prince Drusus. "Don't you agree?"

"Hm?" He broke his staring reverie to look around, glance toward Dawn, then back at me with a partial smile. "Oh, um, yes."

I clasped my hands tightly in my lap and vowed not to give him attention the rest of the night. Foolish, foolish man. Then I looked up at the assortment of food and spotted my favorite.

"Cake!" The table tittered their amusement as I eyed the fluffy white dessert with sweet cream drizzled over top. I'm fairly sure the sight caused my eyes to twinkle.

"Not until after the meal, darling," Mother said with fondness.

As dinner progressed, I remained silent with my head down,

eating every bite of fish and greens on my plate as the men spoke of Roman conquests and expansion, wondering when everyone would finish so we could cut into the cake.

"You have quite an appetite, Psyche," Dawn's prince murmured from across the table. "How do you keep such a figure?"

He likely meant it as a compliment, but my cheeks heated, and Dawn's face fell again. Half of her food was untouched.

"She is young still," Miracle said, giving me a wink. She had plumped up the slightest bit since marriage, especially in her hips and chest, and I looked forward to the day when I would as well. Thankfully Father asked the suitor his opinion about weaponry, and the men went back to war talk.

Once "pleasantries" were over, and I'd devoured my delicious plate of sticky cake, I couldn't excuse myself from the table fast enough. Followed closely by Boldar and his two younger guards, I headed straight for the one place nobody would find me.

The archery range.

I wasn't able to take a solid, full breath again until I passed through the stone archways into the open-air courtyard surrounded by the castle walls and lined with windmill palms and long feather grasses.

It was always empty this late in the day. During the early hours all of Papa's soldiers were out there honing their skills, arrows whizzing toward fake soldiers and horse targets made of hay. I chose one of the smaller bows from a wall of weapons hung on wooden racks and examined the quivers.

"Must you?" Boldar asked.

I understood his apprehension. When I was eleven, Papa found me sparring with a ten-year-old boy using real swords. Dull, but real. I'd never seen my father turn so red, nearly purple.

"You could hurt yourself!" he'd shouted, no doubt worried I'd somehow mar my skin with scars.

"But look, Papa! Watch how good I am! No boy can best me!"

He'd snatched the hilt from my small hand and frowned. "A woman with a sword is as useless as a teat on a boar. Get inside with your sisters. Don't you have music lessons?"

The only thing that kept me from touching a sword again was knowing the boy I'd sparred with had been whipped. I'd talked him into fighting me, and he'd been punished for it. I'd given Papa the silent treatment for weeks afterward, then taken up the bow instead, a solitary hobby. After I became quite good, I announced at dinner one night that I'd taken up archery in secret, and nobody could stop me.

"Archery?" Miracle had laughed. "Will you chop your hair and join the army?"

"Don't jest!" Mother chided, clearly horrified at the possibility of my ruined hair and need for rebellion.

"If ever we are attacked, I will join the archers to protect our home."

"You most certainly will *not!*" Papa had bellowed.

Dawn had giggled behind her hand as I stared him down until he softened and shook his head with a huff. I'd been twelve at that point, already appearing older than other girls my age, able to stop men in their tracks when all I wanted to do was run barefoot with my hair down, tangled by the salted winds.

Five years later, my arrows always found their targets. I took pride in the *twang* of a strong release, each *thwump* of the arrowhead embedding into the hay, and the thrill of challenging myself to shoot faster from farther away.

When my quiver was empty, my chest rose and fell with exertion. I looked at the three guards. They comically stood side by side, armored arms crossed, surveying arrows sticking out from the dummies' eyes.

"If only half my men had such steady arms and impeccable

aim," Boldar murmured.

I walked to the hay figures to retrieve the arrows. "I wish to go to the market tomorrow."

All three guards groaned. The seaside market was always bustling with islanders, foreign travelers, and soldiers. In the past year, the number of visitors had drastically risen.

"They will be looking for you," Boldar warned. "*You* are the reason they come."

I swallowed hard, regret slithering through me. For over a year, I'd doubted and denied the claims that people came to our island from far and wide to see me. I was a mere mortal girl. The very idea was ridiculous. And then the gifts began. Each week, Boldar gathered wreaths of flowers, small hand-carved maidens of wood I assumed were me—the long hair being the giveaway, and even live goats and sheep adorned with ribbons. He brought the offerings from the castle grounds entrance to me.

Papa and Mother laughed with glee as each week the gifts became more preposterous.

"You're their own personal goddess in the flesh," Mother had said, running a hand over my hair. I'd yanked away from her at the dangerous comparison.

"I am no goddess. I don't want any of this!"

"Don't be ungrateful," Papa had chided.

"It's not a matter of gratefulness," I'd told him. My hands were in fists of frustration, words of explanation eluding me. "It's just...*wrong*." How could they not see?

But Mother had only laughed as if I were being silly, and Papa kissed my head, telling me not to fret over harmless flattery. After that, I ordered Boldar to donate any live gifts back to the market folk. As for the other baubles, I didn't even want to see them. I was certain my parents were giving far more than this in their offerings to the gods, and I hoped Venus felt honored that my "gifts" were given back to the poor.

I looked at Boldar now, the worry in his eyes stabbing me with guilt.

"I can't stay cooped up in these walls forever," I said. "You know I'll lose my mind." I chewed my lip in thought as he frowned. Two months ago, when I had visited the market I was swarmed. Nobody wished me harm, but it had frightened my guards. In retrospect, it had been quite comical to see the three strong men being swept away from my side by peasants and street people excitedly trying to get closer to me. But that was the only humorous part about that day. I'd been sickened by the push of bodies, the tear-filled eyes devouring me, the voices calling my name in absolute reverence.

I shivered at the memory. "I'll tie back my hair and wear peasant's clothing." All three men chuckled, and I glared at them. "Why is that amusing?"

"Because no clothing will hide your face," the youngest said.

"I'll wear a hood of muslin cloth and keep my head down."

"We'll have to bring more soldiers," Boldar insisted. "I won't be separated from you again."

I sighed. "If I'm crowded by an army of soldiers it will draw attention. You can alert the others and have them spread about the market or somewhere nearby, if you must, but give me space."

Boldar grumbled, making me smile up at him.

"Just think," I told him. "In a year I'll be married off and you won't have to be ordered about by me anymore." The thought soured my mood.

His menacing scowl fell away, replaced by something akin to sadness.

"I know," I said, patting his broad shoulder. "I'll miss you too."

Chapter Three

Handsome Stranger

OH, HOW I ADORED THE MARKET. THE LYRICAL SHOUTS of vendors' voices on the air. Laughing children running about with honeyed faces, waving sticks fashioned with ribbons. The scent of everything from shellfish to fresh herbs to food stalls where onions sizzled in deep pans. I smelled everything I could get my hands on. Bottles of lavender water. Candles with rosemary-infused wax. Mint oils to rub on one's chest and feet during the sickness season.

I kept my hood low and my face down. Now and then I'd slide coins across a table to obtain items I knew Mother would never buy: deformed bottles and hand-colored scarves imperfectly sewn by local women with arthritic fingers and not enough money for proper glass forges. Mother's goods came only from the mainland.

I felt the presence of Boldar and the other guards—more men than I'd requested—but they kept their distance. Their eyes on me felt overly obvious, but people were so involved in their own business that nobody seemed to notice. They would never expect one of the princesses to be walking alongside them at the market in a plain cloak that hung low over her face. The thrill of it never ceased.

Two hours into my excursion, and my basket was nearly filled with interesting, one-of-a-kind items. My favorite stall was saved for last. I approached the trinkets, reaching out to touch a wooden flower.

"Don't touch unless your hands are clean," the old crone snapped. "And I've got a stick long enough to whack anyone who tries to pocket the goods." The vendor rapped a thick stick upon the table's leg.

Without raising my head, I replied, "Yes, madam."

Then she was quiet, allowing me to browse the animals and items, ranging from the size of an actual cat to as small as my palm.

"Do you carve them yourself, madam?" I asked.

She grunted in response. "My husband and son do."

I ran my finger over the beak of a wooden gull. "They're quite good."

Another grunt and we spoke no more. I grinned to myself as I took up a tiny mountain lion cub. That was the exact moment I felt another person sidle up beside me. I tilted my head just enough to see the form and arm of a man. He took a lion bauble in his hand, running a finger along the mane. A bizarre sense of affection and heated, buzzing sensuality came over me and I had to swallow, shocked at my ridiculous reaction to a stranger. His hands *were* nice, and his forearms appeared strong, but such a tiny glimpse hardly warranted my body's strong response.

"Just looking," he said, his harmonious voice giving me a jolt. I nearly looked up, but realized he was talking to the vendor, not me. "I've never been to your island. It's quite beautiful. I'm here for the day, passing through."

Gods alive, his voice. It was warm and sultry, making me shiver under the mid-day sun. His accent was…worldly. Definitely a traveler. It'd been a long while since a male had piqued my curiosity. I turned a tiny fraction to try and see as much of him as I could without showing my face. His build was semi-tall and lean. I felt such a strong pull to move closer and look up that I scolded myself internally.

"That's a cute one you've got there." His perfect hand pointed to the cub between my fingers and I gasped inaudibly, setting it down quickly. I checked to be sure my shawl was still in place, as if that would avert his attention from me.

"Sorry," he chuckled. "Didn't mean to startle you."

He spoke to me so normally, his voice lacking the mesmerized awe to which I'd become accustomed. I let out a shallow laugh of relief, realizing he hadn't recognized me.

"It's okay," I finally responded, picking up the wooden cub once more. "This one reminds me of something that happened when I was a child."

"And what's that?" He leaned forward enough for me to see the bottom half of his face. I bit my bottom lip, momentarily stunned. I wasn't one to care about male beauty. Most of the handsome boys and men I'd met in my life had egos to match, and I found prideful males to be undesirable. That wasn't the impression I got from this stranger. I was actually considering telling him the story, which made me laugh again, my nerves fraying. Oh, Hades, why not? I peered down at the cub, remembering.

"When I was small, I came across an injured mountain lion cub and brought it home. My parents were furious and scared to death—its claws were enough to shred me—but I insisted on nursing it back to health. So, I did. And it never once scratched me, though I can't say the same for my room's furniture. I cried when I had to set it loose."

I waited for him to laugh. To exclaim how foolish the female mind was. When he didn't, curiosity got the best of me, and I lifted my chin enough to look at him. I'd only intended a quick glance, but the full effect of the handsome stranger's dark features had my eyes darting back to him as soon as I'd pried them away.

For a long moment I searched his face as he searched mine. Whenever I met a male, it began with a sliver of hope that he might see past my appearance. That hope was never long lived. Each and every time, their eyes, then their bodies, then their minds went through a sickening sort of metamorphosis. I waited for the man's dark eyes to glaze over, his mind to turn to enamored mush, and his body to spring into lustful possession, but he remained upright and clear eyed.

My heart set out on a nervous jog that turned into a sprint. What I felt from him was curiosity. Interest. Those were new to me. I had to look away. The handsome stranger still hadn't responded to my childhood tale, and I began to feel like an idiot.

"I know," I said, giving the precious cub one last look. "It was silly."

"What?" His chin moved side to side. "No. I don't consider a tender heart to be silly."

He didn't? Who was this man? I allowed myself to fully stare at him. In that moment, it was as if the two of us were in a bubble. Even with my face lifted, on display, nobody noticed me. Not the stall owner. Not passersby. Even my guards were keeping their distance. I felt miraculously alone with him. Intimate, even, especially as he studied me. I needed to know everything about him. We both opened our mouths at the same time.

"Where are you from?" I blurted as he asked, "What is your name?"

What is your name? Of all the questions he could ask. My parents said my name was well-known, even deep into the mainland. I dropped my eyes. I couldn't chance telling him who I was. Not yet.

"I'm nobody," I whispered. He blessedly didn't press, so I peered up into his tanned face again. "What is your name?"

"Leodes," he said.

Without meaning to, I repeated his name back to him, tasting each letter… "Leodes."

His eyes widened the tiniest bit, his reaction making me smile because it all felt so sincere. I'd done a lot of people-reading in my life, and I thought…my gods…this young man might like me. Me. Not Princess Psyche, the name and human idol. Just a girl in a cloak talking about nothing.

But as I stood staring at his open face, it was like a sudden shadow passed over him. His body stiffened. His throat bobbed with a hard swallow.

"I've lost track of time. My boat will leave without me."

My mind raced, panic overtaking me. He couldn't go yet! I had to find out where he was from without being too forward. I began to babble without thinking. "I didn't mean to keep you with my stories, sir. Thank you."

"For what?" he asked.

"For…" What could I say without sounding desperate and sad? Well, I'd been honest so far. May as well continue. "Listening." No male had ever truly listened to me. The kind of listening that went hand-in-hand with caring.

And just as I was about to ask from where he hailed, his eyes bore into mine and an urge hit me with acute power, shrouding all my other thoughts. There had been one area of the market I'd avoided—the animal farmers. And I suddenly had a huge desire to visit the pig stall. Why? I blinked. Piglets! Yes, that's it! There had been other things on my mind I'd wanted to ask him, but they seemed of little importance now. I *had* to see the piglets.

"I must go, too," I told the intriguing stranger. "I wish you safe travels."

He turned from me, and I turned from him, lowering my face and tugging the hood of my cloak lower. As I walked, feeling sluggish and heavy, my mind became as muddled as the port on a foggy morning. I couldn't think. All I could do was move through the throng of people to the pig stall on the other side of the market. I barely registered my guards following me, still keeping their distance.

I stopped outside of the stall, the pig excretions burning my nose. My arms and legs weighed me down, and my skin prickled as if I'd just walked into a patch of shade after being baked by the sun. I blinked, confused. I needed to be right here at this moment, but why? It was like the sensation of being stuck inside a dream. I felt as if I were being watched, but I couldn't move my head to peer around, or get my limbs to work.

The pig farmer caught a glance at my form as he shoveled a mess of hay into a cart. "What do you wannn..." He peered closer and must have seen I was a young female, though I kept the top of my face hidden. "Hello, my dear." His gruff voice turned sickly sweet, churning my stomach.

What *did* I want? My eyes moved across the area to where the larger pigs and piglets had been penned. One spotted piglet, in particular, was running in circles in the small space, bumping the door and sides until the door fell open and he came sprinting out. I nearly giggled at his adorable snorting sounds of freedom.

The farmer turned and shouted, "Damned vermin!" and kicked the piglet, making it fall to its side with a loud cry.

A guttural scream escaped me, and I covered my mouth as he manhandled the baby pig back into the pen, shutting it with hands that appeared swollen. Then he jutted out his belly with his hands on his hips, giving me a grayish smile of rotted teeth. I dropped my hands as my head seemed to clear a fraction.

"You didn't have to kick the poor thing!" I shouldn't have spoken to him, but in my anger, I'd blurted it out. At least I kept the top half of my face hidden.

"No worries, Miss, they don't feel pain the same as us."

"I don't believe that."

"Say, what's your name, Miss?" The pigman licked his lips. "You seem familiar."

My name. *My name.* What in great Hades was I doing here talking to this cruel man? In a flash, my mind cleared, and I straightened, feeling my strength return just in time for a strong wind to whip through, clattering stall hangings and forcing people to grab belongings. My hood wrenched back, and I turned, hiding my face, but my hair was loose. I felt it lash out around me, the leather strap coming loose to unleash the long strands. I rushed to snatch my hair and shove it back into my hood, yanking the fabric over my face again. The pig farmer let out a gasp, and I turned from him. I had to get out of here.

"Hey!" the farmer called out as I turned, which made me move all the quicker.

He shouted again. "Don't you know it's rude to walk away from a man without responding?"

I hardly cared how rude I appeared. I don't think he figured out who I was, only that I was a young woman. I saw Boldar's feet nearing me, but he didn't stop. He seemed to want to shut the farmer's mouth, so I grabbed his arm and hissed, "Let him be."

"What were you even doing there?" he asked.

"I...I don't know. I suppose I wanted to see the piglets."

But I was deeply shaken the entire walk back to the castle. What on Earth would cause me to want to leave the presence of the handsome stranger, especially when I'd wanted so badly to learn more about him, and to bring myself to the pig stall instead? My heart stuttered as my stomach swam sourly. Is this how people felt when their minds began to go? Was I ill? How could I let go of an opportunity to know a man who saw more in me than my looks?

I halted and turned to my youngest guard, the fastest runner. "Do you recall the man I spoke with at the wood carving stall?"

His eyebrows drew together. "I believe so."

"His name is Leodes. He was set to board a merchant ship. Run to the port and find him. Learn where he is from and where he is headed. Delay the ship if you must. Do you understand?"

He didn't appear happy about it, but he nodded. "Yes, Princess."

"Quick! Go!" He left us at a sprint and I let out a sigh. Perhaps all was not lost.

Boldar grumbled. "Your father will not approve of you seeking a strange merchant."

I hardly cared. "He will if he's rich."

Another grumble. "Come along."

I allowed the guards to lead me the rest of the way, hope filling my heart to overflowing.

I will find you, Leodes.

I sent up a silent prayer to Venus, the goddess of love, as I paced within the palace gates.

"Princess, I implore you to come to the castle," Boldar begged. "It could take a long while for him to check every ship in the port." We'd even sent a crew of others to help him search. That was an hour ago. I sat on a low stone wall making a ring of flowers from the wild weeds.

"I am perfectly safe right here within the walls, Boldar. Leave me if you must."

He let out a masculine sigh and sat. I pressed my lips against a laugh when his stomach gurgled with hunger. "Oh, go on. I've held you back from the mid-day meal."

"No." He crossed his bulky arms. "I want to see what this Leodes fellow's reaction is when he realizes the famed princess has called him back."

My face flamed as I concentrated on the flowers. What would Leodes think? Would he act differently once he knew who I was? A pang of guilt lodged itself in my ribs at the thought of negatively affecting his work by delaying the merchant's vessel.

The sound of pounding feet and hushed voices had Boldar and me standing at attention as the young guard and the others made their way through the gates. My gaze darted around for Leodes but he wasn't among them. The young guard found my face, then Boldar's and he shrugged, shaking his head.

"Checked every single vessel, your highness, from large to small. Only one Leodes was aboard a merchant ship, but he was an old man. I'm sorry."

Disappointment washed over me like a hot, angry rain. His vessel must have left the moment he'd boarded. I wanted to cry. How could my mind have become so addled in the presence of a kind, interesting man? I wasted a perfectly good opportunity. I would never understand the decision I'd made today. And I had a terrible feeling it would haunt me for a long while to come.

CHAPTER FOUR

INTERFERENCE

AWN'S WEDDING WOULD BE THE START OF MY YEAR OF courtship. That was usually how it went. As one princess married, all eyes immediately moved to the next in line. A row of suitors had been waiting to dance with Dawn at Miracle's marriage celebration. I couldn't help but be curious and nervous about who might show interest in my hand.

For months I'd secretly imagined the handsome foreigner in the market to be a prince in disguise. Gods, I'd give anything for him to appear at the celebration. *Leodes.* I replayed our meeting over and over again in my mind. In those first days I hardly slept, so overcome with thoughts of him. The way he'd looked at me, seeming to perceive more than my outward beauty—his sincere interest when I spoke.

Realistically, I knew I'd never see him again, but I couldn't help but fantasize.

Mother made me wear my finest new dress to Dawn's wedding. I planned to steer clear of her husband, Prince Drusus, who turned into a gaping buffoon every time he laid eyes on me. I truly hoped my sister would find joy in those fields of olive trees and grape vines. I hoped he would be more attentive to her there than he was here on our island.

After the ceremony, the masses gathered in our open-air courtyard of marble floors. Climbing rose vines wound their way around white pillars that held up grand arches, the warm air filled with rose fragrance. I attempted to make myself scarce so as not to take any attention away from the couple, but Mother was keen on parading me around to every family with an available son. Intelligent conversation was too much to hope for, no matter how hard I tried.

"Prince Lucius," Mother said to a light-haired man. "Meet my youngest daughter, Princess Psyche."

"How do you do?" I smiled. "Are you the Lucius known for his skill with architecture?"

"The only architecture I can fathom at the moment is you." I held back a groaning eye-roll as he peered from my toes to my gold-leafed crown.

"Oh?" I asked. "Have you forgotten the beauty of the aqueducts you had a hand in creating?"

"The gods perfectly sculpted you, *Psyche*." The way he whispered my name had me forcing back a cringe.

Mother elbowed me, and I cleared my throat. "Thank you."

It's not that I was ungrateful, but it irked me knowing I couldn't tell any of these men about the mountain lion cub from my childhood and expect them to listen and appreciate the story. Yes, that had become my standard. Low, and yet still virtually impossible to meet.

"All they care about is how I look," I hissed to Mother as she moved us along.

"That is their first impression," she hissed back. "Allow them to be impressed. Their love of your personality will come once they get to know you."

I wanted to believe her. When it came time for dancing, I shooed my mother away, to check on Dawn. This was really the time when I longed for friends. Someone to giggle with like a normal girl. Peering around, so many eyes were on me. Some appeared mesmerized, staring, while others were curious or lustful. But nobody approached, male nor female.

I tried to catch the eye of a girl I'd met last year, but she quickly looked away. I smiled at another girl, the daughter of another island king who I'd swam with as a child, but when I began walking toward her, she quickly shifted into a larger group. My stomach sank like a rock in the lagoon. At past parties, when a female was forced into my presence, the conversation always ended up being about my grooming routine. How did I get my hair to shine? What did I put on my skin to make it glow? How much time did I spend in the sun? Exactly what did I consume between sun up and sun down each day?

A prickle on my neck told me someone approached from behind, but when I spun there was no one. Just an open, empty archway opening into a dark hall. I grasped my neck and swallowed.

When I turned back to the crowd, one of the younger princes from the northern lands took two tentative steps in my direction. Thank the gods. Standing alone for such a long time was awkward. His parents urged him forward, watching the show as if he were a gladiator attempting to capture a lioness.

I stood taller and gave him a smile, which seemed to bolster his confidence because his shoulders loosened, and he took several more strides toward me. Then, to my confusion, he seemed to jerk and lightly trip, blinking rapidly as a younger princess from the south rushed into the space between us. They locked gazes, and I swear it felt as if they were colliding and sparking right before my eyes. My heart sank as they tentatively smiled, both bashful and uncertain, their eyes overcome with exaltation. Within seconds, pure, unadulterated love—lust?—filled both of their faces, as if no one else in the room existed. Hand in hand, they made their way out to dance.

What in Olympus had just happened? I could have sworn he'd been looking at me, heading my way. Even his parents appeared baffled. I covered my mouth to hide a laugh. Mother made her way to my side with a friend, noticing the couple. "Prince Darius Costos is dancing with Senator Loukas's daughter? Huh. I could have sworn they'd promised her to another…"

"Well," said her friend, "those two certainly seem to be a strong match." The woman looked at me, a flash of something dark crossing her face. "I would have thought every eligible man in the room would be lined up to dance with your youngest."

"Yes…" Mother smiled at me and peered unsurely around the room. "Perhaps they're nervous to approach. I suppose I'd better take the reins myself. Excuse us."

I wasn't thrilled at the idea of being lauded around the room again, but I did want to meet people. We first approached an older senator and his second wife, who was even younger than the son they introduced me to.

"Stavros Manolis, this is my youngest daughter, Princess Psyche." Mother beamed.

The tall, broad-shouldered son blinked his eyes and when he opened them his entire demeanor changed from haughty to drained of all energy.

"Yes, lovely to meet you," Stavros said. "I'm famished. I see they're carving the roast pig now." His eyes were sliding past me as he spoke and soon his body was leaving us as well. His father's face was horrified, and the young bride pressed her fingertips to her lips.

"Not what you were expecting, hm?" she teased me from the corner of her mouth as Senator Manolis plied Mother with apologies. "You're probably not used to being turned down."

I wasn't, but it didn't upset me as much as her hurtful reaction. Something about tonight felt…off.

"Yes, it's quite refreshing," I told her with a smile. "Come along, Mother. We'll meet him after he's eaten."

When we walked away, Mother hissed, "We will *not* go back to him. How incredibly rude! That rat-faced mongrel—"

"It's fine," I promised, trying to calm her. And then Mother was dragged away by Dawn to meet obscure new relatives.

The entire night turned into a comedy of errors. Every single set of parents who seemed about to approach with a son was either intercepted by another woman or abruptly turned away, opting for more wine or to watch the sparring that had broken out between several guests wanting to showcase their skill. There was no end to interferences that stood between available men and me. But love was undoubtedly in the air. There were more new couples dancing, gazing and kissing than I'd ever witnessed at a gathering. Parents were up in arms about the sudden infatuations garnered that evening. Apparently matches were being made that were never meant to be.

I found myself backed up against a cool pillar, watching the spectacle with amusement at first, which eventually morphed into something heavier. Even my own family, all four of them, stood at the front near the musicians, laughing together with Dawn and Miracle's spouses, chatting about the wealth of new gossip. And if I were to approach them now, I had no doubt the entire mood of the group would change. Was I destined never to laugh with another? To always feel alone in the midst of so many? I didn't feel the need to wed the way my sisters had, but I desperately yearned for true companionship.

When my chin began to quiver, I made my way to the dark side of the pillar to get a hold on my emotions. I would not cry at my sister's wedding celebration. This day was not about me. I took several deep, cleansing breaths and was suddenly overcome by that sensation of being watched again. This time it was much closer, my flesh pebbling with awareness. I squinted into the nearby shadows.

"Hello?" I whispered. The internal stirring was gone as quickly as it had come, leaving me sagging. Something was wrong with me. I felt caught in a slow dream. I needed to lie down.

I jumped when I caught sight of a figure standing by the farthest pillar, my eyes squinting until the form took shape. In a blur, I recognized that dark hair. Those dark eyes. The same dark, sensual feeling sliding over me as it had that day at the market. For a moment, I was stunned immobile, and then my heart slammed wildly.

"Leodes?" At the sound of my voice, he moved into the marble courtyard with the partygoers. I darted out through the archway, but lost sight of him in the crowd.

I ran, my chest heaving with exertion and excitement. He was here! I couldn't believe it! Ignoring shouts of my name from Mother, I moved through the people, not able to keep the smile from my face. Then I nearly plowed into the giant chest of Boldar and tried to rush past. He grasped my wrist.

"Your mother is looking for you. Why do you run?"

I stood on my tiptoes trying to see over his shoulder. "Boldar, I'm looking for the man from the market. The one at the woodcarving table. Do you remember? Leodes was his name."

Boldar's brow creased. "He's not here."

"Yes, he is! I just saw him!" I worried my hands, fiddling with the sash of my dress as my eyes darted back and forth over the faces. Where had he gone?

"I've been at the entrance with the guest list all evening, only just relieved."

"Let me see the list." I took off toward the entrance of the courtyard with Boldar on my heels, calling my name. When we got to the largest arch of all, I took the list from the confused soldier and scanned the names.

"Princess Psyche." Boldar caught up and sighed, crossing his arms and allowing me to peruse the list. I ran a finger down the familiar names.

"No," I muttered to myself. "He's not on here." I eyed the new soldier. "Do you recall letting in a young man with dark hair? Cream colored toga with a brown belt? His name is Leodes. Perhaps he was an unexpected guest of another?"

The soldier looked scared out of his mind as he stared at me. "I-I don't believe so, your highness. I've only let in one older couple since I took position."

I cursed quietly and press the list back into his hands, scanning the people again. My heart still hammered, and my blood felt hot and thick. I'd seen him. I *had*.

"Psyche!" Mother's voice jolted me, and I turned to face her.

"Mother—"

"Why are you not at the party? You have more guests to meet."

"Mother, I stood there for ages and not a single person asked me to dance. They are here to see Dawn be married."

"Don't be ridiculous."

She grabbed my hand, and with the first step we took a wave of exhaustion crashed over me. I stumbled into the wall as my vision became splotchy, and I vaguely heard Mother gasp. Boldar caught me and held me to his chest. I blinked and wanted nothing more than to sleep in his arms.

"Oh, my darling!" Mother cried. "Boldar, take her to her room and fetch the nursemaid to tend her until I can get away." She ran a hand along my cheek with worry before rushing off, and I let Boldar lead me out. I felt almost immediately better once I was away from the courtyard, able to walk on my own, my head clearing.

"Have you been sampling the wine?" Boldar asked.

"No," I whispered.

"Hungry, then?"

"I ate." But something had not been right tonight. "I feel fine now."

He let out a harrumph. "You made yourself sick to get out of a bit of dancing?"

"No." I crossed my arms, frustrated that I couldn't reply truthfully without making it seem as if I'd lost my mind. And perhaps I had. "I haven't been sleeping well. I just need some rest."

"Well, you shall have it." Boldar opened the door to my bedchamber and I entered.

Before he could close it behind me, I turned and grasped the edge of the door. "If you see the man, Leodes, from the market, you must get me."

He tilted his head as if I'd lost my wits. "Princess. He's not here."

"Promise me, Boldar."

He huffed. "I promise." Then he closed the door.

I moved to the edge of my window, throwing open the wide shutters to invite the sea air to dance around me, moving my skirts against my skin. The gray castle cat, Stormy, who preferred my room over all others, leapt onto the ledge to garner my attention. I scratched behind her ears for a while, staring out at the sea in thought. When she bored of me, I twirled on my feet, head back, the air sliding like a physical thing over my arms and neck. Bright stars twinkled over the ripples of water below, always moving, never still, like the heartbeat of our world.

I didn't speak to the gods nearly as much as I should. Guiltily, I leaned from the window and sent my words of worship on the wind: "Jupiter, god of the sky and king of the gods, I thank you for your creation. I thank you for the wind, my only dance partner this night. If it be your will, I pray for a true love to dance with me someday." I kissed my fingertips and stretched my hand from the open window, letting the breeze catch my offering to send it high.

CHAPTER FIVE

SUITORS

*A*FTER THAT FLUKE OF AN EVENING, APPREHENSION SHROUDED my courting period. It was hard not to think about it nonstop now that Dawn and Miracle were both gone, and Mother set her sights solely on me.

"Oh, how I've dreamed of your courtship since you were a child!" Mother took my hands as she and I sat in the garden looking over a scroll of possible suitors, listed from best to absolute-last-case-scenario. Mother chatted on, telling me tidbits of gossip about each man as my shoulders slumped further and further.

"Adrian Galanis is the talk of Athens—gorgeous head to toe!—and he knows it. Some say he's ruined several well-to-do marriages." My stomach lurched. "But have no worries, darling. If anyone can keep his eye and set him straight, it's you. Sit up straight, dear. Oh!" Her slender finger found another name of interest. "Calix Floros comes from a strong line. It's rumored he'll be in the Senate soon. Gods know, half the bureaucrats in Athens have had their pockets lined with his father's bribes."

I made a face of disgust. "Are there any on the list who aren't filled with greed or cursed with a wandering eye?"

"Pshaw!" Mother waved a hand as if I'd made a joke. "No family is perfect. Don't be so picky! If you're not satisfied by gorgeous, powerful men, perhaps you'll enjoy the company of Orrin Castellanos, the scholar."

I narrowed my eyes, remembering that name from Miracle's

wedding. "Didn't he court Dawn? Didn't she cry and beg Papa to turn down his offer because he was likely too old to sire children?"

"He's forty-three, not quite on his deathbed."

Actually, his age had been Dawn's excuse. What she really didn't like was that the scholar couldn't see to his feet past his belly, and his bald head was covered in sun spots. I recalled feeling bad for him at Miracle's wedding because he seemed jolly and kind, but Dawn wouldn't dance with him. I'd been young. Only fifteen, and already a spectacle. But if I remembered it correctly, he was the only man who managed to carry on a semi-normal conversation with me, after a bumbling start with mottled cheeks.

"What number is he on my list?"

"Oh, don't be ridiculous, he's not on your list!" She *whapped* my leg gently with the feather quill. "I was trying to put things in perspective. We've chosen the best for you, darling. Only the best."

"Mother..." I sat up straighter and braced myself. "Is there a rush for me to marry?" Her mouth bobbed open, and I hurried on. "I'm just saying, let's not force it. I don't *need* to marry."

"Psyche, really! Every woman needs to marry."

I sighed at the unfairness of it. "An extra year or two with you and Papa wouldn't be too much of a scandal, would it? We can travel and meet people. A natural courtship progression would be more palatable than this." I brushed a hand across her list of men.

Mother tilted her head and smiled at me, then patted my cheek. "This is fun for me. Finding husbands for my daughters is my joy—my only true job, really."

"You're a queen. You have many important jobs."

She waved that fact away. "None more important than this."

"Mother, please." I took her hand and held it tightly until she looked at me again. "I don't want to rush this. I want a husband who loves me, not a man who sees me as a prize of some sort."

"Okay, darling." She patted the top of my hand with her free one. "I will make you a deal. Allow me to continue the courtship, asking men to visit and meet you, but I will speak with Papa about not rushing the actual wedding part."

"Thank you!" I beamed at her, but she shook her head.

"This is not an endless agreement. By the age of twenty, we must choose, together, and you must marry. Preferably someone who can further Papa's standing. You want that, don't you?"

I swallowed the bile rising up in my throat but nodded my agreement, and she kissed my head. One way or another, I'd become someone's wife. There was no getting out of it.

Chapter Six

Faithless

"**W**HAT DID YOU *SAY* TO HIM?" MOTHER ASKED, PULL-ing her shawl closer against a blast of chilled wind as we walked the stone path from our living quarters to the dining area.

"I said nothing that would cause such disinterest in me or turn his eye to his bath maid instead," I assured her. My appeal to her to slow the process of my courtship period had gone un-heeded. She'd rushed head-in, bombarding me with man after man, failure after awkward failure.

The latest suitor had been one of mother's last hopes for a suitable match. As a bonus he was a warrior of high ranking in the military with bloodlines that traced back to ancient Athens. I'd quite liked the look of his strong thighs. Our initial meeting had been positive, even hopeful—he'd only gawked at me two long minutes before gathering his wits and being able to carry on a conversation. But last night while everyone had slept, he found Boldar and explained he was leaving, hand in hand with the bath maid we'd assigned him. A girl even younger than me. Boldar said his eyes were crazed and he couldn't stop proclaiming his love for the girl.

If I wasn't so scandalized and concerned for mother's state of mind, I'd have laughed at the irony of one lost suitor after an-other, and me supposedly the "best catch" in all the lands.

"How is it possible?" Mother exclaimed, raising her palms to the world in frustration. "To choose a plain-faced servant of the

Metics class over a Princess!"

"She *was* a kind soul. And I wouldn't call her plain-faced," I said in her defense, but Mother raged on.

"The fool! And now I have to find a replacement maid!" Mother's shouts were lost to the winds. A storm was blowing in, and from the churning, sooty look of the skies, we'd do well to stay inside the remainder of the afternoon. We rushed through the doors of the dining hall, held open by two soldiers, and exhaled loudly in the sudden quiet of the windless room.

Both of us shook out our shawls and placed them across the backs of our chairs, joining Papa at the table. He sat heavily, elbows on the table, peering at us menacingly over his goblet of wine. From the droop of his eyes, I was certain it wasn't his first drink.

"What did you say to him, Psyche?" Papa accused.

I turned to him as if my eyes could lash back. "I said nothing to turn him away! I was cordial and kind and, and—"

Papa slammed a fist to the table, making Mother and I jump and his wine slosh up like a red wave on an angry sea.

He pointed a finger at me. "You must be sabotaging our efforts in some way!"

I trembled inside because Papa never spoke harshly to me. "I swear to you, Papa. I'm *not*." But I understood his frustration. It had been nearly a year. Soon, rumors would start to spread.

Mother took my hand and spoke gently to Papa. "Could it be they are too intimidated by such beauty?" He grunted, and Mother continued. "Ever since she's grown breasts no man has been able to talk to her like a normal female."

I pressed a hand to my forehead and rubbed it down my face. "Every woman has breasts, Mother."

"It's not just that, Psyche," she told me. "It's the entire package. The more you become a woman, the less men know how to behave around you!"

"They treat you like a goddess," Papa said quietly, almost reverently, but with a hint of regret, as if the thing that had always pleased him had turned to strike him with hidden fangs. Part of me rejoiced that they were finally beginning to see the burden of it.

"Then perhaps we should make a special offering to the gods, something even more than usual, as a family," I suggested.

Mother's eyes snapped to Papa's and they appeared strangely hesitant.

"An offering," Mother said, as if it were an altogether new idea. "It couldn't hurt."

Papa looked away, down at the table, around the room at the hanging rugs, then down to his cup. I couldn't understand their odd reactions.

"Is something wrong?" I asked.

"Of course not," Mother quickly responded. "There's just been a bit of talk lately. People from the mainland coming over, spouting off about our 'superstitions' and the changing ways of the new world."

I glared now. "What superstitions? About the gods? That's sacrilege, Mother! I hope you're not paying them any mind."

I stared back and forth between my parents who shrugged and shook their heads, pulling their faces to the side. A horrible thought punched my innards as the walls shook with a bellow of thunder.

"How long has it been since you gave an offering?" As a minor in the family, it was left to my parents to pay our debts to the gods and goddesses at the altar. I attended and participated in the festivals, but now that I was entering adulthood, I would soon go independently of them.

Again, those gestures of nonchalance. Mother waved a hand.

"The last festival, I suppose?"

Shock razed my skin like I'd skidded across coals. "That was at the start of fall! It's nearly spring!" They should have been worshipping and giving gifts several times a month on behalf of our family! My last meal turned to rocks, and I grabbed my stomach.

Mother sighed with exasperation, fiddling with her skirts. "Darling girl, things have been so busy with trying to find you a suitable match. I've never been so exhausted!"

I gaped at her, then Papa, who nodded. My gods. They'd been faithless. A pit of dread opened inside me.

"It's no wonder our efforts have fallen flat." I stood abruptly, my eyes scanning the room for something to give the gods before landing on the bejeweled gold cuff on Papa's wrist. I held out my shaking hand.

"Give me your cuff."

He reeled back. "Pardon?"

"Papa! We need to make an offering—now!"

"It can wait until after the storm." And to back up his words a bolt of lightning filled the room with brightness before crashing in our ears seconds later, shaking the room.

I reached down and wrestled the cuff from his wrist. He barely fought me, just laughed as if I was being ridiculous. Then I turned to Mother's shocked face and pointed at the golden snake that wound around her upper arm. She placed a protective hand over it.

"Are your treasures more precious to you than my life? Our future?"

Now it was Mother's turn to laugh at my dramatics. "Of course not. Please sit and relax and I swear to you we will gather a proper offering first thing in the morning."

I pressed a hand to my forehead and whispered, "It will be too late." In truth, I believed it already was. My eyes burned with fear, filling with unshed tears, and Mother reached for her upper arm.

"Please, Psyche, don't cry. Here." She placed the winding gold in my hand, folding my fingers around it and rubbing my skin with tender affection. Her eyes were soft and regretful. I had a feeling her regret had everything to do with my sadness and nothing to do with offending the gods. I would rather it have been the other way around.

I swallowed hard and turned from them, forgoing my shawl. Both of my parents made sounds of despair as I ran for the doors, but neither stood to stop me. A guard opened the door for me, peering over at my father for instructions.

"Accompany her to the altar," Papa said, resigned.

The winds hit me in a rush, rain pelting my skin with the sting of a hundred tiny daggers. I lifted an arm to shield my eyes and ran. Several times the winds blasted me, offsetting my balance momentarily, making me slip on slick stones. But I never stopped.

At the altar, I climbed the wet steps then fell to my knees in the rounded center of pillars under a domed roof. I let out a small cry at the two measly piles of soggy offerings. This altar should have been filled with bounty.

With trembling hands, I laid my two gifts in the center of the circular room, open to the elements, rain slashing sideways to smack at me.

"Forgive us, please," I shouted over the howling storm. "Please accept these offerings and know that there is more to come. We—" I had to stop and swallow. "We honor you. All we have is for your glory."

A gust of wind rocked me to my side, and over the din of noise I heard a sickening *snap* and *whap*, followed by the yelling of my guards. I lifted my head in time to see an unrooted palm tree fly against the outer pillars as if trying to fight its way into the altar area. A strong arm came around my midsection and lifted me from the ground.

"We must go!" Boldar shouted.

I didn't argue. He and four other guards surrounded me, and we shuffled our way clumsily down the path back to the castle, my hair whipping all of us like a live, angry thing. We'd barely reached the stone entrance to our palace when my eyes filled with blinding light. An explosion loud enough to burst the insides of my ears lifted all five of us off our feet, throwing us through the castle doors. A shock of heat filled the area before dissolving into a chill again. But the rumble of crashing sounds continued, and even through the rain we nearly choked on ash and dirt. I waved a hand in front of my face, trying to see.

What in the great name of Jupiter had happened?

"Lightning strike!" Boldar yelled, on his feet, lifting me again. And as the dust finally began to settle, I squinted into the darkness. Through the sheet of rain, under the angry gray skies, our altar lay in crumbled ruin, smoke warring with the falling moisture. I smacked a hand over my mouth to hold back a cry of anguish. My parents could speak of superstition all they wanted, but I didn't believe in coincidence. Our offerings had been denied in the most powerful of messages.

And now I had no doubt. I was cursed.

CHAPTER SEVEN

THE ORACLE

THE RAIN DIDN'T LET UP UNTIL EARLY MORNING AND SLEEP never found me. My only relief was that I didn't have to beg or convince my parents—when they set eyes on the altar wreckage, they took one long look at one another and paled, realization dawning on their faces.

"We travel to Miletus at first light," Papa had said, his jaw set before stalking away from us.He never took defeat well. Even, apparently, against the immortal gods. And while I didn't want him to suffer, I hoped he would be truly humbled. If he brought his mortal pride into that ancient temple tomorrow, it would further insult the gods. Even kings could be made into fools.

I was ready to go. I'd been ready for hours, donning my most modest dress and plain shawl, my hair piled neatly atop my head in a way befitting of worship. And then I'd gone around my room and gathered every worthy item: jewels, a fine body wrap sewn with gold thread, dazzling hair pins, and hand carved boxes. These were all things meant to accompany me to my marital home someday. Things that would add to my worth and dowry. Without all of this, I could only hope my good name and my beauty would be enough to land a decent match. If the gods allowed.

The muscles of my abdomen seized tightly at the thought of the gods and their wrath last night. Deep in my marrow I knew this was our last chance to please the gods. If they found our worship and offerings anything less than perfect, it wasn't just

me who would be cursed. I had no doubt our entire island king-
dom would suffer. With a snap of their fingers the immortals
could tell the waters to swallow our land and every being on it.
No castle on a hill was too high for them to transform to rubble.
Civilizations rose and fell at their whim. How my parents had
forgotten that fact I had no idea.

I jumped at the sound of a light tap on my door. Instead of
calling out for them to enter, I opened the door myself. Boldar's
grim face greeted me, surveying me from top to bottom.

"You are ready."

"I am," I answered, bringing my basket of goods. He winced
when he spied my offerings, regret in his eyes as he took the basket from my hands, but he said nothing as he led me to my parents in the courtyard. The dark crescents under their eyes were
an indication they slept as little as me, and I was glad of it. Papa
gave me a nod, and Mother tried to smile at me but failed horribly, her mouth only managing to quiver instead.

Beside them was a cart covered in cloth. A shining hilt pro-
truded from one corner and I covered my mouth against a gasp.
The sword had been in our family for countless generations. Papa
had won battles with that sword in his hand. As much as it pained
me to think of giving it away, I was glad to see he was taking this
seriously. Not a single material item was worth more than the
lives, health, and happiness of our people and homeland.

The walk to the barge was a somber event. Dark clouds
still roiled in the skies above us, the grounds sodden with the
aftereffects of the storm. Rivulets of water ran down the streets,
and the morning was hazy gray. Guards pushed the cart and
pulled our best animals behind us. Our finest steed. Our best
milking cow. Fatted swine and the fluffiest of sheep. Our sweetest
little lamb. I couldn't allow myself to think of their sacrifice. For
their sake, I was even more frustrated with my parents that it'd

gotten to this point.

The waters were rough. We normally wouldn't venture out this soon after a storm, but we clung to the sides of the boat and gritted our teeth against the rolling waves, the smack of the boat up and down, jarring my back. After a while I stood, finding my bent knees took the impact of the rough waters better than my spine. Mother had closed her eyes, prone to seasickness. Papa stared, stoic, out at the sea, his expression never changing as we sighted land.

At the dock, I pulled a shawl around my face against the biting winds, hiding as much of myself as possible. The guards pressed back any locals who recognized us or wanted to greet us, but I felt their eyes watching as we boarded a large chariot pulled by two steeds. It would take several chariots and trips to get all of our party and offerings to the temple.

We made our way down the bumpy lanes of the fish markets to the temple of Apollo, complex god of the sun, music, art, archery, plague, medicine, and most importantly for our family at the moment, prophecy. Today we sought the powerful and ancient oracle of Apollo for wisdom and knowledge about how to get back into the good graces of the gods, and what the future might hold for us. For me.

I stood between my parents on the chariot, one hand holding the rail to keep myself steady, the other holding the shawl at my neck. The horses were swift, and I closed my eyes against the cool air hitting my face. Above us the clouds were still dark and angry. We rounded a corner and the large dome of Apollo's temple came into view on the raised hill, strikingly light against the wrathful sky, held high by giant pillars in a circle. Our temple had been a smaller replica of this one, but it hadn't come close to this majesty.

I itched to fall on my knees and beg forgiveness. Peering at both of my parents, I daresay they were not eager for the same thing. Mother's regal jaw was set with worry and displeasure. Papa wore the same unpleasant expression he did when he had to barter and deal with enemies-turned-allies after war. Their lack of reverence made my blood feel electric with nervous energy under my skin. This was not something they could fake.

"No number of offerings will please the gods if you walk in there filled with pride and bitterness," I said against the wind, leaning forward as the chariot inclined.

"Hold your tongue," Mother chided.

But Papa wanted to argue. "Why are we to be punished? We work hard to rule our lands with justice. Surely the gods can see our daily work."

I eyed him. "It takes more than good deeds, Papa. You know this. You must honor them." He stiffened, his knuckles white on the railing until I pried his closest hand away, slipping my small hand into his large, calloused palm.

"Time has passed so swiftly," he told me.

"I know, Papa. And you are busy with more responsibilities than any man I know. Tell this to the gods when you worship today. Explain that time got away from you and you never meant to offend them."

I held tight to his hand until the horses slowed and came to a stop. The three of us were a shame-filled sight as we gathered as much as we could into our arms, the guards carrying the animals. We brought so much that the altar quickly filled, surrounding the stone statue of the deity. And then the hours of sacrifice and worship began. Chanting. Bowing. Kneeling. Singing. Begging. Promising change. All while the winds whistled through the pillars like small screams.

We were exhausted at the end of it, and the clouds still hovered above the temple. In the distance blue skies painted the horizon, but the sun did not show its face over us. A horrible chasm of despair opened up inside of me, causing my body to tremble as Papa helped me to my feet. My knees were numb and painful.

The three of us exchanged somber glances, telling me their level of hope was as low as mine. It was time to see the oracle and learn our fate. How would we be punished? Would the gods take away our lands? Would Papa's reign be tumbled? Would our people suffer plague or famine? I couldn't bear the thought of our small empire, so precious to our family, in ruin.

Gaining audience with the oracle was a difficult task. Only royalty and the very rich were granted prophecy. Our own guards filled the space around us while Miletus guards surrounded the old woman being brought gingerly up the steps. Two younger seers in white robes, marked with shaved heads, accompanied the oracle, holding her hands. The oracle stared with her chin lifted, but her eyes were a milky, whitish-blue.

As she took the final step into the temple the guards spread out, giving the four of us as much space as possible while still circling us. Papa, Mother, and I knelt and bowed our heads a long moment before Papa spoke.

"Most worthy oracle. We thank you. Your time is a gift." Papa raised his head, taking Mother's hand, then mine, and we stood together.

"A most blessed family on a blessed isle." The oracle's voice was scratchy like sand over rocks. I swallowed hard, my heart banging a fearful beat in my chest.

"What is your greatest prayer request?" asked the oracle.

"My wish…my greatest prayer is for my daughter Psyche to have a husband." Papa closed his eyes, and in that moment, I watched as all pride shed from his shoulders and he stood before the oracle as a mere man and father. My eyes burned, and I swallowed back the moisture building as Mother sniffled beside me.

"Princess Psyche." The oracle's voice tilted up at the end of my name as if contemplating. "Indeed, the famed beauty should have a husband by now."

Mother shivered, taking my hand, and Papa lowered his head.

"I fear," Papa choked out, "that I have cursed her with my… unfaithfulness."

I wiped a tear from the corner of each eye before it could fall. I wasn't prone to crying but seeing Papa at such a low point was tugging at my goblet of emotion, causing it all to spill forth.

"The root of her curse goes much deeper than your own actions," the oracle said, making all three of us gasp at the truth. "'Twas the unfaithfulness of you and all your people that brought the ire of the goddess Venus. And 'tis only the one you so love and admire who can be sacrificed to bring blessing back to your lands."

"Wh—" Papa's breath left him in a *whoosh* as he spun to me, eyes wide.

My stomach dipped but I remained still. In my mind, this had been the worst case. I knew the price would be great, and that it would somehow pertain to me. As much as my body wanted to fall and beg, if I did that, my parents would break. I had to be strong for them.

"No," Mother said. "Not Psyche. Not my baby. She has done nothing!" She gripped my forearm tightly, as if she could save me from the gods.

I put a hand over hers. "It's all right, Mother."

At this, the oracle chuckled, and craned her head to the side as if hearing something nobody else could decipher. Her slow nod sent a hot zap of fear across my skin.

"The gods have spoken. Hers will be a funeral wedding to a dark-deeded winged serpent. Many call him a monster. Your dear Psyche will call him Husband."

My eyes fluttered and for a moment the temple spun. I barely made out the sounds of Mother and Papa fighting to breathe, their hands holding me.

"I won't have it!" Papa shouted. I wanted to tell him to keep calm, that even his immense power could not save me from this, but I couldn't find my voice.

"It is decided," the oracle told Papa again, never raising her voice.

"What if we refuse?" Mother asked.

"Then the curse on her head spills onto those who share her blood and all who reside on your isle."

Mother covered her mouth and started to drop to her knees, but Papa lifted her, scowling at the oracle, as if this were her fault, but it wasn't. It was mine. I should have put a stop to the nonsense years ago. I should have insisted Papa forbid the people from idolizing me. My parents thought it was innocent flattery, but in my heart I'd always known better. I had kept too quiet, hoping the issue would resolve itself over time. Now, fear for my parents and our people rose like a wild fire inside of me—a deadly thing only I could control.

"Please," I said to my parents as calmly as possible. "You cannot fight this. It is mine to bear. I can handle it."

His eyes still boring holes into the oracle, Papa yelled, "He will kill her!"

"He will have her as his wife." At that simple statement, Papa flinched, and Mother dissolved into tears, sagging in Papa's strong arms and gripping him with all her might. The pain in Papa's eyes killed me. He was thinking of all that my husband would do to me—the things I couldn't bring myself to imagine.

My husband.

My stomach lurched. A wave of dizziness threatened to knock my feet from beneath me, but I tensed my muscles to stay upright.

A dark-deeded winged serpent.

I would not survive it, that was certain, but I couldn't let my parents see the terror that burned through me.

The oracle nodded slowly, her frightening eyes staring at my own. "On the next full moon, you will climb to the highest point on your isle, alone, and there you will stay until taken to your husband."

"Who will take her?" Papa demanded.

"That is not for you to know."

His jaw clenched. Papa could bully the mightiest warriors in all the lands, but this frail old woman would not be cowed. She spoke with authority of the gods, and what she envisioned was what I deserved. Perhaps my entire favored life had led to such an ending as this. The sardonicism nearly made me laugh with hysterics. I should have ended the people's fascination with my appearance long ago. I didn't know how, but I should have done *something*. I should have been diligent about my family's worship and offerings. But it was too late to go back.

Now I would make the ultimate sacrifice. Gods, help me.

Chapter Eight

Funeral Wedding

THE SUN HAD NOT SHOWN ITS FACE ON OUR ISLE SINCE THE night our altar was destroyed. Papa's builders worked day and night to create a new shinier, larger altar to the gods. In that time, my day of birth came and went, making me an official adult citizen. The altar was finished a day before the full moon. A day before I was to marry a monster.

I was the first to fall to my knees at the new structure. I didn't cry, though all around me people wept. By now everyone knew of my fate. Everyone knew their punishment would be dealt through me. They cried my name, mourning their cherished princess, as if I were already dead. And perhaps I was. I surely felt it.

Deadened.

I hadn't cried since the oracle had proclaimed my fate, her words slamming like a great stone against my nerves, numbing me completely. If I let myself feel, even for a scarce moment, my heart seized from sheer panic.

Tomorrow I'd be given to a monster. A serpent. An unknown mythological creature. And it was a cruel added punishment that the gods wouldn't even allow me to know my husband's identity. It allowed my mind—all of our minds—to create horrifying scenarios. There was no end of terrifying beasts in Olympus. Immortal humanesque beings.

Papa and Mother begged me to leave. They begged me to go in the dead of night. Papa knew people at the far ends of the land, people willing to let me hide away. They would feign my death, he said. As if the gods would not know. As if we'd not been foolish enough already.

No. This was the only way to lift the shade of darkness and bitter winds that hovered above our isle. I would not run from my duty to the people, especially now as their tears surrounded me, realizing the error of their ways. They had forgotten the power of the gods, opting to shower me with their adoration instead. And now they'd been reminded that their princess was very, very mortal. I felt their regret as stridently as if it were my own.

I would bring no finery to my new bridal home. Only myself. I gave all I had at the altar. After hours of worship, I retired to my room for my last night in the lavish home of my childhood. A sleepless night. Stormy did not grace me with her presence that night. Even the animals felt my doom.

In all the marriage celebrations I'd ever attended, I'd never heard the wedding lute sound mournful until this dark evening. Now and again as we walked the path to the mountain, the over-fed clouds would move just enough for the full moon to show its ominous face, reminding us that it was, indeed, time.

I stood tall and walked with purpose, my face shrouded by a gauzy purple veil, but inside I shook like a loose feather in a gale. My fear was a thick, viscous thing inside of me, like sludge in my limbs, and I fought to overcome it. Not a single female face wasn't streaked with tears; not a single males' eyes were not wide with shock and horror.

And yet, we walked.

From the side of my vision, I noticed Boldar's hand in a tight fist at his side. It must have gone against everything inside of him to allow me to go. He'd spent my entire life keeping me safe, more like an uncle than a guard, and now he marched me straight into danger. Pity made me reach down and squeeze his fist. His eyes moved to mine, and the pain I saw there, practically begging me to turn and run, sent a sharp sting through my breast. For once, I would not try to escape. No more playful running.

I swallowed and tried to smile, which brought a tremble to his chin. We both abruptly looked away and I brought my hand back to my own side. He couldn't save me from the fate of the gods. Nobody could. Wind blasted us, lifting loose sand and whipping it against our party.

The path turned rocky, but the lute's sadness never ceased. Its tune warbled through the dense air, surrounding all of us. Breathing became labored as the walk turned into more of a climb, requiring hands now. And when the peak came into view my sisters and Mother behind me began to wail in earnest. Even Papa let out a choked sound. I swallowed once. Twice. Three times, taking shuddering breaths. Boldar took my elbow on a sharp incline, though I didn't need his help. It wasn't my first climb to the peak of this mountain. But it was the first time I'd done it without joy.

He will have her as his wife.

My stomach gave a violent lurch and I paused to close my eyes. I hadn't eaten in over a day and didn't want my body to bring up the terrible acid that'd been churning in my stomach. If I began to heave, I might never stop.

"Princess," Boldar said with worry, his hand gripping my elbow.

I blew out a breath and lifted my head. "I'm all right." I continued my climb.

When it became too steep and the lute began to get choppy, I rushed to the front of the party. The music stopped. All eyes lifted to me as I faced their mournful faces.

"I will continue alone."

Papa's stern mouth tried to work, but nothing came out, so I ran to him. My family embraced me, shaking with their sobs, the five of us holding fast. Still, I did not cry. Their love and guilt were palpable things. I could not be angry at their past stubbornness or foolishness. I wouldn't blame them or the people. My heart was too full of fear, leaving no room for anger or blame.

"I love each of you," I said, taking in their faces one last time. Papa. Mother. Miracle. Dawn. Then Boldar. When I turned from them, Boldar tried to follow but I gave his hand a reassuring squeeze. "I must go alone." I pulled my hand from his grasp, looking away from his desperate gaze.

I climbed the rest of the way, my eyes scanning the area with apprehension. Only rocks to be seen. The higher I went, the harsher the winds became, grasping and stripping my veil. I tried to grab it, but the winds took it, leaving my face and hair on display as I fell to my knees at the top of the rocks.

As the skies darkened further, I watched the lights of gas lamps and torches begin their slow descent. The path of light moved farther and farther away. And with each retreating step, my heart grew heavier, pounding louder. Hearing a noise, I turned, crying out, but I was alone. Just me and my terror. All around me became blackness, and as the last of the lights disappeared from sight, I finally let loose the emotions inside of me. Every single thing I'd been holding back rushed to the surface, flooding out of me, wrenching my voice from my throat.

On that rock I cried. I bawled, overcome with dread, sadness, and regret. My soul poured out the anger and blame I felt toward my family and the people. This could have been avoided. This should have never happened! This wasn't fair.

I mourned until my strength was gone and I collapsed upon the rock, my face pressed against its cool, worn surface. And then a different wind came. Not cold or hot or rushed. This wind caressed me from toe to scalp, calming me into a deep sleep. And then the wind lifted me and carried me away.

CHAPTER NINE

VOICES

I STRETCHED IN BLISS AS I WOKE, HAVING NO IMMEDIATE RECOLlection of what had happened. In that single instant I was fully rested, more comfortable than I'd ever been. At peace. My fingers lazily moved, twining with velvety blades of grass. And the light beyond my eyelids was as soft as happiness.

Oh, gods.

It all came racing back to me and I sat up gasping, heart galloping. Every scrap of peace I'd felt was thrown from my body, replaced by the panic I'd worn at the rock. But as my fingers gripped the grass on either side of me, and my head swiveled side to side, my mind couldn't grasp what my eyes were taking in.

Lush waves of grass gave way to a mossy bank and a stream that rambled, clear as my own sea. The trees were massive with twisted trunks, making them look as if they'd danced themselves into those beautiful positions as they grew from saplings. Their leaves waved down at me, but none fell. In fact, the grounds were completely free of any leaf or branch debris. Everything about the woodsy area was perfect.

Too perfect.

On closer inspection, the only sounds were the tinkling stream and the rustle of leaves clapping softly against one another. No birds chirping. No buzz of bees. No life other than the plants. The colors, greens, blues, and browns were too vivid and bright. This wasn't my world.

I leapt to my feet, my heart refusing to settle. Where was I?

Why was I alone? Where was my…no. I shook my head. I didn't want to think about the beast. And I didn't want to get my hopes up that this was really where I was supposed to be. Was I somehow being taunted? Teased with a peaceful surrounding before being thrown into a nightmare? It was possible my husband was capable of such cruelty. As much as I didn't want to find out, my stomach gave an ache of hunger and I knew I had to move. I made my way tentatively through the trees, and I swore they moved ever so slightly to accommodate me. When I turned, they seemed to be in different positions, but I couldn't remember exactly. I blinked away the strangeness and continued on.

At one point, I swore I heard soft footsteps behind me, but when I spun, holding my breath, nobody was there. This place—this entire situation—was making me lose my mind. I thought of my family's faces when I'd left them, and suddenly I felt alone for the first time in my life. Truly alone. And though the air was not cold, I wrapped myself in my arms, holding tight against the internal shiver and longing for home.

I continued through the enchanted forest, unable to rid myself of the feeling of being watched, no matter how many times I stared about and saw nothing but trees. And when I came to the edge of the forest at the bottom of a valley where the trees gave way to rolling hills, my fingers fluttered up to cover my lips. At the top of the last vibrant hill was a palace. But not just any palace. It put my childhood home to shame.

From afar, white marble turrets, pillars, archways, and balconies glittered under the sun. A castle far grander than my family's. Each stone was melded together by gold, every doorway edged in precious gems—diamond windows and emerald doors. Yet somehow it managed to be tasteful in its grandeur. My feet moved me up the hill, curiosity driving me closer. Beside the castle was an archery range, vast in its size, with quality targets of stuffed humans and animals.

I was close enough now to make out the main walkway paved in gold. I stopped at the entrance of the sparkling path, stunned. How it all sparkled!

On either side of the path were glorious gardens. Bushes sculpted into giant, wild beasts, creatures I'd never seen but a few I'd heard of: centaurs and satyrs. I recognized the three heads of Cerberus. Beyond the leafy animals were rows of colorful bushes, leaves and petals as bright as if they'd been dyed by a master seamstress. I was drawn to the colors, like nothing I'd ever seen in nature. And for a moment, I forgot to be afraid.

"You like it, then?"

I screamed, nearly jumping out of my skin as I clutched the fabric at my chest, spinning, eyes frantic, seeing no one. The voice had sounded close, right behind me. A deep, rough male intonation. But I was alone!

"Who's there?" I called.

"Be calm," he commanded.

I leapt back at the voice that sounded inches from my face where only air was present. I stumbled a few steps away from the sound, twisted in place, and faced the palace again.

"Who are you?" I didn't mean to yell, but panic gripped me.

It was silent now except for my overly loud breathing. Nobody was there. I was going mad. Now I knew for certain. "Oh, gods," I whimpered.

"Be still." The voice wasn't as close this time, as if giving me space, but my heart still jumped with fright. I stared at the spot from where it emanated on the golden path.

"This is not real," I whispered. "I'm dead."

"Is this how you imagine the Underworld?"

"No." A crazed laugh bubbled forth from deep within me. "Then I've gone mad."

"You have not." His voice, closer again, sent a shiver rippling up my back and through my core. The sound was gravely and low, yet strangely pleasant.

"Then why can't I see you?"

"Because I do not wish to be seen." The voice was beside me now. My instinct was to run, as if I were prey, but I forced myself to remain still this time, tilting away. I had to get answers.

"Why do you wish to hide yourself?" I asked.

"For reasons I cannot say." Now he was behind me, sending a chill up the back of my neck, but I didn't move. He was circling me. I fought to keep my breathing even.

"Wh-who are you?" I asked.

From in front of me now, his voice lowered. Almost dangerous. "I am your husband."

A stab of terror shook me, and I covered my mouth with both hands. My husband. The monster. He was cruel enough to tease me with an atmosphere of beauty and false safety, wanting to savor this moment. I forced myself to drop my hands, stand straight, and swallow my fear. How I behaved now would set into motion our "relationship" from now until I died. However long he decided to toy with me.

"If you are my husband," I said with strength I didn't feel. "Why do you hide yourself from me?"

"I am not permitted to show myself."

That made no sense. "So, you have a master who forbids it?"

He let out a snarl that sent me back a step, despite my vow not to appear afraid.

"I have no master," he said with indignance.

I felt my eyebrows furrow.

"Then you choose not to be seen."

"*No.*" Annoyance. "I am limited as to what I can explain. You will have to...rely on me." His voice twisted after the pause, as if they weren't the words he was looking for.

I snorted with disbelief at the thought of relying on him, then pressed my lips together.

"I will not lie to you, Psyche." He was so close again that I let out a sound of surprise and held up my palms.

"Stay back," I said.

The deep voice chuckled, and I felt the sound rub my lower abdomen. I pursed my lips against the unwelcome clench of muscle in my core. That chuckle...it carried meaning that I seemed to be able to decipher. He sounded surprised when I told him to stay back, almost as if he weren't accustomed to such a command. Like everything else, it made no sense.

"Tell me what the oracle said to you," he demanded.

I cleared my throat and complied, conveying every detail. He was quiet a long while.

"A serpent," he mused.

I tried to imagine his voice linked to a body. Did he have scales? He didn't speak with the slur of fangs, but perhaps he could bare them at will. I shivered and wrapped myself in my arms again.

"And so, you have married a monster, and here you are." His voice was...what? Sad? That couldn't possibly be right. I had no idea how to read him and I was even more baffled when he said, "I have a request."

"Y-yes?"

"I desire for you to...put aside what you *think* you know about me."

What? I blinked in confusion.

"Can you do that, Psyche?"

When I tried to take a deep breath, my chest heaved and shuddered. "I don't know," I admitted. "I will try." Try as I might, I didn't believe I'd ever be able to forget he was a monster, though

I knew it was what he wanted to hear.

"I suppose that will have to be good enough," he murmured like a rumbling purr. "In the meantime, there are rules. Listen closely. You will never, under any circumstances, touch me. I can touch you, but you cannot touch me. Do you understand?"

I had no desire to touch him, but the part about him touching me caused me to grit my teeth.

"Do you understand?" he asked again, more firmly.

I nodded.

"Verbal responses, please."

"Yes," I said.

"Good. Know that myself and my servants will not be visible to you. It is my hope that this arrangement will only be temporary, but that will depend on you."

"What do you mean?" I asked.

"I cannot say."

I let out an exasperated sound, but quickly silenced myself.

"All of these lands are mine and you are free to roam them at your leisure. I have duties during the day, but I will spend the evenings with you."

Oh, darkness of Hades. My mouth dried and my body went rigid with alarm. At my stiffness he let out a low hiss.

"You do not wish to spend time with me." A statement, not a question. And he didn't sound happy. How could he possibly be surprised? I peered down at my feet wrapped in dainty sandals that laced up my ankles. When he spoke again, his voice was hard.

"You will open your room to me each evening, whether it is your desire or not, and we will spend time together."

Again, my chest heaved and all I could do was nod. My stomach took that inopportune moment to make a gargling sound of hunger, and my cheeks heated.

"I forget how fragile humans are. You slept all day. You must eat now."

I blinked, swallowed, and nodded but made no move.

"Well, come on," he said.

"Wait." I took a deep breath. "What shall I call you?"

"You may call me Husband."

I frowned. "You won't tell me your name?"

"No, I cannot. But if you insist on calling me by a moniker, use Leodes."

My eyes bulged, and for a sweet moment my heart thudded in memory. "I cannot call you that." I dropped my eyes. "I once knew someone by that name." What were the chances?

He was silent a long moment, then cleared his throat. "You knew him well, did you? This Leodes?"

I shook my head in remorse. "No, actually. And yet…never mind. It matters not."

Another long pause, and then a gruff, "Indeed. It matters not. Come along."

No touching. No hearing his real name. No seeing him. I didn't understand the mystery surrounding him, but I was grateful he hadn't shown any outward cruelty yet. Perhaps he was saving that for the bedchamber.

My insides trembled as I made my way up the path to the castle fit for Jupiter himself. A paradise that would be my prison. And I couldn't help but wonder how long I had until nightfall.

CHAPTER TEN

NIGHT ONE

WHAT SORT OF MONSTER HAD A LAVISH HOME AND SERvants? None of this was right. I'd expected to be in a cave, on a dirt floor, shackled and in pain. Instead, I sat at a grand round table in an opulent dining room where everything was trimmed in gold. I let out a small yelp of surprise when a golden bowl of soup floated through the air and settled on the table in front of me.

"Princess," said a kind, mature, feminine voice. "White bean and vegetable soup in crustacean broth." Then another floating plate landed gently beside it. "And salted grilled sardines on fresh baked flat bread."

Oh, my goodness, it smelled divine.

"Thank you," I said, but the voice did not respond. The room was so quiet that I peered around. "H-hello?"

"I am here," came the deep voice of…my husband. It sounded as if he sat nearby, but he'd been given no food.

"Are you eating?" I asked.

"I care not for human food, and I do not require sustenance at the moment. Eat."

I stared down at the food, feeling uncomfortable. He could see me, watch me, stare at me. The sensation was beyond eerie. And could I trust this food? What if it was poisoned? I leaned in and gave it a sniff, causing my stomach to constrict at the pleasant scents.

"*Eat*," he repeated, startling me.

I picked up a piece of bread with a fragrant sardine. It'd been smothered in olive oil and I smelled a hint of lemon. My hand trembled as I brought it to my lips and took a tentative bite, holding back a moan of pleasure. It was prepared even more deliciously than that of the chefs at home. When the first bite didn't make me ill or dizzy, I proceeded to eat my fill. A sliced red fruit with white seeds sat on the side of the plate.

"What is this?" I asked nervously. "Ambrosia?"

"No," he replied. "It is tomato from a part of the earthly realm you have never been. Your people do not have it yet, but I think you will enjoy it."

The idea of food from around the world thrilled me, but I held back my excitement and took a tentative bite of the tomato. Slightly sweet and acidic. Very pleasant.

I'd no sooner finished when another plate appeared, roasted figs stuffed with creamy cheese, alongside a flaky, nutty pastry that dripped honey. A steaming cup of tea accompanied it, and though I was full, I continued to eat because I was not looking forward to what might come next.

"Do you require more?" my husband asked, and I shook my head. I couldn't have forced another bite.

"Then come. It is nearly night. We will retire to your bed-chamber."

I couldn't move. Every part of me was as heavy as marble. My stomach turned, a sickening mix of having eaten too much and being anxious beyond belief.

"I…but I'm not tired. I just woke."

"Time works differently here."

I pressed a hand to my lips and closed my eyes. To my surprise, he gave me that moment to gather myself. Also, to my surprise, I suddenly felt exhausted, even knowing I'd been sleeping soundly in the trees not long ago. Still, terror gripped me in tight talons and my body was leaden.

I shook my head. "I can't. Please."

"You will accompany me." He paused as if gathering strength. "Either on your own two feet, or over my shoulder." Each word was slow and deliberate, leaving no room for argument.

I took several breaths in, letting them out slowly. And then I stood, feeling like an invalid with each small, shuffling step away from the table.

"This way." A small nudge at my lower back caught me by such surprise that I let out a squeak, stumbling. He let out a low huff of air as I quickly righted myself, breathing hard and wrapping my arms tightly around my middle.

"Is that how you will react to my every touch?" His voice was low, a mix of anger and disappointment.

I hated the tears that sprung to my eyes, burning, making me want to back myself against the wall and scream. He was a monster. Invisible, yes, but deadly. Powerful. And he was playing some sort of cruel game with me, attempting to lower my guard. Feigning concern. But why?

I couldn't go down that hall. Panic flared to life, and all reasonable thoughts fled.

I made a break for it, sprinting toward the opposite hall from which we'd come. I had only run five paces when I felt my body lifted off my feet at the waist with impossible strength, and placed back where I'd been, facing the other hallway. He didn't let go of my arms as I flailed and tried to stomp his feet. It didn't work. He must have been holding me from behind at arm's length because I couldn't reach him. He gave me one firm shake and I stilled.

A scream wrestled its way from my throat, then he spoke with infuriating calm.

"Walk forward," he commanded. "Into this first hall. You will follow my voice."

I swallowed hard.

"Go," he commanded. I forced my feet to move into the first archway, worried that the more I tried to fight, the crueler he might become. White marble streaked with soft gray surrounded us. Farther into the hall were etchings of scenes made with gold, everything from war and boats in sea gales to lovers entwined, causing me to blush and look away.

"You do not care for that one?" he asked, furthering the heat to my cheeks.

When I kept my head down and didn't answer, he went on. "Rumors say you were a rebellious girl. You had a fire within. Did that defiant behavior not extend to taking lovers?"

My blood was hot, pumping too fast, making my skin feel hot and swollen. The last thing I wanted to discuss with this creature was my love life, or lack thereof. But I had a feeling he knew more than he let on and lying would only make things worse. I slowly shook my head. No lovers.

I waited for his reaction, but he gave none.

"Yours is the room on the left."

I looked up, surprised. Only one door was on the left, meaning that entire side of the wing would be mine. Before I could reach for the handle, the door swung open and I gasped as colors hit my eyes.

"Go in."

I stepped through the door just as the natural light dimmed and smaller lights around the space erupted. I stood, momentarily stunned into forgetting what faced me. My own room had always been beautiful, light and cheery, overlooking the Mediterranean Sea. But this room was twice the size. The far wall had several floor-to-ceiling windows. The tops were stained glass depicting flowers and ferns. All around me were plush furnishings: lounging couches on rich, fluffy rugs, tables with tall, detailed vases holding lavish plants, and an ornate desk. Along the walls were bright, silk drapes. Tiny bunches of oil lamps in brass holders hung from the ceiling at different heights, along with strange pillars of lights along the walls, giving the room a twinkling effect from hundreds of flames.

I stepped toward one of the small, white sticks along the wall, burning from the tip in a small brass cup extending from the wall. When I reached out to touch the dripping white part, my husband spoke close to my ear and I dropped my hand.

"It is called a candle. Another invention your people do not yet have. Wax surrounding a cloth center that burns, melting the outer layer."

Fascinating.

But most breathtaking of all was the bed. I'd never seen one so large. One glance promised me it was the most comfortable bed ever created. The four posters were made of the same trees I'd seen in the magical forest, dancing in all directions and creating a canopy over the downy fabrics.

"It pleases you."

Oh, gods. All the blood drained from my face. Even my fingers tingled. I couldn't look away from the bed, but now it was for a different reason.

The bed.

My marital bed.

I swallowed hard, attempting to wet my suddenly parched throat. I couldn't breathe. I couldn't speak. I couldn't move. My eyes fluttered closed, and I was so tense, waiting for him to touch me.

He was going to touch me.

With his scales.

Talons.

And fangs.

"I can smell your fear, Psyche." I sucked in thin air. He was close. So close. "Do you know the scent of fear?"

I gave my head a single shake.

"It smells like onions, sliced and left to rot."

Fantastic. I smelled horrible. If only it would deter him.

He let out a long, guttural sigh. Was it frustration? He couldn't possibly be surprised that I feared him. I was a human girl. A virgin. And he was a mysterious creature of power from the realm of the gods. A human was less valued than even the smallest of mythological monsters. We were nothing more than play things. So why did he react in such confusing ways?

"What do you fear most from me?" he asked.

"I…" Warm air shuddered from my chest as I searched for words that wouldn't anger or offend him. "I don't know."

"Do not *lie*."

My chest heaved for air.

He growled. "Tell me!"

"Everything!" I shouted. "I can't see where you are at any given moment. I don't know when you're going to t-touch me, or, or… what you're going to do to me. I don't know how much pain I can withstand. And I don't know why you're pretending to be kind!"

I fought to take air in and out of my body. The only sound in the room was my heavy breathing for so long that I wondered if he'd left me. Finally, he spoke again, still standing far too near.

"What if I told you I only wished to bring you pleasure?"

His words, low and rumbling, caused a chill to sweep across my skin, bumps blooming. My teeth even chattered, because there was no way our definitions of pleasure were the same. My husband was a sick, dark creature. A patient sadist.

"I see," he said with a deadly calm that made my breaths halt. I'd said nothing. What did he see?

"You are my wife, Psyche. But I will not touch you while the stench of fear is on your skin."

"Then you will never touch me," I whispered.

A growl reverberated from his chest, shaking the floor and making my eyes widen.

"You must *learn* to open yourself to me. There are things I cannot say or explain but know this…the alternative to me is far worse."

"I don't understand." Why must he speak in riddles?

"I have power," he told me. "Power beyond your imagination. I can turn it from day to night." The snap of fingers rang in my ears, and suddenly every candle in the room went out. The light beyond the windows was gone, as black as a starless night. I let out a whimper in the pitch dark and moved back until I was against the wall. But when he spoke again, he was just as close, having followed me forward as if he could see plainly in the dark.

"Bright soul, why must you make this difficult?"

In his nearness, I felt his words on my cheek. A scream immobilized in my throat as I was overcome by the surprising scent of rain and honeysuckle. That was *not* what a monster should smell like. How was he hiding the reek of sulfur and decay? Was he somehow altering my mind and senses? I let out a moan of despair.

This time when he spoke, he sounded a few steps away.

"Sleep." He, himself, sounded exhausted.

What was happening? Did he truly want me to sleep?

"I can't see a thing," I told him.

A golden glow shone from beside the bed—a small candle.

"Go on," my invisible husband said.

I glanced inanely around for him before moving hesitantly over, removing my shoes. When I got to the bed, I let my hands sink into the softness of the blanket. A small sigh escaped me. The material was more luxurious than anything we had, and we had the best man could make.

I turned, placing my back to the bed and crossing my arms instinctually. "Are you…leaving?"

"No."

That was not good. Across from me I heard him sniff, and I wondered if he was smelling my fear again. When I made no move to get in the bed, he spoke.

"What are you waiting for?"

"Please," I said boldly. "Just tell me what you want from me."

"I seek you, all of you, readily given."

Not happening.

"Then…" I swallowed hard. "Perhaps you should give me space tonight."

He chuckled, a sound of disbelief, again surprising me by sounding amazed that I would not want him. Perhaps I was reading him wrong, but I couldn't help the impression I got, that this creature was accustomed to getting what he wanted from women without any fuss. But how could that be possible? Maybe in the realm of Olympus the godly creatures revered the power of this monster, not caring if they were torn to shreds in the process, but he knew nothing of humans.

"I won't be able to sleep with you near."

"I stay," he told me. "That is not negotiable."

Gods, no. He would be here all night. I would never rest.

"Where will you—" I cut myself off from asking where he'd sleep, and he chuckled again.

"I will not join you in the bed until you invite me, wife."

He was deranged. Delusional. I nearly laughed until I found his breath warm against my cheek again, the sweet and natural smell dizzying my senses. I clutched the downy blankets beneath my hands.

"And I promise you this…" His voice lowered. "You *will* invite me."

CHAPTER ELEVEN

BODY, NOT SOUL

I WOKE BLEARY-EYED FROM EXHAUSTION, SOFT LIGHT SPILLING through the windows and filling the room with a loveliness that contrasted how I felt. Then I remembered where I was and sat up with a jolt, my heart like a rusted hammer against stone.

I made it through the first night unscathed! But how?

I did not invite him into the bed, obviously, and he never laid a paw on me, but his self-assuredness set me on edge. There was nothing he could do or say that would ever make me invite him. So why the confidence? What did he know that I didn't, and why couldn't he tell me? What was he planning? I did not enjoy the mystery of it.

Knowing he was in the room with me last night kept me awake far too long. And since I slept fully clothed, the skin under my breasts was tender from the bunching of material, and my shoulder ached from where the pin of my stola dug into me. I would have to work out a way to change into my comfortable nightclothes without his invisible eyes all over me.

I peered around the room.

"Hello?" No response. "H-husband?" Again, nothing. I couldn't bring myself to call him Leodes. I associated that name with someone special. Someone who didn't cause me to smell like rotting onions. Was my marital beast staying silent to trick me? Hoping I would undress in front of him? Well, that wasn't happening. To be honest, I didn't sense anything nearby. Even invisible, he gave off a presence that was difficult to ignore. Still, I felt on edge and wondered if I'd ever be able to relax again.

I carefully explored the room in more detail, opening both of the two doors. One was a lavatory and bath so lavish and clean it sparkled. The other was a closet twice as large as mine at home, with stolas of every style and color, more bright and vivid than I'd ever seen. Each had pins, broaches, and clasps made of gleaming gems, and fine stitching of gold and silver. These were more fashionable than what I'd wear on a special royal occasion. Nothing in the closet was what I'd consider normal, daily attire. These garments were fit for the goddess Venus, a thought that soured my stomach. I couldn't wear these.

I jumped, startled when the door to my room opened and a tray flitted through the air, setting down gently on a table. My heart thumped until the kind voice from last night's meal spoke.

"Your morning meal, Princess Psyche."

"Thank you," I said, then rushed on before she could leave. "What is your name?"

She cleared her throat daintily and said, "I am Renae, but I'm only a servant, Highness."

"Renae. Why can't I see you?"

A short pause passed, then, "I have been spelled, madam. If you cannot lay eyes on the Lord of this home, you cannot lay eyes on anyone."

"Says who?" I tried to keep my voice light.

"Says He, your husband, madam. But even he has rules upon him."

"Rules from whom? A master?"

"Not…necessarily. I can say no more." I heard the hesitancy and guilt in her tone. "I must go. Do you require anything more?"

"Wait." The thought of being left alone gave me a jolt of worry. "What am I to do?"

"You may do whatever you like, Highness. Walk the property. Explore the palace. You are safe here."

"Safe from all but my husband?" It slipped out, and I heard an intake of her breath.

"I can say nothing, Mistress," she whispered. "I will be in the kitchens. If you need anything at all, ring your bell and someone will be 'round to serve you."

Her feet made heavy sounds against the marble floors as she left, like the clacking of wooden shoes. When the door clicked shut, I was overcome with a rush of complete aloneness.

I leaned my palms against the table and fought the welling emotions. I had to be strong. This entire elaborate ruse was no doubt meant to lure me into a sense of safety, and I had to remain on guard. As much as I didn't want to eat anything in this strange place, it was imperative to keep up my strength. So, I sat, took a deep breath, and lifted the lid on my breakfast.

My stomach applauded with a gurgle as the scent of fresh, warm flatbread hit my nose, followed by eggs, peeled tomatoes, and greens.

Like last night, everything was perfectly seasoned with pinches of coarse sea salt. I decided if the food was poisoned, it would be a preferable method of death.

But alas, I failed to die, and was left wondering what would happen next. I was here as a punishment; therefore, it was only a matter of time before the horrors began. I could not allow myself to get comfortable. This was not home and never would be.

I paced the room, so tense that my neck felt like a thickly knotted rope, and an ache threatened to split my skull. I finally stopped and stared from the window at the extensive gardens. How I longed to be out there. If only the thought of walking through the substantial palace didn't terrify me. But it was more than fear holding me back. The idea of walking the grounds was like saying I felt comfortable. That I was making myself at home, which was what he wanted. If I gave him that, I was one step closer to fulfilling whatever master plan he had—the plan to *trust* him.

Madness.

In my infinite stubbornness, I refused to show any level of comfort. I would not lounge on the divan or hum a merry tune. I would not ring Renae for tea. I would not search for a book of philosophy or poetic ministrations to muse over. I would pace this room, silent and expressionless.

So, I did.

Gods, what a bore.

Perhaps this boredom was part of the plan to bend my mind to his will. I had to remain alert. To my shame, a soft knock at the door had me jumping and grasping at my chest, breathing far too hard than the moment warranted.

The door opened slowly, and a gorgeous tea set on a tray came forth, setting itself on the table without a sound other than the wooden footsteps of Renae.

"Tea, madam?"

"Yes, please," I said, wishing I hadn't sounded so earnest, but I'd been pacing for what felt like hours.

A copper pot with vines for the handle lifted into the air and poured steaming liquid into a cup, perfectly steeped. She added the exact amount of honey and milk that I would have given myself.

"There you are," she said. "Anything else, High One?"

I took a sip and accidentally smiled at the delicious perfection. "How did you know this is how I take my tea?"

"Your husband knows much about you."

I paused, uncomfortable at the thought of how he'd obtained such knowledge, before taking another small sip and letting the warmth fill me.

"Madam?" Her voice was hesitant. "You're still in the clothing from yesterday. Let me fill you a bath while you choose a clean dress."

"No. Those aren't mine."

"But they are!" She sounded cheerful. "Each was made specially for you with your exact measurements. He chose the details for every outfit. They're exquisite."

"*He* chose them? My…"

"Your husband. Yes."

I thought of the closet full of inhumanly perfect fabric and couldn't fathom how that was possible.

"Renae…what does he look like?"

"Oh, madam." She sounded wistful. "Even if I wanted to disobey him, the spell would never allow my tongue to form the words."

Curses. "He spelled you?"

"No. There is a spell over him, his home, and all within it."

Disturbing.

"So, what *can* you tell me about him?"

"Nothing at all, madam."

I sighed, vexed. "Any advice, then?"

"Yes. Bathe yourself. And do what he says."

With those unhelpful words, spoken in exasperating kindness, she shuffled away on heavy feet. I sniffed and squared my shoulders, the stubbornness setting back in the moment the door closed.

He already thought I smelled badly, so what difference did a bath make? If he thought I was going to come to his home, enjoy luxuriating baths and fawn over fine clothing until he was ready to strike, he was mistaken. I would not play the pretty princess with him.

I'd nearly drunk the full pot of tea and was sitting full and sleepy when one of the windows began to shake and clatter. It blew open with a gust of fragrant, warm air that lifted my hair and took my breath away. The unmistakable sound of beating wings filled the room, and I stood, spilling my tea as I backed against the wall.

His presence brushed against my senses, nearly physical in its force. Dark Hades...had he *flown* through the window? What sort of horrible creature was he? With a *whoosh*, the window closed again, and the bolt came down. My eyes darted around uselessly. Everything went very still, and I held my breath until the room began to dim. I squinted toward the windows and watched, startled as the bright sky darkened into evening twilight. Candles erupted around the room, flames flickering to life.

"But...there were only a few hours of daylight."

"I prefer night."

He had done that, changed it from day to night, just as he'd said he could. My mouth fell open and snapped shut again. I didn't want him to think I was in awe of that sort of power.

"In your home," he said, "you happily bathed and changed your wardrobe daily, often more than once."

"How do you know that?" I challenged.

"Is it not the truth?" he asked. "It matters not how I know. What matters is why you deny yourself those simple pleasures here, in your new home."

This is not my home. I bit my tongue to keep from releasing the thought.

"Do you believe you are somehow punishing me by refusing to bathe or dress or leave your chambers?"

I lifted my chin, wondering if he could see the involuntary tremble of my muscles and smell the tell-tale scent of my fear. I hated my body for its lack of cooperation.

A gasp was wrenched from my throat as the bathroom door flung open and the sound of rushing water filled the room. Then I let out a yelp when my husband spoke low, close to my ear.

"My wife." I spun to face him. "You will bathe and enjoy the comforts I give you."

I gritted my teeth. "You can force me to do something, but you cannot force me to *enjoy* it."

"Try not to enjoy it then, bright soul." He dared to sound amused.

The air seemed to press against me, urging me in the direction of the bathroom. I tried to dig my toes into the rug, but I slid easily right through the doors until my thighs bumped the porcelain tub. The water still rushed forth from the spout, lightly steaming. How did he get the water to come out already warmed? I knew the wonders of piped, pressurized water, but at home it was still cool and needed to be heated manually.

It did look inviting with a frothy milkiness from vanilla scented soap. I shot a glare toward the doorway, and it shut with a bang, making me jump. The water stopped of its own accord and the room was suddenly silent. I peered around, suspicious.

I felt no presence in the room with me, yet that did not put me at ease.

"Bathe," came his voice from outside the door.

I sucked in a trembling breath and let it out, still glaring at the door.

"Shall I call in Renae to assist you?"

"No," I said ungraciously. I unclasped the pin at the shoulder of my stola and let the silken, dirty material fall down to my waist. I'd never been prone to modesty, but the thought of my husband possibly watching somehow caused me to cover my chest with one arm while I tugged at the rope around my waist with the other. As my stola fell around my feet in a pile, I stepped quickly into the tub and slid down with a *slosh*. I accidentally let out a sigh. The water wasn't normal. It had a thick, wondrous consistency that made me feel cradled and buoyant.

Great Olympus, it was magical. On the other side of the door my husband chuckled, and despite the heat of the water, I shivered at the sound.

I made quick work of my clean up, scrubbing my skin and hair, working very hard not to relax too much or give him the satisfaction of a long soak. The moment I finished I stood, squeezed out my hair, and snatched a cloth wrap from a nearby bench. I rubbed my hair as fast as possible and wound the cloth about my body. When I went still, the door opened, causing the air to hitch in my chest and my heart to gallop.

The air propelled me forward again, a giant, gentle hand pushing me out of the bathroom, through the bedchamber, and straight into the closet. I fought to right myself when the air abruptly left me standing on my own. Three drawers covered in rose carvings slid open, revealing luscious looking sleeping gowns. A wave of sleepiness hit me then, making me peeved since my mind knew I shouldn't be tired yet. This place was maddening. I grasped the closest nightgown, a vivid green with soft cream lacing at the edges and high waist, and slid it over my head, keeping the bath cloth around me until I was fully covered. As the wet cloth fell to the floor, the air lifted it and carried it out of sight.

Then the wind pushed me out of the closet until I was standing directly in front of a massive high-back chair with an indentation in the seat.

"Come now, Psyche," said my husband in an amused rumble from the seat. "You were never this oppositional at home."

His nonchalance over my situation made me want to spit fire.

"Nobody at my home was toying with me like a cat batting a mouse."

"Am I batting you?"

"Yes." I cleared my throat. "Or fattening me up for the kill."

"I see." His voice was deep and lackadaisical. "Your attitude on the mountain when we were pronounced married…you were frightened, but not angry. Not like this."

I lifted my chin, ignoring my continuous trembling. "I willingly gave myself as a sacrifice for the transgressions of my family and people; however, I thought—" My head dropped as I attempted to fight back the emotions that pummeled me now.

"You thought what?" he asked quietly.

Still fighting for composure, I swallowed hard and drew in a breath. "I thought you would have your way with me and dispose of me quickly."

"I see," he said again, this time more firmly. "And your way of dealing with the fact that you believe I am toying with you is to be angry."

I cleared my throat and gave a small shrug. "I suppose so."

"You are not accustomed to feeling anger, are you?"

My eyes welled. I rarely became angry. To feel it so acutely each moment I'd been here was exhausting. The fact that he seemed to know it made me ill. I didn't want to be analyzed. I didn't want him to know me, or anything about me, and yet here he was. Learning me as I learned myself.

"There is nothing I can say that will ease your mind, Psyche. Only time can do that, if you allow it. But time is a fragile commodity, so I hope you will come to terms with our situation sooner rather than later."

I froze as the indentation in the cushion lifted, and I heard the slow padding steps of my husband drawing nearer. My instinct to run struggled against the riddled words he'd spoken. I hated the fact that my gut believed him to be genuine. This entire, horrid situation would be much simpler if my body, mind, and intuition behaved as one, but he had a way of muddling it all with his strange, gentle sincerity. A heap of fear mingled with a sliver of hope. Raging anger battered against a glimmer of tenderness. This had to be his plan.

To drive me to madness.

I closed my eyes and pressed my fingers into my palms, making fists.

"Whatever you're going to do," I said through gritted teeth. "Just do it."

"Psyche…" His voice was pained. *Curse him.*

"Do it!" I opened my eyes and screamed at his invisible features. *"Take me! Hurt me! Consummate this bloody marriage and end my life!"* I rushed forward to pummel my fists into his chest but heard a *whoosh* and felt the movement of air as his body shot up from the ground. He spoke from above me, making me lift my sodden face to the ceiling's gold patterned tiles.

"I warned you," his gravelly voice stated. "Never try to touch me. You have no idea of the consequences!"

I threw my arms out. "Then *you* touch *me*! What are you waiting for, *Husband*?" I spoke his moniker with a sneer.

He landed before me with a *boom*, sending a rumble through the room. I stood my ground, hands still in hard fists, ready for the pain that would finally come. I shook openly now, my breathing ragged, not caring that my hair and face were a disaster. *End this*, I silently begged.

And then something impossibly soft touched my cheek. I swung my hand up to protect my face from him, earning a hiss from my husband.

"Lower your hand, Psyche," he demanded. "And do not move."

With great effort, I brought my arm down and braced myself. I stared ahead into nothingness, my chest shuddering when the softness touched my cheek again. The sensation was unbearably silky. It slid down my jaw with slow affection, beneath my chin, across my throat to the other side of my face. My eyes lifted to where I guessed his eyes might be. I meant it as a challenge, but what happened instead was a rush of unexpected intimacy. In that moment, with the sensation of a feathery touch moving over my earlobe and then down my neck, all anger and fear disappeared. A delicious shiver rose up from the parts of me that had been graced with the attention, and every other bit of skin on my body wept to be touched as well.

"Your soul," he whispered, so close, "is glowing."

My soul? I swallowed, coming back to myself, and stepped away. The peace of the moment shattered like crystalized sugar, cracking and falling all around me. I touched my throat, horrified by how he'd made me feel.

"You can't see my soul." I nearly choked on the words.

"I can," he assured me.

"Oh, gods," I whispered, stepping away, away, away. I'd never heard of a being who could see a soul through one's body. If he could see it, perhaps he could possess it. Devour it. I pressed myself against the bed. "You can have my body, creature of the night, but you will never have my soul."

He spoke my name, whispered it, as if I'd somehow broken him. "*Psyche—*"

A chill of unwelcomed guilt sliced through me, and I pointed to where I knew he stood. "I will never be yours!"

The room was silent and still until a raging roar split the air and the high-backed chair he'd been sitting in earlier flew backward, crashing into the wall. The windows burst open, letting in a hot gust of air. I covered my face with my arms and screamed until all was quiet. When I lowered my arms again the chair had been righted and the windows were closed as if the entire spectacle had never happened. My husband's presence was gone, leaving me in a haze of confused emotions where there should have only been relief.

The madness was setting in. I had to fight it.

CHAPTER TWELVE

ENCASED IN WINGS

I MUST HAVE REALLY UPSET HIM, WHICH BAFFLED ME, BECAUSE HE did not return last night, and I slept soundly. Today Renae brought a morning meal, afternoon tea, and a late day meal, yet darkness did not come.

"Renae," I called before she left my chambers. "Will you stay with me? Play a game, perhaps? I think I saw a white and black board with stones—"

"I'm very sorry, Highness, but I'm not permitted to entertain you. Only your husband can do that."

I felt my face grow into a frown. "But that's ridiculous!" I tried to blink away the fury that filled me.

"Why don't you take a walk about the palace?" she suggested. "You'll find it quite lovely."

"I don't want to find this place lovely," I said. "I hate it here, and I hate him!"

"Very sorry," she whispered, and the door closed.

Everything I'd just eaten turned to heavy mud in my stomach. On top of being scared and suspicious every moment, I was also bored and restless. My body itched to run. The supposed freedom he offered was, no doubt, meant to lead me into a false sense of security, but I couldn't stay in this room one more moment.

Barefoot, I ran to the door and flung the heavy wood open, my heart racing as I searched the hall. Then I laughed out loud to myself like a madwoman, because what had I expected to see?

Nobody would show themselves for whatever odd, mysterious reason.

When my heart began to settle, I ran. My legs moved, the loose, flowing material of my stola never getting in the way. I took no time to admire the glamorous belongings sitting and hanging tastefully around each room. I ran, the marble cool under my feet. I passed rooms meant for studying, lounging, dining, entertaining, cooking, cleaning, bathing, and gods knew what else. I tried to memorize each twist and turn of the massive palace, its multiple winding staircases making me think twice about which way I'd come and gone. I ran until my feet ached, my legs burned, my stomach cramped, and I was out of breath. And then I burst out into the open, sprinting down the steps, falling to my hands and knees in the cushy, bright grass that stretched onward as far as I could see.

Damn the infinite beauty of this place.

Almost immediately, as I attempted to regulate my breathing, the sky began to darken.

"No," I murmured, shaking my head at the ground. "I'm not going back in." I sat on my bottom, pulling my knees up to my chest and wrapping my arms around them. The quiet outside was eerie and unnerving. I peered around. Everything was so still. No wind. No animal noises or insects calling. No people walking or chatting. No sea moving and splashing.

And that quickly, it was pitch black outside. Not a star or moon to be seen. I held my breath and looked around, but it was no use. I knew the doors to the palace were directly behind me, but I refused to stand and fumble my way back to those chambers of doom. Instead, I tucked my head against my knees and held myself tighter, rocking and trying to ignore the trepidation coursing through me. At least the air was comfortable. I could curl up on this grass and sleep.

No sooner had I thought it than a chill prickled my skin and the air cooled. I tightened my grip and it got even colder. My teeth began to chatter as my body shivered.

"Come inside, Psyche." His voice came from behind me.

I leapt to my feet and spun toward the palace where the door stood open and candles began to alight down the hall before me, welcoming us. I wanted to refuse him, but in only a matter of moments he had turned the outdoors into something uninviting. I crossed my arms over my chest and kept my head down as I climbed the set of marble steps and entered the grand doors. Warmth greeted me, and I let out an exhale.

I stopped and peered around. As much as I hated to admit it, I was lost.

The doors closed, shutting us in. Beside me, my husband cleared his throat and I took a step away.

"My behavior last evening was…unbecoming. This is more difficult than I expected."

His words took me by surprise. "What is difficult, exactly? Being married to me?"

He cleared his throat again. "Getting past your fear and mistrust."

I let out a huff of laughter at the ironic humor. "Why exactly do you need to get past my fear and mistrust? What does it matter? How I feel is not going to change."

"You could find happiness here if you allowed it."

"How so? And to what end? What happens when I let myself feel comfortable?" My insides shook as if I were still cold.

My husband let out a deep sigh. I cocked my head in wonder. I never would have believed creatures of Olympus could sigh with exasperation.

"I wish I could tell you, Psyche." His voice lowered. "More than anything."

His voice caused a tremor to run through me, finding its way to my core with a glorious warmth. I shifted my stance to try and ease the building pleasure, doing my best not to squirm. Wait…pleasure? No. I stood taller. Anger quickly took the place of whatever illogical thing he'd made me feel.

"Stop doing that," I told him.

"What?" He dared to sound curious, even innocent.

"You know very well *what*." I crossed my arms tightly, my cheeks heating. "That magical thing you do when you speak, and you spell me to make me feel…" My lips pursed, and I shook my head. I took another step away as he began to chuckle, the sound wrapping around me.

"I am not using magic. Your body is merely reacting to who, and what, I am."

Impossible. "Then tell me; who and what are you?"

"You know I cannot say."

"Of course not," I said, seething.

"I assure you," he said with underlying sensuality and confidence, "your feelings are your own and not forced by me in any way."

"I am no fool, *Husband!*"

"I would never call you a fool, Psyche. You are merely unaccustomed to the physical response of attraction."

My eyes widened, and my face grew hotter.

"I am not—" I sputtered. "How dare you?"

This time when he chuckled, deep and melodious, I marched away from him, getting as far as I could from the alluring sound in the depths of his terrifying voice. When I made it to the end of the hall and turned right, his voice called from where I'd left him.

"My wife…your bedchamber is the other direction." And he laughed again, infuriating me. The fact that a vile, winged serpent could have such an ego was disgusting. *Attraction.* Ghastly!

Once I made my way to the dining room I was able to spot the wing of my bedchamber. I sped up to get there, then remembered my destination was not a safe place, because he would follow me. Whether tonight was the night he would finally show his dark side, or if he'd continue to toy with me, remained to be seen. Either way, it was my fate. I could not escape it.

Nervousness razed me when I crossed the threshold, as if I'd pressed through brambles to enter. My skin stung with fear, my insides roiling. I backed against the wall near my bed, hating that I could not control my body.

"Come sit," came his voice from the doorway, followed by that exasperated sigh again. His footsteps sounded, and a chair pulled back.

I forced myself to unwrap my arms from around my body, and walked forward with my head high, taking the seat and sitting stiffly. The chair across the table from me pulled out and I heard the cushion depress as he sat. I stared at the blank space before me, the wonder of his invisibility never ceasing. My eyes strained to see the edges of him, at the very least, but not a spec was visible.

"I understand you would like to play a game."

My stomach soured, knowing my kind maid had told him. It felt like a betrayal, though I knew her loyalty was to him, not me.

"I wanted to play with Renae," I clarified.

I heard him shift in his seat and the cabinet beneath the table opening. Moments later a board was placed atop the table. Black and white squares, perfectly aligned, and smooth stones peered up at me. I swallowed down a sudden memory of playing stone chess with Dawn. She was a sore loser, so I often let her win, but she was a sore winner, as well, never able to tap down the urge to gloat. Still, I never admitted I'd botched my turns, because once she finished bragging she'd be in the finest mood, dancing me around the rooms and laughing, wanting to cause mischief with me.

"You are glowing. What are you thinking about?"

I blinked away memories of Dawn's rare, beaming smile and frowned. "What do you mean I'm glowing?"

"Your soul."

My heart thumped, then raced. He really could see my soul. The knowledge was sickening and terrifying, but in truth he sounded...in awe. Perhaps it was a sign of how homesick I was, because without meaning to, I answered.

"My sister. Dawn."

"Hm." I couldn't get a read on that response. He separated out the light stones from the dark ones.

"White or black?" he asked.

"Black seems fitting."

"How so?"

"You prefer to keep me in the dark."

The room suddenly flickered as if the sun itself had blinked, and then it went from day to night, candles erupting into flame throughout the room. Sulfur wafted toward me and I sat very still. It took a long moment for him to answer. "That is the way it has to be. It is not about my preference." The lot of dark stones were pushed forward to the edge of the board in front of me. His mood had definitely darkened along with the room.

"By all means," he said. "Have the first move."

I wondered... "How will you handle losing to me?"

A pause, then a burst of gritty laughter, bringing with it the scent of warm honey. That sound, though deep, and even raw, was again melodious. Every single time he laughed, really laughed, the undertones seemed to slink under my skin in all the wrong ways. My blood danced with the notes of his laughter. I remained very still as his mirth attempted to charm my skin, moving over me, in me, through me to unknot every unwanted tightness, and tighten places that I didn't even want to think about. I kept my face expressionless as his chuckles faded and he sniffed the air like a hound.

A deep reverberation sounded from his chest, making me swallow and clench my thighs.

"Fine, I'll go first," I rasped, quickly reaching out to press one of my stones forward with a shaking hand. He knew what he was doing to me—somehow causing my body to betray my mind. Of course, he did, and gods knew he had a keen sense of smell, but I wouldn't give him the satisfaction of acknowledging it again with words or actions.

One of his light stones slid forward. Only safe moves in the beginning.

As I moved a black stone with brown starbursts, I worked up the courage to speak.

"Whatever it is you're doing to me, for whatever purpose, my mind will never bend." I stared at the board. "Even if my body weakens, my mind will not give in."

"That is what I fear."

I peered up at the place where his face would be, wondering what he meant.

"Why do you fear the strength of my mind?"

"Because if you do not *give in*, as you call it, only pain awaits you."

I bristled, bringing my hands to my lap. "That's when you'll punish me? When my body finally breaks, and my mind is still my own?"

"Not I." It barely came out a whisper.

"Not you?" I was beyond confused. "Then who?"

"You know I cannot say," he gritted.

I narrowed my eyes. "Who controls you?"

"I told you, I am my own master!" A bang against the table caused me to jump back in the chair as the stones lifted and fell back down with a clatter, some tumbling to the floor. With a growl, I felt the air around me stir, and the stones rose again, moving back into the exact places they had been before his outburst. I could hear his ragged breathing.

"All right, no master then," I said. "But someone has some sort of control over you."

"It is not *control*," he bit out. "It is something different. Why must you be so inquisitive? Why can you not enjoy the beauty and comfort I have surrounded you with?"

"You are bound," I said, trying to work out the possibilities in my head, my heart increasing in speed with each word that escaped my lips. "A god, perhaps, has somehow bound you with the task of punishing me for the wrongs of my family and people. But it cannot be a simple punishment. No. You are to break me in every way—"

The air around me changed and I gasped. It felt as if I were enclosed in a small space, though I had not left my chair. Suddenly warmer, my breaths coming more rapidly, I knew he'd somehow enclosed us. I froze as his telltale scent of honeysuckle wound its way seductively through my senses.

"What's happening?" I whispered.

"Shh," he whispered. "Psyche…why must you make this so difficult for both of us? For one moment could you *not* strategize all the possible horrors and just let yourself be?"

Tears clouded my vision and I closed my eyes against the burn. "It's not in my spirit to give over easily."

"Tell me something," his low voice said so very close to my face. "What do you envision when you imagine me?"

I shuddered, overly warm, shaking my head. "A mixture of scales and fur in place of skin." I swallowed hard. "Soulless eyes.

Sharp teeth and fangs. Claws. And wings as thick and dark as stained leather-hide."

"I take it that is not your idea of attractive?"

Ugh, that word again! My face must have been answer enough because he burst into laughter, filling our small bubble of space with a blast of pure...gods, what was that? Pure deliciousness for my ears and senses. I grasped my knees through the fabric of my stola hard enough to feel my nails, and said, "Stop that!"

With a gust of air movement, the enclosed sensation disappeared, and I sucked in a breath, peering around. "What was that?"

"You were in my wings," he explained from his seat across from me. "I thought perhaps if I wrapped them around you, you would feel protected." My skin flushed as his words caused a myriad of sensations to overwhelm my mind and senses.

"Well, I didn't," I said, crossing my arms in a huff.

"It certainly made you feel *something*."

"It made me feel ill."

He made a *snicking* sound with his tongue. "Psyche, lying does not become you."

"Well then I shall lie all the more."

He chuckled again, and I scowled.

"Tell me," he said. "Why do you not call me Leodes as I requested?"

The sound of that name caused my chest to tighten with longing and regret. "I told you, I knew a Leodes, so it feels wrong."

"You think you have feelings for him?"

I didn't like his tone, as if he was aware I didn't know Leodes well at all. But he could never understand the connection I felt after one conversation. My crossed-arms tensed, and I bit my lip, refusing to be baited.

"He intrigued you?" When I only shrugged, he went on. "But surely you met many powerful, handsome men who intrigued you. Suitors?"

"I felt nothing for any of them. Not a single one made me feel the way he did."

"Hm."

I hated when he said *Hm*. I couldn't get a reading on that sound.

"What if I told you, Wife, that I know this Leodes you speak of?"

My eyes widened. "That's not possible." But then he went on to describe my Leodes in perfect detail. I clenched my jaw, in shock.

"I make you this promise," he told me. "If you behave, allow yourself to relax, when our time under these circumstances is over, you will see him again."

I struggled to inhale. This was too much to be true.

"How do you know him?" I asked.

"Not important."

"Is he married?"

His long pause made my heart nearly die. "He is very much available to you, Psyche." *Oh, thank the gods.*

I exhaled in a fluster. "I just want to be loved." I covered my mouth, but it was too late. The pitiful words were out there, making me even more vulnerable to my monster husband than I already was.

"I know," he whispered. "Sleep now. We will finish our game tomorrow."

For a moment I didn't move. His words, soft despite the natural guttural rattle in the depths of his chest, caused ambiguous feelings to collide inside me. Did I trust him? Not at all. Did

I fear him? With every piece of me, yes. The worst was yet to come—I knew that unequivocally—and yet I felt calmer. Perhaps it was the false promise of seeing Leodes again. Whatever the reason, I readied myself for bed, peeking over my shoulder now and again, but instinctively knowing tonight was not the night he would touch me.

CHAPTER THIRTEEN

PASSAGE OF TIME

S EVERAL DAYS PASSED WITHOUT ANY UNWANTED TOUCHES. He'd taken up reading to me at night. Poetry and essays out of Rome and Athens. His rumbling, monstrous voice was oddly pleasing, the rhythm of the words comforting. I'd never admit that aloud, of course. In a way, his voice reminded me of Papa's baritone when he'd rail at his soldiers to rally them for battle. I hadn't heard that war cry since I was a young girl, but I remembered the pride I'd felt at the power in his voice.

My husband was nothing like Papa, though, so the comparison fell flat in my heart.

Just as I'd promised, I never invited him to the bed. I wasn't sure where he slept, or if he slept at all, but I always felt his presence in the room, remaining still, as if lost deep in thought.

That night, I climbed beneath the downy covers and settled down, closing my eyes as the candles snuffed out all at once. Unlike the other nights, I could sense him prowling the room. In the pitch darkness, I could not see or even hear him, but that severe awareness was there. I felt him from across the room, near the windows, and then I felt when he was close. His nearness felt heavy this time. He wanted something. With my eyes closed, I felt him walk along the edges of the bed, back and forth. My heart beat steadily, listening to the silence, waiting.

And just like earlier, the air around me seemed to still.

"Husband?" I whispered.

"Yes?" I jolted at the sound of him so near, only a breath

away. There was something akin to hope in his voice that shook me.

My voice trembled. "What is it that you want?" Ugh, why had I asked that? It was more out of annoyance than anything, but I heard him take in a surprised breath of palpable hope. If he wanted me to ask him to bed, he would be left wanting. Not now. Not ever.

"I suppose...I want to touch your face again, but this time with my hand."

I gripped the blanket. "W-what did you touch me with last time?"

"The tip of my wing."

Oh...it had been feathery soft. Could his wings be made of feathers? Not the waxy bat wings I'd been envisioning? I blinked the thought away, making myself concentrate. His wings didn't matter right now. He wanted to touch my face with his hands. Hands that could shred me with their claws. Would he? I somehow didn't think so, but he *could*.

"If I let you touch my face, will you settle down and stop stalking about the bed?"

He grumbled incoherently, then cleared his throat. "Yes."

"Then fine. One small touch. Be fast."

"Be fast? Are we an old married couple already?" He chuckled darkly, and I scowled, sitting up.

"What is that supposed to mean?"

He made a pleased sound as if my question were cute. "You are an innocent."

I worked over the words I'd said and realized what he meant, embarrassment heating my skin.

"Enough. Let's get this over with." I sat up straight, pretending to feel brave when in actuality I would have passed out if I'd tried to stand at that moment. I closed my eyes tightly, grasping the blankets with all my might, expecting the scratch of rough appendages against my soft skin. What was he waiting for? Depths of Hades, how could I have been such a fool to give him permission? I was about to move away and tell him I'd changed my mind when I felt warmth cup my cheek and I stilled. My heart gave a low, slow thud. Then another.

Gods…that did not feel like a monstrous hand. His fingers moved outward, enveloping the skin around my ear, his fingertips—talons?—moving to touch my hairline. And then he added his other hand, and my face was fully embraced. The pads of his fingers moved, and I swore, I could not sense scales, only smooth, warm skin. Thumbs skimmed my cheekbones, then traced my closed eyelids. Nothing sharp. But that couldn't be. How was he doing this? Disguising the feel of his true self?

"You are so soft." His voice was a low murmur. A caress. My eyes fluttered at the scent of summer honey, drizzled fresh from the comb onto my tongue. "Psyche."

I felt his breath against my lips and gasped, coming back to myself. When I instinctively began to lift my arms to push him away, a blast of air smacked my hands down and he released me.

"Must I bind your hands?" he said. "How many times must I remind you—you are not to touch me!"

"I'm sorry!" I scrambled back and pulled the blanket over me. "I forgot!"

"You must not forget," he ground out emphatically. "One touch from you and everything changes. For the worst. Do you understand?"

"Yes!" No, actually, but I believed him because he sounded upset. If I broke this rule, it would change things for him, as well. I wished I could figure out how it all fit together. This mystery of my husband and who ruled him.

He didn't move away. I sensed him still close to me, perhaps even leaning against the bed. His voice softened.

"Now tell me…how would you describe my touch?"

My face heated, and though it was impossibly dark, I dropped my eyes. "I…you…" I swallowed. "Your hands felt normal. I don't understand."

"Hm."

"What does that mean? *Hmmm?*"

"Trust your senses, Psyche."

I quieted and felt him move away.

"I will not *stalk about* anymore," he said, sounding disgruntled about how I'd described him earlier. "Sleep."

I hunkered down, practically pulling the blanket over my head, hoping I could suffocate the uneasy feeling in my stomach. I thought of my husband's strong, smooth, warm hands on my face. What kind of creature *was* he? And exactly what sort of mind-altering punishment was I up against? Was I strong enough to fight this?

CHAPTER FOURTEEN

PLAYTIME

I SLEPT WITHOUT DREAMS. AT LEAST, NONE THAT I COULD RE-call. I slept deeper than any other night I'd spent here. Surprise coursed through me as I sat up, fully rested, wondering why I'd let my guard down so much. It was dangerous. I couldn't help but to question everything, even my own thoughts, feelings, and actions. How much of that was his power influencing me? He was clearly trying to soften me with his odd gentleness, but why? Getting comfortable would be a grave mistake.

Renae brought my morning meal and urged me to explore the property today.

"Your husband will be gone longer this day, to return at dusk."

"What does he do?" I asked, sipping my hot tea.

"Oh, Highness." Renae giggled, and for the first time she touched me, patting my shoulder and giving it a soft squeeze. "You know I cannot say."

I smiled into my tea. "Off terrorizing villages, no doubt."

Renae let out a high laugh. "Some might consider it so. His work is...complicated." She *tsked*. "I've said too much. Listen. Why don't you visit the archery range today? There is a bow just your size. But I should warn you—an enchantment has been placed so that your bow and arrows cannot leave the range. If you try, you will feel an unfortunate zap."

A zap? I shivered. And he knew of my interest in archery? It wasn't something most females enjoyed. It was disturbing how much he knew about me.

"Ring if you need me." She bustled out with the *clomp, clomp* of heavy feet.

I pondered her responses so long my tea cooled. Then I brushed out my hair, dressed in a sky blue stola that clipped on one shoulder with a golden beetle pin, and found my way out of the grand palace.

Just as the other times I'd been outside, I found the quiet perfection unsettling. I walked the gardens, marveling at the plant sculptures of creatures celebrating. They were dancing animals—bears, leopards, and monkeys—with arms and legs lifted in glee. Centaurs with drums and satyrs with lutes at their lips. The garden party seemed endless with hybrid creatures I'd never heard of, every combination of human and animal one could conceive. I found myself imagining the lure of the music as I walked between them, the sounds of their laughter and banter floating up from my imagination. Flowers as small as ants and as large as my head, every color and variety, wound around the gardens with vines that made pathways for my feet. I followed them so far and for so long I wondered if I might get lost.

I finally made my way out of the celebration maze and came upon the archery range. And just as Renae had promised, a bow was waiting in my exact size, finer than any I'd ever beheld. Smooth, light wood, both strong and pliable, with fire-etched vines along its length. I nocked an arrow and steadied my gaze at a life-sized target of a man. I released my arrow with a clean *zing* and gasped at how smooth it sailed, embedding into a shoulder.

Yes, I would enjoy this bow. When I went to retrieve the arrow, I stared in confusion. Over the dummy's heart was a deep crevasse, as if it had been struck there repeatedly. When my eyes searched, I found no other marks on the cloth body except the one I'd made in the shoulder. A quick look down the line of various targets showed more of the same. Only the bull's-eyes had been struck.

"Of course," I muttered. "My husband is a perfect marksman."

I set my bow and arrow back down, shaking off a feeling unease, promising myself I'd return to practice each day.

I next headed for the hills with the forest beyond, beginning at a walk, and then breaking into a run. It felt good to stretch my legs. I ran as fast as my body could handle until I was deep in the swaying trees, breathing hard to catch my breath. When I finally settled, the only sound in the entire outdoors found my ears: moving water.

I walked until I found the stream. It was delightful, running clear over smooth stones. I slipped off my leather flats and stepped into the water, splashing about. But when I thought about crossing to the other side, the water came suddenly rushing up, and the landscape changed from rambling stream to deep river. I quickly swam back, landing in a pile on the bank. The stream was enchanted not to allow me to cross.

I let out a *harrumph*, standing and wiping off my bottom. When I went to pick up my shoes I noticed the water was already gone from my legs and dress. I was completely dry. Definitely enchanted water. I turned toward the trees and found that they had shifted and moved, creating a straight path out of the forest, back to the hills and the palace beyond.

I eyed the forest and gave the trees a grin. "What if I don't want to go that way?" My feet took me between two trees on the side, their branches so low and entwined that I had to bend and work my body between them. A scream ripped from my throat when I felt something straight press against the back of my thighs, pushing me through the gap. Before I tumbled to the ground, roots shot out and spread, catching me in a makeshift cradle. I peered behind me to see the branch that had pushed me retreating. Laughter bubbled through me.

"Thank you?" I patted the roots and got to my feet, watching in awe as they retracted back into the ground.

At that point it became a game. I tried to wiggle my way through the hardest spots I could find, and to my delight, the trees played with me. They played with me! It was something from a dream. I climbed high in one tree as its branches moved round and round its enormous trunk like a spiral staircase. And when I got to the top, it wound vines around my middle and swung me down, making my belly swoop as I yelled with excitement. It was a far fall, but the tree never let me go. Then it swung me up and the next tree caught me.

By the time I made it to the other end of the forest, my face hurt from smiling and my entire body was spent. I was also sweating through my dress, and I loved it. I gave the final tree a hard hug and kissed its magical trunk, rough under my lips.

"I'll be back," I promised my new friends before trudging away, exhausted.

I fell against the side of a green, fluffy hill. I mean, really, what kind of grass was this? If we had this grass at home, we could drag blankets outside and sleep in comfort under the stars. There wasn't a single bug in sight to sting or bite.

When my strength returned, I walked back to the palace. The doors burst open at my arrival and Renae's voice fluttered out.

"Highness! Are you all right! Did they hurt you?"

"Who?" I asked. "The trees? Not at all! We had the most fun!"

"Fun?" She walked alongside me when I got to the hall, the doors shutting behind me. "But those trees have been known to mangle trespassers. They rarely let anyone see them move! I looked out the window and nearly died of the shock when I saw them so active! I even called to your husband—"

"You didn't." My heart gave a hard series of beats.

"I did, and I'm not sorry. He came immediately and laughed at my worry, assuring me you were quite all right, but I couldn't imagine what all the fuss was out there."

"What else did he say?"

"He said, '*Worry not; they are entertaining one another.*'" She said it in his same gruff voice, and I giggled. "Whoever heard of the trees entertaining? And a guest enjoying it!"

"Well, dear Renae, you'll have to get used to it because I plan to visit them every day." I smiled at her scoffing sound and ran the rest of the way to my bedchamber, loving the feel of dried salt on my skin. It reminded me of how I'd felt at home after a day of exploring and getting into trouble, tired and sweaty, my long hair tangled and wild.

But halfway through my bath, my dark mood returned. Yes, I'd adored every minute with the trees, but I couldn't forget what awaited me. My mysterious punishment. As famished as I was from my day of play, I barely picked at the meal Renae left for me. And though it was still sunny out, I opted for a nightgown instead of another dress. I sat, staring off, my hair still wet and unbrushed, when the massive windows opened, and the presence of my husband came *whooshing* in. I wrapped my arms around myself.

"What is the matter?" He was standing over me. I shivered.

"I'm tired."

"It is more than that." I heard him sit in the chair opposite me. "You were filled with joy when I saw you today."

I peered down at the cushion I held on my lap, picking at the tassel. "You watched me?"

"I only had a moment to spare, but yes. I've never seen the trees behave that way."

It felt strange knowing he'd seen me in that state of laughter and smiles, both things I withheld from him. It was like two parts of myself were clashing. I missed the old me. Being on guard and scared all of the time drained the life from me. I rubbed my face.

"Tell me what you want, Psyche."

"I want my family."

"I am your family now."

His words were gentle, but my eyes burned, and I kept my hands over my face. "I want to know what your plan is for me. When you will finally hurt me. When the punishment will be fulfilled."

He didn't answer at first. I sniffed and forced my emotions down.

"I cannot ease your mind." He sounded regretful. "Not with words. What else can I do?"

"I miss…" I stared out the windows. "Animals. It's strange to be outside and not see a single bird or bug or animal."

"Very well," he said.

I peered at where he was sitting. "You'll bring animals here? A puppy? Or a kitten?" A glimmer of glee trickled within me.

"That is simple. Tomorrow you shall have your wish."

That easily? I smiled down at the pillow, and whispered, "Thank you."

"Psyche?"

"Yes?"

"May I brush your hair?"

"Um…" My face went warm and I looked everywhere except in front of me where I knew he sat. For some reason, the thought of having him brush my hair was even more intimate than allowing him to hold my face. I needed to be more careful. "I can do it." And to prove my ability, I grabbed the palm handle of my brush from the side table and began to roughly drag it through my hair, pretending I hadn't just denied him a simple thing. Why did I feel guilty? I had nothing to feel bad about.

My hair was mangled from today's activities. I ripped out tangles until my scalp was tender, then I set it back on the table and cleared my throat. "See? All done. I should go to sleep. Is it nearly night yet?"

At my question, the sunlight disappeared, and the candles lit themselves around the room. "Thank you," I told him, standing stiffly and rushing across the room to climb into the bed, pulling the blankets up all around me. No funny business tonight.

I sensed him move to the bedside. And then he began the slow stalking thing again. My teeth clenched in annoyance. I could see where the edges of the bed moved, the covers sinking down under the weight of his hand as he dragged it along the material. I thought about that hand. It's tender warmth. Its strength. Its humanesque skin.

"Fear is an interesting concept, Psyche, is it not?"

I said nothing, my heart gaining speed.

"Sometimes," he said, "we fear that which we should embrace because we do not know the full truth."

I swallowed, shaking my head, closing my eyes.

"When I touch you," he breathed, "your fear disappears. You enjoy my touch."

"*No, I don't,*" I ground out.

"Your lies are useless." The covers flew back from my body, making me scream. He grabbed my ankle and pulled me forward. I tried to kick out, but he had both my ankles now and he was unbearably strong. When my body twisted, and I pulled at the covers, terrified, he hissed.

"Be still, Psyche. Lay back."

I whimpered, frozen with fear, still twisted sideways with the bedsheets crinkled in my fists. It was happening. He was going to take me.

In a wickedly calm voice he said, "Turn to your back."

"Let me go!"

"I will not. Turn or be forced to turn."

I wanted to fight. Gods, I wanted to fight. But I knew it was useless, and part of me wanted the inevitable to be over and done with. I rolled rigidly to my back, my ankles still in his grip. My night gown was around my thighs.

"There now," he said. My chest rose and fell at a rapid speed. "All I want is for you to feel me."

I held my breath as he released one ankle. I immediately bent that leg to get it out of his reach but realized it caused my nightgown to raise further, so I dropped it again, my whole body shivering. I pressed my knees together as he pushed the long material up a bit more, exposing half of my thighs. Then he stilled, his warm breath against my knee causing me to shiver. Why, *why* didn't his touches fill me with disgust? Why must everything he did feel so *nice*? The nonsensical, methodical way he was fooling my body caused my mind to feel irrational anger.

"You said you wouldn't come to this bed unless I invited you," I spat.

Just as roughly, he said, "What you think is happening is not."

It clearly was!

"You're mad," I said, fighting back tears of frustration.

"Do yourself a favor, wife of mine. Imagine Leodes." With those words, my arms flew up over my head, pinned above me by...air? I struggled to yank them down to no avail, letting out a shout.

I waited for my gown to be ripped away, but it stayed in place. And then the underside of both of my calves were pinned in his strong hands, pulled slightly apart, the heavy swath of my nightgown blessedly falling into the open space to hide my core.

Something unbearably soft and hot was placed against the skin inside my knee.

Air sped into my chest and got stuck there. He was kissing my leg. Oh, gods. Gods! Dark Hades! His mouth opened on my skin and I felt his silky tongue slide along my skin, then his teeth. No fangs? How could that be? The sound of his mouth closing over my skin, like a kiss, came to my ears and a warm shudder ripped through me. His mouth opened again, moving, his tongue sliding, and I felt my body sag as tension fled my being. I had the oddest longing to cradle his head in my hands, but they were tightly bound above me.

I let out a whimper of surprise. This was happening. I waited for each pleasing sensation to be followed by a slice of pain, hot and fast, but it never came. Instead, my invisible husband worked his way up my leg in agonizing slowness, devouring every single bit of my skin in the heat of his damp mouth, that velvet tongue working against me as he nipped and lavished. I squirmed, caught between terror and something altogether different, yet frightening in its own way—the urge to let my knees fall open to him. I'd never expected his touch to feel like this. It made my body come alive in a terrifyingly eager way. *Yes.*

Wait. *No.* Oh, gods.

"Psyche..." He practically purred my name as his lips approached the edge of my nightgown where it had been pulled to cover my core and upper thighs. I had the wicked urge to grasp the material and pull it higher. Shame heated my face at that thought, and I breathed louder. I hated myself in that moment.

My husband moved to the next leg, kissing along the edge of the material, from the inside of my leg to the top, and back. I moaned, tense, as a kindling fire built inside of me. I didn't want this. But I wanted it more than anything. I shook my head. Gods of Olympus, I was panting like a hound after a fox. If I gave in to this moment, it would change everything. There would be a shift in the balance I'd carefully constructed, and I'd never be able to right it. My body wept at my mind's reasoning.

"Stop," I whispered.

"You want me to stop?" His hands gripped my calves harder and I felt his breath against my damp thighs. A rush of honeysuckle, tempting and sweet, rose up to embrace me, hazing my vision.

"Yes," I moaned. *"Stop."*

Immediately, I was released, and my nightgown was pulled down. I scrambled to a sitting position, yanking the blanket up. My entire body quaked, sensitive and prickling every place his mouth had touched. I could hear his breathing from the end of the bed. Cold regret splashed me, and anger settled back in. Anger at him. Anger at myself.

"Get out!" I yelled, my voice breaking. Hot tears of frustration and humility streaked down my cheeks. "Leave me alone!" I didn't care that it was his palace. Or that he swore he'd stay with me every night. I wanted him gone.

"Sleep well," he said. His voice slithered around the room, under the covers, touching every part of me until I had to curl into a ball and cover my ears.

The window burst open and his presence disappeared in a flash, snuffing out the candles, leaving me in complete darkness. I lay there alone, trying to breath, clenching my thighs and crying at the ache of my body, begging for release. I hated him, and I hated myself for wishing, *wishing* he would have finished what he had started.

CHAPTER FIFTEEN

COMPANIONS

A WARM, INCESSANT LAPPING AT MY CHEEK HAD ME HOLDING up a hand and waking with a start. I made a sound of surprise at the golden mass of hair standing over me, practically shaking with delight, its silky, long-haired tail wagging.

"Great goddess," I whispered, then took the puppy's elongated snout in my hands and laughed. "Hello, precious!" I sat up, and the Saluki pup danced around on my lap with its long legs, excited that I was awake and lavishing him with attention. He was short haired everywhere except his ears and tail, which had soft, straight hair that begged to be combed with loving fingers.

I peered around, wondering if my gift-giver was in here, watching, but my vision was blurred by a massive, intricate web stretching between the two end posters of my bed. My eyes darted around until I spotted a gigantic black body with furry legs in the corner of the web. I let out a scream of terror.

"Spider!" The thing had to be the size of my open hand. I grabbed the puppy, who surely could have been wrapped up and eaten by the creature if he got too near. I jumped from the bed.

"Good morning, Princess Psyche!" I spun at the bright sound of Renae's voice behind me, and saw a tray floating toward my table.

"Renae! There's a spider on the bed!"

"Oh, yes. Very grand. I'm not certain I care for human bugs, but your husband said you were missing them."

"I was not missing spiders!" I petted the pup's head, grateful for his calming presence in my arms.

"No?" She sounded worried. "Shall I dispose of it for you?"

"You can't get near it, Renae," I warned her. "Its legs appear as strong as my own. What if it jumps?"

She outright laughed. "I'm not afraid, if that's what you're worried about. I'll get it now."

"Wait! You're not going to kill it, are you?" I wasn't sure I could handle the crunching sound.

She laughed again. "Ah, humans. I'll just set it free outdoors. Is that all right?"

"Yes." I held my breath and cringed as I heard her clomp toward the bed. The spider began to dart across the web, and then it was snatched cleanly into the air, curling protectively in on itself and "floating" toward the window. I didn't release my breath until the colossal bug was out of sight. Renae hummed jauntily and wiped away the web in a rag as I stared, astounded.

"I thought you were a brave girl," she said with no judgment. "Are you truly afraid of something just a fraction of your size?"

I pursed my lips, feeling foolish. "It's just that…they have so many legs. And they're fast! Some spiders can kill with a single bite. They're sneaky."

Again, she laughed. The puppy began to squirm, so I set him down and he bounded forward and began sniffing the air where I assume the maid stood.

"Oh, you furry little thing," Renae said. "You'd better not piddle all over my clean floors."

I smiled. "I'll take him out frequently; promise."

"Leave it to humans to domesticate nonverbal creatures and allow them to sleep indoors," Renae teased.

From under the bed, a white furball with brown, orange, and black spots darted out and pounced on the puppy.

"A kitten!" I screeched, throwing out my arms in delight.

"Oh, yes." Renae grumbled. "Forgot about that one."

I clasped my hands and laughed as the two of them rolled around on the floor, grasping with small appendages and pulling at one another's loose skin with their sharp baby teeth. When the puppy let out a tiny yelp, I reached down and took the kitten into my hands, lifting her to get a good look. She licked her spotted nose, eyeing me in return.

As I stood admiring the kitten an idea came to me. "I think I'll eat outside this morning, so they can run." I set the kitten down and rushed into my closet, quickly dressing. When I started for the tray, Renae gasped.

"Don't even think of carrying that!" I felt a breeze as she rushed past me and lifted the tray.

I opened the door and the puppy bounded out. Though he ran back and forth all over the place, he always found his way back to my side when I made a *snicking* sound.

"See, look, Renae, he's a smart boy!"

"Sure, he is," she mumbled.

The kitten followed closely, now and then batting at the bottom of my stola as I walked, then rushing over to jump on the unsuspecting puppy. I couldn't stop smiling. Whatever dark game my husband was playing, gifting me with these sweet pets would help me make it through. Perhaps he thought he was merely appeasing me, but my strength of mind rose tenfold with the addition of these innocent companions.

When we got to the doors and I pushed them open, my entire face lit up at the sounds of birds chirping and singing their mismatched songs. Butterflies of every glorious color glided over flowered bushes, and dragonflies chased one another, their shimmering bodies and wings zipping past. My puppy and kitten raced out, the cat disappearing into the bushes.

"Yes," I breathed. This is what the place needed.

"Here you are then." Renae set the tray down at a marble table with four round, marble stools around it. "I'll be inside. Enjoy."

"Thank you." I listened to her clomping away and watched the heavy doors slide shut. The puppy sat near my side, looking up at me. One of his long ears was flopped backward. I righted it with a smile.

"What sort of creature do you think Renae is, boy? Something with hooves?" His head tilted, and I giggled. "What shall I call you?" I pulled the shining lid off the tray and plucked out a piece of sausage. One bite for me, one bite for the puppy. I had to be careful not to feed him too much fat and hardly any grains. Mostly lean meat, fruits, and vegetables. When we'd both had our fill, he ran into the maze of bush creatures and lifted his leg for a long while on the depiction of a minotaur—half bull, half giant man. When he finished, he peered up at the sculpted bush and growled, then barked, his tiny hackles raising.

I laughed, smacking my legs. "Aren't you menacing? Maybe I'll call you Mino since you're willing to battle the mighty minotaur." He came running at me. I moved to the ground where we could play together, laughing. The kitten came from nowhere with a sneak attack, joining the fray.

"Look, Mino, it's our own little Sphinx!" I was tickling the kitten's tummy when a sharp sting caught my ankle. I sat up and slapped the spot, then felt another, higher up my leg and stared down to see hundreds, perhaps even thousands of red ants covering my legs and the ground around me. All at once, my legs and feet were on fire. I jumped and ran from the spot, smacking at my skin and then bending to lift Mino and Sphinx. I didn't see any on them, thank goodness, but I was still crawling with ants.

I rushed farther away, up the hill where I could set down my animals and thoroughly strip off my stola. Gods, they had made their way beneath my dress, biting the skin of my thighs and lower stomach. I swiped down my skin, crushing them beneath my feet. Immediately, my lower body began to burn and throb. As I stood there completely naked, trying to catch my breath and taking stock of my tender, stinging skin, I heard Mino let out a string of *yips*.

My heart seemed to stop as I sighted not one, but two fully grown mountain lions at the crest of the hill opposite us. A male and female. Deep Hades. Slowly, barely breathing, I bent and picked up Mino and Sphinx again, grateful they hadn't run off. Then I stared at the massively powerful hunting cats. My heart would not settle, it only thundered harder behind the confines of its cage in my chest.

What had my husband been thinking? Or was this part of my punishment?

"Gods, help me," I whispered. When my young pets began to squirm, and Mino started barking again, I tried my best to shush and calm them. To my horror, Sphinx clawed her way free and took off toward the forest. And worse, her fleeing caused the pair of mountain lions to snap into prey mode.

"*Noo!*" I screamed and charged down the hill, feeling awkward and slow with Mino in my arms. Sphinx was fast, disappearing into the trees. Which way did she go? Oh, Hades! I was going to have to climb a tree, naked, with a dog in my arms! But couldn't mountain lions climb too? The realization threatened to turn my innards into liquid. This could not be happening. The mountain lions were only two trees away, moving like grace on paws. I stupidly peered around for a loose branch to fend them off before remembering these trees did not shed branches. The ground covering was neat and perfectly litter free.

"Help!"

Before I could despair another second, a set of branches

swooped down and wound around me, lifting me off the ground. The mountain lions leaped upward, swiping their sharp nails through the air. They were so close I felt the movement of air against my hot feet. I watched, fighting to breathe, as roots shot up through the ground, thin and gangly, but strong, and formed a barrier around the snarling animals. They roared and hissed, pacing in circles around their cage.

I couldn't help it—I burst into tears. I even kissed the branch that held us, muttering, "Thank you, thank you," over and over. Mino's ears were back in fear, and he dared not try to wiggle from my arms now.

"I have her," a deep voice said. A moment later, I was being passed by sturdy branches into the open air. I braced myself and the puppy for the imminent fall, but felt strong arms surround me. I heard his fingers snap, and Sphinx climbed the tree, prancing out to the limb and leaping onto my shoulder.

"Keep your hands on the pup," he said. "Do not accidentally touch me."

I buried my face into Mino's furry back to keep from looking down as my husband flew us over the hills and back to the grounds of his estate. The moment he set me down, I curled in enough to make sure Mino was covering my nakedness.

"We could have been killed!" I screamed. "Is that what you wanted? To see me shredded?" Betrayal filled my soul, though I knew it was a pointless thing to feel.

"The trees would have never allowed that."

"Well, what if I hadn't gotten to the trees in time? You obviously wanted to see me terrified and suffering. I knew it was only a matter of time before your cruelty showed!" Gods, it hurt, making me realize I'd let my guard down far too much.

The doors burst open and Renae's clomping feet and worried noises filled the air. She threw a blanket over my shoulders and I set down the puppy to wrap myself in it. I glared at the space where I knew my husband stood.

"Your legs," I heard him whisper. I didn't have to look down to know they were bright red and swollen. Now that my blood was not pumping as hard, the pain returned with vengeance.

"I asked a helper to fill the estate with human bugs and animals, as you asked." His voice was terse. "Clearly I should have been more specific."

"Clearly," I responded, though my anger was weakening, giving way to the physical sting left from the ants.

He let out a growling sound of exasperation, muffled as if he were rubbing his face. I would not feel bad for him.

"Come, Mino. Come, Sphinx." I turned and climbed the massive marble stairs to the doors, hoping my pets would follow, which they did. But every step hurt. I could feel my pulse in my ankles, which appeared double their normal size. Dizziness washed over me as I peeked downward. So swollen. I had to steady myself against the wall.

I was not happy when I felt myself being lifted and carried.

"I can walk." I elbowed his chest weakly, and he held me tighter.

"Be still, Psyche. You need healing."

"Why are you here in the middle of the day?" I wondered, as a delirious fuzziness began to set in.

"You prayed to the gods for help, and I was sent."

Interesting. Overwhelmed with pain and ant poison, I tried to be still and to remain alert. My legs began to crawl again.

"They're on me…"

"No, Psyche—"

"*They're still on me!*" I kicked my legs and my husband ceased walking, lifting us into the air and flying the rest of the way to my chambers.

He set me on the bed and my eyes fluttered, the room going dark, then light, and dark again. I barely felt his ministrations along my feet, ankles, and legs until a huge bout of unbearable heat had me struggling to sit up, yelling.

"Shh, lay back. The poisons are burning off."

I gritted my teeth against the horrible sensation. The door opened, and a basin of water on a tray with cloths and a bowl of ointment settled beside me.

"There now," came Renae's voice. A cloth dipped itself into the water, rung out, and moved to cover my forehead. I gasped at the wonderful coolness. With each gentle wipe of my face, the stinging of my legs lessened, and my body became heavy. Renae's footfalls moved to the closet and she returned with a loose, silk gown, lowering it over my head.

"I will handle the rest," my husband said.

Without a word, Renae left us. The bowl of yellow ointment lifted, and I sat up, grabbing it from the air.

"I can do it," I said. "Leave me."

"I allowed you to order me away once," he said, snatching the bowl back from me. "But that is not happening again."

With a softness that didn't match his gruff tone, he scooped out the ointment and rubbed my feet and legs. I kept a scowl on my face, refusing to show any appreciation, which was difficult since my body begged to sink back in relief and pleasure.

A small whimper and scratching sound made me look down to where the puppy had his paws up on the side of the bed.

"Aw, Mino," I said, gutted by his huge eyes and ears pressed back.

"He is worried about you," my husband told me. "But he will try to lick the medicine. *Down, Mino.*"

To my shock, at the small order from my husband, the puppy fell submissively on his back, his tail lightly wagging beneath him. I accidentally giggled for a moment, clearing my throat as I pulled my legs inward, beneath the blanket that was still wrapped around me.

"I will have the dangerous animals and insects taken off the property at once. Are you afraid of mice?"

"No," I said.

"Good. I will keep them, so your kitten can learn to hunt and fend for herself. You named her Sphinx?"

"Yes."

He chuckled, and in that moment, I believed he'd never meant for me to be hurt. Then my mind turned again. He could be the most masterful liar and manipulator of all time.

"What are you thinking right now?" he asked as if he'd seen the mixed thoughts across my face.

I peered down at the blanket. My thoughts were my own.

"I'm thinking I need to dress once the ointment dries."

"Hm." He didn't believe me. And rightly so.

I looked at my legs. They appeared normal, as if they hadn't been massively swollen and red minutes ago. My husband had powers of healing—yet another wondrous, mysterious thing about him.

A small scratching sound came from the door, and it opened, letting in Sphinx. Meanwhile, Mino was still lying on his back, tail moving, staring at the end of my bed where my husband stood. The cat looked at Mino, then peered up at me on the bed with a high pitched mewl.

"There she is," my husband said. And with that, Sphinx stared at the place where he stood, and her ears went back as her tail lowered and she slouched to the ground, then flopped over onto her back next to Mino. What sort of creature could cause such extreme submissiveness in a *cat*?

"Well," he grumbled. "At least he chose well with those

two." His fingers brushed my shin, sending a shiver across my skin. "You are dry now. I take it you did not make it down to the river today?"

"No," I admitted, curious.

"Come with me." His hands went under me as if to scoop me, and I rolled away with a yelp. He let out an audible sigh. "You will want to see this, Psyche. Keep your hands in your lap and let me lift you."

Damn him. My curiosity was piqued. I sat still and stiff, my knees bent, my hands clasped at my chest. And though I was expecting it, my body still wanted to jump away when those strong arms came around me and lifted me.

"Just what are we doing?" I asked.

"You will see."

I didn't hold back my yelp when he lifted me into the air and jumped from the window.

CHAPTER SIXTEEN

RIVER SURPRISE

HE PLACED ME ON MY FEET, FACING AWAY FROM THE RIVER toward the forest. It took a moment for me to gather my wits and balance.

"What are we...?" I began, but felt his hands on my shoulders, turning me. I stared at the river, which had extended itself into more of a rounded body of water. In the center, to my absolute delight, I saw two fins break the surface in gentle arcs.

"Dolphins!"

"Not just any dolphins. Join them."

It couldn't be...a steady thud of anticipation began in my chest as I waded out into the clear waters, feeling smooth rocks and gritty sand beneath my feet. Soon, I was chest-deep, and the dolphins began to circle me, pulling a laugh of joy from my soul as they nudged and bumped me. I ran my hands over them, unable to stop smiling. And then I saw the scar, and my heart tightened.

"It's you," I whispered. Looking up at the shore of the waters, I saw nothing, but knew he was there, watching. "These are the dolphins from my lagoon? Truly?"

"Truly," came his voice.

In that moment, I allowed myself to let go of every fear and negative thought, instead embracing this time that I had with the creatures from my homeland. And as we swam together, them pulling me at times, the three of us splashing and playing, I was able to nearly forget my captivity and all that plagued my heart and mind.

When I was too weary to continue, I kissed them both many times on their smooth skin, and trudged from the waters, turning to blow them kisses. Oh, how I would cherish this and miss them. I had needed their company.

"Thank you," I whispered.

My husband cleared his throat and I realized he was behind me. I turned.

"It was the least I could do." His voice was even deeper and gruffer than normal. He cleared his throat again, as if something were amiss. I glanced down at the way the thin, wet silk clung to my every contour, my nipples puckering upward as if begging for attention. Was he affected by me? I quickly crossed my arms and he cleared his throat a third time. And as I stood there, awkwardly, the water seeped from my skin and gown, returning every drop to the river until I was dry.

"A bit of home for you to keep," my husband said. "You can spend time with them every day."

My head tilted, not hearing him right. "I thought you said the animals would be taken away in the morning?"

"Only the dangerous ones."

I looked back at the dolphins. The clearing of water was large, but it was nothing in comparison to the expanse of sea they were accustomed to. Did they have a family? It hurt to think of taking them from home and confining them here the way I was. I wanted them here with me, but I could not be so selfish.

"Please return them," I said with regret. "They are not meant to be pets like a puppy or a kitten. They are wild and need to be free."

"Hm." He paused. "If that is your wish."

"It is," I said sadly.

"Very well, Psyche. Let us return to your chambers. Hold

your hands in."

"Wait!" I stepped back, my stomach swooping. "Can we walk?"

He chuckled. "If you insist."

Keeping my arms crossed, we made our way into the trees. When I felt something push under my arm to tickle me, I turned, ready to kick my crazy husband, but what I found was a tree branch pulling back.

"Did it just...tickle you?" My husband asked.

I pressed my lips together.

"Unbelievable." Was that annoyance in his voice?

We kept walking, and I had to dodge tickling branches from several of the trees, unable to hold back giggles. My husband grumbled a little and inhaled loudly when we exited the forest, letting it out in a huff.

"Why don't you approve of their playfulness with me?" I asked, my muscles burning as we crested the hill.

"Their touches bring you pleasure." He was definitely grumbly.

My arms tightened over my chest. "It's nothing sensual."

"Yes, I know. But you welcome their touches. They cause you to smile. When I touch you..."

My gut twisted a little at the hurt and jealousy in his tone. What a confounding creature my husband was. My heart gave a small ache, and I was tempted to ease his mood by telling him his touches brought me more pleasure than I wished to admit, but I bit my tongue. Why should I feel the need to ease his mind? He said nothing more, and neither did I until we returned to my bedchamber.

"I can see you are fatigued. I will draw a bath and have Renae bring your meal."

Seconds later, the animals were on their feet, wrestling one another, and sounds of running water came from the bath. I ate and bathed in silence, feeling his presence in the large chair that overlooked my room. I pondered what he might be thinking, and then berated myself for wondering.

After my bath I dressed in a comfortable nightgown and patted my hair dry. I heard my husband stand, and I stilled.

"May I brush your hair?"

A chill scuttled over me. It was the second time he'd made the odd request. The first time I'd said no. But now, after the dolphins, guilt surged inside me at the thought of denying him such a small thing. As much as I wanted to say no, I pursed my lips instead and held out the brush.

I sat rigidly on the bench, feeling exposed as he came up behind me with the floating brush. I'd had my hair brushed thousands of times by others, so why was I so nervous?

He began in the middle, making gentle, yet firm swipes downward to the bottom. When he hit a snag, he said, "Sorry," and kept going. Surprise razed me at the tenderness with which he stroked the brush through my hair, down my back, over my shoulders, even against my neck. The closer he got to my scalp, the closer he got to me, overpowering my senses with his honey-eyed breath. How did he manage to make a mundane task so sensual? Gods, I was breathing too hard.

I stood abruptly and turned, seeing the brush mid-stroke in the air. "That's enough. Thank you." Feeling like a fool, I rushed to the bed and climbed deep within the downy blankets, curling in tight, begging my body to calm down.

I saw the brush lower to the table, and my husband cleared his throat yet again.

"It has been a long day," he said. "Sleep well."

The room darkened, and I heard him rustle into the chair, letting out a soft exhale.

For an odd moment, I felt comfortable, even safe. It didn't last long. I blinked and shook my head, forcing myself to remember my predicament. I couldn't forget. It didn't matter how gentle he seemed. Anyone could pretend. It didn't matter what gifts from home he gave me. I was not safe here. My husband was a monster, and I'd do well to remember.

CHAPTER SEVENTEEN

GUESSING GAME

THAT NIGHT, AND THE TWO NIGHTS FOLLOWING WERE UNeventful. My husband made no attempts to touch me. We played stones, and he never lost, which I found irritating. I had always been the best at that game. And he was unnervingly polite about his superiority, though he did chuckle tonight when I could no longer hide my frustration, letting out a *huff*.

"Does my perfect Psyche have a personality flaw after all?"

I frowned despite his joking tone. "Of course, I'm flawed."

"Perhaps. But you are still the closest to human perfection I have ever met."

I shook my head, bothered to the depths of my soul. That concept of false perfection was what got me here in the first place.

"It is not only your legendary beauty—"

"Please don't speak of my beauty," I said, my heart racing.

"Why?"

"Only Venus is beautiful. I do not compare."

"Hm." I held back a roll of my eyes. "There are many types of beauty, Psyche. You have them all. Your soul…the beauty of your goodness shines from within."

I looked down at my hands in my lap, my mind racing for a change of subject.

"Your lack of vanity is part of your beauty."

"Enough," I whispered. *"Please."*

He remained quiet, and I felt the need to fill the void. "Every human, no matter how perfect they seem, will make a mistake. They will eventually let down the ones they love. Perhaps not on purpose, and not maliciously, but it is bound to happen. People make terrible decisions when they are frightened or desperate or lacking confidence. I am no different."

Again, he was quiet a long while. "That is true of most. But I find it hard to imagine from you."

Before I could say another word, I saw Mino hike his leg on the bedpost from the corner of my eye.

"Mino! No!" I began to stand.

"*Mino.*" The sound of my husband's voice halted the puppy's business and caused Mino to flop onto his back, tucked tail shivering between his legs.

I sucked in a breath when Mino lifted into the air, floating toward a stained-glass window, which swung open.

"What are you doing?" I raced forward just as Mino floated out of the window, his ears back as he looked at me helplessly. "Don't hurt him!"

"Psyche," he said softly at my side. "I am letting him out, albeit the lackadaisical way."

The air froze in my chest as I watched Mino gently lowered to the ground below where he shook out his body, then gave me a questioning glance upward.

"It's all right, boy," I urged, my voice still shaking.

At the sound of my voice, he began to prance around the garden, doing his business and jumping at white moths that fluttered over his head.

"I'm sorry," I whispered. "He was scared."

"As were you." No malice was behind the words, only hurt.

I shouldn't have felt bad for assuming the worst of this secretive, strangely sensitive creature. For all I knew, his kindnesses were an act, carefully calculated actions to get me to trust him so he could strike. Not that he needed my trust to strike. Unless that was part of his binding agreement with his master.

I grasped my head in my fingers. Every time I thought of the various possibilities it made my head spin. It was impossible to make sense of it all.

"What is wrong?"

I shook my head, closing my eyes and opting for honesty. "You confuse me. All of this. I can't understand it."

"As I said before. Trust your instincts. Be like Sphinx."

I peered down to find the traitorous kitten rubbing incessantly against what I assumed was my husband's leg.

A scoff escaped me. "I think not." Then I addressed the kitten. "Have some dignity." She twined herself between his feet and around the other leg like invisible scratching posts, not caring at all about my opinion or the fact that he was a monster. I wondered how it felt. She certainly seemed to be in a state of bliss. Did he wear shoes? He didn't clomp around like Renae. His hands were soft and humanesque, but perhaps only the top of his body was. He had wings. Was he part human, part serpent and something else? Three creatures in one? I wrapped my arms around myself and took a small step away.

Mino let out a high-pitched yelp below as he began to rise into the air, floating his way straight into my outstretched arms. His tail wagged fiercely, and he licked my face as I tried to turn away before setting him down. The moment his padded feet hit the ground Sphinx brought a tiny paw up, whacking him across the snout, and then the chase was on. My laughter rang out, coupled with the chuckles of my husband as we watched the two of them amble across the room. Mino grew frustrated and let out adorable yips when Sphinx jumped on furniture that was too high for him to reach.

When they knocked over a tall, painted vase, I gasped and reached for it, but it went through my fingers. I squeezed my eyes shut in anticipation of the shatter, but found myself swept from my feet, the sound coming from far away. I opened my eyes and found myself on the bed with Mino and Sphinx beside me. The broken vase was in hundreds of pieces on the floor in the corner.

"I'm so sorry," I said, feeling awful. "I won't let them play in the room anymore."

"Do not worry yourself over objects."

"It was clearly priceless," I argued.

"Everything except life is replaceable."

I began to stand, saying, "I'll pick up the big pieces."

"Stay where you are. Your feet are bare and there are slivers. Renae is on her way."

I crossed my arms, contemplating as Mino locked his jaw around Sphinx's neck, only to be batted hard by the kitten's back feet.

My family was rich by human standards. What set us apart from others was not just our titles, but our belongings. Not everyone of high standing in our society had priceless heirlooms. It made me wonder, yet again, about the enigmatic facets of my husband, a beast so wealthy his belongings were of no consequence. That was…beyond rich, and difficult to fathom.

I held both the puppy and kitten in my arms as Renae bustled in, carrying out pieces and then sweeping up the shards. When she was finished, she brought in a meal that I shared with Mino. Sphinx chased Renae and the broom from the bedchamber, probably off to hunt mice.

As I picked at the delicate, flaky fish I asked, "Do you ever eat?"

"I do not consume human food very often," he answered

from across the table.

"So, you eat ambrosia and drink the nectar of the gods?"

"Yes. But I require very little to sustain myself."

"Can I see it? I know I can't taste it, but I'm curious." The food and drink of gods would cause a human to go mad.

"Very well."

A goblet appeared. Not as grand as I would have thought. Simple ceramic with vine etchings in gold around the edges and base. I leaned forward and peered inside, making a small sound from the back of my throat as my body seized tightly. The nectar shimmered like a glittering, soft rainbow of color, moving and shifting. I knew without a doubt the flavor would be slightly sweet, yet refreshing and wholesome. Everything inside of me wanted to reach for it. I needed it. *One small taste....* the goblet disappeared, making me rear back. I hadn't realized how close I'd been. My torso ached from pressing so hard against the table.

"Oh." I cleared my throat.

"Indeed," he said. "That was nectar. Would you care to see a sample of ambrosia?"

After how the nectar had made me feel, I wasn't certain, but the temptation to see it had me shaking my head.

"Do you eat animals?" I asked.

"No. Our sustenance are the trees and fields of Olympus. Fruit and grains. Our land provides everything we need."

"We? You mean immortals?"

He paused. "Yes."

I nibbled bread that I'd dipped in salted olive oil. "If I guess what sort of creature you are, can you tell me if I'm correct?"

"No. But I would very much be interested in your guesses." His voice held a hint of amusement.

"All right." Mino whimpered, and I placed the last bite of fish in his mouth. "Echidna. Half-serpent, half—"

"Half *woman*. Many of the best hybrids are female."

I tapped the table. I knew echidnas were female, but perhaps some of what humans believed was not true? Or there were creatures we hadn't heard of. The oracle said my husband was a winged serpent. That might be so, but I'd felt his hands and his mouth. They were decidedly not the hands and mouth of a serpent. Now I had to wade through what I knew of the legends to try and narrow this down.

"A satyr?" They were known for their sensuality, and my husband definitely gave off that aura.

He laughed. "Satyrs have no wings."

A light of hope flared inside of me. He was not saying yes or no, but he was giving hints.

I swallowed a drink of water, my heart pounding. "Are you Typhon?" Typhon was one of the deadliest creatures of legend, even an enemy of the god Jupiter. He was, indeed, a winged serpent with snakes for feet. Some say he had multiple heads. But were they human heads or serpents as well?

"Interesting choice." His voice sounded dry. "Tall as a mountain, or long as a giant whale. Upper body of a man, indeed, lower body made up of hundreds of snakes. Fiery eyes. Dragon heads for fingers."

I went very still, trying to imagine that creature in my midst. Now my throat was dry. "What can you tell me about his personality?"

"He is a comic genius."

I let out an accidental snort and covered my mouth. "Be serious."

"I am. Impressive sarcastic wit for one who can scarcely talk."

Laughter bubbled out of me, though my hand still cupped my mouth. I had no idea if he was being serious or attempting to joke.

"What other theories have you got?" he asked.

I chewed my lip. "Manticore?"

"Mm. Cousin to the chimera. Head of a human with sharp teeth. Body of a lion. Bat-like wings. Impressive creatures in combat."

I stared at the space where he sat, my insides roiling. Could he be a manticore? Perhaps the serpent part of him consisted of those sharp teeth? I thought I had felt his teeth against my legs that night, but now I wasn't so sure. I tried to relax my face, but my eyebrows were furrowed tight.

"Psyche. Hold out your arm."

"No." My arms went stiff, hands clasped tightly in my lap.

"Your arm." His voice was so firm that Mino flopped to his back on the floor beside us.

My abdomen clenched. "Please. Can you just say whatever it is? Do you really need—" I screamed as a firm force outstretched my arm onto the table where it lay flat, palm down.

"Keep your other hand in your lap," he told me.

I locked my jaw, too terrified to move. Then I felt the heat of breath above my forearm, and the press of teeth. My throat seized up. He had his mouth around my arm, just as Mino had clamped his mouth around Sphinx's throat earlier. And like the puppy's bite, my husband's was not deadly. I tried to catch my breath and take in the sensation of a full set of teeth, top and bottom, holding firmly to my skin. I even stared in wonder at the sight of those teeth pressing down. I could see the imprint. None of them were particularly sharp. No "fangs." And his lips, surrounding the teeth, were incredibly soft and tender. A heated flush suddenly swept over me, making me glad I was seated.

"All right then," I breathed.

He released me, and I yanked my arm back, closing my hand over the damp spot where his mouth had been. I stood and moved away from the table, pacing to the far side away from him, trying to calm my body. I didn't think I would ever become accustomed to his ways of proving points.

"Maybe," I said, swallowing. "You can retract your fangs."

"No creature can retract their fangs. Either you have them or you do not."

"Well, then, perhaps you filed yours down to appear less dangerous."

"No creature of Olympus would willingly destroy the weapons they were born with."

"Then what *are* you?"

His chair shifted back, and I heard him move toward me. I froze in place.

When he spoke, his voice was near and low. "I know it bothers you not to know who and what I am. I know it worries you that I cannot say the things that would ease your mind. I know my excuses seem without worth or substance. If you would only—" His voice cut off with a guttural sound, like his tongue had been grasped.

"Only what?" I waited, listening, shaking.

"Turn around and put your palms against the wall."

"What?" I breathed, the familiar terror rising again. "Why?"

"For once, can you do as I ask without questioning?"

"No!"

"So be it."

The air spun me like a whirlwind, pressing me into the wall until I was forced to push back with my palms. Try as I might, *and I tried*, I could not turn or move. I grunted and gritted my teeth with effort.

"There. Now stay still."

Weak. That was how I felt at that moment, and I hated it. I didn't know what he planned to do, but I was tired of letting him control me. When I felt the air release me, I spun back around and kicked out a foot as hard as I could, raising my fists to fight, but my foot was caught, seemingly by the air, and I was shoved back around by the whirlwind again, my fingers splayed against the wall, feet flat on the floor.

"I applaud your efforts," he said flatly. "Now this time. Do. Not. Move."

I let out a scream loud enough to shake the room. And though I remained exactly where I was, I stomped my foot down with all my might, stomping until it hurt, jarring my bones.

My husband's arms went around me from behind, wrapping securely around my stomach, his chest to my back, and his face pressed into my neck. He was strong. It was the most I'd ever felt of his body. I froze, taking in the sensation of every place where our bodies touched, from the backs of my calves and legs, my bottom, my back and shoulders, to my stomach and neck. Then quiet fell, and I knew his wings had encircled us. A cloud of warm, peppery honeysuckle, like a summer breeze, filled the small space, its loveliness making me whimper.

"Shh," he whispered into my skin.

"What do you want?" I cried, feeling compressed and overwhelmed.

"This," he whispered. "Only this."

He was holding me. Gods, it felt...good. It felt real. I hated how he could cloud my judgement like this. I thought about what he had told me last time. *Do yourself a favor. Imagine I am Leodes.*

So, I did. I closed my eyes and imagined his dark hair and lashes. His handsome face buried in my neck. His strong, sun-golden arms wrapped around me. I imagined he cared. I imagined he loved me as he held me up, murmuring soothing sounds against my skin, and I wept.

CHAPTER EIGHTEEN

NOT PROPER

LEODES SMELLED OF HONEY. I WOKE IN THE DIMNESS OF DAWN, my body damp, my most intimate parts aching. The remnants of my dream fluttered at the edge of my consciousness, the way our bodies had intertwined, never fully coupling. The body of Leodes with the voice and scent of my husband. Why had I woken? I recalled Mino's barking from far away. I groaned, pulling my knees up under the covers. I wanted to go back to my dream.

"I can help if you'll let me."

I jolted with surprise, my entire body shuddering at the erotic undertones of my husband's voice at the side of the bed. Too near. I rolled to face his invisible form and a blast of honey hit me, causing an upwelling of heat to jostle through my body, rattling downward until it settled at my core, purring. A deep blush filled my face, neck, and chest. I had been so overwhelmed with my dream that I hadn't sensed him there.

"N-no," I stuttered, clutching the blankets. "I'm...trying to sleep."

"By denying me," he said huskily. "You deny yourself."

"I deny myself nothing," I lied, ashamed that he could read my need so easily. Damn him. Damn the humiliation.

I sat up, raking my fingers through my hair, trying to get ahold of myself. I schooled my face and pressed my thighs together tightly, but that did not help my circumstances.

"Don't you have to work?" I asked. "It's daylight."

"Tell me your dream." His voice had moved. He was stalking around the bed again.

"I don't recall it."

"Is that so? Something to do with Leodes, I believe. Seeing as how you moaned his name."

"I did not!" Why was I arguing? I clamped my mouth shut, and he chuckled, making his way round to the other side of the bed. "Where is Mino?" I asked.

"Outside with Sphinx." His voice lowered, and I spied an indentation at the edge of the bed. He was sitting very near me. I couldn't understand why my body hadn't cooled and settled yet. The fear coursing through me should have been enough to chase it away. But his nearness was only making things worse, proof that he was capable of enchantment.

"Stop that," I breathed. "Whatever you're doing."

"I am merely sitting and speaking."

"No." I shook my head, a hum singing through my thighs and upward. "You're doing something. Some sort of mysticism."

"I am being myself. Your soul feels me, the real me, and it speaks to your body."

I let out a dry laugh and pulled the covers higher over my breasts, which were feeling more firm and taut than normal. My whole body trembled with fear and desire.

"Trust yourself, Psyche. Trust your soul."

My head shook back and forth. I refused to fall for this. He scooted closer, and I held my breath.

"Do you think I prefer to force you to accept my affections?"

"No," I answered. "I'm certain you would prefer if I'd mindlessly gave myself over and had my mind wiped of my own thoughts and choices."

"You are *wrong*." Anger edged his voice. "But if this is how you insist it must be, I will keep doing what I must."

Just as they had the other night, the covers flew off me, making me scramble and scream, but there was no escaping. Hot hands grabbed my ankles, yanking me down, and then he was on top of me, pinning my arms over my head. I thrashed and yelled, but it only helped him to nestle his strong body between my legs. When I felt an unmistakable male bulge pressed hard against the softness of my own wet, sensitive core, I sucked in a gulp of air and became as still as stone.

We both breathed heavily, his natural scent intoxicating.

"All I want is a kiss," he said, though his body was asking for far more.

My voice shook. "I will never kiss you." But I wanted to. Gods, how could a monster tempt me so? We were both quiet for a long, tense moment.

"Take your feet and run them along my legs."

"What?" Was he mad? Well, yes, probably.

"You cannot touch me with your hands, but your feet are allowed."

He was giving me the opportunity to explore him. A way around the "no touching" rule. I remained still except for the rapid rising and falling of my chest. Did I want to know how his legs felt? It was a moment of truth. Would I feel scales? I closed my eyes, terrified, but steeled myself. I had to take the opportunity.

I tentatively brought my feet inward until my toes touched the bare, heated skin of his lower legs. My breath caught. He was so warm. I ran my toes up and down what felt like a strong, human calf with normal hair. My whole foot pressed against him now, then the other, running down to ankles, long feet, and toes. He felt...nice.

"All right," I whispered, dropping my feet back to the bed. "I am satisfied."

"Are you, though?"

I nodded, feeling inarticulate. I couldn't bring myself to thank him, though I felt immensely relieved. "But I don't understand. Why did the oracle lie?"

"Lie?"

"It said you were a winged serpent."

He chuckled, and the movement in his lower abdomen made him rub against me, causing my entire core to clench and throb. Damn him again!

"Perhaps metaphorical."

"Well, that's unfair," I said. I gave my arms a gentle tug, but he pressed them down harder into the mattress over my head.

"It is time for our kiss." I felt his words against my lips, and my body buzzed.

Terrified, I turned my head aside. "No. No kissing."

"Very well, no kissing." He arched his hips into mine and my head flew back.

"Gods!" I panted, fighting every urge to rub wildly against him in return. "Don't do that!"

"What? This?" His hips circled, grinding our bodies together, the friction coiling my insides in a way I had never experienced.

"Please…please don't."

He sighed against my mouth. "In all of history I cannot recall a time a woman has asked *not* to be pleasured when her body so clearly begs otherwise. Tell me why, Psyche."

My eyes burned with frustration. "I don't trust you."

"You do not have to trust me to use me."

"It would be wrong."

"Wrong how?"

"I c-can't explain it." Oh, hot Hades, the weight of him on top of me was more delicious than any nectar. My head turned back to face him, and to my absolute shock, I felt his forehead lower to mine, then the tip of his nose touched mine. Our breaths mingled, and my heart skipped at the surprising sweetness.

"You have no idea what I would give to see you take your pleasure, Psyche."

I wrenched my head to the side, away from him, my heart pounding now. "Don't say things like that."

Again, he chuckled. "It is perfectly proper for a husband to tell his wife exactly how he feels and what he wants. Leodes would have spoken to you no less intimately."

Leodes. Gods...just the thought of that man's sexy mouth saying such words to me had me sighing and softening.

"Let it all go." His breath was against my neck now, and his hips pressed into mine, sending stars into my sight. "Think of nothing."

"I..." Words failed me when he moved his body in a way that made the length of him slide fully up the slant of my womanhood, igniting every unfamiliar sensation. I had never felt a man against me, even through clothing. I never imagined it would feel like this. My whole body was piqued. Could I do what he said, use him, and not let it affect my mind? What would it hurt? I wasn't giving *him* anything, despite what he might think. It would be for me. I could remain strong. I could do this. Right?

Without another moment's hesitation, I rounded my back to lift my hips tentatively. My husband hissed under his breath and said nothing, but his body took control. Whatever type of hybrid creature he was, if the expertise of his movements were any indication, he had definitely been with women. I would explore my feelings about that later. Right now, we moved together in a dazzling dance, and somehow, we both knew the choreography. I kept my head to the side with my eyes closed. My lips parted as I breathed heavily while he moved on top of me. My body squirmed and arched, my knees up, pressing and feeling his muscled thighs, his strong hips, his flat stomach, his thick man-hood.

The buildup tightened in my lower abdomen, my nightgown damp between us. Every bit of my flesh was on the edge of igniting, and then he picked up the pace, rubbing up and down, hard and fast, lighting a spark in my core that burst into flames. I shouted, my body bucking, but he stayed with me, pressing the full force of himself into my release as it came in waves. It was a whole-body experience, my skin tingling from head to toe in the most gratifying way. So, *this* was what all the fuss was about among chattering ladies.

His cheek was against mine as I came down from my high, my body quivering, and then his lips were hovering over my own.

"And now for that kiss," he whispered.

I was too blissed to think straight. When his lips touched mine, painfully soft and tender and warm, I moaned. It was the cream on top of an unexpectedly rich dessert. He melted into me, and I let him. Gods help me. *I let him.* And his mouth was extraordinary. Full lips. A soft, velvety tongue that reached expertly into my mouth to meet my own. I had received one kiss when I was sixteen—one of Papa's young soldiers on his way to war—but it had been rushed and overly-exploratory. How had my husband, a dark creature of Olympus, learned to kiss and move his body in a way that would please a human woman so extraordinarily?

When the kiss ended, I felt him watching me. My body was already cooling, and to feel his eyes on me made me aware of the wetness between us, my nightgown saturated where our bodies had touched, and the wanton way I'd given over to my basest instincts…with a monster.

"Fear again," he whispered. "It was lovely not to smell it for a few moments."

"Get off me. Please," I begged.

He did as I asked, releasing my wrists and climbing off me with a deep sigh. I heard the *whoosh* of his wings opening and closing in rapid succession and felt the air move. I yanked up the covers and pulled up my knees, wrapping my arms around them. I'd just...he...oh, depths of the underworld! I'd been under a trance. It was the only way to explain it. My face heated red.

"Regret and self-doubt," he muttered from the end of the bed. "Treacherous human traits."

I grabbed my head in my hands. "I won't let you manipulate my mind again."

"Manipulation? That was all you, Psyche," he said. The erotic undertones seeped through his voice as if he were still imagining me squirming underneath him. He was gloating, and it fueled my ire.

"You lie!"

"I may withhold the truth, Wife, but I never lie. Enjoy your day."

He left me, and I sat there trying to get myself under control. My mind reeled, and my body still hummed.

"It's all right," I whispered to myself. "Everything is all right." I had no idea what to believe, but my mind was still my own. It had just been one moment of weakness, that's all. Though I felt shame and disbelief, no harm was done.

It's all right.

Chapter Nineteen

Homesick

I SAT IN BED, NOT MOVING, FOR FAR TOO LONG, ANALYZING EVERY single moment of this morning. Every motivation that we both might have had. Every possible consequence. I turned over each and every detail in my mind, scouring them for ways he might have control over me now after what we'd shared. And I came to one conclusion.

I was fine.

My mind was strong. Allowing myself a moment of pleasure with him, regardless of our situation, did not give him sway over me. Whatever magic powers he had, I was not falling for them. Yes, all right, I'd wanted him, and so I'd allowed myself a moment of weakness. But one thing was for certain: it would *not* happen again. *I* was in control.

Once I finally began to relax, his kiss landed at the forefront of my thoughts. Our semi-coupling had been a purely physical need, but that kiss…it had been timely and intimate. Far too intimate. The only reason it had felt so wonderful was that I'd been completely overcome by what had happened, my body sated, and my conscious thoughts ambling far away. I definitely couldn't let him kiss me again. That was the sort of thing that could hurt me, weaken me. Kissing was for people in love.

We would never be in love.

Outside, far below, Mino began a barking fit. I jumped from the bed and ran to the window, throwing it wide. The puppy was barking up at a centaur soldier tree-sculpture where he'd treed a squirrel. The animal was shaking its bushy tail furiously.

"I'm coming, Mino!" At the sound of my voice he peered up, went still, and then his whole body began to move side-to-side as his tail swung in glee.

I let out a laugh and ran to my closet, quickly discarding the nightgown and dressing in a peach colored, high-waisted gown that sat evenly on both shoulders and swooped low on my chest. I brushed back my hair and wound it in a twist, poking pins through it to keep it in place, then dashed from the room. I needed sunshine to clear my thoughts.

A floating tray was waiting at the end of the hall and I slowed, calling out, "Renae? Is that you?"

"Yes, Highness. Care to eat in the garden?"

"I would. Thank you."

She followed me through the wide halls until we got outside where she sat the tray down on the marble table. Both of us let out startled sounds when the nearby bush shaped as a Pegasus rattled, and Sphinx came bursting out with something in her mouth.

"What have you got?" I asked as Renae made a disgusted sound. Sphinx dropped a dead gray mouse at my feet. "Oh, poor thing." The rodent, not my cat. "Have you brought it as a gift?" She licked her paw and leapt up on my lap, letting me pet her. "Very kind of you, kitten, but it's all yours. I insist." I kissed her head and set her down. She happily took the mouse and bounded away.

Mino sniffed the spot where the mouse had been, then began licking my toes through my sandals, which made me giggle.

"Need anything else?" Renae asked.

I sighed and looked at the empty spot where she stood. "I wish I could see you."

"I'm not much to see, to be honest."

"I don't care how you look, Renae. It's just...strange and lonely to never see anyone. I am glad Mino and Sphinx are visible, but it's hard."

"I can understand how that would be difficult. Are you at least enjoying your time with your husband more now that you've had a chance to get to know him?"

"No," I answered too quickly, thinking about this morning and flushing with heat. I tossed half of a boiled egg to the eager puppy and hoped Renae couldn't see my blush. She let out a small sound as if she did not believe me.

"I wish you were allowed to tell me something about him."

"I wish I was, as well." She patted my shoulder, and I held back the urge to reach for her hand and hold her there. In that moment I longed for my mother. Yes, she'd coddled me and been vain and proud, but she loved me. I never doubted that. Papa too. They must have been so worried. Did they think I was dead? Or tortured daily, at the very least? Pangs of anxiousness and sadness pierced me.

"Oh, please don't be sad, Princess." Renae smoothed the top of my head.

"I wish I could write to my family."

Renae was quiet a long moment. "You should ask your husband."

I snorted with derision. "He would never allow it."

Now she snorted. "Well, you won't know unless you ask." With that, she patted my shoulder one last time and clomped away, back up to the castle. She was right, of course. But if I asked and he said no, I'd be furious. Maybe that's what I needed in order to remember he was a monster. I needed to find ways to make him show me.

I picked at the food. It was strange not to have an appetite. I was always hungry at home. Mealtimes were usually full of banter, gossip, and laughter. Eating alone, even with an attentive dog, was not the same. I gave Mino several more bites and took a few myself before climbing down onto the ground with him. He got so excited, licking my face and jumping over me, back and forth, making me howl with laughter. Even Sphinx came out to rub herself on me and get scratches on her small head.

"Let's take a walk," I told them. "This time hopefully we won't be mountain lion fodder."

We walked together over the hills, the burn of exertion feeling great on my body. I stopped at the archery range to shoot a few arrows, making sure the animals stayed behind me. Then we headed for the trees. I laughed as Mino and Sphinx began to wrestle, only to topple down the hill together in a clumsy heap of fur. They played the whole way to the forest.

When the trees literally turned to me, as if opening their arms in welcome, emotions rose up within my heart. The trees, my pets, and an invisible maid were my only friends. But I shouldn't take any of them for granted.

"Hello, beauties," I said with reverence as I ran a hand up the closest smooth trunk. The tree shivered under my touch, making me smile. From the corner of my eye I saw Mino approach a tree and hike his leg. Before I could say a word, the nearest root rose up and gave the puppy a shove away. He stumbled and yelped, running for me. I squatted and took him in my arms, stroking his shivering body. Sphinx's back went up and she hissed at the tree. She was way too small to be scary, but it was funny to see.

"It's all right, everyone." I looked at the tree. "I apologize. He meant no harm. Dogs are not very smart compared to you or me." Sphinx moved closer, pacing around my legs. "I know you're not accustomed to animals," I said to the trees. "I promise they won't hurt you." I felt sad when they remained still. The trees did not care for my companions. That wasn't good. Awkward, really.

I let out a long huff and patted the tree again.

"I'll take them away and try to visit without them soon."

They made no move, and I turned to leave, the burden of loneliness settling even heavier on me. Mino licked my chin. I waited until we'd crested the nearest hill before setting him down to run beside me again. Sphinx had followed, and they picked up their playful antics once more.

When we returned to the garden my tray of food had been cleared away. I went inside and headed for my room, feeling tired. But rather than get into the bed, I scoured the desk and found parchment and a dip quill with ink. Sphinx jumped on the bed and nestled in. Mino plopped at my feet and fell straight to sleep.

In the quiet of the room, I lost myself in words. I wrote Mother and Papa first, revealing information to ease their minds, while not giving any of the unsettling details, such as the fact that I could not see anyone. *I am well. I believe I am somewhere in Olympus, and I am safe. The food is incredible. My husband does not hurt me, so please don't worry.* I wouldn't lie to spare their feelings. They knew me too well for that. We all knew this arrangement was a punishment.

I told them about Mino and Sphinx. Then I wrote my sisters, chronicling my closet and all the details they would appreciate. I knew none of my family would read these letters, but it made me feel closer to them to write and imagine reconnecting.

As soon as I rolled the final scroll and tied a string around it, my sadness became an even heavier burden on my shoulders. I wondered how my guard, Boldar, was doing, and if he missed chasing after me. I wondered, if none of this had happened, if I would have found Leodes, or if another suiter would have made himself known and I could have had love.

Not all women loved their husbands. I knew that, of course. The lucky ones gave the rest of us something to dream of. Now, the knowledge that I would never have that opportunity added to the layers of hopelessness weighing on my heart.

I bent and picked up Mino's floppy, sleepy body. He gave a wide yawn, showing all his sharp baby teeth, and I took him to the bed where we snuggled together with Sphinx until I eventually faded into sleep.

CHAPTER TWENTY

GAME PLAY

THE MOMENT I STIRRED, I SENSED HIS PRESENCE AND HIS scent, which sent my body and mind into a frenzy of conflicting sensations. Fear was there, always the initial terror that this would be the moment he would strike. But now fright was accompanied by more confusing feelings: wonder and curiosity mingled with the most unwelcome one of all...lust. For half a second, I'd felt happy not to be alone before I remembered that was exactly what he wanted.

He wanted me to need him and rely on him in all ways: food, shelter, safety, and companionship. I could take the first three things without getting my mind and heart involved, but the latter part was more complex. A tiny part of me was actually happy when he showed up after being gone all day. That's the part of myself I had to keep under close watch.

"Sometimes you are at peace while you sleep," he murmured. "But other times, like now, the worry still creases your face, even as you dream."

Mino, who'd also been woken, rolled to his back, his skinny tail twitching with nervous excitement as he stared at the blank space. Sphinx pranced over to him and I watched as her fur smoothed down over her head, neck, body, and up her tail. My husband was petting her.

I sat up, frowning, smoothing back my hair and redoing the twist. I wasn't sure how I felt about being watched while I slept. It was disconcerting, but I suppose harmless. Still, every moment he was with me he was learning me, which was not a good thing. More for him to use against me when the time came.

I scratched Mino's soft, exposed belly, the pathetic pup. He still stared, wide-eyed, and it made me think.

"Do you suppose he can see you?"

"Yes. They both can."

"How?"

"Because I allow it." A strange feeling of jealousy slithered through me. I narrowed my eyes at the air from where his voice carried, and he chuckled.

"Have you been writing?" His tone was careful.

I nodded, smoothing down the fabric of my dress over my knees. "To my family. I miss them, and I know they are worried. I'm sure you would not allow me to send them, but—"

"You assume much."

My face lifted in surprise. "I can send them?"

He paused, cleared his throat. "I will have them sent, but you cannot receive return mail."

He could be lying, despite his insistence that he never lied, but my spirits rejoiced at the thought of my family knowing I was safe. Or, at least, as safe as could be expected.

"Thank you."

"Please do not thank me." He let out a deep sigh followed by a heavy pause. "We need to speak about this morning."

Heat rose to my cheeks as I shook my head and stared down at Mino. "I would rather not."

"I am sure that is true, but I have things to say." His voice trailed off, soft then louder, and I could tell he was pacing as he spoke. "You are already aware there are certain subjects I cannot breach, which makes having any conversations with you difficult."

He paused again, and I nodded that I understood. Sphinx

curled up in my lap, licking her paw.

"What happened this morn, and the other incidences in which we touched, will not happen again. Unless, of course, it is initiated by you."

I let out a dry laugh. "What are you playing at?"

"You always think this is some sort of game to me." He went quiet a moment. "Perhaps that is a metaphor I can work with." He paused again, and I waited, my heart beating faster in anticipation. Finally, he gathered his thoughts and continued.

"Some games are played one to one. For example, Stones." He paused, so I nodded. "And some games are played in teams. What would you say if I told you, Psyche, that I am not—" He made a garbled noise, followed by an ancient-sounding word that sounded very much like a curse. "I cannot say that. All right... imagine a game with two players on a team together against an opponent of one." He exhaled and let it out in a rush, as if he'd finished a great task.

My insides tremored slightly at the strange feeling that we were at an important crossroad. I thought about what he had said. A team of two against a team of one. My eyes narrowed.

"Are you saying we are on the same team? Against another?"

He laughed, then cleared his throat again. "I cannot answer." But he sounded joyful, as if we were on the same page.

"Well, I suppose that would change things," I said, almost to myself. "If it's true." He growled, and my heart gathered speed. "I know you said you can't lie, but you can't blame me for being cautious."

A lower growl this time.

"Does this mean you're being punished as well?" I asked.

His answer was a whisper. "Not exactly." He sounded decidedly sad. I was ashamed of the level his apparent sadness affected me. I felt bad for him for a moment, then shook off the feeling.

Whatever he'd done to be punished, he probably deserved it, just as I did for allowing my family and people to revere me when I knew it was wrong.

"Wait," I said. "What exactly is your punishment in this situation?"

Yet another growl, this one clearly a sound of frustration.

"Why must you think of things in terms of punishment? We are speaking of a game, if you recall. In a game there are rules, and there is strategy."

"There are also winners and losers," I said.

"Precisely." He sounded as if he'd turned sharply to face me. "When I play a game, I do not want to lose. Nor should you. I have never lost." I rolled my eyes to myself as he went on. "And I have realized certain games require gentler strategy than others."

I gazed upward, scrutinizing his analogy. "So, assuming we are a team, and we must work together, what is our goal? How do we win?"

His feet were heavy against the floor as he approached the bed and two indentations appeared at the end where he leaned on the mattress with his hands.

"That is where you must trust your instincts, Psyche."

I fell back with a long groan, holding my head. "This is too much."

"You have no choice but to play. Some games, my wife, have more at stake than mere glory."

That made my stomach hurt. Something bad would happen if we did not win this game. Wait, *we*? Was I truly believing this "team" nonsense?

"What else do you know about games?" he asked. "Think."

I shook my head, letting out a long breath. "Some games are played on a point system. Are there points to be earned in this hypothetical game?"

A negative-sounding grunt.

"No points," I said. "An end-goal, then?"

"Mm." That was not a yes or no, but it sounded affirmative.

"All right, so we are supposedly working toward something. Together." He was quiet, so quiet. But I felt a spark between us. "Can you give me a hint?"

"No," he said. "That subject, above all, is something I cannot go near, verbally."

Damn.

"What else?" he asked. "Think."

"So pushy," I whispered as Mino stood and shook himself out, looking around, probably for a place to relieve himself. Before I could get up, Mino was lifted into the air toward the open window. The pup was still not used to this. His ears were back, and he peered over his shoulder at me helplessly.

"It's okay, boy," I said, trying not to laugh. I stood and went to the window to watch the puppy be lowered to the ground as I thought. "Some games have time limits, goals they must achieve in a set time. While others, like stones, have no limit. You play until someone wins."

"*Yes.*"

"So which type is ours?" I asked. "Do we have a time limit?" He was quiet again, and the silence ratcheted my anxiety. "How long, Husband?" When he still didn't answer, I wrapped my arms around myself. "I see. Not long then." His continued silence was all the affirmation I needed.

"What does your sensible gut tell you, Psyche?" He stood close. So close I could smell him when the breeze from the window caressed us. I had to swallow.

"I don't know," I whispered, but that was a lie. My gut told me to trust him. To learn him the way he was trying to learn me—that our end-game somehow vastly relied on building trust.

My gut said he didn't want to hurt me, a concept that was the opposite of what I'd firmly believed when I arrived. Could I trust my gut now, or had my instincts somehow been compromised along the way? I didn't know, but I believed unequivocally that I did not have all the time in the world to contemplate it.

Either I would choose to believe my husband and do my best to act as his teammate in this mysterious game, or I would continue to listen to the paranoid voice in my head saying to fight him until the bitter end to save myself.

It was time to decide.

CHAPTER TWENTY-ONE

INSTINCTS

$\mathcal{A}$S I SAT THERE CONTEMPLATING, MINO WAS LIFTED BACK into the room. All at once, the bedchamber went dark as pitch, and the candles bloomed to life along the walls. My heart gave a great pound and I backed away from where I'd been standing near my husband.

"Psyche," he said, disappointment in his tone. But he seemed to understand my trepidation, because he spoke softly now. "There is something intimate about darkness and candlelight."

I nodded. "I'm going to wash up." Then I hurried away to the closet to grab a fresh nightgown, taking it to the bathing room where I closed myself in. My body shook as I ran a damp cloth over my skin and brushed out my hair. I could not bring myself to believe him about not touching me anymore. Once I was dressed, I hurried back through the room to my bed but stopped short when I saw the indentation on one side, the cat curled up above the indentation in mid-air, and Mino on his back in the middle, appearing to get his belly rubbed. Was Sphinx laying on my husband?

"I will sleep beside you," my husband said matter-of-factly.

My mouth fell open and stayed that way for a long moment.

"Y-you said you wouldn't come to the bed unless I invited you." And yet twice he had done that very thing, coming into my bed and forcing affection upon me.

"What I specifically meant, dearest wife, was that I would not consummate our marriage until you requested it."

It felt as if a flame had been lit beneath my skin. I stared down at the edge of the bed, chewing my lip, heart galloping. He had to know I would never request that to happen, but he spoke with his usual characteristic, perplexing confidence, as if it would eventually be a sure thing.

"Tell me why you have decided not to touch me again?" I said, then quickly added, "I am not complaining. I'm simply curious." My weight shifted from one foot to the other.

"It felt ingenuine," he answered. "To force it."

He sounded so sincere. It drove me mad that he did not consistently remain in the villainous box within my mind. And then he amended, "As with any game, if your strategy is not working, you must rethink it."

Ah. So, his forced affections were not having the desired effect.

"It *was* wrong," I told him, earning a low grunt in response. "But I do not understand your ultimate goal. Was it to..." I blushed. "Make me want you? Physically?"

He was quiet a long time before solemnly replying, "I cannot say."

Of course, he couldn't. For once, I found myself wishing I could know, not just the truth, but his heart. His true thoughts and feelings, all of them.

"Are you really going to..." I waved a hand at the bed. "Sleep there?"

"I am," he responded. "And you are going to sleep..." He patted the open spot beside him. "Right there."

I glowered, not caring for this at all. Mostly because it forced me to acknowledge the flare of anticipation his nearness brought.

"Put these on so you do not accidentally touch me." A gorgeous pair of iridescent gloves appeared from nowhere in front of me. I startled, giving a small jump.

"How did you...? I cannot sleep in gloves."

"You will find they are quite comfortable."

I crossed my arms. "Perhaps it would be simpler if I slept on the lounger."

"Put on the gloves and get into bed, Psyche." His forceful tone irked me to no end. My arms tightened across my chest and my lips pursed.

"There are limits to my patience," he warned.

I did not trust this. Not at all. But I loathed when he forced me to his will and would prefer not to feel powerless like that again, so I huffed through my nose as I yanked the gloves on. Damn them for feeling so wonderful. They were lightweight, yet when I touched my hands together, I could not feel a thing through them. I roughly pulled down the blanket and climbed in.

Mino jumped up, turning 'round and 'round as he pressed against me, tongue lolling, begging for pets. It was hard to keep my grumpy disposition with his loving, carefree attention. I sighed and tried to focus only on him, but it was impossible not to feel my husband's invisible eyes on me, laying so close.

Sphinx, apparently perturbed by the puppy's antics, leapt across the space to pounce on him, her tiny paws wide. My husband and I both laughed as they rolled around between us making adorable growling sounds. After a while of this, I found myself sinking down and getting comfortable. I wondered if my husband had propped his elbow to hold his head as I did while he watched the precious spectacle. I wondered if his wings were folded neatly on the bed behind him or if they hung off and trailed the floor.

What did he look like?

Were his eyes warm and kind or beaded and calculating? Was his head covered in scales and horns or the hair of a man? Most importantly, who had control over him, and why?

"What are you thinking right now?" he asked.

I decided to answer without holding back. "I was thinking of you, and what you might look like, and how you came to be in this situation with me. I would like to know your story." I felt splayed open just then, vulnerable.

"And I would very much like to share every detail with you. Someday, if our team wins, I will."

I regarded his presence and felt the wall of fear slipping. I had worked so hard to hold it up, expending every last bit of my energy, that my body all but sagged with relief as I let it go. Perhaps this would be my greatest downfall, this very moment, when I finally decided to push past my trepidations.

"I'm going to trust my instincts," I said softly. "Maybe that makes me a fool, but I cannot continue to live in fear. I was not built that way. I want to trust you. I want to…work with you. As a team. To do whatever it is we are meant to do."

A grateful sound escaped his throat. "I know I said I would not touch you," he breathed. "But I must."

I went very still and closed my eyes as I felt his large, warm hand touch my cheek and hold the side of my face with utter gentleness, his fingertips slipping into my hair. Would he kiss me? My chest rose and fell in a shudder as I recalled the feel of his lips.

No. No, I didn't want that. I shouldn't. It was one thing to work with him to achieve a goal, whatever that elusive goal might be, but I had to keep my mind clear. This twisted lust I sometimes felt did not belong. It was misplaced emotion—a product of madness caused by an outrageous situation. I would not waste another moment feeling guilty for what had happened, but I also could not allow myself to indulge those sorts of thoughts, husband or not.

"You often overthink," he said with patience, his hand

dropping away.

I shook my head. "There is no harm in caution. Especially when my life and well-being are on the line."

"Hm." My lips twisted at the sound, and he asked. "Why are you making that face?"

"I hate when you say, *Hm*."

He had the nerve to laugh. "My hands are tied. Figuratively. You know that."

"It is still annoying."

Another laugh from him had me shaking my head again and trying not to smile.

"You know," he said, "If there is something you want...*anything*...you need only ask." I got the distinct impression he was talking about what had taken place between us in this bed. He may have promised not to do it again against my will, but he was still hoping for more. I cleared my throat.

"I want nothing."

"Shame."

I rolled my eyes. For a creature of Olympus, he was such a man.

"Continue to follow your instincts, Psyche," he whispered. "Even if they go against your need for precaution. You will not regret it."

I hoped not, because at this point, my instincts were all I had. But I was not going to indulge in any misplaced desires that might arise along the way, no matter how much he wanted me to. From here on out, my mind would be clear. I would work with my husband as a teammate, but that was all. No kissing or touching or anything of the sort. And please gods, no more dreams of Leodes.

Chapter Twenty-Two

Speaking Without Words

I T WAS BIZARRE TO WAKE IN THE DAWNING LIGHT WITH A PUPPY curled against my belly, a kitten beside my head with her tail draping my throat, and a heavy, warm hand over my waist, his leg pressed against mine from behind. I lay there very still, soaking in the sensation.

Why did he have to feel like such a normal man? A monster's touch should never be so comforting. Would it be okay to pretend, for a brief moment, that he was Leodes? No, not Leodes; thoughts of him got me into trouble. But a man. A respectable man my parents had married me off to with their blessing. A man who cared for me and would always look out for my well-being. A man who would eventually fill my belly with his seed to make us a father and mother.

No. Not that last one. I'd hardly given any thought to motherhood, so I wasn't sure where that came from. No pretending. This entire line of thought was not beneficial. I would drive myself to despair thinking of that which I would never have. My life had no room for childish daydreams anymore. Dreams were not harmless. Desires were a danger.

I felt my husband's fingers flex on my waist, his leg stiffening just before he stretched, wakening.

"Good morning," he said, wafting warm honey my way. Who wakes with perfectly scented breath? My creature, apparently. It was dizzying.

"Morning," I mumbled, keeping my face turned away.

He patted my hip and I felt the bed shift as he climbed out, causing the animals to stand and stretch, yawning. Mino shook out his ears.

I also got to my feet, about to take the puppy out when the door opened and Renae entered, carrying in a tray.

"Good morning, Princess," she said. "Here is your morning meal. Come with me Mino and Sphinx; time to go out."

They both seemed excited to leave the room, bounding away.

I removed my gloves, setting them on the bed and rubbing my hands, feeling shy.

"Sleep well?" he asked.

"Fine. You?"

"Better than fine."

I held back a smile, and asked, "What will you do today?"

"Work for my allotted time, and then return to you straight away."

I peered down at my toes as they dug into the soft rug of woven, colorful wool.

"What will you do, Psyche?"

I had no answer. Every morning I was awash in melancholy. Of all the times of day, mornings were the hardest for some reason. Perhaps it was knowing the day held no hope of seeing people. Just me, two animals, and the trees, who did not care for said animals.

"What is the matter?"

Could he not see it? "Loneliness, I suppose."

He paused. "You are accustomed to companionship."

"Are you not?"

"No."

I frowned.

"On occasion," he amended. "But not daily."

It was hard to explain how I felt when we were so different, especially knowing it made no difference. Nothing would change. I meandered over to the tray and lifted the lid, picking at a ripe berry. Even its mix of sweet, tart juice on my tongue did not raise my spirits. The tea pot lifted, and a stream of steaming light brown liquid poured into a cup, followed by milk, then it moved toward me. My husband was serving me.

"Thank you." I took it and added a large drizzle of honey. "I'll feel better after some tea." I held the cup in my hands and blew at the steam, feeling silly that he was probably watching me with pity. Assuming he felt pity for me. That was the ambiance he gave off anyway.

"I have to go." He sounded regretful.

I took a tentative sip of the hot liquid and it immediately soothed me a fraction. "Have a good day at work."

"I will tell Renae she can play games with you if you would like."

"How generous of you." I gave a small smile and he sighed before leaving.

Weren't we the picture of domesticity?

Moments after he left, Mino came running back into the room, and I fed him. As I watched him, I battled the gloom inside me. I had never been prone to depressive bouts before I came here. As much as I wanted to climb back into bed, I would not let myself give in to the sadness. I went outside with Mino and Sphinx and ran with them, playing, even rolling down the hills with them. Strangely, not a single grass stain marred my silk stola.

I stopped at the range as I did every day, honing my archery skills. I wondered what bow my husband used since only my own was present. When I'd hit the target three times from three different positions, I left the range to find the animals.

Both were thoroughly exhausted, so I brought them to my room and went to see the trees, as promised. I was nervous, fearing they might still be upset, but they welcomed me with open branches and were happy to swing me and let me climb, even brushing their leaves over my hair, lifting the strands, which I had left down. It was the touch of a friend, and I adored every moment.

The last thing I did before retiring back to the palace was to dip my feet in the moving stream. I found that if my intentions were not to try and cross it, the water did not rise. It seemed to know. Sentient waters. Sentient trees. Such a wondrous place. If only I had someone to share it with.

I took my time walking back to the grand palace, finding hot food awaiting my return. Mino was doing his best to climb a chair to get to it. I was ravenous this afternoon and immediately sat down to eat, taking bites and sharing with both animals until it was all gone.

We were about to retire to the inviting bed for a nap when the window opened, and I felt my husband's larger-than-life presence. A bubble of giddiness rose up and I smacked it down. Yes, I had agreed to work with him as a team, but it was nothing to get excited over. For all I knew, I was being fooled, but I was choosing not to bother with those thoughts as well.

"You look spent," he said. "Perhaps a bath?"

That did sound nice. I probably should not climb under the covers with dried sweat covering me. I gave a nod, and soon the sound of running water filled the room. Like every time he had run a bath for me, he left me alone and closed the door, but I couldn't help but wonder if he was somehow spying. He had seen me nude the day of the ant bites, but it hadn't been a moment of sensuality in the least. Never before had I been bashful of my nakedness; the people of my culture were not modest, but the thought of him seeing me without clothing made my skin prickle with nervous awareness.

I became mindful of the heaviness of my breasts and the way my waist swooped in, then flared out over my hips. The way my thighs lightly brushed, and how my hair fell with a delicious tickle across my back and arms. What would he think of the way my nipples pebbled into tight pinkish-brown buds?

I blinked the thoughts away and slid into the water, holding back a groan of pleasure. Nothing mattered less than what he thought of my body. I was being ridiculous. Perhaps I should ask him not to touch me while we shared the bed. The affections were going to my head, a dagger to my logic.

But if I were honest, it was more than the physical affections. On its own, his touch was not enough to affect my mind. It was his attention that was wearing at my wall of resolve—attentions that reminded me, against my better judgment, of Leodes. Either my husband was a better actor than any in Greece, or his concern for me was genuine. His questions, his conversations, his complete focus on my interests and well-being…it was flattering in a way I wished it wasn't. It felt as if he cared about me as a person, not a princess. Of course, it could all be a part of my husband's dark, ulterior motive—a thought that sent a sour stitch of disappointment through me.

I sighed and sank deeper into the warmth of the bath, pushing those thoughts away.

The water soothed away my anxieties as I lathered my skin with lavender and vanilla. When it began to cool, I climbed out and patted myself dry with a thick, warm cloth, squeezing my hair. I stepped from the steaming bathing room, wrapped in the fabric, and immediately felt my husband's eyes on me. He was hard to ignore as I made my way toward the closet.

One heartbeat later, I had a moment that can only be described as spontaneous madness. Without thinking on it, I dropped my towel, not looking his way, heading nonchalantly into the closet with my naked body fully on display for him. An unmistakable intake of air came from my husband where he stood at the windows before I disappeared from his sight. My heart was like a gong in my chest over and over as I fumbled to dress, suddenly terrified that my small show would bring him over here in expectation of something more.

Stupid, Psyche, why must you be so impulsive?

I felt like an idiot as I forced myself to walk back into the room, my cheeks hot, pretending it had been nothing at all. A small gasp parted my lips when the room went dark like a starless, moonless night. When the candles did not light as they usually did, I knew I had made a horrible mistake. Should I apologize? No, I had to feign innocence.

I forced out a whisper. "I cannot see."

"Pity." His voice was directly in front of me, startling my senses. My whole body went on high alert. "Because I have made myself visible."

Visible, standing right in front of me, and I could not see him. My lips pursed in annoyance.

Something soft pressed against my hand, and he said, "Put these on."

The gloves. My hands trembled as I slipped them on. At no point did my heart settle its steady pounding. I was torn between acknowledging the mistake I'd made and being too prideful to bring it up.

Stupid, stupid, stupid.

"You must be tired." He was being so matter-of-fact.

"Are you...angry?" I asked, trying to prepare myself for what was to come.

His chuckle was deep, reverberating through me. "Anger is far from what I feel."

Oh, deep Hades. I had aroused him. Why did that come as

such a surprise? Clearly there was some dark part of me that had wondered what he thought of me, physically. Unlike other men, he never harped on about my appearance. Funny how those other men used to irk me so.

"What do you want?" I asked defensively.

Again, with that damned chuckle. "What do *you* want, Wife?"

My heart danced on its toes and spun, but I said, "Nothing."

His humor was not deterred by my attitude. "Nothing? Well, if you insist. Let us get you into bed for a bit of nothingness."

Sarcasm. He placed a hot hand at the small of my back, forcing me to suck in a breath as he led me through the room to the bed. I heard him lift Mino and set him on the bedding. I grabbed the blanket, throwing it back and getting myself quickly under it. His footsteps around the bed were even, and then the weight of the soft padding shifted when he climbed in. Mino settled at our feet. I had no idea where Sphinx was.

For the love of Olympus, heart of mine, be still and relax!

I lay clutching the blankets at my shoulders, staring up into the darkness, unable to see a thing.

"I could have sworn you were exhausted." He was facing me, and his voice still held humor. I should have closed my eyes and pretended to sleep.

"It is not fair that you can see me," I said grumpily.

"Of course, it is not fair. Did you believe this arrangement would be fair?"

I crossed my arms like a petulant child and he laughed as if it were adorable. I uncrossed them.

"Come now, Psyche," he soothed. "There must be something you want. Something that will help you relax."

My thoughts immediately went to his lips, and I flushed, shaking my head.

"Have you not enjoyed any of our time together?" he asked. "Is there nothing you like about this place? Please. Tell me. I am truly curious." There went his curiosity about me again. The level of interest and attention that other men never showed. Damn him.

My teeth clenched as I struggled to find the right words to explain the ambiguous feelings I had about him and my grand prison.

"I feel as if I cannot trust what I feel." I shook my head. "I know that makes little sense. Nothing makes sense here! Sometimes I think Cupid has infected me with his bow, or I've been slipped drops of nectar in my tea. My thoughts do not feel like my own."

He was quiet for so long, I almost reached out a foot to see if he was still there.

"I assure you," he said softly. "Neither of those two things has happened. All of your thoughts, everything you have felt, are your own."

My belly turned with nervousness and a tickle of unwanted pleasure. I believed him. I hated that my instincts so strongly believed him and that my heart was desperate for it all to be true and real. I wanted to be on a team with this infuriating creature. That, above all, made no sense.

"Do you have horns?" I asked in a rush.

He laughed, something he seemed to do a lot of at my expense.

"Sit up a moment, Psyche. Face me." After a moment of hesitation, I did as he asked. "Keep your hands down." I pressed my gloved palms into the bed at my sides, then held my breath.

The air escaped my lips in a shudder at the feel of his face pressed against mine, cheek to cheek. He was warm, so warm. His skin was smooth and supple. Gently, he rubbed downward, until his breath was against my neck, and then he angled his forehead against my throat. I lifted my chin to feel him against my neck. No horns. Just heavy, silken waves of hair caressing and tickling my skin. Gods…I wanted to bring my hands up to touch him and feel that hair between my fingers, but I dared not.

He had proved his point, but I didn't tell him to stop, nor did he seem to want to. I felt him leaning closer, his hands pressing into the bedding on either side of me. And then his lips touched my throat. A tiny sound escaped me. I clenched the covers in my fists, feeling that delicious build-up in my core again.

"Satisfied?" He breathed the word near my ear.

"No," I breathed back, and then my eyes went wide. "I mean *yes*. I am satisfied to know you have no horns or scales on your head."

He chuckled, staying near, the layers of his voice cutting through my defenses.

"Very good." His lips grazed my collar bone, and I felt the urge to lay back and welcome him on top of me. I resisted. "May I keep tasting you?"

I flushed from top to bottom. "W-what do I taste like?"

"Everything sweet. Berries. Melon. Even nectar."

"You smell like honey." I did not mean to say it. I was overwhelmed.

"Would you like to taste me?" he asked.

"*What?*" My mind immediately went to some very intimate acts. "No. I've never…I can't."

And then his cheek was at my cheek again and he chuckled. "You can."

I remained still as he moved his jawline against mine until our chins touched, and then he lifted his head so that my face was in the crook of his warm neck. I pressed my lips to his heated skin, his heady honeysuckle scent making my eyes flutter. And then I opened my mouth and let my tongue touch him. We both moaned, and he pressed into me. Gods, he tasted sweet with a hint of salt, and I knew for a fact he was not human. I'd never licked a man before, but our skin most definitely did not have *flavor*. He was like a living honeycomb.

I kissed along his neck, up to his jaw. He moved, anticipating where my mouth wanted to go. When I got to his earlobe, my teeth grazed the skin there as I took it into my mouth and dragged my lips away. He whispered my name and shuddered. Everything in me felt animalistic and proud that such a small gesture could bring about a reaction from an immortal. I should have stopped then, but I was too far gone. I tilted my head to his cheek, and he moved, letting me trail a line of kisses across his face to the edge of his mouth.

My heart expanded, and all of my feelings crashed down. What was I doing??

"I am scared," I whispered.

"I know," he whispered back, but he didn't move away. Neither did he push. We stayed exactly like that, our breaths quickening against one another's cheeks until I finally decided to move.

My lips touched his with shy tentativeness. I expected him to take over as he'd done before, but he remained still as if urging me to explore. I threw all my fears and trepidations aside and opened my mouth against his, lifting my chest as I leaned forward.

Now he moved, and gods it was so hard to keep my hands to myself. He took my face and together we fell back, our lips and tongues moving against one another's with barely sustained need, gulping breaths.

"My hands," I moaned.

His face lifted from mine. "What is wrong with them?"

"I want to touch you."

"No," he growled, grasping my gloved wrists and pulling them above my head. Then he kissed me with a fierceness that had me wrapping my calves around his legs to keep him close, wishing I could pull my long nightgown up and out of the way.

What were these thoughts?

My husband shifted off me, moving to lay beside me and hold my wrists with one hand. I heard a snap of fingers and felt a sudden coolness against my skin. I lifted a knee and realized my nightgown was gone. I let out a surprised shriek and brought up my legs.

"How did you do that? I...I'm not...I..."

"Not ready to be naked in my presence again?"

Oh, he thought he was very clever bringing up my moment of indiscretion earlier. I squirmed, feeling hot now.

"I am not ready to, you know. I didn't mean—"

"Not ready to consummate. I understand. I told you; I will not have you as my wife until you ask. But I have other adventures in mind for us in the meantime. Unless you object?"

His voice shifted as he spoke, and I felt his hot breath hovering over my breast. My mouth opened, my whole body going taut.

"Psyche...?" My nipple puckered. "Is that a yes?"

"I—all right," I whispered, but I had not been prepared for how it would feel when his mouth covered the tip of my breast. My back bowed up as I gasped and writhed. He held my sensitive flesh in his hand as his mouth worked, tongue moving, lips sucking. Then he moved to my other breast, working pure mysticism on my skin, pulling back to leave both my buds damp and sensitive from his expert mouth.

I breathed as if I'd run for the cliffs.

"I cannot say all the things I wish to say." His voice dropped deeper and huskier, sending a ripple through me. "But if you listen, Psyche, listen to my touch...perhaps you will hear."

His hand lay heavy across my ribcage. I felt each long finger and the graze of his smooth palm as he moved over my skin with something akin to reverence. It was the only word I could think of to describe his touch. His hand roamed me with patience, as if not wanting to miss a single spot of my stomach and waist. Gooseflesh sprouted across my skin, the tiny hairs standing up as a delightful chill spread over me.

His hand moved over my hip, rubbing small circles on my thighs. He let go of my wrists, apparently trusting me to keep my hands to myself, so he could lavish my body with both of his hands. It was difficult not to lift my hips and silently beg for more of his touch. I had no idea it could feel like this. I never dreamed I would want to be touched by him. Replacing my fears with something far greater was exhilarating.

His hand roamed down my inner leg, beneath my knee, sliding upward until he cupped my thigh, holding me like that. "Tell me what you want, Psyche."

Embarrassment filled me. "I do not know, Husband."

"Yes, you do," he whispered. "Tell me."

He continued to cup my thigh, his fingers so very close to my core.

"I want you to keep touching me," I whispered.

His hand slid upward. "Always tell me." And then he pulled my thighs open just enough to run his thumb gently down the center of my folds. I grasped the pillow underneath my head and held it tight. He leaned down and pressed his lips to mine, whispering, "Have you ever been touched here?"

"No," I breathed, and to show him what I wanted, I lifted my hips. A guttural sound came from the back of his throat, so sexy. He kept his face near mine, our breaths mingling, as his thumb was replaced by a finger that pressed downward, finding the moisture that had gathered for him.

Like before, he let out an ancient-sounding curse, and his finger moved in a small circle, teasing me. I arched my back and his finger slid into me, making me cry out. As his hand found a delicious rhythm, touching sensitive places inside of me, the pad of his thumb discovered the top bundle of tension at my center and began to rub in a circular motion.

"Oh, gods," I moaned. "Yes…Husband."

He kissed me, his hand moving more aggressively as I bucked up to meet him, still marveling at this openness between us, this *rightness*. With his hands and mouth, he built me up, bringing me to a mountaintop and then exploded my senses in a lightning storm of pleasure. He once again had to hold my wrists above my head as my whole body rocked. And with every shudder and yell that came from the depths of me, he kissed my lips, one after another, until I calmed, breathing hard.

He pulled my bottom lip between his, stretching it a tiny bit and letting it go. His hand that had tended to me so well, was now at my waist, holding me close. He kissed my cheek, and lay beside me now, his fingers trailing my belly as I continued to come down from the summit to which he'd brought me.

He had asked me to "listen" to his touch. So, what had I heard? Was it my imagination, or had every single movement he'd made tonight seemed to say…he cared? How could that be? I had believed with everything inside of me that he was an evil creature. Could I have been so wrong?

"You are thinking," he said. "Say it out loud."

I shook my head, trying to work out the kinks of confusion.

"Say it," he urged, taking my face in his hands. "Say it before you lose your nerve."

"You care," I told him, my whole body shaking now. "You

care about me?"

The long pause terrified me, and then he let out a sound of laughter that was pure joy. He kissed my lips, then my cheeks and my forehead.

I would take that as a yes.

And for the first time since I had been forced to marry, and carted off to this strange, mystical land, I did not feel alone.

CHAPTER TWENTY-THREE

HUSBAND

WHEN I WOKE IN THE SOFT LIGHT OF THE NEXT MORNING, his invisible hand heavy on my waist, a small smile graced my lips. How quickly things had changed.

"Good morning, Wife." He sounded fully awake.

I rolled toward him, holding my hands together at my chest, and stared straight through the spot where he lay. His body's indentation was there. His presence was there. And his scent was definitely there.

"Is it strange?" he asked. "Not to see me?"

"So strange." Because, though I had felt most of his body against other parts of my skin, there was still a touch of fright in the mystery of the unknown.

"Would it matter if I were unattractive to you?" His curiosity was endearing.

It did not take me long to think about it. "Other aspects of a person are far more important."

"Hm."

My lips pulled to the side and my eyes narrowed. "What? You don't believe me?"

"Any normal human woman would be disappointed to have an unattractive husband."

"Even the most beautiful of men becomes hideous if his character is hateful and disgusting."

"Well said," he whispered. "Not every man can look like Leodes."

"Why must you always bring him up? Are you jealous? You, with all your power?"

He laughed, the sound sending reverberations through my heart and down through my belly, even lower. When he quieted I heard him breathe deeply, and I pulled the blanket higher, as if it might hide the scent of my body's reaction.

"You are blushing." He ran the back of his fingers down my cheek and I shivered.

"I am not used to this."

"An innocent in so many ways," he remarked. "Always fascinating."

Mino, waking now, made his way over the covers and came up right between us, stretching, yawning, and then wagging his tail as he licked my face. When my husband laughed, Mino flopped straight to his back, and it was my turn to laugh.

Sphinx, who'd been off who-knew-where, leapt onto the bed and curled herself on what I assumed was my husband's stomach. She appeared to be floating in the air.

"She really likes you," I said.

"Yes, well. She is brave. Most animals fear me, but felines, in general, do not seem to know their place. I woke with her across my face this morning."

I giggled. "Our tiny queen."

"So she believes." I watched the kitten's fur flatten out in a line down her back as he petted her, which set off a rattling purr from her chest. "You are more at ease today than any day here."

I stared down at my gloved hands. "I don't want to think about it. If I think about anything too hard, my mind fills with doubt and worry. I can't live that way anymore."

"Good choice." He spoke close to my face, and I saw Sphinx leap from his lap as he pushed me back, holding my wrists beside my body and kissing me.

Yes, this was what I needed. To feel and not think.

But the kiss ended far too soon, with my husband saying, "I must go." He placed one last kiss upon my lips before climbing from the bed. The disappointment I felt surprised me. I wanted to sit there and wallow, but Mino was dancing around the bed in circles, so I jumped up to take him out.

"Here," my husband said, picking Mino up in his arms. "Let us walk out together." So, we walked, him holding Mino, and Sphinx prancing along behind us. I kept my fingers folded together in front of me, fighting against the urge to reach out for his arm. When we got outside, the weather was perfect, of course, and my morning meal was waiting for me.

"'Til tonight," he said, and placed another kiss against my lips before the sound of flapping wings filled the air and he was gone.

My heart sank as the familiar loneliness washed over me like a heavy, scratchy cloak. I took a deep breath and let it out slowly. I needed to be stronger than this. My circumstances were completely different, far better, than what I assumed they would be when the oracle had told me my fate. It was imperative that I remain positive and grateful. I'd chosen to believe that my husband was on my team, and together we would do our best to overcome our opponent.

And who might that be?

I contemplated as I ate and fed Mino. My husband was powerful. He'd become offended when I'd once alluded to him having a master. Who could wield power over such a mighty creature? Only a god. Or goddess.

I shivered. It made sense. My family and people had surely offended the goddess Venus when they had turned their attentions to me instead of her. Was it Venus who somehow controlled mine and my husband's fates? What did she want from us? If she had simply desired to torture me, why hadn't she chosen a despicable creature for me to wed? It was all so baffling.

The doors to the palace opened and the tell-tale clomp of Renae's feet sounded. A checkered stones gameboard floated down the steps. I smiled.

"Good morning, Renae."

"Same to you, Princess." She pushed aside my tray of food and set down the gameboard. "Did my ears deceive me or did I hear laughter in the halls this morn?"

I thought about our walk together and warmth filled my chest. "Yes. We had a nice morning."

She let out a matronly burst of laughter and clapped her hands. "Shall we play?"

"I would love that." I scooted closer and set up my side of the board.

We played for a while—maybe an hour?—talking about my life before I had been brought here. She was especially keen to hear about how I'd vexed the guards by running off on adventures. When I tried to talk about her life, she always veered away from the subject. I adored Renae, but one-sided conversations lacked true meaning. I forgave her, knowing she was bound to whatever rules also bound my husband.

"Well, you beat me soundly," she said, tapping the board. "I never was great at stones."

"Let us play something you enjoy more," I suggested.

"Oh, I enjoy it just fine," she told me with a laugh. "I don't mind losing. But I had best get back to the kitchens." She patted my hand and took the tray with her.

"Do you need help in the kitchens?" I asked, desperate not to be alone.

"Certainly not!" This time she patted my head. "You relax and enjoy the day."

If only I could enjoy it. Too much relaxation all by yourself was a bore. Still, I stood and walked toward the hills, going about my daily routine and finding comfort in it.

Do not take it for granted.

The day passed slowly. I even napped in a treetop, waking to find myself protected in a bed of twined branches. They hadn't wanted me to fall out. As always, I kissed the trunks before I left them.

Back in my room, the animals crashed on the bed from running and wrestling all day, and I climbed into a hot bath. Like yesterday, I had a heightened awareness of my body. My husband had awakened my womanhood, opening a new world to be explored. The idea fascinated me, bringing about opposing feelings of shyness and excitement. I ran my hands over my silken, wet skin. As I got to the place where his fingers had been last night, I heard a rustle in my bedroom: the window opening.

I went still, listening to Mino's whimpers of excitement, and my husband chucking in a low voice, saying, "Yes, boy, Papa is home."

Papa is home.

And if I weren't already feeling pliable, those words melted me into mush.

"Is your mother in the bath?" he said, making Mino yip and cry in that happy puppy way of his. "Oh, you think I should go see for myself, do you?"

I bit my lip, nervousness flooding me as I covered my chest and crossed one knee over the other. Silly, I know, since he had already seen me naked, but it felt different in the bright light of day.

His footsteps sounded deliberate, as if he wanted to make sure I knew he was coming, and then his voice came to me from the open doorway.

"Mm. Good day?" How could such simple words feel like molten sensuality to my ears? I stared at the seemingly empty doorway, marveling at how thoroughly I could *feel* him.

"It was fine."

"Just fine?" He sounded closer now, and I closed my eyes when his hand brushed the wet hair back from my shoulder.

"Lonely."

He quietly brushed my hair from the other shoulder and began to massage them. I let out a small groan of pleasure as his fingers kneaded my muscles with the perfect amount of pressure.

"I told Renae she could join you. Did she?"

"We played a game of stones, but she couldn't stay long. And, of course, she cannot open up to me, so…"

"So, you are lonely."

Yes. But I wanted to be positive. "I am better now." I reached up to touch his hand. All at once I remembered the rule as he hissed, and his hands left my shoulders. I sank lower, pulling both my hands into my chest and making an anguished sound.

"I am sorry!" I said. "I'm so sorry. I forgot." I had not touched him, but my whole body shook, making the surface of the water ripple.

"That was close," he whispered, and I swore I heard anguish in his own voice, as well.

"I will be more careful," I promised, still hugging my hands under my chin.

He touched my head. "No harm was done."

The water felt cold now. I stood on unsteady legs, still covering my chest, and he handed me my wrap.

"Thank you," I whispered. I dried myself quickly, but when I headed for the closet to dress, my husband's warm mouth caressed my ear.

"Is that necessary? For you to dress?"

I flushed, clinging to the soft cloth around me. "Are *you* clothed?"

"Do you wish me to be unclothed?"

My face was on fire. "Well." I swallowed. "It seems only fair."

He paused for a moment before I heard the rustle of clothing, and then a soft *thwap*. My eyes widened as his pile of clothes became visible on the floor: a rich brown chiton, pleated neatly and edged in thick, gold thread. It was large, the size that would accommodate a tall, muscular man. Two sizeable sandals landed on top.

I covered my mouth to hide the wide smile.

"Happy?" he asked huskily.

Mino jumped down from the bed and ran to the pile of clothes, taking a sandal into his mouth and shaking it.

"Oh, no!" I giggled with surprise.

"Mino," my husband said. "*Sleep.*"

The puppy dropped the sandal and flopped down right on the discarded chiton, falling fast asleep. My eyebrows went up. "That is useful."

"Will you sleep in your wet towel?" he asked.

"Is it time to sleep?" The room went dark and my heart jumped. "I see. All right. Then, I suppose I can get rid of this." I tossed the damp cloth in the vicinity of the bathroom entrance. I was jittery, pretending to be confident, but I was certain he could perceive my nervousness.

"Your gloves," he said. I felt them against my hands and took them, sliding them on. "But do not let them give you a false sense of security. You must get in the habit of keeping your hands to yourself."

I nodded, but silently pouted.

"Now, now," he said, and then took my plumped-out lip between his teeth before taking my mouth with his. I fisted my hands at my sides, trying really hard to focus on not touching him, even though everything inside me said to throw my arms around his neck and pull him closer.

He walked me backward until my back was against the wall, and kissed me soundly, our tongues and bodies rubbing. I gasped when I felt his hard length pressing along my middle, my whole body alighting at the knowledge that we were naked together, and I had an effect on him.

As we kissed, he turned me toward the bed, placing my back to him, and guiding my hands to the bed so that I was bending over. Then he kissed a path down my back, over my hips and bottom, until his face found my place of need. He positioned my feet wider.

I nearly collapsed at the feel of his tongue, so warm and perfect, sliding up the delicate folds of my core. He held my hips as I cried out, grasping the blankets in my fists, pressing back for more. As a scorching heat built between my legs, an emotion so intense I could hardly contain it welled up inside me, and I called out.

"*Wait.*"

He rose, and I sensed his face beside mine. I continued to grasp the bedding in my hands. I was so tired of being afraid. Of holding back. My husband, this being, had more than proven himself to me. I wanted more—to give more, to receive more—I wanted it all.

"Tell me what you want, Psyche. Tell me how you feel."

"I…I want you." I said it out loud. It felt surreal.

"Are you inviting me into the bed, Psyche?" An air of masculine arrogance rose up, and I pulled my lips to the side, remembering how many times he assured me I would do just that.

"Yes. I am ready to be your wife in every way," I murmured. "Bed me."

With a great growl of victory, he took my hips and lifted me onto the bed, then lay me back and began kissing me again, lifting my arms over my head so he could kiss down my neck, lavishing both of my breasts with his mouth. I was a sopping, mewling mess by the time he nested on top of me.

My blood was hot, and my skin hummed in anticipation. I waited for him to align himself with me, but he continued to kindle the fire within me until I was ready to overheat.

"Please, Husband," I begged.

Then he flipped us so that I was on top, and my arms raised into the air as if suspended by ropes from the ceiling—not uncomfortable, but definitely secure.

"You will be in control, Psyche. Your timing. Your speed. It will hurt less this way."

"I don't know what to do," I said, bashful at the thought of taking control. I was sitting across his abdomen, his manhood laying heavy against my lower back. The thought of what was about to happen made me tremble. His hands rested firmly on my waist.

"I will guide you. Raise up onto your knees."

I did as he said, my breaths coming in short bursts.

"Shh," he murmured. I felt his hand move to grasp himself, and with his other hand he moved me back until he was lined up with me. He held my hip tightly as he ran the tip of himself back and forth up my slit, which was already slick for him. Then I sank down a tiny bit, shocked at the pressure. I pushed a bit more until he slid past my entrance. We both cried out and he tightened his grip on my hips.

"*Psyche…*" It was a plea.

My knees clenched around his waist and I sank further, leaning forward to get a more comfortable angle.

"Gods," I breathed heavily, working my way down the length of him until he was fully inside my body, filling me. In that moment I felt as if he were touching every single part of me.

My husband let out a string of gorgeous, unearthly words that went straight to my head. He sounded overwhelmed with awe and pleasure, exactly as I felt.

He gave a small buck of his hips as if begging me to move, so I did, tentatively at first, and then with more confidence as I found a pleasing rhythm and an angle that rubbed perfectly against my most sensitive spot.

I breathed, moaning words, wishing so desperately that I could touch him. His hands roamed enough for both of us, and his hips circled in a way that complimented my movements. Together we pressed and slid and moved our bodies. As good as the other night had been when we'd rubbed through our clothing, this was a million times better, his body inside of mine, touching parts of me I didn't know existed, pleasurable spots that overrode any twinges of discomfort and stretching.

As I felt the pleasure at my center building, I moved faster, sounds escaping my throat. A wildness overtook me, and I couldn't hold it back.

"Husband…I…I…"

"*Yes*," he ground out.

I completely let go, his strong hands holding me against him as I let out a surprising yell, my entire abdomen seizing with clenching, delectable madness. Over and over I pulsed around him until the waves got smaller and I wanted to collapse.

His voice was tight. "I have never been more thankful for my ability to see in the darkness."

And with that comment, he held my waist tighter as his own hips rocked up and I felt his thickness throb hard inside of me. I moaned in small spurts, unexpected bouts of pleasure hitting me all over again as he pumped upward until we were both spent.

He sat up, still inside of me, and my legs twined around his back. My arms remained in the air as he kissed me, wrapping his arms around me. We were both lightly sweating. I could not believe it. We had consummated our marriage, and it had been me who asked for it, just as he'd promised I would. But the moment left no room for fear or suspicion.

"What do you feel?" he asked. "Tell me your exact thoughts."

"I am happy," I said, still trying to catch my breath, surprised to find I *was* truly happy in that moment.

"Happy." He sounded...disappointed, which sent me into a tailspin of worry.

"What do you wish me to say, Husband? I am glad. It was wonderful."

His forehead touched mine and he placed a gentle kiss on my lips. "Happy is good." But he didn't sound as if that were true. He'd wanted a different response.

"I'm sorry if I have displeased you," I said.

"Never."

My hands were released, and he lifted me from his lap, making us both gasp. He turned me so that my back was to his chest and we were snuggling on our sides. He held me tight, and I wished more than anything he could tell me what he was thinking and feeling too.

He kissed my neck and whispered, *"Happy,"* as if tasting the word. "You have given me a gift," he whispered.

I wanted to touch him more than ever—to turn and take his face and tell him I'd been given a gift, as well—but there was something almost sad and desperate in the way he held me so hard. I couldn't help but feel that we were running out of time, and I was missing the bigger image of this game we were stuck in.

We were husband and wife now, in every way. I'd faced my fears and overcome them. He had earned my trust. So, what was I missing?

Chapter Twenty-Four

Happy

Despite the wonders of last night and feeling connected to my husband in ways I'd never been with another soul, this day was my worst one yet. I felt beyond alone. When I sat on the hill and cried, Mino sensed my sadness and climbed onto my lap, licking my cheeks with his ears back.

"Oh, you sweet boy. You know I am sad, don't you?" I petted his head, holding him close. "I am so glad I have you." When my tears dried, he bounded away after a white moth.

I curled up in a ball on the side of the hill and stayed there, losing all track of time as I reminisced about home and my loved ones. What was life without other people? Even when they drove me mad, I still wanted them in my life. I'd rather be in a rundown shack surrounded by the people I loved than to be in a palace alone.

Tears found me off and on throughout the day as I lay there feeling sorry for myself, and then hating myself for being pitiful. Why couldn't I snap out of this despair? I wished my husband did not have to work. I wished he could stay with me throughout the day, or I could accompany him. But that was not right. I had always been independent. To feel as if I needed him here with me to be happy was wrong.

I stood, shaking out my arms and breathing deeply. This was no time to lose myself. Everything was going to be fine. It had to be.

For the rest of the afternoon I did my best to stay busy and remain positive. I counted the good things about my life, taking note of every tiny comfort. It got me through the day without any more tears. But when the windows of my room opened wide and I felt my husband's presence whoosh in, I ran to him, clasping my hands behind my back, needing his touch.

My cheek found his chest and I pressed against him, closing my eyes. He was very still for a moment, as if surprised, and then his arms went around me. I felt his lips on top of my head.

"Has something happened?"

"No," I said. "I just missed you."

"Psyche." He sounded sad, and he kissed my head again.

"Make it dark," I begged.

He did it without question. I went up on my toes, tipping my face to his, and he took my lead, kissing me deeply. His hands held my upper arms, pulling me closer while helping to keep my hands down. It was torture not to touch him.

"Take me to the bed," I whispered against his mouth.

One of his hands lifted to cup my face. "Are you certain nothing happened?"

"I am certain, Husband. I just need you."

He questioned me no more, unclasping the pin at my shoulder and tugging down my soft stola until it fell to the floor. My gloves appeared at my fingertips and I quickly pulled them on. We kissed fervently as he backed me up to the bed, then lifted me so that I was sitting on the edge as he leaned against me, still clothed, his fine fabric nuzzling my nakedness.

"I have been worthless today," my husband said, sliding lower to cup my breasts and take one into his mouth. My head fell back, and I grabbed the edge of the bed. "I have done nothing but think of you."

"Now you are here," I said. "And you can do more than think."

He grabbed my waist and threw me onto the bed with inhuman strength. I bounced and smiled, so damned happy to have him there with me. So happy to be feeling something good, something that wiped out all other thoughts. So happy he was more than willing to comply.

"I want you in control this time," I told him as I fisted the bedding at my sides, arching my back as he kissed my belly button. "I trust you."

Those words made him growl and hold me tighter, nipping my skin with his teeth before coming up to kiss me again. I moaned when I realized he was naked above me. My legs opened, wrapping around his strong hips, feeling his thighs and manhood against me.

"Please," I begged, trying to move my hips.

He chuckled. "I need to ready you."

"I *am* ready."

His hand dipped down between us and he made a deeply masculine sound in the back of his throat when he felt how wet I was. I blushed, wondering if he thought me too wanton.

"Is that...shameful?"

"*Never.*"

He grasped my wrists and yanked them over my head as he pushed into me, my whole body contracting, overcome. My feet wrapped around him to hold myself steady as he rocked above me, pulling nearly all the way out, then pushing back into me with forceful thrusts. The friction, and the way he dominated me made me breathe loudly, whimpering affirmative sounds as I was caught between mild pain and the promise of wild bliss.

"I want to touch you," I begged.

"No." His teeth clamped on my neck, his tongue hot as he pulled his mouth away.

"Please...oh, gods, let me touch you."

But he only held my wrists tighter, tugging my arms up, pounding harder into me, faster, rocking us. All at once my core ignited, sending sparks through my limbs, causing my body to jerk beneath him, and my throat to release every blissful, animalistic sound inside me. But this time, he was right there with me, his pleasure spilling into me, our bodies reaching and grabbing and holding tight to every sensation. And nothing in the world was more sensual than the sounds he made against my ear, his heated honey scent sliding over me. It took a long while for us to both settle down.

"I was not very gentle," he said in a low rumble of remorse.

"It was just as I wanted," I assured him.

Tears slid from the corners of my eyes as I tried to catch my breath. He kissed one side of my face, brushing away the tears with his lips, and then the other.

"Your feelings, Psyche," he breathed.

"Happy," I whispered. "So happy."

He sighed, his head sinking into the bedding beside my head, his body heavy above me. And once again, I had a feeling my response was not what he wanted to hear. A moment of panicked hopelessness seized me. I had given him my body. I had given him my trust. I had come to rely on him and to feel happiness with him, but it was not enough.

"Are we going to lose?" Another tear slid down each cheek.

"No." He released my wrists, but I kept them above my head as he took my face, wiping away my tears. "We are going to win, Psyche." He kissed my lips. "We must."

CHAPTER TWENTY-FIVE

PROMISE

HAPPINESS WAS, OF COURSE, FLEETING. IT FLED FROM ME each morning as my husband left my side. Each day I became more and more desperate for his companionship. I wanted our bodies touching every moment we were together. I yearned all day for him to be inside of me, for our breaths to intertwine, for his hands to caress me, his lips to kiss mine. I felt as if his attention in the darkness of night could chase away all the despair I felt during the day.

And each night after we made fervent love, he would ask for my feelings. I answered truthfully, always: joy, bliss, satisfaction, even ecstasy. No amount of positive affirmation seemed to appease him. I felt him growing more and more frustrated.

"What is it you want from me?" I had shouted last night.

"You know I cannot say!" he had yelled in return. And then he held me, rocking me, kissing silent apologies across my face until the frustrated tension eased from my being.

This morning I was awoken to his thumb rubbing gently back and forth over my hip. I felt fully rested, but it was still pitch black. He did not want to turn on the sun yet—he was not ready to leave me.

"What are you thinking, Husband?" I whispered into the darkness.

"If only I could say," he whispered back. His solemnness hit me in the chest. "You tell me you are happy, but you are not."

Guilt tugged at my gut. "I *am* happy when we are together."

"And when you are not with me?"

I pressed my lips together. "I attempt to keep busy, and I am grateful for the love of Mino and Sphinx, even Renae, but…"

"But?"

I swallowed the burn of moisture. "The loneliness is overwhelming."

I heard him rub his face, sighing deeply. "You miss your home."

"My family." I choked up. "My sisters. What I wouldn't give to see them once more." Saying the words out loud, picturing their faces, brought the emotion to the surface and I inhaled, exhaling the emotion away.

He pulled me close, my back against his chest, and held me.

"What if I promised to bring your sisters here for one hour? Would that suffice?"

Hope reared up, causing me to drag in a breath of shock.

"You can do that?"

He paused. "Yes."

I sat up, facing him, though I couldn't see a thing. "All this time I could have seen my sisters?" The truth of it hit me with a painful smack.

He cleared his throat. "There is no rule against it, but it is not best for our situation."

My forehead furrowed. "This is like you keeping Renae from playing games with me. You want me only to yourself!"

"Of course, I do," he growled. "You forget what is going on here!"

A chill ratcheted up my spine. The game.

"I have been forced to make decisions that I believed would help," he said stiffly. "In retrospect, not all of those decisions have worked."

I couldn't help the small grin that graced my lips. He was

apologizing, and he clearly was not accustomed to admitting when he'd been mistaken.

I bounced a little. "So, they can come? Truly?"

"Yes, Psyche," he said on an exhale. "Just this once. I beg you to make the most of it."

I let out a small, excited screech. "I want to hug you!"

"Do not dare." He chuckled, and I clapped my hands.

My sisters! Oh, glory!

Vibrant excitement filled me. I grabbed the covers and leaned forward, searching for him with my face. He helped me out, landing his lips on mine with a laugh.

"You had better dress."

"Not yet," I said, leaning forward to touch my tongue to his.

He made that satisfying sound in the back of his throat and my body warmed, tensing and preparing.

"Psyche...I must go very soon."

"Husband..." There was one position we hadn't done yet. I turned on my hands and knees and peered back over my shoulder in the darkness. "Not yet." My heart gave a pound of nervousness followed by flutters that made me short of breath.

I heard his wings flap as he came up on his knees behind me, running a firm hand from the back of my neck, down my spine to my bottom.

"Are you being a bad little Princess?" He grasped my hips and yanked me to him, pressing himself flush against the line of my core. He was hard and ready.

"Only for you," I said, brazenly rubbing up and down his length.

He entered me from behind and I gasped at the new sensation, feeling fuller than I ever had in our time together. At first his strokes were unhurried, pulling all the way out and sliding back in with agonizing slowness, as if both savoring and preparing.

But then his baser instincts seemed to take over, and I had to hold tight to the blankets as he thrust into me, smacking his hips to my bottom, rocking the whole bed.

It was sensation overload; the friction hitting my sensitive spots just enough to set me over the edge. We found our summit together, riding the waves of pleasure until he all but collapsed on top of me, pressing my belly into the bed, his chest against my back. I felt the air tighten as his wings surrounded us, combining our breaths in the small space, dizzying my head. He kissed the side of my face, and a deep feeling blossomed throughout my entire being.

The feeling was the most intense I had ever experienced: a mix of devotion and protectiveness. My heart pounded fiercely at the thought of what I had come to feel for him. Love.

"Tell me, Psyche," he said in my ear, as he did after every lovemaking session.

I swallowed hard, suddenly terrified and filled with doubt.

"I..."

He pulled back, his body tensing. "Yes?"

A tremble coursed through me. "I liked that."

His tension went slack. He placed a soft kiss to my hairline and pulled out of me on an exhaled breath. But he said nothing. I felt his weight shift as he climbed from the bed.

I sat up and pulled the blanket over my lap. A fragile outer layer formed over me as I questioned everything. Was I mad to love him? He was my husband and he had proven his devotion to me, had he not? It was only logical that our time together would turn to love. So, why was I hesitant to tell him, or to even feel it, for that matter?

Dim light filled the room through the windows, waking Mino, who had magically slept through our morning escapade. Or maybe my husband had silently commanded the animals to remain asleep. Sphinx rubbed against my back with a loud, high meow, and Mino excitedly jumped into my arms, his tail smacking back and forth. I petted them both and wished them good morning.

"I will let them out," my husband said, kissing my forehead and lifting both animals. I giggled at their floating bodies. "Get yourself ready. I will arrange passage for your sisters now."

I covered my mouth to hide an enormous smile. "Thank you, Husband."

"Do not thank me," he said with gentleness.

I felt the suctioning sensation of complete aloneness when they left the room, but for the first time since I'd come here, I was not plied with horrible solitude. I jumped from the bed, running to wash and find just the right dress—something pretty, but not too fancy—and then for my hair.

I had never wanted for anything in my life, and yet, I had never felt whole. Ironically, at that very moment, I felt for the first time as if I had it all. My health. The care and comfort of a partner. Sweet animals that adored me. And now the companionship of my sisters. Wealth beyond measure seemed the least of my blessings. It was all about the other souls in my life.

I finished my hair with a delicate crown of brass vines that sat daintily across my head, nestled into my dark waves.

"Oh, Princess, look at you."

I turned toward Renae's voice in the doorway to the bed-chamber. "Am I presentable?"

"The smile," she said. "It sets you apart."

"You are too kind." I clasped my hands together to resist hugging her.

"I will be setting up a brunch meal for you and your sisters. Can I bring you tea and something to eat before that?"

"No, thank you. I'm too excited to have anything just now.

Brunch sounds perfect!"

I practically danced my way out of the room, humming a tune that I adored as Renae giggled behind me. She was most likely laughing at my inability to keep a tune or rhythm, but it mattered not. She'd never seen me like this, of course, because I had not felt this happy since I arrived. Now that I knew it was possible to see my family, perhaps next time I could request Mother and Papa to come. The thought of being able to see my loved ones, even if it were only now and then, would make future days here far more bearable.

Outside, I swept Mino up into my arms and showered his face with kisses, laughing as he squirmed like mad to try and repay the favor. The garden looked especially beautiful and inviting that morning as I set Mino down and we played a game of chase until Sphinx burst out from within a Pegasus's leafy leg to pounce on him. I marveled at how they'd both grown a little, appearing longer and lankier. How long had I had them now? It seemed to have happened so fast.

I was still pondering the passage of time when I heard a commotion from afar and stopped to listen. High, feminine voices came from the direction of the hills. My face split into a gigantic smile and I grabbed the lower layers of my stola, ready to run.

My sisters were here.

CHAPTER TWENTY-SIX

DAWN AND MIRACLE

"Is that her?" I heard Miracle say.

"It is! Psyche!" Dawn yelled, and the three of us were running, them down the hill, me up it, until we collided in a tight embrace, all three of us crying.

"Oh, how I've missed you," I cried. "Tell me everything! How are Mother and Papa?"

"Is it really you?" Miracle pulled away and took my face. "Our parents will be worlds better when they hear of our meeting."

"Oh, Miracle!" I could scarcely see her through my wet eyes. "I never thought I'd see you again!" I grasped her again, kissing her cheek, and then doing the same to Dawn, who gawked at me, holding me at arm's length to let her eyes roam from my tiny crown to my leather sandals that tied up my calves.

"How…" Dawn's voice trailed off as her arms dropped. "But you look so well!"

"I *am* well." I smiled and nearly laughed at their shocked expressions. "I hope you have not worried too much."

"Of course, we have!" Miracle said, her voice quavering.

I took her cheek in my hand, sad to know she had suffered.

"Worry no more, Sister. Come, Renae has prepared a meal. I will tell you everything."

I took both of their hands and practically skipped between them as they walked, murmuring in awe about the grounds. They both gasped as Mino ran up at full speed, jumping and sniffing and going 'round in circles of excitement.

I let go of their hands to pick up the puppy. "This is Mino, short for Minotaur. Isn't he just beastly?" His tongue lolled out as he licked clean up my cheek, and my sisters laughed, still appearing shocked and unable to process what they were seeing. I couldn't blame them. I set down the pup and took their hands again. The sooner I could explain everything and set their minds at ease, the better.

Dawn gaped at the walkway. "Is that gold? Truly?"

"It is," I said, slightly uncomfortable with the strange look upon her face. I felt almost…guilty. "Come on." I led them forward.

When we got to the table, I was glad to see it was already set with a mouth-watering assortment of finger foods, sweets, tea, and wine.

"Come, sit!" I led them each to a seat and sat before them. "Tea to start? Or straight to the wine?" I didn't drink wine, as it soured my stomach, but both of my sisters adored it.

They looked at each other, and Miracle was first to shake her head.

"I'm not sure we should be eating or drinking anything here."

"Not to worry," I assured her. "It is all human food. No nectar or ambrosia. I eat it every day." I popped a roasted, stuffed fig in my mouth and said, "Mmm." I could not stop smiling.

"I am really not hungry," Miracle said as Dawn shook her head. "I ate when I first woke, before the strange man showed and told me I was being summoned to see you."

I patted my mouth with the napkin, my stomach sinking at her seriousness.

"I apologize," I said. "I hope you didn't have important plans that were interrupted. I was not certain how this would work."

"I thought you were dead," she whispered, her voice cracking. "I thought I was being summoned to get your body. He would tell me nothing. Not where we were going. Not how you were. Only that he was taking me to see you and I would be home by nightfall. So ominous." She covered her mouth, and I saw that Dawn's eyes were watering, just as my own were. I reached across the table and took both of their hands.

"I cannot imagine how frightened you were. And knowing how these immortals are, you probably weren't given much of a choice."

Dawn said, "He blindfolded us and took us into the air! I had never been more terrified. I was sure it would be my death."

I tried not to smile. "Do you know who it was?"

"He called himself Zep," Miracle said. "He was a creature of few words."

I had no idea who that was. I shook my head, then lowered a healthy piece of pork down to Mino.

"I apologize again. I told my husband this morning how lonely I was for you and he shocked me by saying you could come for a visit. I couldn't believe it. I have missed you both so." I swallowed down the emotion, wanting them to see that I was fine and feeling strong. But they knew me better than that. They had always been able to see the fissures in my personality better than anyone else.

"Please, darling sister," Miracle said. "Tell us everything from the moment you arrived."

I held my hands in my lap as I began, chronicling the days of fright, and how my husband was only ever gentle and kind and tried to touch me in pleasing ways. I was careful not to give too many details of his sensuality. I was close to my sisters, but we'd never been that type of close.

"And once I began to give him a chance, I found that we cared for one another, and I trusted him. He may be a creature of the godly realm, but he is no evil monster."

"Wait." Dawn stopped me. "You have never touched him with your hands or seen him?"

"Not once," I said. "But I learned there is reason for it. And this is where things get mysterious and tricky. My husband is a powerful creature of Olympus—I'm not certain what, exactly—but he can control the atmosphere here. This land is his." I waved my arms. "But someone, somehow, has either cursed him or bewitched some sort of deal upon him. Someone has power over him, and the two of us must work together to break it."

My sisters shared a wide-eyed look. I wished they would not appear so spooked.

"I know this is hard to believe. Trust me, I'm *living* it, but everything I'm telling you is the truth." I explained the game analogy to them, but skepticism was all over their faces. I began to feel panicked, talking faster and using my hands to explain, but Miracle buried her face in her hands and Dawn grimaced.

"It is too late," Miracle murmured into her hands, and when she looked up, it was at my other sister. Dawn nodded, grim.

"What is too late?" I asked.

She cast me a look of pity. "Psyche." She took my hand. "There are...rumors."

"What rumors?"

"About your husband."

My heart, which had been steady this entire time, began to trot.

"What about him? I already told you, the 'serpent' part of the oracle's claim was metaphorical. He is like a strong, powerful man with wings. Not like any sort of creature we learned about."

She peered at Dawn again, and I really wished they would stop sharing those damned conspiratorial glances, as if I couldn't handle whatever knowledge was between them.

"What is it?" I said, using all of my self-control not to shout.

"Have the two of you...been intimate?"

I blinked, the heat rising to my face. "He's my *husband*," I said as way of explanation. I pulled my hand from hers and began pouring myself a cup of tea while they exchanged yet another look. This time they did not bother to try and hide their horror.

"He forced you," Miracle said with anger.

"No, he did not," I assured her. "He waited until I was ready. It was my choice."

"Your choice?" Dawn asked. "You chose to have a monster rutting over you—"

"It's not like that!"

Her eyes widened. "You take pleasure from him?"

"He is my husband," I said again, flushing. "Do you not take pleasure in yours?"

Dawn's eyes lowered to her lap and I felt a prickle of pity as I remembered Prince Drusus. Probably a selfish lover.

"Oh, Psyche," Miracle whispered.

I should not feel ashamed. Of course, they wouldn't understand. They had never spoken to him. They had not lived these awful days, not knowing what to believe, thinking they would be shredded to death at any moment. They had no idea the tenderness of his touch or the softness of his lips. That type of affection could not be faked.

"There are things you need to know," said Dawn. Her voice was stiff, like how she used to sound when she was jealous, but she couldn't possibly be jealous of me in this situation, could she?

"One week ago," she said stiffly, "we came together as a family in Athens to make sacrifices on your behalf. Papa was begging the gods to release you." I covered my mouth at the thought of our father doing that, and Dawn continued. "An old woman was there, a seer. She told us of your *husband*."

My mouth went completely dry at her ominous tone, but I

couldn't bear to lift the teacup with my trembling hand.

"Her tale is ringing true with what you have told us," Miracle said, picking up the story where Dawn left off, speaking more gently. "She said that he is a creature of many faces, able to change his appearance at will. But his true form, the one he takes while sleeping, is the serpent."

"Everything is all right," I assured them and myself. The thought that he could shift, that he was a serpent at night, was unnerving, but it was not the worst thing possible, was it? I started to lift the cup to wet my parched throat when Dawn began again, her words coming faster.

"His goal is to lure you into a false sense of security, Psyche. To gain your trust and seduce you, body and heart. Once you completely succumb to him, giving him your heart, that is when he will strike. He thrives on human emotions. He is a soul-sucking beast!"

Her eyes were wild, and I dropped the teacup over the saucer with a clatter. My hands shook, and my heart raced. *Soul-sucking.*

"That is not true!" I shook my head, sickened by the old doubt rearing its head again. "I will not believe some crone's gossip!"

Miracle stood and came around to me, kneeling at my feet and taking both of my hands in my lap. "You must believe us, sister. What reason would we ever have to cause you undue pain? Look how you tremble. You know there is truth in our words."

I shook my head and shut my eyes. *"No."*

"This is no way to live, sister," Miracle said. "I know, and I am sorry. I wish I could steal you away this very moment, but we both know I cannot. You must be strong. Can you do that for us? Because the seer said one more thing."

I sniffed, my chest heaving. "What?"

"She said his powers over you cannot last forever. If the creature cannot seduce you into loving him within a certain time, his power over you is lost. We aren't sure what that means, but we are hoping you will get to return home. Or be released to live your own life in this realm at the very least. Can you do that, Psyche? Can you stay strong, my love?"

A sob choked out of me, and Miracle came up on her knees, hugging me hard. I hugged her back. My heart felt as if it were being cleaved completely in two. How could this be? How could my instincts have been so wrong?

"If you have any doubts remaining," Dawn said fervently from the other side of the table. "There is one way to prove this to yourself."

"How?" I asked.

She smiled, and it was the cunning grin she used to give me when she wanted to do something that would get us into trouble.

"At night, as he sleeps, light a flame and have a look at his face."

My heart jumped inside my chest. "What if he wakes?"

"Only light it for a split moment, just long enough to get a glimpse of his face, and then quickly blow it out. But if he wakes…" She pulled a small blade from her pocket, and bile rose in my throat. "Stab him here." Dawn pointed the tip of the knife in the tender spot under her chin.

Nervousness wracked me. Our two primary rules: I could not see him, and I could not touch him. If I broke one of those rules, the game was over. Unless he'd made up those rules and the game so that I wouldn't discover his true self. Oh, gods. My stomach lurched at the thought that the man I'd come to love had been fooling me in the worst sort of manner. I pressed a hand to my abdomen.

"I do not have means to light a flame," I said. "He lights and extinguishes them all with his powers."

Dawn and Miracle both reached into their pockets. Of

course. I had always kept fire starters in my pocket at home, too. I took Miracle's flint and oil-dipped pine stick with a shaking hand, feeling as if I might pass out. She covered my closed hand with her own.

"You were always fearless," she said. "Remember who you are. You are that same girl who kept every guard at the castle on their toes. You are the soul of our isle. You are Princess Psyche. You cannot let him win."

I nodded, though I felt none of that strength right now. I didn't want to believe them, even when it made sense, which it did. I wanted to run over the hills and through the trees, straight into the river and let it rise over my head.

No. I brushed away that thought. Hurting myself was just another way to let him win. Dawn slipped the blade into my palm, and I pocketed all of the items, sick to death.

The door to the palace opened, and we all jumped to our feet.

"Renae?" I called.

"Yes, Highness," she responded from the steps. "I am very sorry to interrupt, but the carrier is here and will await your sisters at the foot of the hills. I do hope you enjoyed your time together." Oh, heat of Hades, she sounded so believable. Did she know the truth of my husband? Surely, she must. The two of them together had soundly tricked me, and the bitter sting of betrayal cut deep. It felt as if I had lost two people I'd come to love.

She clomped back inside and shut the doors, and I turned to my sisters, hugging them fiercely. I didn't want to let them go. They pried themselves away, calling back to me with worried eyes and encouraging words as they left. The carrier, Zep, or whoever he was, remained invisible to me. When my sisters were out of sight, I crumpled beside my chair, all of the heartache, loneliness and deception building up to a rolling boil inside of me.

I lifted my face to the sky, that false, vivid blue, and I screamed.

CHAPTER TWENTY-SEVEN

ONE LITTLE CANDLE

WAS IT REALLY ONLY THIS MORNING I HAD FELT LIGHT-hearted and filled with hope? Even the animals could not break through to me as I dragged myself to the bedchamber with no will to eat or bathe or even think. I felt as if I would die if I didn't learn the truth.

Was my husband the malicious soul-sucker my family believed him to be? Or was the seer a madwoman? If only so many of her details did not coincide perfectly with what I knew of him and our situation.

I sat as still as death in a chair, hugging my middle, my eyes unfocused. I desperately wanted to erase the entire conversation from my mind. My heart ached, and I questioned everything, even my own character, because part of me would rather have died with my heart full of love for him than to find out the truth.

A wave of nausea rolled over me and I closed my eyes, rocking back and forth. The remainder of the day slipped through my fingers as I chanted silently in my mind, *"It cannot be true. He is not a monster. Please, let them be wrong."*

"Princess?" Renae asked softly from the doorway.

I startled, tensing, my eyes shooting open.

"I am sorry to disturb you, Highness. Can I bring you tea and something to eat? I noticed the brunch food was untouched."

"No," I said, feeling cold. "I want to be alone."

"Very well." She sounded sad. She was a very good actress. Even Mino and Sphinx trotted out of the room after her, leaving me.

I stared about the room until I spotted the smallest candle in a hand-holder on the desk. Quickly, I stood and plucked it from its place, moving it to a table closer to the bed, then shoved the flint, pine stick, and knife under my pillow. My pulse raced, and I felt as if I might choke. I knew, deep in my soul, even if he were truly evil, I would not be able to stab him. The blade was useless.

I went to the windows and opened them wide, watching Mino run below. My heart gave a squeeze. What would happen to my sweet animals if I were killed? If I'd been thinking straight, I might have sent them home with Miracle and Dawn to be sure they'd remain safe. My fingers touched my lips as I watched them play, rolling in the soft grass together.

Awareness filled my chest and a great flapping sounded from afar. Both of the animals stopped to peer up, and then lowered to their bellies, rolling onto their backs. The unmistakable sound of my husband's laugh rose up, tickling my skin before the happy sensation turned into a rock in the pit of my gut. Did he know I was watching? Is that why he put on such a display, petting the animals?

Murmured voices rose now, but I couldn't make out the words. I believed he was speaking with Renae. Moments later, a great flapping sounded again, and the puppy and kitten were rising into the air toward the window.

He was coming. My innards felt as if I were jumping, though I stood in place unmoving. I stepped back, crossing my arms as if I could protect my heart.

"Psyche." It sounded like true worry in his voice. Damn him. "Renae says you were quite upset when your sisters left. I worried it would be difficult for you."

"Yes, well." I cleared my throat, trying to cease the quaver of my voice. "I will be fine. I'm just tired now." I turned and went to my closet, closing myself in and quickly changing into a nightgown. When I came out, I climbed straight into the bed and pulled the covers up to my chin, rolling into a ball on my side. I felt for the objects under my pillow, making sure they were hidden. Guilt filled me. Sphinx nestled above my head, and Mino behind my knees.

He would never buy that I was sleepy. I was far too tense, and the scent of fear was undoubtedly wafting from me. I held my breath when I felt him sit on the edge of the bed before me. His hand brushed back the hair on my forehead and I nearly burst into tears at the contact. It felt so real—his concern—and yet I wanted to recoil from him.

"Wife," he whispered. "Will you not speak to me?"

I had prepared what to say, but when it came out it sounded rehearsed and fake. "I thought a visit would be good, but it makes me miss them even more. I am afraid they will forget me."

"Hm."

My teeth ground together. His hand continued to stroke my hair, and I wanted to rail at him to leave me alone. That touch only muddled my mind further.

"Did they say something to upset you?" he asked. I cursed his perceptiveness. "Because this seems to be something more than simply missing them."

"N-no." My heart took off at a gallop. He'd done well learning me. Lying to him was useless.

"They do not believe that I am what you say I am." His touch continued to be gentle, and his words were soothing. I buried my face deeper in the blankets so that only my eyes were showing, and I wouldn't look at him. I had to answer. I had to put him at ease.

"A woman frightened them at the temple. A seer. But I told them she was a mad old crone."

His hand went still on my head, which made me hold my breath.

"A seer." He chuckled darkly, then stood. His footsteps were not as light as usual. His wings made rapid *whooshing* sounds as if opening and closing in agitation. "I should have known better. What a fool I was." It seemed as if he spoke to himself, not me, until he said, "The opponent found a loophole, knowing I would be weak."

"What do you mean?"

He was quiet. "The seer was not what she seemed. She was a ploy. I can say no more." A shout of complete frustration escaped him, making me jump.

Immediately, he was on the bed crouching over me, his wings enveloping us in a silent cocoon, his full lips kissing the side of my face as he pushed back my hair.

"I know you were frightened." He kissed me again and let out that ancient curse, his head turned to the side. His voice held a desperation that wrecked me. "You must not ask me for visitors again. Not until the game is complete. You have been right to trust your instincts, and I was wrong to go against mine. It will not happen again." As he held me, hot tears stung my eyes. I wanted to believe him. I had never wanted anything more. But those feelings of trust had been loosely woven, at best, and now the threads were too frayed to repair without proof.

"Can we sleep?" I asked. "I will feel better tomorrow."

For a long moment he was quiet, the air heavy between us. Then the room went dark and I felt him shift over top of me, moving to mold his body to mine from behind. His hold on me was tight, as if fraught by worry. I did not doubt his high emotions for one moment; it was the motivation behind the emotion that I doubted. Was he upset because he knew his dark plans had been foiled; because our opponent had gotten to my sisters and me, causing me to question what was between us? Or because he was truly worried about my well-being and that we were now set back from our game's "goal?"

All I knew for a fact was that if he was an enemy, he was the most dangerous enemy possible, because when I was with him, my heart, my body, and my soul wanted him. Even now, I felt myself melting into his touch, wanting to pretend my sisters had never come and poisoned me against him. I wanted to ease his mind.

"Everything will be all right, Husband," I whispered.

He held me tighter. "Do you recall the elements of a game that we spoke of?"

I thought about it. "Opponents and teammates?"

"Not that one."

"Earning points or having an end goal?"

"No. What else?" He sounded almost panicked.

"Having a time limit?"

"*Yes*." My chest jumped when his face pressed against the side of my head, his despair apparent. "Go back in your mind to this morning, before your sisters came. Can you feel it?"

The burst of love that had overcome me. Oh, how I wished I had not pushed for their visit. I swallowed and whispered, "Yes."

"Go back to that place in your mind, Psyche. We have worked so hard. *Go back*."

"I want to." A tear slipped from my eye, and he wiped it away, kissing the spot. I wanted nothing more than to go back, yet here I was, at an impasse. As we lay together with his arms and scent surrounding me, options of how to move forward tumbled through my mind. What was I to do? What was I to believe? In the end, one thought blinded me, overpowering all others.

My soul was too high a price to pay for a possible false love. Sleep was a long time coming.

A zap of panic woke me in the darkness of night. My husband's breaths were steady behind me. I remained still for a moment, wide awake, my heart beating like a Gladiator's in the stadium.

It was time to discover the truth.

I took my time slowly nudging myself out of his hold, waiting to see if my movement would wake him, but he was sound asleep. I silently tip-toed to the table, feeling in the dark for the candle's holder. I found it and rushed quietly back to the bed. I slipped my other hand under the pillow, pulling out the lighters. Holding my breath, I angled the tip of the oiled pine stick to the rough flint and pressed hard, swiping to the side. The small crackling sound made my heart skip a beat, and the sudden bright light near my eyes caused me to blink.

I lowered the tiny flame to the candle and lit the wick, my hand shaking like mad.

Moment of truth.

My hand slowly raised over the bed, and my other hand covered my mouth against a gasp of astonishment as my husband's form became clear in the dim light.

Gloriously golden skin was on display, not a single scale in sight, the muscle defined and apparent. His masculine hand stretched out, near me, his fingers splayed over the spot where I'd been sleeping. His hair reminded me of ice—a divine color I'd never seen on a human. But his face…

In the back of my mind a voice was screaming for me to put out the candle, but I was too mesmerized. His face was perfection. Every defined angle. The darkest, thickest lashes. And those bow-shaped lips. They were as full as they felt, and so beautiful my chest ached. Behind him lay giant, majestic wings of white, tipped in smoke gray.

This was no monster. My eyes darted to beside the bed and took in the golden bow and a quiver of ornate arrows. A tremor ran through me as realization slammed my soul like a tidal wave.

My husband was a god. The god of love. Cupid himself.

I yanked the candle back to extinguish it, and as I did, a drop of hot wax dripped straight onto my husband's hand. It happened so fast, and yet so slow.

He sucked in a sharp breath and his eyes opened. I froze, falling into those blue depths, more exquisite than anything I had ever seen.

"Psyche?" he whispered, his eyes going to my face, then the candle. "What have you done?" His voice, full of horror, was not the voice I'd come to know. It was as if the rough, scratchy layers had been scraped away to reveal the sensual melody hidden underneath.

I shook my head, stepping back, shaking, my jaw unhinging and my voice dead. In my movements, the pillow had shifted, and Cupid caught sight of the blade.

"Were you to kill me, Wife?" His eyes bore into mine, the pain there causing my mouth to open and close, my head to shake back and forth. "You know I am immortal."

"I know," I whispered. "I was...I *would never*—" Again, I gaped.

He leapt from the bed with inhuman grace, wearing a warrior's pleated wrap around his waist. Landing before me, he blew out the candle and grasped my upper arms, giving me a small shake in the darkness.

"Quickly," he said. "Tell me how you feel, Psyche."

"I am sorry!" I wanted to collapse. I had been so wrong.

"Not an apology! Your feelings!"

"I feel *horrible*," I shouted.

"Your feelings about me!"

"*I love you!*" As soon as I said it, I knew it was what he wanted all along—my love. And I knew, without a doubt, that it was too late. "I broke the rules." A sob of disbelief and shame tumbled from my throat. "Oh, gods! What have I done?" I wanted to sink to the ground, but he held my arms tight.

Daylight filled the room, and my husband still stood there before me, larger than life, so real and beyond beautiful.

"I will fix this." With a fierce look, filled with all the things he had never said, he turned and bolted through the room, through the window, wings tucked tightly behind him and then shooting outward in an ethereal arc when he hit the air. I could only stare as he flew away.

Fast clomping came from the hall and the door to my bed-chamber burst open. A short, rotund, middle-aged woman stood there. Well, a woman on the top half, and goat on the bottom half. She smacked a hand over her mouth as I looked her up and down.

"Renae?"

"You can see me? The binding has been broken!" A pretty smile filled her face until I collapsed into the nearest chair, heaving for air. I barely noticed Mino jumping at me excitedly, and then running to hike a leg on the bed.

"I have ruined everything," I said, my breaths coming fast and short. "I—I…" I pointed to the candle on the floor, hot wax splattered against the marble.

She stared at it, her hand on her chest, shaking her head. "You didn't." She turned saddened eyes on me. "Oh, dear. It was your sisters, wasn't it? I knew something bad had happened!"

"I should never have doubted."

"Oh, Princess." She knelt and hugged me, rubbing my back. I didn't deserve her kindness. "You must go to the temple of Venus." She pulled away to hold my shoulders and look into my eyes. "Go. Beg for her mercy. Tell her how you feel for her son!"

"But I broke the rules! What will she do to me?"

"I don't know," she said frankly. "May the gods have mercy." Renae kissed my forehead and called to the windows. "Zephyr!"

I stared as the god of the west wind flew gently into the room, smaller than Cupid, his hair and wings dark in color, his face lovely and delicate. He nodded at me.

"Zep," Renae said frantically. "You need to take Psyche to the temple of Venus at once. She broke the binding. There is no time to waste."

"Where is Cupid?" His melodious voice was soft and comforting.

"I don't know! Take her—go!" She shoved me toward him and he lifted me easily.

"Maybe I should wait for him to return?" I began, but he was already lifting me into the air. "Renae!" I called. "Take care of Mino and Sphinx!"

She bent and lifted the puppy as Sphinx leapt onto the window sill. The three of them watched Zephyr fly me away. I held tight around his shoulders and pressed my forehead to his neck, praying silently all the while.

Cupid, my husband, forgive me. Venus, celestial goddess...hear my heart.

Part Two

CUPID

One Year Earlier…

"Love looks not with the eyes, but with the mind
And therefore is winged Cupid painted blind.
Nor hath love's mind of any judgment taste;
Wings and no eyes figure unheedy haste.
And therefore is love said to be a child
Because in choice he is so oft beguiled."

~William Shakespeare, A Midsummer Night's Dream

Chapter Twenty-Eight

Goddess Impostor

CUPID PERCHED HIS LITHE BODY IN A TWISTED, THICK OLive tree overlooking a winery and inn. More often than not, humans disgusted him, yet he could never stay away. The very idea of their souls was fascinating, especially since he was the only god who could sense that brightness or dimness from within each human. It helped him decide who to punish and who to gift.

But mostly who to punish.

He was not permitted to kill their mortal bodies and send their souls to the Underworld, but he could bring chaos to their dull lives by playing on their emotions. Most knew him as the god of love, but he was more than that. He was the god of sensuality and eroticism. With his nature, wreaking havoc on humans was too simple.

Right now, he spied the wife of the winery innkeeper stomping grapes with two fellow employees, skirts lifted to their thighs, as her husband entertained prestigious guests inside. Indeed, the night before he had entertained the daughter of a guest once his wife and the girl's parents had fallen asleep.

For a human male, the innkeeper was attractive, but his soul was muddied by vanity and a constant need to have his physical prowess validated. It was this weakness—the human male's blatant desperation—that earned the wrath of the youngest god.

Cupid's fingers ran deftly up and down the strings of his bow as he pondered his arsenal of tonics. Along his low-slung belt, he carried potions with the ability to temporarily heighten almost any human emotion: anger, sadness, humor, regret, and yes... love. Though love, being complicated, was the most temporary of all. Love started as a series of attraction followed closely by interest, then adoration. But then love morphed into something more significant, requiring action, not just feeling. Humans had to choose each day to continue on that path of devotion and loyalty, and often it was simply too much work for their meager minds and bodies.

No creatures were as easily bored, distracted, or ungrateful as humans. Except, perhaps, gods.

But gods were not weak, and Cupid would never love. Not in the foolhardy way humans did. Unlike them, he was immortal and never in a hurry. Never hasty. Never in need of *validation*. His confidence was as eternal as his body. Someday his perfect goddess would be created, and they would find one another. His mother would be sure of it—a flawless match. Cupid had faith in the future. For now, he was content to meddle in the lives of those on Earth, and when the urge took him, to shift into his mortal disguise and sate his appetite with human women.

In fact, the innkeeper's wife was looking more attractive the longer he watched her dancing in the fruit, legs staining purple and red, a light sheen of sweat along her brow. He had punished many mortal men by having their women for a night. Cupid had always enjoyed the causticness of it. Where his true form was golden and awe-inspiring, his chosen human form was dark and intriguing. Both stunning in their own ways, but human women cherished a dangerous challenge.

A light tingle along his skin alerted him of the presence of another god. He turned on his branch to find his mother approaching, a vision of beauty gliding across the swaying grass, slowly being lifted by small clouds that puffed into and out of existence with each graceful step, like a staircase leading up to his perch in the tree.

The goddess of love was able to take away the breath of even the mightiest of gods. To Cupid, her presence was the ultimate comfort, for she alone loved him. He could tell from the pursed pout of her lips she was not pleased.

"What is it, Mother?"

Instead of answering immediately, she glimpsed the women below, nearly finished with their grape crushing.

"Why do you humor yourself in such a way, my son?" She touched the bluish-white waves that framed his face, her eyes searching the pronounced bow of his lips, turned down. "I worry you spend too much time among their kind and not your own. Are you lonely? Shall I speak to Jupiter about a match for you?"

Cupid took her hand, giving it a gentle squeeze before dropping it. He would not ask the king of the gods for anything. The last time he'd gone to Jupiter, hoping to find out his true paternal parentage, the god had laughed in his face and said, "If your mother does not know which of her many lovers sired you, then it is not your fate to know either."

As far as Cupid knew, Jupiter was not one of his possible fathers, but the king of the gods had been burned by the exploits of Venus and was forced to put out one too many firestorms started by her antics. So be it.

"No. It will happen on its own when the time is right."

"A romantic," Venus said, earning a glare from her son that made her laugh.

A bird flew near, alighting itself on a nearby branch to catch Venus's attention.

The goddess peered up. "Winged creature, if you relieve yourself anywhere near me I will smite you."

The bird puffed up its feathers and flew away.

Cupid grinned. "Be kind to the poor beasts."

She eyed his feathers with admiration—snowy white, edged in smoke gray, his wingspan impressive. "You are the only winged creature I trust."

Silence fell until Cupid asked, "Why have you sought me, Mother?"

All traces of humor and ease faded from her face. "I have been wronged by a human, and I seek your help."

Cupid's hand tightened on his bow. "Who has dared wrong you, Mother?"

"A girl." She practically snarled the words, and Cupid's brow drew tight. It had been over a century since a human had earned his mother's ire. He couldn't imagine what a mere girl could have done to catch the attention of Venus, much less upset her so.

"Tell me everything." And so, she did, beginning with the island where the girl resided, and he stopped her. "Wait. Did we not visit there recently? The king and queen with pure souls?"

"Yes," she spat. "The very same ones who had been trying years for a child. The queen was barren, so I blessed them with fertility. Now they have three daughters, and the third believes herself as beautiful as *me*."

Cupid laughed outright. "How old is this silly girl, Mother?"

"She is not a simple, *silly* child," Venus assured him. "She is nearly of marrying age. And for the past year she has accepted gifts from the people that should have been for me. She has turned the eye of my worshipers, stealing my offerings and relishing praise meant for me. My alters in the surrounding area have been bare. They say..." Venus stopped to compose herself. "They say she is more beautiful than me."

"Impossible." A name tickled the back of Cupid's mind, a name he'd heard murmured among humans in passing. "Is she, by chance, Psyche?"

Venus's eyes blazed. "Of course, you have heard of her! Have you seen her? What are her flaws?"

"No, Mother." Cupid shook his head. "I have never seen her." The name Psyche had stood out to him because it translated to Soul. Now, hearing of her vanity and audacity, the name was ironic. Her soul would have to be completely polluted to think she could compete with a goddess.

"What would you have me do?" Cupid asked. Girl or not, he would punish the imposter goddess, reminding her exactly who and what she was.

A wicked smile played across the naturally red lips of Venus. "I would have you humiliate her. Make her think she has fallen in love with the most hideous and vile of men. Someone far beneath her station. Make her devotion for him so powerful that she would elope with the monster to break the heart of her parents who turned their backs on me, forgetting the blessings I gave them."

Cupid nodded, his wicked grin joining hers. "Consider it done."

CHAPTER TWENTY-NINE

FRIENDLY FIRE

It was not the first time Cupid had been sent on a mission by his mother, and he was certain it would not be the last. It honored him to be trusted by Venus above all others.

The moment Cupid spotted the island from afar he was reminded of when he had been there last. Everything from the briny warmth of the air to the layout of the long island, starting flat at one end with fields and orchards, and layering upward to the summit of its palace and royal fortress surrounded by rocky edges that fell majestically into lagoons and gully caves. He thought it was breathtaking then, for an Earth place, and it was just as gorgeous to him now. It soured his attitude knowing the rulers had forsaken their gods, especially his mother who had taken time to personally see to their fertility.

After today they would realize, too late, the error of their ways.

It seemed only days had passed since he had been there, but in human time it was at least twenty-five years. A blink of an eye in a god's time, but long enough to make humans forget. That was the problem with humans. Well, the *primary* problem. They so easily forgot. Over and over the gods showed themselves, proving their glory and might. But all it took was the short passage of time for humans to begin questioning again—for them to start believing themselves superior to those they could not see, and wondering if the gods were indeed real, only to come running to the altars when tragedy and famine struck. The gods wearied of this vicious cycle. Someday, if the humans were not careful, the gods would cease to show themselves at all.

Cupid landed at the edge of a craggy cliff, scouting, then shot up to crouch on the edge of the royal walls. Humans couldn't see him unless he wished it so. He peered down at the soldiers practicing with swords for yet another war in another age on another land. As long as there were humans there would be war.

The god flew over the ramparts then into the castle, searching for the youngest princess while also keeping an eye out for any hideous male he encountered to become her "love." All it would take was a whisper in the male's ear to coax him close enough to Psyche, and a prick of his arrow for her to open her eyes to the foul man. Cupid took his time and savored the search.

It turned out she was not in the castle like he had expected. His immaculate hearing picked up her name farther down the hill, past the rows of cliffside houses to the market.

Perfect, Cupid thought. He would catch her in the act of accepting worship from the people. Perhaps if he were angry enough he would show his true godly self for the first time, frightening the people nearly to death and causing odes to be written about his might and splendor for centuries to come.

Nah.

The more faithless humans were, the less the gods were willing to prove themselves. To glimpse a god was a gift beyond measure. Rarely did a human deserve such sanctity.

Cupid pulled in his wings and drifted down beside a stall emitting a stench that made his eyes water. One look through the slated cracks of wood and he nearly laughed out loud. The pig farmer was up to his knees and elbows in feces, his pockmarked face red with frustration as he tried to catch the swine. His soul was as dark as the grime that covered him. He swore with every filthy word known to man, gritting his gray, half-rotted teeth.

When he finally captured a creature, holding the piglet against his rounded belly tightly enough to make the animal squeal in pain as he cursed it to the nether regions of the Earth, Cupid knew.

This would be Psyche's husband.

Now all he had to do was find her and lead the two of them into a nearby vicinity so the pigman's face would be the first the princess saw after being struck with Cupid's bow. Too simple. Vengeance belonged to Venus.

Although the god could make himself invisible to the human eye, his physical body was still very much present. Not wanting to be touched in his true form, even accidentally, he shifted into his Earthen form. Brown hair in waves around his face. Brown eyes with dark brows. Leaner muscle. Less height. Thinner lips. Plain cream linen draped across his shoulders and wound around his waist held by a simple rope. Worn leather sandals. Many men wore their weapons as part of their attire, but Cupid could not disguise his bow to look anything other than majestic, so he kept it invisible against his back. Although he considered this form minimal, it still received him no end of attention from humans. He could not help the vitality he gave off.

Cupid merged into the mass of bodies hocking goods and bargaining. Smells of fresh mackerel and sardines wafted past. A warm blast of yeast. Pungent smoked eel and sun-ripened citrus. The god took in the Earthly sights and smells, ignoring the eyes that landed on him and lingered, their souls a mix of light and faded. None were especially bright or dark. His eyes were peeled for crowds around a single person, but oddly the atmosphere was usual human commotion. Nothing stood out the way a princess's presence would warrant.

He was about to open his senses to see if she'd gone back to the castle when he rounded a corner to a street of housewares, clothing, and colorful adornments and nearly collided with a burly man in plain clothes, who stood at attention like a guard. The man looked him over, giving him a nod when Cupid passed some silent test. A guard in disguise? The man's eyes went straight forward again, and the god followed his gaze to a stall selling hand-carved animal trinkets.

Cupid sucked in a breath and nearly stumbled back. He could not recall a single time in his existence when he had been without grace.

But neither had he ever seen a soul so bright.

The glowing woman leaned over a table, her face and body covered by a plain shawl. Her hand, which appeared lovely and young, lightly touched the face of a cat bauble. Cupid's heart, which rarely ever changed its forlorn, steady beat, was pumping too fast.

He surveyed the situation. As Cupid's eyes flitted down the path of vendors, through the crowd, he spotted at least five other broad, plain-clothed guards and soldiers going back and forth between watching the girl and surveying those who passed her.

This was Princess Psyche. In the pit of his stomach he knew it. And though her pure soul should not affect his mission, it did. Why was she hiding herself? To have a moment of selfish peace before garnering the attention of the market goers? It made no sense. The more he thought about the description his mother had given him, the more he knew this young woman could not be the girl he sought.

"Can I help you find something, sir?"

Cupid, taken by surprise, gazed at the guard and realized, gods above…he had been staring and so lost in his mind that he moved closer to the girl without meaning to, drawing attention to himself.

"No." The disguised god gave the soldier what he hoped was

a friendly smile. "Just browsing. Thank you. So much to see."

It must have worked because the man relaxed a fraction. "First time on the island?"

Cupid gave a tight smile, finding it uncomfortable to lie, though he would do it if he must. "Passing through."

The soldier bid him good day, and Cupid made a snap decision. He had to see the face of this girl. He had to know for certain. And no matter what, regardless of whether or not his mother's information had been partly mistaken, he would carry out this mission to completion.

Cupid approached the table, keeping space between them, and picked up a detailed lion carved from wood. The stall owner eyed him.

"Only looking," he told the old woman. "First time on your island. It is quite beautiful. I'm here for the day, passing through." The old woman grunted in response, not interested. But the girl had shifted slightly in his direction. Cupid spotted her nose, not pointed but not too round either. Perfectly sculpted.

Behind them the guard shifted closer, and the god pushed back with his mind, silently telling the man, *"Step back. Look away. There is no danger here."*

The guard immediately obeyed.

Cupid turned his attention back to the table. The girl still held the small cat.

"That is a cute one you have there," he told her, edging closer.

The girl's grip tightened on her shawl with one hand and she abruptly set the bauble down.

"Sorry," Cupid chuckled. "Not my intention to startle you."

She let out a small laugh that pleased Cupid's ears, making him blink.

"It's all right," she said in a voice both husky and soothing, picking up the cat once more. "This one reminds me of something that happened when I was a child."

"And what was that?" Cupid leaned forward just enough to watch the girl pull her plump bottom lip between her white, straight teeth as if considering. His insides jumped, and he blinked again.

Gods, what in Hades was wrong with him today? It was just a human girl.

Again, she released a breathy laugh, almost nervous. She surveyed the cat, which he realized now was more of a lion.

"When I was small I came across an injured mountain lion cub and brought it home. My parents were furious and scared to death—its claws were enough to shred me—but I insisted on nursing it back to health. So, I did. And it never once scratched me, though I can't say the same for my room's furniture. I cried when I had to set it loose."

Cupid stared at the tiny bit of her profile she allowed to show. Then he stared some more. She hesitantly turned enough to glance at him, and he watched with immense satisfaction as she did a double take, forgetting herself and showing the oval of her face within the cloth. He jolted with something he'd never felt in all his long years of existence. The sensation was so foreign he couldn't begin to put a name to it. Her eyes, so round, were a mix of golden honey, amber sap, and sunshine. As bright and beautiful as her soul. Her lashes stretched wide like dark butterfly wings. This was definitely, without a doubt, Psyche.

The stall owner gasped at the girl's raised face and began to point, but Cupid cut her off mentally—*"Look away. She is a normal girl."* The woman's eyes and hand dropped.

"I know," Psyche said sheepishly, peering down at the figurine once more. "It was silly."

"What?" he asked. Oh, the cub story! Cupid shook his head.

"No. I do not consider a tender heart to be silly." He meant it and truly wished it was not the case. He needed her to be inconsequential.

She tilted her head and stared back at him now, studying him. He wondered why she scrutinized him so. What did she think when she looked upon him? Was she suspicious? Did she not believe his words to be genuine? He wanted to understand this look from her. He wanted to know and understand everything about her. His thoughts gave him a shot of chilling fear.

No.

He did not need to understand her. Nor did he need to know her. This ended now.

"Where are you from?" she asked at the same time he said, "What is your name?"

The girl peered down. "I'm nobody." A non-prideful response.

His heart clenched tightly in his chest and he forced himself to breathe.

"What is *your* name?" she asked.

"Leodes," he answered automatically, using the Earthen name he always gave.

"Leodes," she repeated with a sweet smile, and the way it sounded from her lips made him overly alert in all the wrong places. That was not part of the plan.

"I seem to have lost track of time," he told her stiffly. "My boat will leave without me."

Disappointment flitted across her face as she gazed at him now, full on. "I didn't mean to keep you with my stories, sir. Thank you."

"For what?" he asked.

"For...listening."

Odd. A princess surely had an arsenal of listening ears at any time. He let out a breath, fighting instincts that fired up inside of him before pushing forward with his thoughts. He had a mission. He must put his misgivings away and trust his mother's instruction. *"You will visit the pig stall. Now."*

Her eyes glazed, and it gave him an ill sensation. He'd never felt regret or remorse for any mission, and he dared not start with such foolishness now.

"I have to go, too," she told him. "I wish you safe travels."

He could not bring himself to respond. Cupid tore his eyes away and walked heavily in the opposite direction. A single glance behind him showed the guards all moving to follow her, leaving no doubt this was the third princess. The princess who calls herself "nobody," takes pity on stranded animals, and hides her beauty. A girl with the brightest soul on the island, who his mother mistakenly believed to be cruel and selfish.

It mattered not how the girl caused him to feel. Or how she seemed unworthy of punishment. Cupid's place was to obey. His mother trusted him, and he trusted her.

Cupid gave his head a hard shake and stalked behind a stall, shivering as he shook off his human glamor and filled out his true form once again, remaining hidden from sight. He yanked the bow over his head with more force than necessary. On this day he didn't bother bringing his vials. He had dipped his arrowhead straight into Venus's own fountain that morning before leaving Olympus. The tip of his arrow was poisoned with the most potent love potion.

One scratch and the glowing girl would be in love with the pigman.

He ignored the churn in his abdomen and bent his knees, leaping onto the stall roof, then gliding from one rooftop to the next, flying the last bit until landing on the flat roof of a barn within shooting distance of the pig stall.

The man was shoving a different squealing piglet into a wooden crate as Psyche approached. Cupid held his breath as he watched how she walked with natural grace, almost gliding along the pebbles and dirt as smoothly as his mother.

No. That was the same foolish comparison the humans made, and it angered him that he could understand now how the rumors came to be. He had not even seen the girl in full, and he was overcome. He could only imagine how the stupid humans felt. Cupid grabbed his forehead and closed his eyes a moment. He needed to finish the job and get far away from this damned isle.

"What do you *wannn*...hello my dear." The pig farmer had noticed her. A chill raked up Cupid's spine at the way the man leered, showing all of his graying teeth. The guards gave one another concerned glances, all stepping a bit closer. Psyche was still under Cupid's spell standing at the stall, presenting her back to him as a perfect target. He could not wait a moment longer.

Without taking his eyes off her form, Cupid reached back and pulled the arrow from his quiver. No more delaying the inevitable. Squatting, he aligned the tip of the arrow with the part of Psyche's back where her heart lay. He would not think about how brightly she shone, especially in comparison to her future mate, dim in every way—the man whose filthy hands would soon be all over her.

Hades.

Cupid wiped his brow. Was he sweating? Was that a tremor in his hand? What fresh madness was this?

When he looked back, the pigman shouted and kicked a piglet who'd managed to pry its way from a crate. Psyche bellowed a cry and covered her mouth. Her heartfelt reaction to the treatment of the animal gave Cupid pause. Would her emotion be strong enough to break his verbal spell? How would she react to the pigman? He stared in fascination, his bow drifting downward as he allowed himself to watch for one more indulgent moment.

Just one.

She really was a mesmerizing sight. Her guards all watched from nearby, seeming baffled as to what she was doing there.

Finally, she dropped her hands, making tiny fists, and raised her chin. "You don't have to kick the poor thing!"

The pigman's eyes narrowed and he forced a laugh. "No worries, Miss, they don't feel pain the same as us, you see?"

"That is not true."

"Say, what's your name, Miss?" The pigman licked his lips. "You seem familiar."

She stiffened, the motion bringing Psyche to her full royal posture just as a wind gusted, her hood falling back to reveal rich waves of honeyed brown hair, shining like silk kissed by the sun and sea. The breeze picked up her hair, pulling it from beneath the cloth and blowing it out from her body. The farmer gasped, and the god gaped as she tried to wrangle the long strands back under her hood. Gods of Olympus, she was a *sight*.

A sting of pain caught Cupid on the knee and he hissed. What in darkness? Cupid peered down at the cut in his skin, now tingling. His arrow, no *Psyche's* arrow, hovered above the spot where blood pebbled to the surface of his skin, then immediately healed over. In a moment of confusion, he looked back down at the pig stall and saw Psyche turning, shaking her head as if bewildered, then he saw her face. A rush of strong emotion hit him like a hurricane, swirling furiously around him, forcing his breaths to come in gasping waves, his eyes widening, his heart soaring.

Oh.

OH.

His knee. His arrow. Psyche's glowing face of perfection. His mind expanded, stretching wide enough to take in all of Earth and Olympus and all of the worlds beyond. The feeling strained his mind and heart, muddling everything he had ever known. Cupid began to tremble. He could not look away from the small sliver of her heart-shaped face beneath the hood, those soft and lush lips, and her creamy hands.

He loved her. There was not a single, miniscule part of him that did not love her. The feeling was all-consuming. A devotion more powerful and wondrous than anything he had ever known.

Somehow, his mind-spell over her had been broken much more quickly than normal, and she seemed to want to get as far as she could from the stall. She moved faster when the pig man shouted after her.

"Don't you know it's rude to walk away from a man without responding? Hey!" He glared at Psyche's retreating back. When the largest guard passed her, heading toward the stall to deal with the mouthy farmer, the princess grabbed his arm and begged him to leave it—the pig farmer had no idea to whom he spoke. Within seconds the remaining guards were surrounding her as well, and they rounded the corner out of sight.

Cupid flew down at top speed, still invisible, and crushed his golden fist into the pigman's face. The farmer, having no idea what hit him, flew back into the hay and manure, grabbing his face and yelling, flailing in pain and alarm.

Nobody shouts at my love, Cupid thought.

His love...yes. Nothing had ever felt more right.

Psyche didn't know it yet, but she was inescapably his. And he was hers. Nobody, not even his mother, would lay a hand on her.

CHAPTER THIRTY

MOTHER DEAREST

CUPID CAUGHT UP TO PSYCHE AND HER GUARDS, FLYING above them as she moved quickly through the crowds, her head down, face and body hiding behind the large, loose shawl. When the guards moved closer, she waved a hand as if to keep them at bay. They arrived at the gated entrance of the royal living area, and Psyche paused to look upon the massive pile of items against the wall.

The god realized with a pang that these were the offerings his mother spoke about. Baskets of fresh fruits and vegetables. Bushels of wheat tied with twine. Shiny bits of jewelry and gems. Handwoven rugs of fine quality and color. Yes. Psyche deserved all of this and more. But to his amazement, she gave her head a sharp shake and barked something at the largest guard, who gave an order to a younger soldier before escorting the princess on while the younger guard began to gather the items. Cupid scowled when the guard momentarily touched her lower back. If he did that again, the god would snap the man's fingers.

Glancing back, he saw that the younger soldier was not carrying the offerings through the palace gates. Instead, he headed down a smaller path toward the squat homes that leaned against one another, one sea storm away from toppling over.

Cupid's heart constricted. His love was giving her gifts to the poor.

His mother's information had been so very wrong. He wanted to pummel whoever had spoken ill of Psyche. She could do no wrong. Cupid would clear up this entire mess, and all would be well.

Once he saw her safely into her home, Cupid flew swiftly, crossing the layers of atmosphere between the realms that only gods could see, passing from Earth to Olympus. It took only seconds for his eyes and nose to adjust to the brighter colors and more vibrant scents. He flew straight to the seaside villa of Venus, surrounded by fields of flowers and covered in lush vines.

He was out of breath when he landed before his mother, but not because the trip had winded him.

"Mother!"

Venus's hand flew to her chest and she let out a startled laugh. "Son! Why do you look as if all the spirits of Hades have risen? Did you accomplish what you set out to do?"

"Listen." He took his mother's thin, but strong, shoulders in his hands. "We had it all wrong. Princess Psyche is not at fault. She has no interest in the offerings—"

"Cupid." The goddess shrugged out of his grip, her face stern. "What in the name of Olympus has gotten into you? You are crazed! Is that sweat on your brow?"

"No, Mother, please." He closed his eyes, grasping his hair, desperate to make her understand. "She is good. Her soul is…" He let out a deep sigh, remembering. "The most beautiful soul I have ever seen."

When Cupid finally opened his eyes, his Mother was gaping at him as if looking upon a stranger. A particularly odd stranger. She shook her head slowly.

"Do you mean to tell me you did not do as I asked?

"Did you not hear me, Mother? Her soul—"

"I do not care. Her parents also had bright souls. Do you recall?"

Cupid shook his head. He had to make her understand. "Not like hers. Nothing like hers."

Venus scoffed. "Her feeble soul will be sullied in the blink of an eye, Cupid. Do you deny she has been given offerings? That she is but a false god?"

"She does not accept their gifts. She gives them to the poor."

"They are *my* offerings. They should not be going to any humans!"

The mother and son faced off, standing close, both speaking in raised voices.

"Then punish the people, not Psyche!"

Her voice lowered a dangerous notch. "How dare you question me? I will punish everyone on that forsaken island *and* their beloved princess."

Cupid gripped his hands into fists. "I will not allow you to hurt her."

A bubble of laughter rose up from Venus, but her face held no amusement. "*Allow* me? Are you hearing yourself?" The goddess's hands lashed out and shackles appeared on her son's wrists. Her hands flicked again, and he flew back, crashing into the wall, struggling to break the manacles.

"No!" Cupid rushed to his feet, only to be bound by the waist and ankles, yanked back and pinned against the wall by his mother's immense power.

She glided forward, her face a mask of terrible anger. "Are you so weak as to fall for a pretty human face? Is that what this is?"

"I love her!" he shouted, panting for breaths.

Venus jerked as if struck, and for a moment her mouth hung open. Then her eyes darted to his bow and quiver, squinting.

"There is blood on your arrow." Her eyes narrowed, and she began to shake as she stared. "Who did you strike?"

When his mouth clamped shut, she moved to him, crouching close and stroking his cheek with gentleness. "Cupid?" Venus cupped his chin. "You know you have my heart more than any ever has. There is nothing I would not do for you."

He all but crumbled under her touch and kind words. All of the fire left his body and he slumped into her hand.

"Whose blood is on your arrow, son?"

Cupid swallowed hard. "My own."

Time seemed to pass in slow motion as Venus processed this information. And this time when she began to laugh it was genuine, earnest humor. She kissed his cheek and rolled back on her haunches, laughing so hard she had to grip her stomach. Cupid glared at her misplaced hilarity. He had never seen his mother in the clutches of such merriment. He gritted his teeth, wishing it would pass.

"Are you quite finished?" he asked when she finally began to gasp and sit up, wiping tears from her eyes.

"Oh, Cupid. Darling." She brushed his cheek again. "You know I cannot let you go until the effects have passed."

Cupid frowned, yanking the chains. "Mother, no. I must go!"

All humor left Venus's face. Her soft touch turned to the rake of a fingernail along his jawline.

"I know what is best for you. If my potion lasts three months on the average human, you should burn through it in a fraction of that time. Not to worry. I shall care for you until you are yourself again."

"I have never been more myself!" He attempted to stand and failed. "Let me out of these!"

She *tsked*. "Once your self-inflicted wound has healed and

you see clearly again, you will complete the task I gave you."
Venus stood, peering down at her son's frantic eyes, as blue
as arctic waters. "Princess Psyche will marry a monster as
planned."

"Mother, no!" He struggled, every muscle tensed, bulging
with useless power. "I will never do it! Do you hear me? *Never!*"

Venus walked away from her son, taking her time, never
looking back as his pleas of agony filled her chambers, rattling
himself to the bones.

CHAPTER THIRTY-ONE

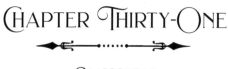

OMISSION

I T HAD BEEN NEARLY A YEAR SINCE CUPID HAD LAID EYES ON Psyche. Eleven human months. The arrow's elixir had long since worn off, leaving behind a haze of memory of the weeks afterward. If he had not been so dazed by the strong tincture, he would have known better than to challenge his mother. Handling Venus was a delicate act, one at which Cupid was a master, but he had failed miserably the day he had struck himself like an amateur, ending up chained. He would never lose his head like that again.

Now, he did as his mother asked, keeping Psyche from finding love or a good marital match, though now he did it for his own reasons unbeknownst to his mother. He could never tell her that long after the effects of the love potion had worn off, his feelings of intrigue for the human, his fascination with her soul, his need to watch her nurturing animals and appreciating the beauty of nature only grew. And grew. Blooming into something far stronger, richer, and more magnificent.

His love for Psyche mirrored his mother's hatred for her, in reverse. Their sentiments were both filled with passion, though Venus made hers known while Cupid kept his hidden. In his pocket, he often rubbed the wooden mountain cub bauble. He had gone back for it when his mind righted and had been surprised to find it still for sale. Now the trinket never left him, a constant reminder of her sweet soul.

Ultimately, Venus still wanted the youngest princess to marry a monster, but she was entertained in the meantime with tales of Psyche's "misery" from the mouth of her son. At first, he did not believe his actions were causing her true misery, only mild confusion and irritating dramatics. After a year of his meddling antics, however, he began to see the toll they were taking on the princess.

Cupid ached, knowing it was his actions that had caused her smile to disappear. He had kept Psyche, and every possible suitor, from falling in love with one another. He had lured the men to other women with his whispers and arrows. He had even allowed himself to be spotted by her in his Leodes form during her sister's wedding, wondering how the sight of him might affect her.

To perceive her excitement when she spotted him had been even more satisfying than he had envisioned, though the self-indulging moment had filled him with unfamiliar guilt afterward. The moment, when he followed her back to her room and witnessed her breakdown, had been the closest he had come to revealing himself to her, an act that would have crushed every ounce of trust between him and his mother.

The balancing act of keeping both women he loved happy was becoming precarious. Impossible.

"Did she cry herself to sleep again?" Venus asked, sipping her goblet of nectar as she lounged on the soft grass by her fountain.

"Just as the night before and the one before that," Cupid told her, not exaggerating when it came to Psyche's brokenness. He would have to put a stop to this soon. With each day, her despair deepened. It became more and more difficult not to show himself or comfort her in some way.

"And do the people still leave gifts for her?"

Cupid swallowed. His mother could detect lies as easily as any other god. Cupid was clever with half-truths, simply omitting the parts that would make her unhappy.

"Yes, Mother. The people are still unfaithful."

Her pretty mouth pursed. "And my nearby altars are still barren. Just as I should have left their queen's womb. So be it." She narrowed her eyes at Cupid, and he held his breath. It always shocked him to see her beauty transform from warm to shrewd so quickly. "I bore of toying with her. It is time to end this."

Cupid's jaw tightened, but he gave a nod of understanding. He had to be cunning where Venus was concerned. He would have to find a way to appease his mother, and still claim Psyche as his own. "I will seek the perfect husband." The words would have burned his mouth if he were not certain he would never allow her to be hurt. And if anyone were to be her husband, it was him.

His mother's head tilted, her perceptive eyes taking him in. "In all this time you have not yet found a man miserable enough to punish the woman who makes a fool of us?"

He gave an indifferent shrug. "I have been focused on other factors."

"Really." It was a soft declaration, not a question, and the gentleness of her tone put him on edge.

"I will start today." He began to pack his things when her voice rang out to him again, sending a chill up his spine.

"If I find that you linger too long, I will take care of this myself."

Cupid roughly shoved an arrow into his quiver. "Your lack of trust is disheartening, Mother."

She sat up. "You are right, my dear son, because trust is everything. And I lost a piece of yours when you came out of that trance. Do you think I am not aware of your lack of enthusiasm for punishing this human who hurts me every day? Do you have any idea how my heart breaks to feel I have lost not only the people's love but yours?"

Her eyes welled with emotion, the sight punching Cupid in the chest.

"My love has always been yours," he told her with every ounce of devotion he had for her. "But we do not share a mind. I swore to avenge you, and I will. In my own way and my own time."

She stood gracefully, moving closer, her eyes fierce. "What is your way? Hm? Tell me your plan. Why do you stall?"

Cupid gritted his teeth, swinging the bow over his shoulder. "Your questions are insulting—"

"You still want her!" Venus all but growled like a lioness on the warpath. "Admit it! And do not dare to lie!"

The god's chest rose and fell too quickly. He had been hoping with all his might to avoid another confrontation with his mother, but she was unflinching where Psyche was concerned.

Venus's eyes fluttered shut. "I will never forgive her for the rift she has caused between us."

Cupid surged forward, her undue hatred for the innocent girl making him lose his wits. "She has done nothing. Not to you, not to me, not to anyone!"

"You believe you have encountered a perfect human?" Venus laughed.

"I never said she was perfect." Though, she was as close to that notion as he had ever found in a human or god, for that matter. Oh, how he had wished she would do something horrible—it would make the situation far simpler—but each day her words and actions only softened his heart further, drawing him in.

"Then tell me, precious son, what are her shortcomings?" Venus crossed her arms, head tilted in a challenge.

Cupid opened his mouth, but his mind slowed. Stars and sky. What were her faults? "She...cannot carry a tune." That was true, but he found himself holding back a smile at the thought of her discordant humming as she walked the castle lands or singing to herself in her room, making the cat dart under her bed. How could he find such a mundane flaw to be so adorable?

"That is all you can manage to fault her?" Disappointment tumbled over Venus's features as her arms fell to her side. "She will grow old when you blink, son. Her beauty is not long for this world."

"I care not for her beauty," Cupid breathed, remaining steady. It was her soul that drew him each and every day. Her soul that nourished him as the sun sustained a lonesome tree in a field. "I beg you to see reason. We can find another way to punish her parents and the fools in town who worship her."

Venus took her son's face in her hands, peering up at him. "Everything I say and do when it comes to you is said and done in love. Someday, I trust you will see my actions for what they are."

This time Cupid was prepared for his mother's wrath. He'd been drunk on love potion last time, but now his mind was clear. When Venus struck out, Cupid flung his arms to the side, breaking the shackles before they could buckle around him. Venus stepped back, her glare as sharp as daggers. Part of his heart was murdered by that look from her.

"I am not your enemy," he told her. "Nor will I be your prisoner."

She flung out her hands, manacles appearing from nowhere. But Cupid did the same, his power causing the shackles to fly from his ankles before they could connect. Venus frowned at his control, her eyes welling again.

"She does not deserve your touch," his mother whispered. "Do you not see that I am trying to keep you from heartache? One look at your face and she will be mesmerized by your perfection—aroused by your essence. No mortal can love you. Not in the way you seek."

Her words struck him precisely as she had intended, for it was his deepest fear to never be truly loved.

"Then I will not allow her to see my face."

Venus's eyes narrowed in suspicion. "You jest."

"No." He eyed his mother with full seriousness. "Tell me you will allow me to try, without interference, and I will prove myself, and her in the process."

She glared. "You are proposing a compromise? A bargain?"

This was highly dangerous territory, but he could see no other way. His nod of agreement was rigid. A roll of parchment appeared in one of Venus's hands, an inked quill in the other. A slow smile crept onto her face as she brushed the feather across her delicate chin. "There will be rules, of course."

"I have no doubt there will be." He had seen his mother strike bargains with others and it was never in their favor.

"You will have a time limit of two human weeks to make her love you."

He schooled his face. "Make it two human months."

"One," she compromised.

He gave a stiff nod, and she wrote the rule on the parchment.

"She must declare her love verbally within one month. Agreed?"

With gritted teeth, he nodded, and she wrote.

"She will not lay eyes on you *or* place her hands on you."

That gave him pause. "But I can touch her?"

"Yes."

"Agreed. Let us sign." He reached for the quill.

Venus laughed and turned away, tucking the scroll to her chest. "Oh, my boy, I am only getting started." She paced, enjoying herself far too much. "You cannot tell Psyche your identity or mine. She, her family, and all those pathetic townspeople must believe you are a monster. Even your voice shall be altered."

She giggled when she spotted the terse frown on his face. "Do you doubt your abilities to woo a woman with a few small restrictions?"

"She will be terrified."

His mother lifted an eyebrow, grinning wickedly.

"Is that all?" he ground out.

"I think not." She went on to outline the many things he could and could not say or do. No comforting her with words like, "I will not hurt you," or, "You are safe." So many details. This would not be the simple mission he had had in mind, but he was the god of love. His true intentions would shine through and speak to her soul; he had to believe that.

"If you fail after one month's time or any of these rules are broken, she becomes mine to punish as I please."

Cupid stood ramrod straight. "I will never allow you to kill her, even if I fail."

"I never said I would kill her," she admonished. "You know that is not my style. My punishment of the mortal will only happen if, and when, one of you breaks the heart of the other because that is what is in store for this cursed match. At that point, you might not care quite as much."

"I will care!" he all but snarled. "Amend your words."

Venus spun a hand in the air, thinking. "Then I will give her a journey. A series of tasks to complete. Something to push her to her mortal limits." When Cupid attempted to argue, Venus held up a finger. "This is perfectly reasonable."

The god pressed his lips together, discerning, tunneling his way through his mother's proposition to find all the possible ways he could fail and put Psyche at risk. Venus would never make a deal unless she believed she could win. He could not pretend it did not hurt that she thought Psyche would never love him, and that heartache was inevitable, even though logic told him it was the mortal girl who his mother doubted, not him. It still stung. Venus had always been his greatest ally. Now, in his first venture of love, she was to be his greatest foe.

"Do you agree to these terms?" she asked.

"You are not to come to my lands during the month or send anyone."

"I agree," she said.

Cupid stood before her at full height, unsmiling, more apprehensive than he had ever felt. "I agree, as well."

They both signed, then clasped one another at the forearm. An invisible band of godly magic warmed their joined limbs, sealing the deal. Both would have to honor their end of the bargain, and he hoped to the skies beyond that his mother would not find a loophole to cause trouble. Venus wore a mixture of expressions that her son couldn't quite read. Worry for him, perhaps? But it warred with her utter contempt for Psyche. Cupid would prove her wrong, and when he did, she would come around to accepting the woman he loved. She *had* to.

He gave a curt nod and turned to leave.

"Oh, and Cupid?" He peered over his shoulder at her motherly smile. "When she proves to be a mere mortal, incapable of what you desire, I will accept your apology."

Cupid huffed through his nose like a bull and charged away from the infuriating goddess. He opened his wings in a *snap* to spray water from the fountain in every direction as he headed to prepare his home. As he flew, he wondered how he would earn the love of a mortal woman, who thought him a monster, and then he remembered this was Psyche. The girl who took in mountain lion cubs. She wasn't as easily frightened as most.

At least he hoped she wasn't, because love could not grow where fear and distrust had lodged. He could only hope her instincts were strong.

CHAPTER THIRTY-TWO

ONE MONTH

THE TASK OF WOOING PSYCHE WAS THE MOST DIFFICULT undertaking of his immortal life. For the first time in history, Cupid found himself surprised over and over again and ultimately humbled. Was this what it felt like to be human? Impossible time limitations looming every minute of every day? Lacking the charm of a mesmerizing voice and perfect physical prowess?

On day one, the way her bright eyes had flickered around his being with sheer terror—that had gutted him and caused his first moment of self-doubt. Then, to add the stabbing fact that she fancied herself in love with the fake human version of himself, Leodes? The cruel paradox! Especially as time wore on and her body gave itself away, softening to him even as her mind begged her to keep him at arm's length. He had nearly been driven mad by the succulent berry scent of her arousal, winding itself around him like a flowering vine that would strike with thorns if you dared a caress.

It had been one mishap after the next, a learning curve to be sure. He had attempted to show her how nice his affections could be. *Let me kiss you, hold you, bring you to the apex of pleasure,* but no! His ministrations were felt as forced and unwanted, riddling him with guilt. *Let me bring you the bugs and animals you miss so much,* but no! Without specifying what creatures to secure, the dim-witted Zephyr had brought flesh burning ants and cats that could eat his wife whole.

But he had no time to learn and try again. Each mistake cost him precious time. And Cupid was not accustomed to making mistakes. Indeed, he was not accustomed to consequences of any kind, causing his patience for the process of falling in love to be weak at best. However, at no stage did his feelings for her lessen. Often, to calm himself while she gave off fumes of anger and fear, he would rub the mountain cub bauble in his pocket, reminding himself what was at stake, and to be patient.

His chest ached thinking about that first time she sought his mouth, wanting to kiss him. How his heart had become a radiant starburst within his chest at the small act.

Cupid knew love. Love was his job. He knew Psyche loved him two days before she had realized it herself. They were down to mere days until the month would be over. Days! He was desperate to ease her mind, so she would voice those feelings. That was all she had to do. Say the words. If only he could tell her!

But it did not work that way with humans. They had to be shown. One had to prove oneself beyond measure, and even then, they doubted.

He was at this state of desperation when Psyche admitted how horribly homesick she was. To be honest, in all the time he had studied her, Cupid had never taken much notice of her sisters. He did not know their personalities. The fact that Psyche missed them made him believe they must be similar to her.

It went against his every instinct to allow them passage. Venus had not given a rule against visitors, and Cupid knew why. Visitors would make his wife miss home and could possibly fill her mind with doubts and fears. Visitors would complicate their delicate arrangement. He had purposely limited the amount of his staff she could speak with for this very reason. But those limitations had backfired. He believed her extreme loneliness was the one thing standing between them, so he made a rash decision.

One hour was all it took. Psyche did what no other being, mortal or immortal, had ever done.

She broke Cupid's heart.

He would never forget how gorgeous she was, leaning toward him, long hair falling around her, awash in the dim candlelight, her eyes vivid with awe. Cupid had not realized at first what was happening until her expression changed to horror, and her bright soul took on a dulled haze of regret.

The candle.

Her eyes looking directly into his.

The knife.

The panic Cupid had felt as he jumped out of bed had been monumental. If he had extracted that pure emotion and shot it down from Olympus, an earthly city would have crumbled to ruin. So he had carefully hidden it within himself as he took his wife's arms.

"Quickly," he had said. "Tell me how you feel, Psyche."

"I'm sorry!"

"Not an apology! Your feelings!"

"I feel *horrible*," she'd shouted.

"Your feelings about me!"

"*I love you!*"

Yes. His chest had filled with heat as his immortal heart expanded. Glorious Olympus and all that was eternal! Hearing those words had made him want to cry. Could he cry? He never had before, but his eyes burned in the strangest manner.

Psyche had broken the rules, ending their deal, but she said the words out loud just minutes afterward. Would his mother have mercy? Doubtful. But perhaps he could strike another deal!

"I will fix this," he had promised Psyche, quickly leaving to catch his mother before she came to them. As long as he kept Venus away from Psyche, his wife would be safe. Nobody could pluck the goddess of love's heartstrings quite like her son. He would fix this.

He knew the moment he touched down at his mother's elaborate fountain that it was too late. Her chariot of precious gems and the rainbow-necked doves that pulled it were gone. Cupid had no doubt she had immediately left to claim her rightful win when she felt the pull of the broken binding.

The god of love cursed into the skies as he flew faster than his wings had ever moved, back to his palace. Why had he left Psyche there alone with no one to guard her? How could he have been so impulsive? Would his wife think quickly enough to hide herself? Not that the goddess would be outsmarted, but if she gave her the runabout until he could arrive…

He nearly tumbled to his knees as he burst through the bedroom window, righting himself and coming to a stop in front of Renae's trembling form.

"Zep took her to the temple of Venus to beg mercy."

"No…" His heart gave a great lurch. "Of all the places, Renae."

"I didn't know what else to do, Lord of Love!" She was still shouting her apologies as Cupid sped from the room, heading for Athens.

PART THREE

PSYCHE & CUPID

"When I was from Cupid's passions free, my Muse was mute and wrote no elegy."

~Ovid

CHAPTER THIRTY-THREE

TEMPLE OF VENUS

Psyche

ZEPHYR SET ME DOWN WITH EASE ON A HILL NEAR THE TEMple. I thanked him quickly and ran. It wasn't until I was in the presence of other people, their eyes raking me, that I became aware of my hair, askew from sleep, and my white dressing gown. So many people! The presence of other humans after being alone for weeks was overwhelming. Add their stares and whispers as I pushed through them, terrified about what was to come, and every fiber of my being wished to run and hide. From the people, from the goddess, from everything.

But I had to be brave. Venus would not reward cowardice. I had nothing to hide. I loved her son dearly, truly, and I would make her see that. She was the goddess of love, after all. She, above all others, would feel the truth of what was between Cupid and me. Game be damned.

All around the temple were piles of offerings: bags of grains, tables laden with shining coins and jewelry, fine looking sheep and a goat. The bleating and neighs of animals rose up and joined with the mixed songs of birds and voices of people. My ears rang with the cacophony. I stepped through an arched opening where drying flowers hung upside down in bunches, their mild fragrances still lingering.

My heart rattled like a snake's tail in a cage as I rushed down the narrow hall, entering into a room with an incredibly tall, domed ceiling of gilded bronze tiles. Thin lines of light spilled forth through slats in the marble walls, and my nose stung with the heady sharpness of burning incense. I ran forward through the gathered people to the steps of the altar, falling to my knees in front of a large statue of Venus. Her arms were outstretched, holding many doves, her face of perfect symmetry lifted.

When I opened my mouth to speak to her, an uncontrollable keening sound poured from my lips. Every sorrow, every regret, spilled from the depths of my soul. I didn't care that I was frightening people, causing them to whisper and move away as if I were diseased. My eyes shut tight and my hands pressed the cool floor, head bowed. I could not have lifted my face if I'd wanted to. I had never felt so heavy.

"Oh, goddess," I whispered. "I should have known the faithlessness of my isle. I should have been more aware. The blasphemies of my people are on my shoulders. I accepted the punishment. I married what I thought to be a monster. And my goddess, oh mother of love and beauty, I came to love your son having no idea who he was. I have never loved another, nor shall I ever. But I wronged him. My fears, and the worries of my unwise sisters who knew no better, bested me. Even as I broke the binding, I loved him. I should have told him! I was a fool! Oh, please forgive me. Please, goddess! I beseech you."

"Comely words."

The scratchy voice had me raising my chin enough to see the bare, wrinkled feet of an old woman in a worn-out wrap dress. My eyes drifted further up until our eyes met, and my breath halted. Those dark, sunken eyes gave her away. This was no mere, weak woman. This was a woman of power, and the energy she gave off was not gentle.

"Are you the seer?" I asked. "The one who spoke to my sisters?" The one who fed them lies? Anger gripped me in its burning hand.

"The very one," she murmured, her dry lips lifting in a smile that hardened my innards. This woman worked for Venus. She had interfered on her behalf, hoping the fear instilled in the hearts of my sisters would somehow make it back to me. My heart ached knowing it had been my own error in judgment. I'd begged for them to come. He had been trying to please me.

"Everything is my fault," I claimed.

"Indeed," the woman agreed.

From down the long, narrow hall, my name was bellowed, causing the woman and I, along with every person in the temple, to turn. Was it him? My husband? Surely, he would not show himself to all these people! I leapt to my feet, trying to see over the crowd.

"Leave us!" the old woman shouted, her voice reverberating painfully around the room. When I turned to her, I saw that her eyes had taken on the milkiness of prophecy and power. The worshipers became a crush of voices and bodies, pressing out of the room. When they had all exited, a man pushed his way into the atrium, his dark eyes ablaze, and my heart became faint. I blinked.

"Leodes?"

His eyes roved over me, as if assuring himself I was okay, and then his attention turned to the old crone, who let out a dark laugh.

"It is too late," she said. "You can see the manacles of *De servo corrupto* about her neck and wrists." What? I glanced down and saw nothing. "I am her master now, and no immortal, even you, can hide her as a fugitive. I will have my way."

I backed up, away from them both, confused and overwhelmed.

"Leodes?" I whispered. This time, when he looked at me his

eyes penetrated my soul, causing the flaming of awareness of understanding to course through me like a blaze. "It's you..."

"It is me," he whispered.

No. I covered my mouth. Leodes had never been a mortal man, only a pretty illusion I had fallen for. Cupid, a form shifter. A god. But of course. My heart had been with him all along. That meant the old woman...

"Mother," Cupid pleaded, turning his attention to her and verifying my suspicions.

In a flash of golden light that made me flinch, the crone turned into a woman so beautiful, it hurt to gaze upon her. Each time I tried to focus on her features, they shifted. All at once, she was fair and dark, her hair cascading like a shimmer of spices, feathery light and straight, then heavy with raven curls. She was all forms of beauty, from wispy to curvaceous, petite to tall. My human eyes could not comprehend.

"Oh, goddess!" I fell to my knees again.

When Cupid spoke this time, his voice was the melodious tones I had heard beneath the gruffness of my monster husband's words. I tipped my face up to see he'd taken his true form as they faced off, each filled with unfathomable power, his wings spread about behind him, trembling with tension.

"Stop showing off and take a form," Cupid commanded. "Have mercy on Psyche. She has admitted her love."

I dared a glance to see the goddess take the form of a Greek woman, tall and imposing, with lustrous black hair and skin of smooth, light copper. "Her mockery of a declaration came too late, Cupid. She broke the binding agreement. Now she is mine."

"You said there would be tasks," he said, his mouth tight. "What are they?"

She smiled, and the room seemed to glow. "Each task will be revealed in time." When her face turned down to examine me, I dropped my eyes. "I see she whored herself to you before affirming any sort of supposed love."

To hear her description of our time together caused my heart to crumble in shame and hurt.

"You do not know what has happened between us," Cupid said through clenched teeth. "Do not dare to insult her in such a way!"

"I *know*," she drawled with a dark edge. "Because she carries your seed. No doubt to try and win my favor and pity, but it will not work. As far as I am concerned, the child is a bastard, no grandchild of mine."

I clutched my lower belly, a tremor of surprise running through me. I was pregnant? When I peered up at Cupid, the way he looked at me with unreserved tenderness and helplessness made me cover my mouth again, holding back a deluge of emotion.

"Mother," he whispered. The simple plea broke me. How could his mother deny him anything?

"*No!*" she snapped. "You have proven yourself to be foolhardy and soft! I am ashamed."

Cupid rounded on her, making her step back with his ferocity. "Do not dare look down upon me for loving another. You, of all beings! You, with your infinite wisdom about love, and yet you have lost more lovers than any immortal."

"I have *lost* nothing! No single being is worthy of all the love I have to give! It is my right to love as many as I please!"

"And yet, if I love one, you deny me."

"There are so many worthy goddesses and demigoddesses to choose from, son." Venus pointed down at me. "And you choose *this*, a lowly human. The one human who has hurt me beyond any other. How do you think that makes me feel?" She sounded choked up, and it crushed my heart to know I had come between them.

"Let us make another compromise," he said.

"Here is your compromise!"

She flung a hand to the spot beside me, and a massive diamond-headed snake appeared. Its wide head raised high and stared straight at me. Everything I knew about coming across snakes in the wild told me to remain still and calm. But we weren't in the wild, and I had not been expecting this, so my body reacted. I screamed and shifted backward, causing the snake to dart toward me.

"No!" Cupid sprang forward.

The snake disappeared just as Cupid became rigid. My scream began anew as a thin, golden rope wound its way around my husband, from his ankles to his chest, fast like a whip. Struggle as he might—I could see the battle in his face and shoulders—he was not escaping.

"Don't hurt him!" I begged. "Please!"

She shot a dark scowl at me. "Unlike you, faithless one, I would never hurt him. He agreed to this, and I will not have him interfering. Your first task begins now."

Venus snapped her fingers, and my stomach dropped as everything around me changed.

Chapter Thirty-Four

First Task

Psyche

M Y INSIDES *WHOOSHED* AS IF WE HAD MOUNTED A HILL IN A chariot and were plummeting steeply down the other side. My vision was a blur, and as it cleared, I spun, finding myself in a well-lit storehouse of some sort with open windows. All around me were heaps of wheat, barley, millet, vetches, beans, and lentils, all spilled out and flowing together in mixed piles.

It was quiet, but when I strained my ears I could hear the distant cooing song of majestic birds. Venus appeared beside me, giving me a fright.

"These are my grain offerings," she explained. "However, my doves are picky, and each loves a different type. For your first task, you must separate these grains into their own piles."

My eyes widened. It was a large room. It would take days, if not weeks to accomplish this. I swallowed hard and nodded. "Yes, goddess."

"Very good." She gave a dark chuckle of delight. "I shall attend a celebration banquet. You have until I return at nightfall."

She turned to leave, and my heart staggered. "Pardon? My lady of love...you mean I must separate it all today?"

"That is exactly what I mean. And if you fail, there are a myriad of things I can choose as your fate. None of them is death—that was my agreement with my son—but trust me, dear..." She leaned close, a burst of dewy, lily scent striking my nose. "You will wish you were dead."

She glided gracefully from the room, and my heart began to slam in my chest. All my thoughts were incoherent as I stared around blankly. I could not move. Where would I begin? It was too much! An impossible task.

Compose yourself, Psyche! I grasped my head, taking several deep breaths before crouching and beginning to sort. It was not only my life on the line. If what Venus said was true, and I believed it was, I was pregnant. My fingers shook, dropping several grains as the pressure of the situation rained down on me. This would never work!

I needed a better plan. I stood and ran, gathering an empty barrel from along the wall for each type of grain, lining them up behind me. They were heavy and unwieldy, leaving me sweating. I pushed back my damp, ragged mess of hair and began sorting as quickly as my fingers would allow.

With each hour that passed, I tried desperately not to look at the piles yet to be sorted. The amount I had finished compared to the abundance remaining proved my efforts would be wasted. Several times sobs of despair rose, threatening to choke me, but I shook my head and continued. For Cupid. For my love. For our child.

Cupid

"I am trying to decide between slavery in the moors, prostitution in Rome, or truly marrying her off to a monster of Olympus." Venus stroked one of her oversized doves as she sat outside of Cupid's cell, ignoring how his fists were clenched.

"She would enjoy prostitution far too much, I think." Her son growled from deep within his chest, and she held back a smile. "I think the irony of a true beastly marriage would be the most fun."

"You dared to tell her you would never hurt me, but you lie." His voice was as sharp and scathing as a razor. "Nothing would ever hurt me more, and I swear to you…you will be no mother of mine if you go through with such a cruel punishment of the one I love."

Venus's eyes darkened. "I never believed a child of my own flesh could be as fickle as other men. But I will forgive you. Over time we will forgive one another. Her life will end as quickly as a wind's whisper across the earth, and then you have eternity to heal and see the situation with clarity. You will realize I am doing this for both of us. The hold she has on you is not healthy."

"You speak as if what I feel is a madness, but it is not. It is *love*."

"Is love not a madness?" She tilted her head. "Tell me, when was the last time you used your arrows of love to truly bring a couple together, to strengthen them, rather than to punish another or cause strife?"

Cupid's lips pursed in displeasure. He sat on the floor of the cell, arms draped across his knees, with his head laying back heavily. "I have changed. I have no desire to use love as a weapon anymore."

"How precious."

"Mother, be reasonable!" Cupid lurched forward, grabbing the cell bars, his eyes wide. "She carries a demigod within her! My child! Your own grandchild! No matter what you say, I know you must care. Think about it, Mother. Let yourself imagine cradling your own grandson in your arms."

"Enough! I will not think about the bastard child, created with the single intention of trying to manipulate me. I already told you—"

"I swear, if anything happens to her or my babe—"

Venus stood. "I bore of your melancholy dramatics. The sooner this ordeal is over, the sooner we can move on and regain what we once had before *she* ruined it all."

"Jealousy has never been a good look on you, Mother."

"All the more reason to snuff out the cause. Now if you will excuse me, I have a banquet to attend."

She turned in a swish of robes and left him on his own. Cupid gritted his teeth and gripped his hands into fists, striking the ground hard enough to make the room shake. He stood and peered through the small window to the storehouse below. Through the long sets of windows where doves could fly in to feed, he spied Psyche on her knees, her hands moving rapidly. His chest became impossibly tight. She was trying so hard, and for what? They all knew a mortal could not accomplish such an endeavor.

He slid back to the floor, pressing his palms into his eyes until his acute hearing picked up a tiny scratching sound at the window. Cupid stood again and found a black worker ant crossing the sill. Before his mother had decided to move the storehouse to her lands for the doves, she had brought in a few harmless bugs from Earth for them to eat. Often immortal birds from all over Olympus came to hunt the bugs that could not be found anywhere else in the immortal lands.

Most of Cupid's powers were unable to work in the cell—his mother had warded against that—but there was something he had not tried. He whispered to the tiny insect in his godly voice, and its black body gave a tremor before climbing quickly out of sight, and down the side of the tower room. Cupid watched avidly, listening for sounds of his mother, but she was not nearby. To his complete joy, thousands of black ants climbed the walls of the storehouse, entering through the windows, and began to make quick work of separating the grains. He watched as Psyche leapt to her feet in surprise. Once she realized they were helping, she crouched down again and continued working, as well.

Yes, he thought, *go, go, go!*

As night began to fall, Psyche collapsed onto the floor, holding her face as the ants receded out of sight, finally finished with their task. Cupid, who had been restless the entire time, also slid down to sit, laughing with relief.

Psyche

I had never been more nervous. Though the task was complete, and Venus had given no rule against receiving help, I feared she would not honor my win. I stood pacing until she stepped into the room, candles sputtering to life along the walls. I dropped to my knees as I beheld the goddess, crowned with a rose garland, smelling of sweet balm. Her expression of smugness dissolved into shock and anger as her eyes darted around the room.

"I see," she said. "Who came to help you?"

"No person came, goddess."

"Was it Zephyr? Sneaky little wind god?"

"No, goddess. I swear it."

Venus breathed quickly, peering about for something, anything, out of order, but all was pristine.

"You think yourself clever, do you?" She glared down at me. "You and my son?"

"No, high one. Truly, I am not."

"We shall see."

The goddess reached into a fold of her dress and took out a small, dark hunk of bread, which she tossed hard at me. Then she flicked a finger and a wooden cup of cloudy water appeared on the ground.

"Your next task begins at sunrise. You will sleep here."

Famished, I fell onto the dry bread and ate every crumb before gulping down the water, which tasted like a fishy lake. Then I nestled my tired body onto a large bag of wheat with my hand draped across my belly.

"Someone is looking out for us," I whispered to my unborn child as I thought about the ants, grateful beyond measure. Would I be so lucky next time? If this task was any indication of what was to come, it would only get worse.

CHAPTER THIRTY-FIVE

SECOND TASK

Cupid

I N THE NEXT ROOM, HIS MOTHER HUMMED A LIVELY TUNE AS she readied herself that morning. Her pitch was perfect, but it grated on his ears.

"What is today's task?" Cupid called out through the bars.

"Well, my dear, I would tell you, but *someone* seems to have a habit of interfering."

Cupid scowled, thinking of her disguise as the old seer. "You interfered first."

"And now we are even." She blew him a kiss from the door-way, sending a breeze of lilies his way. He turned his head away from it.

"Mother…"

"Good-bye. I will be certain to relay every detail when I return."

"*Mother!*"

Moments later he watched from the window as she gathered Psyche from the storehouse below. Had his mother even fed her? His wife appeared bedraggled and frail in her night-gown, despite how she held up her dainty chin as if filled with purpose. The sight of her caused a chasm to open inside him, rapidly filling with a flood of fear. Cupid tried to shout to her, but his words reverberated back at him like an echo. He cursed and banged the window as the goddess's chariot took to the skies with his mother and wife, arcing toward the forest of Olympus.

Psyche

If my situation were not so dire, I might have enjoyed the magical chariot ride. It was truly a spectacle worthy of the goddess of beauty. The oversized doves with colorful necks flew and landed with smooth, steady precision. I stepped from the bejeweled carriage into the forest behind the goddess, trepidation stealing my body warmth. I crossed my arms and peered at the trees, but they gave off an ominous air, not the feel of comfort I had felt from Cupid's trees. Oh, what I would give to have them here right now!

The sound of rushing water came to me, and I saw a river with a meadow and a grove just beyond it. I walked behind Venus to the river's edge, my heart thrumming. I followed her eyes across the river to where golden-fleeced sheep glittered under the sun. From tiny lambs to mother sheep and large-horned rams, the magical animals idly munched on the grass.

"Here is your second task." Venus snapped her fingers and a large wooden pail appeared by my feet. "You will cross the river and fill that pail with golden wool."

I bent to pick up the pail, peering around for sheers or a knife.

The corners of her full lips tipped upward as if knowing what I searched for, and I was hit with the splendor of her beauty, even while she was being cruel. The set of her eyes, cheekbones, and mouth were perfection.

"I shall do it, my goddess. I shall prove myself to you. Thank you for this chance."

She frowned. "Do not attempt to run away. I will find you."

"Of course not, great mother of love."

She made an annoyed sound and turned, gliding away from me back into the trees. Over her shoulder, she said, "As much as I would enjoy staying to watch, I have things to do. I will fetch you after dark."

Once she was out of sight, I shook out my arms and did a series of meditative breathing. I could do this. The river would be the toughest part. It looked to be deep and fast moving. I would have to swim harder than ever. If only I had my full strength. I shook with hunger and thirst, but I dared not eat or drink anything in Olympus.

I peered out at the sheep, serene and gorgeous with their golden fluff. There had to be more to this. Yes, it would be hard to get wool without shears, but I could tug through with my fingers and pluck it if necessary. The sheep would not be happy, and it would wound my soul to hurt them, but they would survive. So, what was the catch?

Remembering how the river had been enchanted on Cupid's property, and the trees sentient, I decided to give something a try before I dived into the undertaking. I crouched, petting the mossy grass at the bank while peering down into the blue depths of the gurgling water.

"Hello, magnificent river." I felt silly but continued anyway. "I would like to cross. I need to get to the glen on the other side to perform a task for the goddess Venus. Will you grant me safe passage? I promise to be as careful and gentle as I can. It will be an honor and a privilege to feel your grand waters around me, like a mother's embrace."

All at once, sounds of nature rose up, the whisper of reeds and trickling of water, coming together in harmonious pitches to form intelligible speech. My eyes widened, and I stilled to listen.

"Nay, Nay, Psyche, have a care. These are not gentle sheep. The flock will destroy any who set foot in their grove during the light of day. The rage of bloodlust is their nature."

My gut gave a violent tremble. "Oh, dear. Are you…a river god?"

"I am. Your passage will be granted when the sun begins to lower, and the animals nestle into sleep. Even then, it is not safe. You will gather your wool from the bushes and trunks of trees where their bodies have brushed."

"Oh, thank you!" I bent and kissed the wet place where the water met the pebbled sands. The river danced, lapping at my fingers and lips before receding. Now I had to wait out the day and hope I would have enough time to gather bits of wool when the sheep bedded down. I, myself, was sleepy, but I feared the myriad of things that might happen if I napped here. Any creature of Olympus could happen upon me. I could oversleep. It wasn't worth the risk. I paced the river's edge, my bare toes loving the contrast of warm pebbles and cool water. Now and then I peeked at the sheep. The rams had taken notice of me, coming closer to their side of the river and sniffing the air, huffing through their noses with looks of evil in their eyes.

Never before in my life had I thought an animal possessed an evil look, even those mountain lions. There was a distinct difference between evil and having a hunting instinct. These creatures were not what they seemed. Their beauty was a deadly lure.

I decided to move closer to the forest as I waited out the day.

Cupid

Cupid paced the cell. And paced. And paced some more. He did not think he would ever forgive his mother for what she was doing to Psyche and his child, and for the demeaning humiliation of being jailed.

He was so busy cursing her name to the edges of Olympus that he almost missed Zephyr outside his window, knocking at the soundproof ward. Cupid nearly leapt from his skin, jumping forward and mouthing to his friend.

"Forest!"

Zep mouthed it back slowly, and Cupid read his lips, nodding. Then the god of love used his hands to pretend to eat and drink. Zep pointed at Cupid in question.

"No." He shook his head. "My wife. Psyche needs food. And help!"

Zep gave a nod and sped away. Cupid clapped his hands together once, grinning like a boy. Zephyr would be smart and make himself scarce where Venus was concerned. With the god of the west wind on her side, he felt confident Psyche could pass this test, whatever it may be.

Psyche

I never had a chance to scream as a sudden hand was placed over my mouth, and a warm breath of wind coasted past my ear.

"Shh, Psyche, it is Zephyr."

I spun to face him and held back the urge to hug him. "Oh, I'm so glad to see you!"

He handed me a round of flatbread that had been sliced on

one end to be opened and filled. I spied meats, soft cheeses, and sliced vegetables.

I took the gift from his hands and held it to my chest. It took all of my self-control not to scarf it down that very second. He next handed me a pouch of water.

"I cannot stay," he said. "Venus will feel my winds and be angered. What is your duty here?"

I explained to him my task, and before I could tell him about the river god, he said, "I can fly you across, but not until the golden sheep are asleep. They will devour you. And the river will not take kindly to human touch."

"About that, I spoke to the river god, and he spoke back to me, promising safe passage."

Zephyr's eyebrows drew together as if doubtful. But when he glanced over at the rushing river, a stream of water rose up into the air, formed the shape of a hand, and waved at him. At the look of surprise on Zep's face, I nearly laughed despite the dire, sour feelings riddling my insides.

"Well, that is...highly unusual," said the god of the west wind. He raised an eyebrow at me, impressed. "It seems fate is on your side, so I will leave you now. I wish you luck, love of Cupid."

I couldn't help but smile at the moniker, though the moment of warmth quickly cooled when I remembered how my mistrust had caused all of this. Zephyr turned and rose in a rush, spinning like a sea funnel before disappearing from sight.

Food and water in hand, I sat amongst the trees and ate every bite. Once finished, I stood and paced to bide the time, glancing anxiously at the sheep every few minutes. Time was a strange thing in Olympus. The sun never moved from overhead. It simply appeared and disappeared, though Cupid did allow it to dim in his land. I wondered how much longer I had until Venus would return, and when the sheep would ever tire of eating and take a rest.

I took to speaking to my belly as if the tiny speck within me could understand the dilemma we faced. Though I felt no different, and my stomach had not yet begun to swell, it was oddly comforting knowing I wasn't alone. At the same time, that comfort morphed into distress, knowing my life was not the only one at risk if I failed.

Finally, finally, the sheep began to slowly make their way from the open grove into the nearby trees to lay. My blood moved in a rush beneath my skin, nervousness etched into every fitful movement. When the last of them had made their way to bed, I tip-toed my way through the soft grass and knelt at the river's edge.

"Beautiful river," I whispered to the water god. "I think they are sleeping. May I have the honor of passing?"

That same swishing sound of reeds and trickling came together in my ears, saying in a garbled whisper, *You may.* I held my breath as the water slowed and shallowed.

"Oh, thank you!" I whispered, taking up the bottom of my dingy nightgown in one hand while I held the pail in the other, on my hip. It was heavy. I crossed in brisk steps, stepping on the smooth rocks that were somehow dry on top. When I got to the other side I blew a kiss of gratitude to the river, and it seemed to swell for a beat before returning to its rushing movement once more.

I held my breath, a beat of fear striking me as I turned to face the meadow and bordering forest. The golden shapes of the sheep, nestled in sleep, were too close for my liking. I would have to work fast. I darted through the large expanse of grass, stopping at every bush to pull golden threads that had snagged on leaves and branches. My heart never stopped thumping in my ears and throat as I raced about, casting surreptitious glances toward the grove as I went.

After I'd scoured every bush in sight, my basket was only half full. My blood pounded in wild fear. I would have to get closer to them. The bottoms of the trees held large tufts of glittering wool stuck to the bark.

I forced my breaths to be steady and silent as I walked slowly, my every sense on high alert, working together to watch, listen, grab, move. I made quick work, and my basket was nearly full. *So close, so close...*

The final tree had enough fleece attached to overflow my basket. I stepped gingerly toward it. My fingers closed around one, two, then three tufts, and I pressed them onto the top of my pile, exhaling slowly. The closest sheep to me was a lamb, and I couldn't help but marvel at the tiny, wondrous creature. In sleep, it looked so peaceful and innocent, but I knew better. I took a step backward, keeping an eye on it, then another step.

Snap.

A twig. Of all things! Why couldn't this forest be like Cupid's, where there was no shedding of the trees? I froze in place as the tiny lamb's head rose heavily and turned to me. Even through its droopy, sleepy eyes, I saw the realization take place, and the red of bloodlust come to life. I froze, petrified, hoping it would go back to sleep. Instead, it let out a demented *baaa*, that was too deep for such a small creature. My chest gave a painful bang and I grasped the pail with both arms, turning, and sprinting at full speed.

I never turned to look. I didn't need to. I could hear them.

A dissonance of rickety *baaa's* and quick stomping feet rose up behind me.

"River god!" I shouted, praying it would have pity on me once more. "Help! Please!" The basket was too heavy, and I kept stepping on my damned nightgown!

Would the animals follow me if I leapt into the river's depth?

They were so close! Would the river consume me whole, rolling me under until its water became part of my body? What about my baby? Cupid's child? My despair crashed down on me as I neared the bank of the river.

I watched in wonder as the water rose up like a great sheet, my awe turning into horror as the liquid arced over top of me like a massive wave. I crouched, covering my head, but not a drop hit me. A great rushing sound came from behind me and I spun in the dim light, watching as the water formed a wall to stop the evil sheep.

"Thank you!" My voice was hoarse as I shouted my appreciation, running forward through the rocky riverbed until I was on the other side again. I didn't stop until I got to the trees, then I turned, panting for air, and watched as the wall of water receded into its bed. The sheep ran about bucking and kicking their back feet angrily, shaking water from their fleeces. I covered my mouth as I laughed in shock and gratitude. Someday, in some way, I wanted to thank the river god properly.

The smile was still on my lips when Venus's grand chariot appeared from nowhere, coming to a stop just before it ran me over. I jumped back, holding the pail close, but nearly falling on my rump.

Venus towered over me in the glittering, bejeweled cart. An absolute scowl marred her beauty when she laid eyes on the pail of golden wool in my arms.

"My goddess," I said, bowing low as I set the pail before her.

I stayed low to the ground, my head bowed, my heart hammering my chest like a blacksmith forging a shield. She took her time exiting the chariot and gliding to stand over me.

"Who helped you?"

The fierceness in her voice caused me to shudder with fear.

"I gathered the wool on my own, goddess of love. I swear it."

Her words came out in slow, enraged spurts. "Spoiled girl. You. Are. *Useless*. I know you did not do this alone! You are incapable of doing anything for yourself! Well, you can rest assured..." She sounded as out of breath as I was, her anger sending a chill over me. "You are on your own for this next trial, for I daresay nobody will help you where you are going."

Chapter Thirty-Six

Servants of Venus

Psyche

THE GODDESS PUT ME IN A CELL ON HER PROPERTY. I SAT on the cool, stone ground, one hand on my belly, my head leaning against the wall as I thought about my husband. Where was he? Was he captive, like me, or had he come to his wits and had a change of heart? I'd hurt him with my distrust. I'd ruined everything we'd precariously built. My eyes squeezed shut, fighting the burn behind my lids, sorely wishing I could turn back time and choose love over fear.

I was so tired. So very tired.

"There she is, Sorrow," said a small, childlike voice. My eyes popped open and I gasped at the sight of two willowy wisps on the other side of the bars. The women were identical in body with long, stringy yellow hair, their eyes like bottomless pits, skin pale and ashen. The only difference was that one wore a crimson dress and the other dark blue. I hadn't even heard footsteps! I scrambled to my feet.

"Not as beautiful as they say, is she, Sadness? We shall have to remedy that."

The women smiled, sending a wave of frigid fear cascading over me.

"Who are you?" I asked.

"We are Sorrow—"

"—and Sadness." Still, they smiled. "Servants of Venus. Here to beautify you for your next journey."

I shook my head. "No, thank you."

"We take our orders from the goddess of all things beautiful," said the one in red, Sorrow, I thought.

They opened the cell and glided in with bags in their hands, closing the door before I could even think of fighting my way past them. I held up my palms in warning.

"Do not touch me." I pointed at the door to my cell. "Just get out and leave me be."

They both giggled, the sound high and creepy. And then Sadness, clad in deep blue, pulled out a gleaming pair of shears, opening and closing them with a *ssssnip*.

"First for your hair cut."

My bowels turned over and I clutched my stomach. I had never been in a fight, other than innocent swordplay years ago. But these two were frail enough. Even in my state of exhaustion and pregnancy, I felt confident I could fend for myself against them. Although those shears looked sharp. That would be a problem.

"Get out," I said again. "No haircut. I want nothing from you. *Leave me.*"

"Stay still, human," Sadness warned. "Or Sorrow will have to hold you down."

I lowered my voice, feeling as if I had sprouted spikes like a porcupine. "Do not come near me."

"Keep her still, Sorrow."

The waif in red came at me, and I lunged forward, a scream tearing from deep in my throat. But what I encountered was not a weak maid. She had the power of Boldar. Damned immortals! I screamed and fought as she took me by the arms and shoved me to the ground. I pulled my legs in and kicked her hard in the stomach several times, making her mouth open in a yell to reveal jagged teeth.

We scrabbled, both kicking, screaming and scratching. When she let go of one arm to smack my face, whipping my head to the side, I grabbed a fistful of her hair and yanked hard enough to fill my fingers with the greasy strands as she screeched into my face. I nearly vomited at the sensation of causing pain to another.

But then they were both on me, turning me to my stomach on the floor, pinning my arms to my sides. One of them yanked my head up by the hair and smashed the side of my face into the floor. The pain radiated out from my cheekbone, across my scalp, and down through my body.

"Be still!" one of them raged at me.

With a sob of frustration and pain, I went limp, loathing the feeling of defeat.

And then the haircut began, and I screamed anew. I felt them grabbing great chunks of my thick locks, tugging against my scalp as the shears made their grinding snips. When they nipped the edge of my ear, sending another fiery burn of pain through my body, I struggled again, shrieking with fury, trying to turn, but it was useless. They giggled maniacally at my efforts.

"Such an improvement, would you not say so, Sorrow?"

"Oh, yes, dear sister. Masterful skills on your part. And now I get to do her makeup."

They turned me roughly, and I caught sight of my piles of hair as I felt the cool ground against parts of my scalp. My face was streaked with tears of anger. When Sorrow leaned over me with a pot of something red, I spat in her face. Her soulless eyes widened, and she bared her sharp teeth before leaning in to bite my shoulder. My back arched and fought with every muscle in my body, but Sadness was on top of me, feeling as if she weighed five times her actual weight, her skinny hands gripping my wrists with the power of ten soldiers.

When Sadness finally let up on my shoulder, I felt the warm rush of blood seeping out, through my dressing gown. My eyes fluttered as a wash of pure exhaustion came over me, my body trembling. She roughly rubbed strange creams in circles over my cheeks, then smeared some sort of powder on my eyelids. Lastly, they slathered paint across my lips.

"And now she is properly fit to see our lady of love," one of them said.

I tried to shuffle upward and crawl to the door when they released me, but they were too quick, and I was far too slow. I ached everywhere. Taking stock of the damage done, the pile of blood-soaked hair was the least of my worries. In my burst of energy while fighting, I had not felt my body being banged against walls and the floor, but now I felt every bit of it: every scratch, welt, and bruised piece of flesh. The worst was my cheekbone and eye, which were swelling, causing me to squint on that side. And my shoulder...great Hades. Those vile witches.

I sat against the wall and ripped the bottom of my dressing gown, which was already in tatters, pressing the handful of fabric to my shoulder to staunch the flow of blood. After a long moment, my hand began to fall as my eyes drooped. I knew I needed to stay alert, but my body begged for rest. An ache had begun in my head, and I had to close my eyes. I brought up a hand and wiped at my mouth, smearing red paint all over the back of my hand. I let my arm drop.

I'm not sure how long I dozed before a small intake of breath woke me. I tried to open my eyes, but only one would cooperate. I lifted a hand and felt the right side of my face completely swollen and tender to the touch. I hissed at the contact, then peered up at the bars of my cell with my good eye.

Venus, in all her magnificent glory, stared down at me in

shock and something else—pity? The look was gone as quickly as it appeared, replaced by a sneer.

"You should not have attempted to fight them, mortal."

My lips pursed. "Would you not fight if two strange women attempted to cut your hair?"

She glowered. "I would never have done something so awful as to put myself in your position."

I looked down, shame filling me.

"Shall I call Cupid in?" she asked in an overly-sweet tone.

Call him in? Was he walking about the property? Disgrace continued to fill me, this time at the thought of him seeing me degraded in this way. Would he be disgusted? Did a small part of him feel I was getting what I deserved for disobeying him? Gods, I had taken a knife from my sister and kept it under my pillow! How betrayed he must have felt! I turned my head aside and closed my eye.

"No," I whispered.

"You do not wish to see him?" she asked.

I wanted more than anything to see him, but did *he* want to see *me*? He was a god, and not just any god. The god of desire. He could have any woman, and yet I had feared him and taken him for granted, breaking one of his simplest rules. It must have felt like a slap to his face. No, I could not blame him for not coming to me here, but neither could I handle his rejection face-to-face right now. The thought of it hurt worse than every physical ailment I suffered at that moment. I shook my head slowly, carefully. She *tsked* and sighed.

"Very well. I will give you this day and night to heal. You leave in the morning."

"Where will I go, goddess?" My eye opened, but she said nothing. With a flick of her finger, a piece of brown bread and water appeared at my side, and she glided out of the room, leaving me to ponder my fate and deal with my pain.

I took small bites of the dry bread until it was all gone, and then I drank the murky water, my throat hoarse from screaming. Overwhelmed in every way, with my heart broken at the knowledge of what I had thrown away, I curled up in the corner and slept like the dead.

Chapter Thirty-Seven

Beauty No More

Psyche

WHAT IS GOING ON? GODS, MY HEAD! I WINCED FROM THE stabbing pain, and then gasped from the strain the small movement had brought. The events from yesterday tumbled through my memory like sharp rocks.

From my place on the floor in the corner, I lifted my heavy head and peered toward the bars of my cell. My eye was still swollen but it had gone down enough for me to crack it open. The rest of my body hurt even worse than before.

Venus stood, unsmiling, looking down at me. Her presence was a glowing, colorful haze, like a misty rainbow against a soiled background. My hair on the floor was now a drab, raggedy pile, the blood a dark stain. I glanced to the side at my shoulder long enough to see scabby teeth marks through my torn gown.

"I almost pity you," Venus muttered. "But then I recall how you stole from me and broke my son's heart."

There wouldn't be a day of my remaining life or afterlife when I did not regret both of those things. I moved to my aching knees with considerable effort, then lowered my torn hands and blotched face to the ground.

"I never meant to hurt either of you, goddess, I swear it. And I fell in love with him, not knowing he was a god. Even when I believed him a monster, my heart knew better. I will be sorry all of my days."

"Yes," she whispered. "You will, I am afraid." But she seemed to have lost a bit of the anger she'd held so close. Still, I kept my head down, afraid to raise her ire again, until I heard her say, "Eat."

I raised my head enough to see the brown bread and cup of water again, so I did as she said, taking great pains to remain on my knees as I ate. She waited quietly without moving.

When I finished, the meager meal sat in my stomach like a wet stone as I awaited further instruction.

"Today," she said softly, "you will fetch something for me." She paced, gliding with grace from one end of the bars to the other as she explained.

"I have lost a touch of my luster while dealing with this situation. As a goddess, I can give and receive beauty from other goddesses. You will take this box to my dear friend Proserpina, goddess of agriculture, and tell her I require the immortal beauty ointment." An ornate box appeared in her hands, and my heart gave a start. Proserpina? But she was the wife of Pluto, god of the underworld. She spent half of the year in Olympus and the other half in Hades. Surely, she was in Olympus at the moment.

A tired smile appeared on Venus's lush lips, and I knew, without a doubt, she was asking me to go into Hades.

"But goddess, Beautiful One, h-how will I get there? Please instruct me, and I shall do anything you ask."

"You are a smart human, are you not? Did your parents not grant you the best of tutors? I am certain you can figure out how to get to the underworld." And there it was. What she had wanted all along.

The only way to enter the underworld was to die.

I was shockingly calm, as if my body had known all along and had accepted this fate before my mind had.

"Worthy Venus," I whispered. "How will I return to give you

the ointment?" Nobody who died ever left the underworld. By the way her small smile spread, she knew this as well and was not concerned about the box or its contents.

"I am sure you will find a way. You have come this far."

My head was so heavy. It took too much energy to hold it up, so I let it fall to my chest as I muttered in anguish.

"Why not kill me yourself, goddess? I have displeased you. You have every right to punish me, even take my life if that is what you wish."

"I am the goddess of fertility. I *give* life," she said as if offended by such a question. "I do not take it."

An accidental giggle bubbled out of me and she glared. I covered my mouth. This was what I knew of gods. They were master wordsmiths. With them, everything was semantics. Venus had orchestrated every event that would lead to my death; however, she would take no responsibility for my actual loss of life. It had not been her hand to hurt me in any way, or to kill me. I dropped the fingers from my mouth and looked her straight in the eye.

"Even without your blessing, I love your son. I will love him every day of my life and eternal death. And our child, your grandbaby..." I clutched my stomach. "Its blood is on your hands, no matter how far removed you are from the events that will kill us."

Her eyes brightened like the bluest depths of a flame. "Silence, foolish girl. You have been clever thus far. Have you no confidence remaining in your waste of a body? Oh, if your people could see you now. You are no beauty." She spat the words as if they could hurt me, but I shook my head, lifting my chin.

"It is you who cares about beauty, not me. I would choose to look this way every day of my life if it meant I could birth this child for Cupid before I die."

Her voice rose. "You only gave your body to my son so you could use a child to manipulate me!"

"That is not true! I would never do such a thing! He earned my trust and my heart, even before my mind was willing to admit it, and what we shared was *real*—"

"No more!" Her jaw clenched. "You are a lying, filthy imitation of beauty. I will not listen to your falsehoods for another moment." She raised a finger and I felt my lips become heavy. I tried and failed to open my mouth, huffing through my nose instead.

The bars of the cell slung open, making me fall to the side to avoid being hit.

"Get up. We leave now. Sorrow and Sadness will escort you to the chariot." The two waifs came from around the corner, smiling, and I stood as quickly as my sore body would allow. I followed Sorrow as Sadness walked behind me. Neither tried to touch me, though I watched their every move. Even in my wretched state, I would fight them all over again.

When we left the building, I saw we were in a patch of woods out of sight of her grand estate. That meant Cupid had not been nearby after all. A pang of worry filled me as I was herded onto the obscenely picturesque chariot. Where was he? Did he know what was happening? Did he care?

I tried to open my mouth to plead with the goddess to let me see him one last time, to apologize, but it was no use. We lifted into the sky and I left my heart behind.

We departed Olympus, venturing through a brief, strange tunnel of frigid nothingness between worlds. Although I had been watching every step of the way, the entire journey jumbled in my cognizance like a dream as we entered back into Earth's realm, and there was no way my human mind could have recalled the direction back to Olympus.

We flew above mountains, cities, and villages before coming to rest at the edge of a cliff overlooking rocky shores and rushing, wild ocean. Beside us was a tower of stone. I wanted to ask where we were, but my mouth was still enchanted shut.

I remained still as I watched Venus staring out at the ocean from her high perch in the chariot. She was quiet for a long time before surprising me with soft words.

"All I ever wanted from humans was their love. Their adoration. It does not seem like so much to ask, so difficult a request, being a goddess of Olympus, and yet…" Her hair lifted, shimmering like threads of gold and bronze. I shivered, both from her speech and the sea breeze. "Since the dawn of time I have given much of myself. Each time I place a blessing in a woman's womb, each time I touch a child's head with beauty to make their lives a little simpler, or grant love to a widow, their joy and gratitude fill me with hope. Hope that they will remember me. Hope that they will continue to honor me."

My heart contracted at the mourning in her voice. I could not imagine that existence. Of course, she would be jaded. It was clear from her tone that her efforts were lost and forgotten more often than not. My family was probably one of thousands to do the very same thing. I blinked rapidly to clear my eyes.

"Have you any idea, Psyche," she went on, "how it feels to be asked to prove yourself over and over again? By those who are beneath you, no less." She laughed without humor. "Those whose lives you have touched, they will forget you when you go, or betray you if you stay. How stupid your people were to worship you; your beauty is fleeting. Mine is forever."

I wrapped my arms around myself, a heaviness overtaking my chest. As she spoke, the angry tone faded into a deeper sense of woundedness. My lips were still sealed shut, so I could not respond, even if I had the words. When I thought she was finished, she said one more thing that chilled me.

"I try to love them, to woo their love from them in return, but humans only respect those who lord their power, not those who show love. They want to be afraid, and that is something I will never understand."

Not all of us, I wanted to say. But she was right, too right. Fear was something we could understand, trust, even cling to, while love was complicated. It required more from us. How long had I held on to my fear in the face of Cupid's love? It all made me incredibly sad.

Venus turned her head to me. "It is time. I trust you will figure out this journey, Princess Psyche." She placed the box in my hands. All the negativity was gone from her eyes and demeanor, leaving behind a pure utterance of beauty and love that came off her in pulses of energy, causing my eyes to burn and my heart to race in great *thumps.*

"I give you two words of advice. The first is not to open the box once you have given it to Proserpina. Its contents are not for the eyes of humans. And secondly, what you seek for your task is in the tower beyond." I followed her eyes to the ominous, tall tower of stone before she turned her eyes back on me. "Off you go."

I stepped down, my breaths coming to me in shudders. It was not until she lifted off and left me that my jaw unhinged, and I opened my mouth to fill my chest with fresh air.

I stood there, peering around at my barren surroundings, feeling alone. The goddess's words came back to me: *What you seek for your task is in the tower...*

Yes. Of course, it was. I peered over the edge of the cliff. It was possible that if I jumped from here, I would tumble, breaking bones and hurting myself beyond measure, but not die. I eyed the tall tower, and numbness crept through me. When I had shed every bit of emotion, all that was left was an awareness of the chilly air on my exposed skin.

Holding the box with one hand, I lifted the other to my

head and my chest heaved at the feel of my chopped hair. Some chunks were three finger-width's long while others were near my scalp, nipped by the cold air. My hand shook as I brought it down from what was surely a macabre scene on my head.

It matters not, I told myself, because I was fairly certain what Venus wanted me to seek in that tower. *You are about to die.*

Chapter Thirty-Eight

The Tower

Psyche

D O NOT THINK.
Do not feel.
Keep moving.
What you seek for yourself is in the tower.

I opened the wooden door of the tower with a *creak* of rusted hinges. Dusty air filled my mouth, and I coughed as I came to the spiral staircase of stone steps and began to climb.

Despite the strong hold I thought I had on my emotions, a tremble began in my core as I ascended. I blamed the pregnancy. At that point, the child was all I cared about, and this was not fair to him or her.

Venus had made it seem as if there was a way to return from the underworld. But would I be in spirit form? Would Proserpina take pity and ask Pluto to return my spirit to my body? What if I decided to turn, right now, and run? Run as far as my worn feet could take me? I paused, the stone steps cool under my bare feet.

How long could I hide from the goddess? Would Cupid look for me? Would he be disgusted by my cowardice? A choked sound ripped from within my chest and my feet began to move again. I kept one hand on my stomach with the box tucked against me, and the other on the wall, leading me up, up, up until I reached the top.

The room at the top was simple and circular, with no

furniture and one single window overlooking the sea. Could I do this? Could I jump to my death to get to the underworld?

What you seek for yourself is in the tower.

I moved to the window sill and held the side, looking out. A wave of dizziness hit me, and I clutched the stone sill. A rush of panic made me gasp and lean back. Gods above! I was so high up, the sea a raging ink blot below. I gripped the stones and combed through the words of Venus.

What you *seek*... What did *I* seek? I sought a way to complete this task without dying. I sought a life for my child. So, was this a riddle or a cruel impasse?

Venus created all of these hardships for me to face, and even allowed her servants to beat me, but she would not lay a hand on me, much less kill me. The goddess of love could not stomach death and violence. I let out a caustic laugh as the wind whipped my face.

The realization fortified me. If Venus sought my death, she would have to do it or order it herself. I would not take my life or that of my babe. There had to be another way to complete this task, and I would find it.

"*Oh, poor wretch.*" The voice sounded ancient and gritty like stones grinding together.

I turned, stumbling away from the open window onto my bruised and swollen knees.

"Who is there?" I called, wincing and pushing to my feet as my eyes scanned the empty space.

"*I am the watchtower of Taenarus. Why dost thou forsake thy life?*"

The tower was speaking to me? Would there never be an end to the wonders? The tower believed I had come to jump.

I swallowed hard. "I must complete a task for the goddess Venus. In the underworld."

"*Mortal, if thy spirit be separated from thy body, thou shalt never return.*"

My gut clenched in anguish. "She advised me to come to this tower. She could only mean for me to die."

The rumbling chuckle made me want to cover my ears. "*Or to speak with me.*"

My pulse began to race beneath my skin. "Why, honorable tower, would she want us to speak?"

"*Because I can tell thee how to reach thy destination with thou soul and body intact.*"

Was it possible?

"*Listen and heed, for I weary of speech.*"

I went very still, focusing with all my might, afraid to hope.

"*Venture to the city of Lacedaemon, where thou will obtain two coins for the Charon to ferry thou across the River Styx, and two sop cakes—one to give Cerberus to allow thy entrance into the palace of Pluto—and one to be allowed out. When thou returneth to Taenarus, thou wilt find a hole in the cliff where none dare to risk. This is the entrance for souls into those infernal shades. The underworld is a treacherous place with souls full of avarice. Guard thy coins and sops, for the spirits will attempt to steal from thee. Now, go.*" His booming voice softened. "*And be well.*"

I wanted to ask for clarification, but the tower's spirit was fading.

"Thank you." I pressed a hand to the stone, clutching the box to my chest and leaning my forehead against the cool wall. "Thank you, Tower." The floor gave a tremor and tufts of hair lifted on my head as if the tower had sighed. I rushed from the room with renewed hope, all but flying down the stairs, quickly finding the path to the city of Lacedaemon. All of my pain and ailments were forgotten as I ran, expending what little energy I had left.

When I reached the outskirts of the city, my body ached anew. As the first person laid eyes on me, a man, I became acutely aware of my appearance, for no man had ever looked upon me with such disgust. His nose scrunched, repulsed, and he hurried off. I nearly laughed, which turned into a desire to cry, because the monumental task ahead of me was made all the harder by how I now looked. I would have to beg, and for once in my life, people would not be so willing to give me what I wanted.

It was a shameful feeling to realize what an easy life I'd had in comparison to others—humbling beyond measure. As I walked further into the city's dirt streets, even beggars looked upon me with morbid curiosity, trying to see past the chopped hair, swollen eye, and bruised body.

I stood against the outer wall of a thatched building selling wares. First thing I needed to do was secure the box. People would think I'd stolen it. I'd seen some of the other beggars pull up the top layer of their dressing gowns to make pouches for their few belongings. I pulled my raggedy gown up on the side, revealing my calves, and tied the fabric around the box. It was unwieldy and uncomfortable, but it would do the job for now. A middle-aged gentleman, soft of belly and friendly-faced, began to pass. I reached out and gently touched his arm, saying, "Please, kind sir—"

He let out a yelp and pulled his arm away, as if I were a contagious leper. His benevolent appearance changed to disgust as he scowled and marched away, brushing off his arm.

How would I ever make enough to buy cakes with two half-pence to spare?

As the day wore on, I tried everything. Conversation. Flattery. Nothing worked. The longer I stood out there, the more exhausted I felt, stooping and shifting my weight. Two streets away, I had passed a woman singing a cheery tune and getting coins, but my singing would surely send people even further away from me.

"I don't know what happened to you, Miss, but I can see someone has done you wrong. Here." I faced a woman in a faded, but fine toga, her black hair streaked with strands of white that made her appear noble. She handed me a cream-colored shawl.

"Oh, thank you!" I said. When I smiled, my cheek and eye zinged with pain.

"May the gods have mercy on you," she said, already walking away.

"May they, indeed," I whispered. I made quick work of draping the shawl over my head, tying it at the nape of my neck to hide my tattered hair situation. It made me feel ten times better. I stood straighter.

The next people to pass were a mother about Miracle's age with a young daughter holding a small book of poems. I recognized the author at once.

"Good choice there," I said, pointing to the book. The mother gave me a worried look, glancing at her daughter and beginning to tug her faster. But before they could get too far, I began to recite.

The mother stopped and turned in surprise, and the daughter beamed up at the woman, then me.

"That one is my favorite!"

"Me too," I said, leaning my hands on my knees. "I can see you are a very smart young lady."

The mother blinked at me, her eyes scanning my nightgown and beaten features. "How does such a cultured woman take to the streets?" She quickly closed her eyes and shook her head. "Never mind. I probably do not want to know."

"You wouldn't believe me if I told you." I tried to smile, though I was certain it warped my face even worse. I could tell her my name, and there was a chance she'd have heard of me, but she would undoubtedly think I was a lying halfwit.

"What happened to your eye?" the little girl asked. Her mother began to shush her, casting me an apologetic look, but I answered.

"I took quite a tumble, but I assure you, I will be fine. With a little luck, fate will help me up and I will make amends."

The woman studied me. "You do speak beautifully." In a quieter voice, she asked, "Who did this to you? A lover? A boss? Are you a runaway slave?"

I shook my head, still wearing a small smile. "My mother-in-law."

Her eyes widened, and she let out a huff. "In that case…" She pulled out two shiny, large coins, and I clutched them to my chest, overwhelmed by her generosity. "Back on your feet, you go." She lifted her chin and gave me a conspiratorial grin.

"I cannot thank you enough, Miss." I bowed my head. "May the gods bless you and your precious daughter." I looked at the girl once more. "Keep up the reading." She nodded, curls bouncing.

As they walked away, I stared down at the coins and closed my fist around them. It was enough to buy the two sticky cakes for Cerberus and have coins left over for the ferryman. Gratitude welled inside me but never turned to joy—not when I knew I was one step closer to the underworld, a place where no mortal had ever gone and returned with their soul intact.

Perhaps Cupid would never have me again after what I had done, but I would prove my worth to him. To Venus. And most importantly, to myself.

Chapter Thirty-Nine

Third Task

Psyche

A HOLE IN THE CLIFF WHERE NONE DARE TO RISK. *WHAT DID THAT even mean?*

I stood at the edge of the cliff in Taenarus near the Tower. It was night now, but the moon was full, and the sky was clear. As I stared out at the dark water and the shadowy, rocky descent, I had never felt hungrier or more spent. My mouth had filled with moisture when I walked into the bakery, but the owner had not been happy to see a threadbare, dirty customer. He attempted to charge me an outrageous sum for the cakes. It was far harder to barter as a beggar than a princess. I finally talked him down just enough to have two coins left over, but there was not enough for me to buy food for myself. Thankfully I had found a fresh stream along the way to fill my belly with water.

As I explored the ledge of the cliff, I spied a narrow, steep pathway hidden by brush. It was enough room for one person to shuffle downward. I slipped the coins into my makeshift pouch with the box and held the cakes gingerly between my fingers as I scooted along the constricted path, nudging overgrown vines out of the way. Not using my hands to steady myself made me feel off-balanced. I concentrated extra hard to keep my footing.

A hole in the cliff. That had to be a cave. I moved slowly along the path but up ahead I could see there was a curve, and something blocking the way. As I approached, I squinted in the darkness and discovered it was a mass of thorny sea brambles.

Of all the horrid luck.

I avoided those at all cost. The stickers were murder on bare feet. How would I get past them?

Where none dare to risk. I repeated that line in my head. Any sane person would turn around at the sight of those briars. Could this possibly be what the tower had meant? The closer I got to the brambles, the stranger I felt. My heart began to skip, then race. A strange sentience overcame me, like a warning, telling me to turn back. I tensed, catching my breath, and forced myself to trudge forward again. Tiny steps. I was almost to the wicked brambles.

You will fall! A voice shouted in my head and I jerked to a stop, leaning against the rock. *Go back!*

My eyes darted about, and my ears were on alert for the strange source of my panic, but nothing at all was there. Still, I couldn't quite seem to catch my breath.

"No," I whispered into the darkness. "I cannot stop."

I urged myself forward, clamping my jaw shut against the urge to scream in terror as I sidled up to the malevolent, overgrown sticker bushes.

I reached out a trembling arm to push aside the bramble, prepared to tear my hand away, but what I encountered instead of thorns was a soft sheet of leaves that easily parted under my hand. Confusion filled me. I crept forward, pressing into the canopy of tangled branches that felt nothing like it looked. Darkness engulfed me. Still, I pressed on.

My blood pumped wildly as I stepped out of the curtain of darkness. A sharp gasp caught in my throat when I realized I was inside a cave. Dim, thick candles aligned the walls with what appeared to be hundreds of years of wax drippings piled underneath them like the buttressing of massive trees. One more step inside had my vision clearing, causing me to press my back against the wall in surprise.

People! So many people! Where had they come from? It looked as if they were coming in through the same entrance to the cave that I had taken. But there'd been no one outside. Or had there? I brought the back of my hand to my mouth. Peering around now, they were not like me. They appeared solid at first glance, but the longer I stared, the more they seemed to blur along the edges.

Spirits.

I held the wrapped cakes in my hands, trying not to squeeze them, and began to shuffle along with the mass of souls. I kept against the wall. When they brushed up against me, it was the strangest feeling—almost like the soft rub of a cat's fluffy fur—not quite solid. I shivered and hurried along, feeling the clink of the box and coins in my gown's pouch. Ahead, my eyes beheld a frightening sight: two sooty stone gargoyles, so large their heads scraped the cave ceiling. Their eyes roved over the souls coming in. As I neared, their staffs sliced downward, halting my entrance and startling me to pieces.

"What is your business here, live one?" came a booming voice.

Once I gathered my wits again, I told them, "I come with a task from the goddess Venus, to get this box filled by Proserpina." I took out the box with shaking hands and held it up for them to see. After a long moment, the staffs raised, and they said nothing more. Spirits spilled past me, and I moved tentatively forward, my heart erratic as I passed through without harm.

Outside of the opening, souls went in different directions, as if they instinctually knew or were being silently guided to their proper destinations.

We were in a giant underground area with tunnels along one

side that spilled a constant stream of spirits. It was difficult to see. The only lights were scattered candles along the walls, and glowing stalactites overhead. Liquid dripped down stone walls into guttered ruts that ran along the floors. I spied a long line against one wall where sounds of running water drew me.

As I moved toward the line, a man pushing a cart of wood stepped in front of me and the whole thing toppled. He let out a strangled sound and stooped, then grabbed his back. I couldn't understand why a spirit seemed to be working down here instead of going to his destination, like the others.

"Please, Miss," he said, beseeching me. "Can you help? If I bring this to Charon, he will allow me passage."

My heart squeezed with pity. I wanted to help him, but I dared not set down the cakes. And I remembered what the Tower had told me about not stopping for any reason.

"I'm so sorry," I said. "I have to go."

When I attempted to pass him, he snarled and threw his arms out to grab me. In his semi-solid state, it was enough to make me stagger backward and fall on my bottom, barely keeping the cakes in my hands. To my horror, I heard the clang of a coin falling from my ratty pouch.

His eyes widened with the avarice the Tower had warned me of, and I quickly huddled my body over top of the fallen coin, lowering my face to pick up the coin with my lips. I pushed it into my cheek with my tongue and threw back an elbow to get the soft spirit off me. He fell harder than I had intended, proving to be as frail as he looked, and I tried not to feel guilty.

I stood and ran to the end of the line, my body shaking all over. I carefully transferred one of the cakes into the crook of my other arm and dug down into my pouch. Securing the other coin, I pressed it between my teeth and cheek with the other one. Then I held the cakes like fragile treasures and waited.

My eyes darted all around, not trusting a single soul. Spirits were quick to fill the space behind me, but the line moved surprisingly fast. As we neared the front of the line, I saw the River Styx flowing out through a darkened tunnel, and running along the wall, far down out of sight. It was hard to gauge distance in the darkened space, but the river was wide. The gurgle of the water sounded sluggish, not welcoming.

As I moved forward, I watched souls reach out holding coins to a dark figure as the boat appeared before them. That's right, *appeared*. One moment the boat was there, and the next it was gone. Then back again. Two souls away from the front, and I was able to take a good look at the fabled Charon, ferryman of the River Styx.

Though he appeared tall and thin, one shoulder stooping, the magical power in his person was undeniable. He wore a black robe with a hood, but his face was not hidden. His drooping skin held the gray pallor of death, his eyes as deep and soulless as Sadness and Sorrow's. Every part of me wanted to turn and run from his presence, but I steeled myself to move forward until it was my turn.

I stepped forward when the boat appeared, rocking to and fro. Charon stuck out a bony hand that looked as if he had been submerged in water for hundreds of years. Balancing both cakes in one hand, I pulled a coin from inside my mouth and placed it on his palm.

"Been a while since I ferried a live one." His voice was like sticks rubbing together. He needed a drink of water worse than me.

Charon's dead eyes seized mine as he motioned one arm to beckon me onto the boat. I held my breath and stepped past him, sitting on the small seat. I had always imagined his boat would be huge, ferrying many souls at once. Everything about this was bizarre.

He pushed off from the bank with his oar, and I tensed, expecting us to disappear in a blink of an eye like the others, but we simply moved along the river at a normal pace. I shivered as we got farther down the river.

"Pardon me, worthy ferryman." My words were slightly garbled with the coin in my cheek. "Why did we not disappear like the others?"

He paddled slowly. "Time works differently for those on the river."

Still holding the cakes, I crossed my arms, chilled to the core. The darkened tunnel had me spooked, giving off the sensation of passing through spiderwebs. When I saw something come out of the water beside us, I was already screaming before I could make it out.

A hand.

Then a head. A man! He grabbed my arm in a grip that felt stronger than the old man spirit from before. I struggled, still screaming and nearly squeezing the cakes to mush. I wrenched myself from his grasp. The sudden loss of my arm caused him to fall back into the water.

"Oh, my gods!" I stood, peering around as Charon kept rowing, his eyes straight ahead. In the water, I could make out other bodies. Terror froze me as solid as ice. Hands reached, their mouths open in silent screams, their eyes pleading.

"It is their eternal punishment," Charon commented.

"Gods above," I whispered. This was more than a nightmare. This was the true fate for these souls; they would never wake up from the torment. What had they done to deserve it? I shook my head.

As uncomfortable as Charon made me, I decided to stand with my back to him, so I would not be taken by surprise by any more of the dead. It was a good thing, too, because another man, his long hair and beard stringy from the thick water, was able to pull up on the boat side to look at me, his hand reaching far too closely.

"Help," he croaked. "Please, help me."

As I stared at his desperate face, my eyes burned and something inside my chest twisted painfully.

"There is nothing I can do," I whispered.

He wailed as he was pulled under by something beneath him. My stomach lurched, and I fought to remain standing. After what seemed like an eternity, a shore appeared in the distance. I stared, glad to have something to take my attention from the morbid waters. Unfortunately, the view became more unbecoming as we neared.

The shore was filled with souls overlapping one another. To one side stood a massive dark stone castle partially built into the walls of the cave—the palace of Pluto, god of the underworld. A shiver ran through me. Would I meet him? I hoped not.

In front of the castle's grand entrance, between onyx pillars, was the legendary three-headed dog, Cerberus. He was even larger than I had envisioned, with muscles that bunched in his back and legs like tree trunks. He snapped at souls that got too near. I glanced down at the cakes in my hands with worry. How would one tiny cake suffice all three heads of that beast? And not just once, but twice? Everyone knew the creature would not allow a human to pass within reach without mauling them to bits.

I drew in a cool breath and held it until my chest hurt before letting it out slowly. I had come this far. There was nothing to do now but trust the tower's advice and keep going. When we pulled up to shore with a light thump, I turned to Charon.

"I will be returning soon. I have another coin for you."

His scratchy chuckle made me want to cover my ears. "If you say so, mortal."

I climbed out gingerly, stepping onto the damp sand and rushing away from the waters. When I turned, Charon and the boat were already gone. Panic threatened to climb into my throat, but I swallowed it down and turned to survey the scene. On one side was the castle. On the other side was an ancient soul standing on a raised platform surrounded by countless tomes: the judge. For each soul, he found their name and pointed to which entrance they were to take. The path to the right of his dais was a bright, gleaming archway to Elysian Fields, the heavenly place for blessed souls. To his left was the dark and murky entrance to Tartarus.

When souls refused to go, gray-winged dragons rushed down from jutting ledges in the cave's wall, and grasped the souls with their talons, tossing them through the Tartarus doorway as the souls screamed. No way was I going near that podium.

I skirted the edge of the water and the mass of souls until I neared the palace. Cerberus's heads came up immediately as if scenting me. Three pairs of eyes opened wide, and he began a ferocious round of barking, snarling, and howling, pulling on the massive chains that restrained him. I jumped, thinking for a moment he would break his bindings, but he remained secured. I moved closer, muttering useless things to the creature, trying to calm myself.

"I have a little something for you. Good boy."

When I got close enough, I bent to the ground and unwrapped one of the cakes with a shaking hand. Then I stood and launched it at the dog, realizing why one cake was better than three. The heads began to fight, thrashing at one another. I was completely forgotten.

My feet began to sprint before my mind had even caught up to what was happening. I ran around the beast, my breaths hitched with fear. When I got to the grand, obsidian doors, it took all of my self-control not to bang on them. I knocked politely, if not rapidly, peering over my shoulder at Cerberus, whose middle head was licking its chops while the others snarled at it.

The door opened and a satyr who looked much like Renae stood there. Only this servant was not smiling.

"Hello. I need to see Goddess Proserpina. It is urgent. Goddess Venus requires something from her." I wiped my sticky free hand on my filthy nightgown, then I reached into the pouch and pulled out the box. One glance at it had the satyr nodding and opening the door to let me in.

Deep Hades. I was in Pluto's palace! I had made it! Safely inside, I slipped the coin from my cheek and let it drop into my pouch.

I followed the solemn servant through the halls. Much like the halls of Cupid's home, these had paintings and murals of war, but these were far darker, gorier, the faces elongated and made more grotesque by the spattering of candlelight flickering at odd intervals. Layers of dust seemed to have collected on everything in sight. I looked away, facing forward. It was even colder in here than it was outside.

When the satyr opened a door and beckoned me in with a single wave, my spirits lifted. The room was brighter, filled with hundreds of candles that warmed the space. Everything was clean. Gleaming candelabras and silver platters were set out on a long table. In the middle of the room was a grand, plush chair of rich cream fabric. In it sat a vision of sweetness that caught my breath. Her skin was dark mahogany, her large eyes a soft green, lips pink. The Goddess Proserpina appeared as young as me with her hair pinned up in black ringlets, her body petite and innocent in appearance, with dainty ankles crossed.

My eyes met hers only for a brief moment before I lowered mine and rushed forward, falling at her feet.

"Oh, goddess. I am beyond honored to be in your presence. I am Princess—"

"*Princess?*" Even her voice was youthful, high and pretty.

"Yes, wondrous one. I know I do not appear so, but I am Princess Psyche, a mere mortal as you can see. I am on a mission from your dear friend, the goddess Venus, to obtain a bit of your beauty in this box."

I held the box up without lifting my head, and she took it.

"My, my," Proserpina said. "I cannot recall the last time Venus needed help. She must be going through a difficult time. What have you done to her, girl?"

I gritted my teeth as a multitude of emotions swam within me like lethal sharks, their tails whipping.

"I am the wife of her son."

Proserpina gasped, paused, and then giggled. "Cupid has taken a mortal? Oh, the outrage!" She sounded utterly delighted by this bit of gossip. "That must have smarted his poor mother. No wonder she is in such a state as to require my essence."

I heard the box snip open and felt a *whoosh* of magical wind warm my skin before the box clicked shut again. A nudge at my shoulder had me lifting a hand to receive it.

"Thank you, great one." I began to stand, but she stopped me.

"I never have visitors. Stay a moment. Tell me the tale of how you and Cupid came to be. I find my own company to be tiresome."

I understood that feeling. Although I could not stay long, her request seemed heartfelt. Who was I to deny her? So, I began my tale, starting with Venus's blessing to my family. It felt good to say it all out loud. Even the horrible parts were somehow cleansing. Proserpina listened avidly, now and again making small sounds. Tears streamed down my cheeks when I admitted how I had broken my husband's trust. I went on to tell her of my tasks and my encounter with Sorrow and Sadness.

At the end, she was quiet a long time before regarding me with softness and asking, "What, mortal princess, would you say is your greatest regret in all of this? Losing your beauty? Being forced to face these fearsome tasks?"

"No, goddess. My first regret is earning the ire of the goddess who granted me life. She never deserved that. But my biggest regret is hurting Cupid." My voice caught, and Proserpina hummed her feelings.

"It seems he has forsaken you. Yet, you still love him?"

I wiped my eyes against my shoulders. "I will love him for all my days and into eternity."

"Believe it or not, mortal," she said gently, "even a god is capable of forgiveness. Unfortunately, sometimes it can take centuries. I should know. After what Pluto did to me, tricking me into being his wife…" Her lips pursed, then pulled to the side in a grin. "But now, there is no one who affects me as he does. None one I would prefer." Her eyes became dazed and sultry for a moment as if imagining him. My cheeks heated.

"I am glad to hear that, High One."

She pondered. "Do you believe you will be able to leave the underworld with your soul intact?"

"I can only hope, goddess."

"None have before you. Indeed, I find myself hoping you will. I wish to see how this tale proceeds. In the meantime, you must eat. I have an assortment. Stand."

I had been kneeling, hunched over for so long, that an embarrassing sound of pain escaped my throat when I tried to stand. Every part of me was stiff and sore. My energy was depleted, my mouth parched.

"Meats, oils, flatbread, wine, and fruit await." Proserpina

motioned toward the table of food, but I felt unworthy to eat at the feast of a goddess, especially in my state.

"Harvest Mother," I begged. "I am undeserved. Have you any brown bread and water?"

Seeming to understand, she made that humming sound again, and a plate appeared with the rough ground bread Venus had been feeding me. I never let go of the cake in my hand as I used my other hand to devour the bread and drink the water.

"I must go, goddess." I clung to the box. "I cannot thank you enough. If I make it through this final task, I will make an offering on your behalf as soon as I possibly can."

"Indeed. One last thing before you go. You are aware that the contents of the box are not fit for a mortal, correct?"

"Yes, goddess. Venus told me."

"Good." She smiled, and warmth like an autumn breeze spread over me, smelling of sweet hay and sunshine.

I bowed my head one last time before the servant led me out, back to the doors of Pluto's palace. I never saw him, and for that I was grateful.

The moment I was ushered out, the satyr shut the door, not bothering to see if I was eaten alive. I gave a shout of fright when Cerberus nipped closely at my legs, and without thinking, I threw the other cake, still wrapped. Like before, the dog leapt for it, his heads thrashing. I had not given myself much room to slip past and ended up getting smacked with a massive paw that left a stinging scratch up my arm and across my cheek.

I ran until I was out of its reach, then lifted my hand to my face. A long welt was already raising, but only a touch of blood showed on my fingers. I sighed heavily. I was alive. That was all that mattered. And now, without the cakes, my hands were freed. I would hold the box to keep it from banging against my leg as I walked. I took the coin out of my pouch and put it safely back inside my mouth.

The souls crowded me as I walked, their emotions rising like scrabbling vapors to fill the dense air with a feeling of dread and anticipation. I tried to make my way back to the river, becoming confused and turned around. Their emotions raked at me, and I felt the urge to drive forward with the souls being shepherded into the lines.

No, I told myself, pushing against them until I finally broke free into an open space. To my surprise, a woman sat in the opening with a spinning wheel. She appeared frail like the earlier man with the wood.

"Miss," she pleaded while she spun. "I am so weary. Help me, please. Just one moment while I rest. Please."

The dreamlike feeling of floating came over me, and I wavered. She was an old woman. I had to help her. I began to reach for the spindle, and then stopped as her eyes widened in victory.

"No," I said, shaking my head clear. "I cannot stop."

"Give me your coin!" She leapt on me with the same might as the old man had, knocking me to the ground as I clutched the box. "I saw it!" She screamed, ripping at my dress. Even in her half-solid state, she was strong and mad with greed. It felt wrong, so wrong, to hit an old woman, but so be it.

I brought the box up and whacked her in the face, earning an *oomph*, then elbowed her chest. When I rolled to get her off me, I felt the coin slip to the back of my throat, choking me. I leaned forward, coughing until it spewed from my mouth. We scrabbled ferociously, and when my hand enclosed over the sandy coin, she grabbed the shawl, ripping it from my head and stumbling back. I stood and ran, leaving her in a heap on the ground.

I had to get out of this hell before I lost my sanity.

I stumbled along the shore, feeling half dead, until I saw the boat flash into existence, releasing a shuffling soul.

"Wait! Charon!"

His bony face turned toward me from under the draping hood, and a ghoulish smile slowly flitted onto his face. I held out the coin as I sprinted the last few steps, out of breath.

"Please," I panted. "I need to get back to the other side."

"Well, well," he said. "This is a first." He plucked the coin from my grip with wrinkled, stick-like fingers and moved aside for me to board. I nearly broke into a bawling fit at the relief of being on the boat as he began to row. Like last time, I stood with my back to him, clutching the box and watching the writhing waters. Every sting and ache pulsed at the surface of my skin and deep into my muscles, causing my eyelids to droop. My body begged to collapse into a deep sleep.

Not yet, I told myself. *We are so close.*

I couldn't seem to catch my breath. We moved up the darkened tunnel on the enclosed river, and my body started to shiver violently against my will, as if the shock of all that had happened was crashing down on me.

We had barely pulled ashore when I was clambering out, falling to my knees and pushing up with my free hand. I had to shove through the throng of souls, their hopelessness enveloping me and threatening to turn me back. I focused, pushing forward, turning to the side to slide more easily along the dirt wall. Once I was through the crowd, I spied the giant gargoyles at the arch where I had entered, and the mass of souls passing through was even thicker.

Filled with terror, I approached the gargoyles with the box held up for them to see. Their eyes followed me as I pushed through the throng of souls and edged myself against the wall, pressing in despite the objections of the spirits. I let out a sharp breath when I passed the gargoyles. My body begged to let go and be swept off where I could stop struggling and sleep, but my mind fought.

So close, so close.

An animalistic sound of desperation tore from my throat when I saw the cave's entrance covered in briars. A last burst of energy rushed through me, pushing me forward until I was through the throng, shoving the faux sticker brush aside, and collapsing on the thin ledge of the cliff. The feel and sight of the spirits were gone.

I let myself lay there and sob, my body wracked with a myriad of pains and an overload of emotion. I was alive! All at once, I realized I would be returning to Venus. I had made it through her tasks. My life was spared, and I would soon be a mother. Oh, the glory of it! Could it really be true? Gratefulness, like a fragrant flower, flowed through me.

But what would this mean for Cupid and me? Would he be proud of my accomplishments or was it too late? The look of hurt and disappointment when he'd woken to find me staring at him would forever be scarred into my memory. My husband in all of his immortal perfection. How I'd betrayed him. Me. A mortal woman who didn't deserve the attention of a god, much less his love. I had horribly hurt him, and now look at me!

I touched my face, swollen now on both sides, and my hair. Oh, gods. Disgrace pummeled me. I was hideous. The irony of it cascaded heavily around me. I had always resented the fact that my appearance was the only thing people found worthy about me. But now, my head spinning with the hiss of self-doubt and paranoia, I couldn't help but wonder: Who was I without my beauty? A torrential firestorm swirled in my head, loud and painful, and I gripped my shaggy hair.

Cupid could have any woman, mortal or immortal. After what I'd done to him, and what had become of me since, what could possibly make him want me now? The thought of his disappointment stung deep within my abdomen, digging upward toward my heart like a dagger ready to pierce. Desperation coated my every thought and emotion, making it impossible to grasp anything beyond it.

As hopelessness gripped me, making me tremble, a warm reverberation began to sing to me from my lap. My eyes drifted down to the box. In a hazy blur of pain, I pushed to sit up, cradling the box in my lap. I could scarcely hear the sound of waves on rocks below through the rush of blood in my ears.

The box. The box. It wanted me to open it. It called to me, enticing me, the way the nectar in the goblet had. I wanted to throw it to the sea, but I had to bring it back to Venus.

You are ugly. I tried to swallow, to shake the voice from my head. *But you do not have to be. Your beauty can be restored by one miniscule swipe of my contents.*

No, no, no. I couldn't! The contents were meant for gods, not mortals.

Nobody will know.

"I will know," I whispered, my teeth clenched. I just had to stand. But weakness overcame me; the toil on my body had been too much, my mind not far behind it.

One look at you, and he will question it all. He will see your mortality. Your haggard future appearance.

My chin dropped to my chest in defeat, because I believed it. What I'd had—what I had ruined—had been too good for a mere mortal. The desperation inside me spoke louder, every self-doubt and fear rising to a shouting crescendo in my soul. I clutched the box, taking a deep breath into my chest and holding it.

One tiny drop will not hurt a human. Take it. Restore what little dignity you have left, and go about your life, renewed.

Cupid would never want me again, but I had to face him and his mother. As it was, I couldn't walk, my wits had left me, and I was hideous. Useless. Unworthy.

Do it.

My fingers trembled at the edge of the clasp.

"Just a drop," I whispered, my voice shaky and hoarse. "Just a drop."

I cracked the lid of the box. A bright flash assaulted my eyes, and all at once my exhaustion became a burden I could no longer carry. I felt my torso tilting to the side as the sun began to wink to life lazily over the horizon, and I succumbed to what I realized, too late, was the sleep of the dead.

CHAPTER FORTY

RISE OF POWER

Cupid

THE GOD OF LOVE AND DESIRE PACED HIS CELL. HIS MOTHER had been gone nearly two days. Every horrible scenario had plagued him during her absence. Where was Psyche? What was happening to her? How was she handling it? He had seen a fire in her during their time together, and he hoped her will to live was as strong in these trials.

When his ears caught the faint beating of dove wings from afar, Cupid raced to the window and shouted a beastly sound. His eyes raked the skies until he spied the chariot, but when he squinted, he only saw one soul—his mother's.

A strong fist squeezed Cupid's heart. "Where is she?" he shouted at the skies. Even from afar, his mother lifted her chin, her eyes going wide as she gazed upon the wing of her abode where he stood, watching. What was that expression on her face? He had never seen it before, and he did not like it.

When the goddess finally made her way inside, a soft pink frock over her shoulders, their eyes met through the bars. Cupid held his breath. His mother lifted her chin as she had done on the chariot.

"Are you thirsty?" she asked politely.

"Where is she?"

"I imagine she is nearly finished with her final task." She set down her frock, carefully arranging it on the back of her divan, not meeting his eyes.

Cupid narrowed his eyes to slits and spoke with careful deliberation. "Which was…?"

Her eyes held his now, but she lacked the ego and vindictiveness she had possessed when he last saw her.

"What has happened?" he asked, his anxiety rising.

"You agreed to these terms, Cupid. Do not forget. We bound ourselves."

His voice lowered to a fervent hiss. *"What has happened?"*

"I am afraid she is no longer the beauty you left behind."

A slither of apprehension climbed his spine. "You hurt her?"

"I did not touch her!" Venus raised her chin again. "She would not comply with Sadness and Sorrow when they came to ready her. She should not have fought—"

"You let those revolting creatures touch her?" Cupid felt his eyes bulging as he grasped the bars tighter, shaking them. "Where is she?"

"Cupid—"

"Where is she?" he bellowed, causing her eyes to flutter closed.

"I sent her to retrieve a box of beauty ointment from Proserpina."

The ground seemed to shift under Cupid's feet, making him unsteady. "Proserpina?" *No. NO,* he thought. It could not be. "From the home of her mother, Ceres?"

Venus swallowed, her dainty throat rising and falling. "She is currently with Pluto."

A deadly calm washed over Cupid and he felt something rising within. "You sent her into the underworld, from whence no mortal has ever returned. Is that what you are telling me, Mother?"

"I brought her to the tower, and I trust that the spirit of the structure gave her solid instructions of how to enter and return."

"Oh, you trust that, do you?" he asked. Still, he felt the storm within himself building, a tremble beginning in his core and spreading outward to his limbs. "And you sent her to retrieve the essence of goddesses, which human eyes cannot look upon without falling into the sleep of the dead?"

Venus stepped closer, jutting out her chin in self-defense. "I gave her orders not to open the box. I told her it was not for human eyes."

A rumble of laughter rose in Cupid's sternum. The thing growing inside of him was filling his head now, making him feel light, clearing his mind of all but his own power.

"After all of this," Venus whispered. "After she proved herself unworthy, you still want her? What about me, son? What about the way she and her people hurt me? I am the one who has ever been by your side. Your advocate in all ways!"

"Until I found love! And then what, Mother? You refused to listen! Psyche was never your enemy!"

"She will die in a blink, Cupid, and then what? I am trying to protect you! Love between mortals and gods is foolhardy at best! It is time for you to let this go. You have lost her. She is not for you."

"I will love and mourn her every day," he whispered.

"You are just a boy! I know what is best for you! Soon, all will be right again, and you will see. You will realize my love for you is steady and true, and I would never break your trust—"

"You already have! Do you not see it, Mother?"

Venus clenched her jaw, her eyes filling with moisture. "Choose your words carefully, Cupid. I am eternal, and I am your mother. The choice is clear."

"I choose my wife!"

A vicious, howling fist of power surged through Cupid. The roar that tore from his throat shook the entire estate, blasting the bars off his prison cell. His power crushed the wards Venus had erected, throwing her off her graceful balance, onto her backside where she scrambled back against the wall, eyes wide.

The god of love was breathing hard, stepping over the threshold, his eyes bold and blazing as he peered down at his mother. She lifted an arm as if in fear. Indeed, his smile was wicked. The day had finally come that his immortal magic exceeded hers. Never again would she be able to keep him from his heart's desire.

He had nothing more to say to her. Cupid left his mother cowering as he lifted into the air and flew toward the mortal lands and the Tower of Taenarus. A deep part of him knew it was too late. Humans did not enter the underworld and leave again. Oh, his beautiful soul. The thought of what she had seen and been through since leaving his palace ripped at his heart. Why had it taken so long for his power to overwhelm Venus's hold and break him free? Why had he doubted it was even possible? His love for Psyche had set him free, but it was too late. He would forever lament the events of the past year.

Cupid lost the only soul he had ever loved. He had failed her. She had died alone, suffering in fear, and he was to blame for allowing his ego to agree to that accursed bargain.

Cupid's mood was grievous when his eyes landed on the tower in the distance. Despite the bright sun shining over the sea, the scene felt dark and foul. Waving an arm as he flew, clouds were pulled from surrounding cities, cramming together over the waters to blot out that blinding sunshine and turn the day gray.

He made it to the edge of the cliff and swooped downward at a sharp angle. There was the ledge and the long line of spirits being led into the underworld. Suddenly, his breath caught, turning to fire in his chest. A small body lay near the entrance.

Cupid dived, lowering his feet to land in a crouch by the broken, feminine body.

His keen eyes took in the sight, but his mind denied what he saw.

This human's soul was dim, nearly dormant, and as gray as the storm clouds he'd gathered, lacking hope and joy. Her hair had been roughly chopped, covered in dirt and dust. Her body was frail, her chest barely rising and falling. Scratches and bruises marred her skin, her nightgown torn and filthy. One of her ankles appeared swollen and purpled, turned at a slightly odd angle.

A shock of varying emotions kicked Cupid between the ribs as he swooped down, kneeling at her side.

Her face was turned down with an arm draped over top of her head. His mother's box sat open near her fingers, the glow of goddess beauty ointment shedding a light that would cause the sleeping death to any mortal who beheld it. But Psyche would never have opened it. She was too cautious for that. She must have tripped and fallen, the box accidentally opening.

No matter. She was alive, though barely, and he would tend her. He knelt and closed the box, shoving it aside, and reached under her arm to lift her head.

"I am here, beloved. I am—" His voice hitched as he glimpsed her face. Unrecognizable. Her eye was nearly swollen shut, skin discolored by a deep scratch up her cheek. He wanted to kill something. When he got his hands on Sadness and Sorrow, they would wish for death.

He placed his wife's head in his lap and set to work. First, he healed her face, relaxing a fraction when she began to look like herself again. Then he held her ankle until it mended, and the swelling receded. His hand roamed her skin, stitching up gashes and scrapes that would have stung any warrior. Lastly, he closed his eyes and concentrated on the curse that wrapped around her soul. For him, it was as simple as sponging away a layer of grime from her being, but he concentrated hard, wiping his hands over her face, his fingers rubbing her eyes, clearing away every last vestige of sleep. When he finished, her chest rose in a deep intake of air, and her eyes fluttered open. Most importantly of all, her soul lightened, though it was not nearly as bright as usual.

He could only imagine what feelings she carried within that would cause the dimming of her soul. More than anything, that hurt him. But she was alive. She was gazing up at him in confusion, and he wanted to squeeze her. Instead, he held her head in his hands, rubbing his thumbs across her ashen cheeks.

"I have you, Psyche. You are going to be all right. You did it."

"Cupid?" Her whispered voice was scratchy. He needed to get her water and food immediately. But to his surprise, as she became aware, she turned and buried her face in his lap, curling in on herself, covering her head and crying miserably. "Please do not look upon me!"

Sour bile rose within the god at this reaction.

"What is this?" he said. "Why would you ask that of me? I am your husband!"

"Cupid, please!" She pulled her head from his lap and placed her forehead to the rough ground, bowing before him as low as possible. "I am not worthy of you. My regrets are too heavy, my shame too great. I was a vain fool to try and take a drop of your mother's ointment. I was not in my right mind!"

Now his face twisted as a grave sensation caught him.

"You opened the box?" He grasped her arms, trying to lift her though she struggled against him, hanging her head. "You thought to take some of the goddess beauty for yourself? But *why*, Psyche?"

"Why do you think?" she cried, frantically meeting his eyes. "Look at me!"

His eyes never left hers. *"I am."* Cupid released her arms and took her face in both hands. She closed her eyes as her body shook with wracking heaves, and he whispered, "Open your eyes, Wife."

Eyes still shut, she cried, "How can you still call me that?"

"Open your eyes."

She did, but slowly as if afraid.

"Do you still fear me?" he asked.

"N-no. It is not that. How can you not see? I am so far beneath your station. I had to beg in the streets!" The words came out in strangled anguish.

"And was there anger in your heart while you begged?"

She stilled at the question. "No."

"Did you go into the underworld, Psyche? All the way to the palace of Pluto, and back again, as no mortal human has before you?"

"Y-yes," she whispered.

Cupid pulled her to him, burying his face in this miraculous mortal's neck, and she embraced him too. They trembled as they clung together at the edge of the bluff.

As if coming back to her mind, she said, "But you deserve the best. Everything about me is...breakable."

He reared back, a look of anger causing her to gasp and drop her eyes. Cupid lifted her chin roughly. "Do not look away from me. Hear what I say, Wife, and do not dare to question my words."

She swallowed, her eyes wide as she gave a tiny nod.

"It is your soul I love. I am a god. If I wished, I could mold your body, cause your hair to grow, change color, cover your skin in a flush of sunshine." He gripped her harder, putting his face close to hers. "It was never your face that drew me. Not your hair. Or the curve of your hips. It was *your soul*. And you are not broken. Even after everything! You have no need to doubt."

Her eyes clouded as hot tears streamed unbidden down her cheeks. "But...I hurt you with my mistrust. I didn't declare my love when I should have. I..." She gritted her teeth. "I allowed my vanity to cause me to open the box. Even my soul is tainted now."

He grinned because as she admitted to those wrongdoings, her soul lightened before his eyes. Not as brightly as it had the carefree day at the market but glowing in a way that caused his own heart to swell.

"Still gorgeous," he whispered. "With each life experience, you will make a choice. You will react. You will decide if you hold on to anger, regret, and hurt, or if you will embrace their counterparts. I think I know which type of person you are."

The ghost of a smile flitted across her dry lips. She placed a hand over her lower stomach and looked down at the flat expanse, then back up to his face. Joy rocked through him at the reminder of their progeny, such a powerful emotion that the clouds split in the sky and sunbeams flowed over them, causing Psyche to squint and shiver in his arms.

"Will you take me to your mother?" Psyche bent and lifted the box. "I am ready to see this through."

Cupid smiled and gathered his wife into his arms, holding her close and relishing the feel of her soft cheek against his shoulder, then he took to the skies.

CHAPTER FORTY-ONE

CHOICE

Psyche

EVEN WITH MY HUSBAND AT MY SIDE, I WAS TERRIFIED WALKING into the home of Venus. We had first made a stop at Cupid's palace, where I quickly ate, bathed, and dressed, taking time to pet a very excited Mino as Spinx wound herself over and over through my legs, calling up to me with her *meows*. Oh, how I'd missed them!

I declined Cupid's offer to regrow my hair, clinging to that facet of my mortality, and opting for a silk scarf over my head instead.

I had seen in Cupid's eyes that he did not want to leave just yet. His seductive gaze lingered over me, landing back on my eyes, and a curl of heat burrowed at my core. He really did want me. In his full glory, wings draped regally behind him, it was nearly impossible not to slip right out of the gown I'd just donned and climb into his strong arms.

But I wanted my mind and conscience to be clear first. I had to deal with his mother.

So, here we were.

We walked through a high-ceilinged atrium and through a columned walkway to a sun-drenched opening in the center of her property. A gleaming fountain stood in the middle, mesmerizing me, proving that something stronger than water flowed from its bowels. I tore my eyes away as Venus glided from behind it, her chin tilted up, her arms crossed. She gave no hint of how she felt as her eyes landed on me.

"You made it out." She looked at Cupid. "See, son. All that commotion for nothing."

He took a step forward, but I grasped his wrist. "Your box of ointment, goddess."

Her eyes flitted downward as I moved forward, holding it out. For a moment, she looked as if she might blast me away with her power, but I moved forward with careful, steady steps, stopping close enough for her to accept the box. She took it and eyed me.

"Congratulations, mortal girl."

In a torrent of bravery, I responded, "Thank you, Mother."

Her eyes widened and blazed, making Cupid chuckle and move forward to join us. He wrapped a hand over my shoulder.

"Is that all?" Venus asked. "I am very busy."

"One more thing," I said, placing a hand on my abdomen. "Is the child all right? After all I've been through, I cannot help but worry."

Venus took two shallow breaths before her eyes lowered to my belly, a quick glance, then back up to my eyes.

"Everything is fine. You carry a resilient soul." She peered at her son again. "I am not surprised."

A smile of relief beamed from my face as I thanked her and smiled up into Cupid's beautiful eyes. My heart ached to look upon him and receive his gaze so richly in return. He gave my shoulder a squeeze.

Both Venus and Cupid lifted their eyes to the sky, foreheads scrunching.

"Who could that be?" his mother whispered.

I strained my senses but could not hear or see a thing. Cupid took my hand and led me back a few steps until we were under the protective awning. He stepped slightly in front of me as a massive carriage of gold and bronze set down from the sky, drawn by two large, immortal war horses with hooves and teeth that could slice. In the chariot was an enormous male in grand, gilded attire, leaving no doubt in my mind he was a god of the highest power. His beard and hair were thick, perfect waves of rich brown. In his hand was a lustrous thunderbolt as large as a staff. He turned an eye to Venus with a nod, then Cupid, and then me.

By instinct, my hand slipped from Cupid's and I slid to the ground, bowing on my knees, my head down, my heart beating as if I were winded. My body and soul knew without a doubt— this was the god of the sky and thunder—Jupiter himself.

"The rumors are true," his glorious, rumbling voice said, making me shudder. "Cupid has taken a mortal female?"

"I have, Lord Jupiter," my husband said with pride that made me melt further into the marble floors. "Her name is Princess Psyche."

"Ah. *Soul.*" I felt the king's eyes boring into me. "Stand, dear Psyche."

Cupid took my hand and helped me to my feet. I was still weary and weak, though free of pain now. It took all my effort to look at Jupiter. Gods, he *glowed.* To behold such a supreme being was too much for my senses.

"Though, I wonder," Jupiter said. "How much of what I heard was truth, and how much was gossip? Enlighten me, Venus."

The goddess lifted her chin. "I certainly shall."

She began her side of the tale, and in truth, it was embarrassing to hear her speak of the faithlessness of my parents and people.

When it got to the part about Cupid attempting to strike

me with his arrow to make me fall in love with a loathsome pig farmer, but accidentally striking himself instead, I gasped and stared up at him. Was that a blush clawing up his neck to his cheeks?

I recalled that day. The strange yearning to see the piglets. It made me short of breath to think what would have happened if Cupid had struck me.

Jupiter chuckled, grasping the edges of the chariot as mirth overtook him. Apparently, the thought of Cupid acting a fool in love was amusing to both him and Venus, but the thought sickened me. Was that why he loved me? Because of the tincture?

"But long after the effects of the potions wore off," Venus said, "he still acted strangely, dragging out his task. I knew something was not right."

"He still loved her." Jupiter peered between the three of us, then back at Venus. "Fascinating. Go on."

Cupid squeezed my fingers, and I exhaled. It wasn't the potion. His mother continued, detailing exactly how Cupid had sent every eligible suitor running from me, and then outlining their bargain. I felt ill by the time she finished. Together, they had toyed with my family, playing with those suitors and my life as if we were inconsequential. To them, we were nothing.

I was nothing.

I pulled my hand away from Cupid to wipe my face, which was dry, and then I crossed my arms. When I did not reach for his hand again, Cupid gave me a tight-browed glance. I kept my eyes on Venus as she spoke.

She'd disguised herself as the old crone and given my family false information about Cupid, hoping I would beg for them to visit, knowing my husband might succumb to my wishes.

Then she outlined the tasks. Jupiter's face was lit up as if watching a theatre performance or gladiators in the arena. I had mixed feelings about being fodder for the gods' entertainment, although I knew that was what humans were for. It was impossible not to take it personally.

As she spoke of the tasks, Cupid stepped away, his arms crossing.

"And so, I left her at the tower with the box and instructions, and today she returned to me, the task completed."

Her words were matter-of-fact, not letting on how she felt about my success. I felt Jupiter's eyes on me.

"Tell us every detail of your journey."

Could I refuse? I wanted to but dared not. The entire ordeal was beyond humiliating. I started with how I had been beaten by the servants of Venus. She held a hand over her chest in innocence while Jupiter raised a disappointed eyebrow and Cupid's hands tightened into fists.

I went on, telling every detail as he had asked, though I could not muster any excitement. I gave the facts, rather monotone as I stared dead ahead at the fountain, not caring if the king of the gods enjoyed my retelling or not.

I probably should have cared.

When I finished explaining how I had awoken in Cupid's arms, I swear Jupiter's eyes were gleaming. Was it possible my journey had pulled at his heartstrings?

"I told you not to open the box," Venus scolded.

"You did," I agreed. "And I regret it for many reasons. I was not in my right mind."

"Let me ask you this," Jupiter said. "After all you have been through, more than any mortal woman I have known, how do you feel now about our god of love?"

I swallowed, looked at my sheepish husband, then back at the king of the gods.

"I find it disheartening that the god of love could cause so much suffering. Not only in my life, but the lives of others." I felt Cupid stiffen beside me.

"I have always wondered the same," Jupiter said, eyeing Cupid. "But it was only a matter of time before he succumbed to the greatness of adoration himself. He was merely awaiting his perfect match—a woman who would make him work for her love. A woman with the strength of heart to take on a goddess and face death, then live to tell about it. Ah, yes, mortal, our Cupid has been waiting for *you*."

I dropped my eyes as emotion overcame me, heating my chest and causing my limbs to tingle. A response eluded me. I wanted to believe the king of the gods. Indeed, what he said should have filled me with humbled appreciation. But as much as my heart wanted to grasp those romantic words and cling to Cupid, there was new information to consider.

My head tilted up to Cupid, and the absolute plea in his eyes nearly broke me. I pressed my lips together.

Venus stepped toward Jupiter. "Tell me you are not encouraging this."

"I am more than encouraging it," he said, turning his attention to Cupid and me. "I am offering a gift to the couple, if they so choose to remain married after all they have been through."

My heart gave a start, and I shared a curious glance with Cupid. He raised a shoulder and sounded like an innocent boy in a man's glorious body as he spoke.

"I want nothing more than to be with Psyche."

All eyes landed on me. Confusion clouded my head, squeezing, causing me to close my eyes and drop my chin. "I...don't know. I need time."

Cupid's audible intake of air gutted me. He was scared.

Venus made a wrathful sound of disgust. "You reject the love of a god? My son? He could have any woman—"

"Mother, *please*," Cupid said.

Jupiter held up a hand. "She has been through much. I daresay she needs a moment."

I flashed him a quick, obliged rise of my lips that slipped away. "Yes, king of the gods. Thank you for understanding. But I need more than a moment." I braced myself to be brave. "Would it be possible to return to my isle while I think?"

Jupiter chuckled. "The heart of a queen, this one."

Cupid's eyes bore into me, but I dared not look at him lest I make a rash decision. Jupiter snapped his fingers and Zephyr appeared. "Take the girl back to her isle."

"Psyche," Cupid whispered in anguish, the single word crushing my chest. I stared straight ahead.

My family and people had done much wrong, but so had Venus and Cupid. It would be necessary to wade through all of these conflicting thoughts and feelings before I could move on. The things Cupid had done, even in the name of love, had inadvertently hurt me and others. A god or not, I had to show him I wasn't going to abide by that. I walked to Zep, letting him take me into his arms and straight into the skies, without looking back.

CHAPTER FORTY-TWO

HOME AGAIN

Psyche

ZEPHYR SET ME DOWN ON THE EDGE OF THE DROP OVERLOOK-
ing the lagoon, as I had asked. I patted his shoulder and
thanked him. With a nod, he set off, raising the ends of the
shawl over my head, and causing my skirts to twist around my
legs. I smiled weakly at the cloudy sky where he'd disappeared,
feeling a strange sensation of imbalance, though I'd stood at that
ledge hundreds of times before.

I was at a new precipice. I had a choice. If I wanted, I could
stay here on this isle and become a spinster, raising my child
where I'd been born. Nobody would fault me after what I'd been
through. Rumors would swirl unabashedly, and people would
pity me, but I didn't care about what anyone thought anymore.
Not even my parents or sisters. It only mattered what I thought.

I turned and jumped.

When I hit the water, I had hoped to feel as carefree as the
last time I'd taken that leap, but as I came up and gulped the fresh
sea air, I only felt heavy and tired. And then I wondered if the
jump had hurt the baby. Surely not. But I realized with a pang of
sadness that it might be the last jump I made. At least for a long
while. I was not the girl I used to be.

I was too weak to tread water for very long. My sea friends
seemed to instinctively know this, because they showed up, nudging me, allowing me to hold their fins as they pulled me ashore. I

thanked them with soft kisses and lay on the shore there catching my breath. Then I trudged up the path toward my family's lands, securing the damp shawl over my head again.

The first bright sensation of joy hit me when Olive and Berry came baying down the path, ears flopping, recognizing me at once. I bent to scratch their ears, laughing as they plied me with wet kisses, causing me to wonder about Mino and Sphinx. How I missed their sweetness. Would they remember me? The hounds joined me as I walked the path.

It had been cloudy when I arrived, and now the skies darkened further. All around me I frowned at the yellowed grasses. At this time of year there should have been flowers blooming and green lushness all around, but the land appeared famished. Apprehension filled me.

Nearing the guarded tunnel into the royal fortress, I opted for covering my face with the shawl and continuing into town instead, the dogs on my heels. I walked through the market and the streets, keeping my head down. It was as I feared. The people appeared frail and hungry. Baskets usually overflowing with food wares were low, their fruits and vegetables pale and shriveled. Prices being shouted were higher than usual. A blight had overcome the isle.

When I came to the gates of our castle, I was relieved to see no piles of offerings.

"Sorry, miss, but you'll have to move along," said one of the guards. I approached the gates and pulled back my shawl, revealing my face and ragged, wet hair.

"Where is Boldar?" I asked.

The guard's eyes squinted in confusion and then widened.

All at once, he was being shoved aside by a huge hand. I looked into the wide eyes of Boldar, whose mouth hung open as he stared at me.

"Princess!" He wrenched the gates open and dragged me inside, clutching me close to his chest in an embrace. I held him in return, letting his unconditional love flow over me.

"But what are you...? You escaped him!" He pulled back, holding my shoulders to look at me. "What happened to your hair?"

I pulled the shawl back up. "Take me to my parents. I will explain everything."

It was a tale I only wanted to tell once.

The reunion with Mother and Papa was bittersweet. While it was wonderful to see them and to know they had turned their lives back around, they seemed to hold a sadness in their eyes that would not leave, and I knew my own eyes were the same. We had all changed, and it could not be undone. Even the castle seemed forlorn in a way it never had before I'd gone. I spent the afternoon purging the story from my soul without stopping, even for the sticky cakes the kitchen staff brought out.

"A god," Mother whispered, raising a shaking hand to cover her mouth. "I cannot believe it. But we thought...oh, Psyche!" She grasped my hand and I held hers tight. Papa appeared ashen, dabbing a cold sweat from his brow.

"Tell me what has happened here," I said.

Mother and Papa shared a sad glance, my father pressing his lips tight and shaking his head.

"We have not seen a ray of sunshine since before you left," Mother said. "We beg the gods daily for mercy. The temple is filled with what little we, and our people, can offer."

A bout of illness shook me, and I closed my eyes. It was as I feared.

"I will join you at the temple tomorrow." Exhaustion overpowered me. "I must rest."

"Yes, of course," Mother said, still shaken. "You and the

babe." Her eyes were filled with tears as she embraced me again, placing a hand against my stomach, warm and loving.

My parents helped me to my feet and stood silent as Boldar led me to my rooms, where I climbed on top of the bed without bothering with blankets and fell fast asleep.

I woke with Smokey the cat purring and sprawled across my face. I gently slid from underneath her, feeling parched and hungrier than ever. But greater than my need for sustenance was my need to honor the gods.

After dressing and running a brush through my hair, I found Boldar and he led me to my parents, who were already at the temple. I brought the cake, which I so desperately wanted, but would fast for the remainder of the day.

I bowed between my parents, my head down on the cool temple floor, open to the shady skies and cool winds.

"Proserpina," I said, remembering the wife of Pluto's smile. "I was humbled and beyond honored to meet you. I come to you now with my parents, giving all that we have, and forsaking my hunger, beseeching you to bless our lands. Our people and our leaders, have seen the errors of our ways. Yours is the glory, whether you take pity on our isle or not. We will honor you."

We remained on our knees a long while as priests and priestesses chanted and burned incense, wafting the smoke around the temple. We worshiped for so long that my knees ached, my stomach twisting in on itself with hunger. Then warmth hit the back of my legs just as the priestesses and priests cried out.

We lifted our heads and turned to see the beam of sunlight breaking through the clouds, shining on the temple. Mother cried out, bowing again to kiss the temple floor.

"She has heard you," Papa whispered.

We watched in awe and wonder as the dried vines along the edges of the temple began to fill out once again, brightening from brown to green, blossoms of red and lavender sprouting and opening before our eyes. Every human soul in the vicinity cried out. Cheers could be heard outside of the castle grounds.

"Thank you," I said, lifting my face to the sunshine. "Let us remember."

When all offerings had been burned and thanks had been given, I trudged back to my room once again, falling into the bed where I slept until the next morning. Immediately upon waking, nausea rolled through me and I dashed from the bed to a bowl in the bathing chamber. When I'd finished heaving, I touched my stomach.

"There you are, little one. Still with me, I see."

And despite the ongoing feeling of sickness, I was ravenous.

It was time for those cakes.

I ate and drank my fill, and to my surprise, slept for another hour. When I next woke, I felt more like myself than I had in a long while, free from any fear, though something was decidedly missing. I felt like a visitor in my home, but not because of anything my family had done. Something inside of me had changed. I was a woman now.

Mother sent in a maid with shears to even out my hair. As it grew, I quite liked the way the short strands curled around my face and neck.

For those first few days, my parents and Boldar did not bother me, only checking in now and again with silent glances, as if assuring themselves I was really there, really alive. I was glad for the space, because my pregnancy sickness hit with full force during that time. And then my sisters showed, apparently having received messages from Mother about my arrival.

They both kissed me and swept their eyes over me. I felt numb toward them, which caused me remorse. It was not their fault for the part they played in my mistakes. They had been tricked by Venus. But I couldn't help but wish they had listened to me and trusted my instincts instead of making me question my feelings for Cupid.

No, I told myself. They were not to blame for my actions. I tried to shake off the negativity and enjoy their visit.

"I have news," Miracle said over tea, beaming. "I am finally with child!" I cheered. They had been trying for years. Dawn made happy sounds and I jumped to my feet to hug Miracle.

"How magnificent, Sister!" I said, taking her hands. "We shall be mothers together!"

Miracle's brows tightened. "You are pregnant?"

"Did Mother not tell you?" I looked between the two of them, both shaking their heads, though Dawn's frown turned to more of a scowl as the news set in.

"How perfect," Miracle said, squeezing my hands and drawing me in for another hug. "I am so glad to see you are happy. Our children will grow up together! As it should be."

"Married to a god," Dawn said. "Carrying a demigod in your womb. Yes, how wonderful for you, Psyche."

Miracle and I both turned toward her harsh voice. The look of envy Dawn gave me soured my stomach and I wondered if I might be sick again. I had spent the whole day so far feeling ill and was only now able to eat.

"Dawn," Miracle warned. "Psyche has been through much. None of it was her choice. You would do well to show some care." But Dawn continued to stare at me.

"Born beautiful. Married to an immortal. All the while the people were worried and feeling sorry for you. Mother was barely able to leave her bed, while you were whoring with—"

"That is enough!" I stood shaking, peering down at her. "It was one thing to deal with insults from Venus, who did not know me. But you have known me all my life, Sister. If you do not see my true heart by now, you never will!"

She stood, as well. "If you go back to him, you are a fool! You are nothing but his plaything! A poppet he will bore of and discard the moment you begin to grow old. And you *will* grow old, Psyche. Your body will stoop and wrinkle, just like the rest of us! Your beauty will not last forever!"

I gaped at her angry, red face.

But before I could say a word, the windows blasted open and a wind swirled like a funnel, billowing our dresses and raising our hair from our heads. The small cyclone circled Dawn, making her scream and grasp her gown. The overwhelming presence of my husband filled my mind and heart, caressing my skin from toe to scalp. As quickly as he had come, his presence was gone, leaving my sisters panting and clutching their chests, and leaving me with a deep longing before I returned to my senses.

Was Cupid spying on me? The fiend! Why should I be surprised after learning he had haunted this castle my entire year of courtship? Like everything he did, I was partially flattered, and partially maddened.

Dawn pointed a trembling finger at me. "You are cursed!" Then she ran from the room. Her judgment dug into my chest as sharp as a dagger. My own sister.

I reached for the chair and sat heavily, my head reeling. Miracle fell to her knees before me, taking my hands and kissing my fingers. In her eyes I saw true understanding.

"Do not hear her words, spoken in jealousy." She smiled up at me. "You are not cursed, little sister. You are deserved. You are blessed."

CHAPTER FORTY-THREE

WASTED MINUTES

Psyche

I NEEDED OUT OF THE CASTLE. I NEEDED TO WALK. BOLDAR FOL-lowed me, without question, as I donned the hooded shawl and plain sandals. It was market day, and I longed to lose my-self in a throng of people, their voices and clacking carts drowning out the sounds of my own thoughts.

First, I walked to the corner where the pig farmer kept his stall. I remained out of his sight, but my breathing became heavy as I stared at the man Cupid had chosen to make me fall in love with. Ghastly. How close I had come to being his wife. It sickened me. I peered up at the nearby stall's roof where he had most likely perched, drawing his bow, accidentally striking his own self.

A smile crept onto my face just before a sense of awareness had me sucking in a breath. I turned quickly to see Leodes stand-ing there across the way, leaning against a battered stall wall, his arms crossed, sexier than any human form deserved to be. I glanced over at Boldar, who stared hard in the opposite direction.

"Have you enchanted him?" I accused.

Leodes, *Cupid*, shrugged. "You do not need his watchful eye. I am here."

I crossed my arms. "You are supposed to be giving me time and space."

Again, he shrugged, then grinned, sending that familiar curl of need through me. Cupid, the god, was all light and beauty. This version of him was wickedly dark, bringing back those memories of innocent pining. I swallowed and held fast to my shawl.

"I did not want to strike you, Psyche." He jutted his chin toward the pig farmer. "I was smitten from the moment we spoke." Leodes pulled something small from his pocket, tossing it in the air and catching it, then holding it between his fingers. My mouth opened at the sight of the tiny wooden mountain lion cub.

"It has become a bit worn," he said, admiring it. "Not a day goes by that I do not look upon it, rubbing where your fingers touched, remembering your childhood tale."

I lifted my chin, pretending I wasn't affected. "You should not be here. Shame on you." My words were weak in every way. Especially as he strode toward me, the muscles in his legs above his knees flexing with each step. My heart clambered as blood moved quickly under my skin.

He practically pinned me to the wall without ever touching me, his presence overwhelming, his dark eyes boring into mine.

I worked my lips, forcing out the words. "Even if I tell you I don't want to be with you, you will never leave me. Will you?"

"Never." His grin was dark and sensual. "But if that is what you choose, I will not show myself again."

Oh, and what a great pity that would be.

I blinked and stood taller. "And if I take another husband?"

The humor left his features and his eyes hardened, darkening. "I would not show myself."

But he would be there. He would know, and it would hurt him deeply. He would be jealous. A flush of lust for this man, this god in disguise, danced through me with sultry movements.

"I will give you time, beautiful soul." His eyes raked me from top to bottom, as if seeing straight through the fabric to my flushed skin beneath. "I will not show myself until you request it."

"Wait."

Leodes turned, unable to disguise the hope in his eyes. An impishness filled me.

"I want my pets. Mino and Sphinx. They should be here with me."

His jaw flexed, and he nodded. "It will be done."

He turned from me and walked from the small alley, causing Boldar to shake his head and scour the alley in confusion. My knees shook, and I pressed my thighs together.

"I am ready to return," I whispered.

That night, I locked Smokey out of the room. I opened my bed-room window as wide as it could go and climbed between my covers, waiting in the near-darkness.

It didn't take long.

A breeze gusted through the space, rustling the curtains hanging around my bed, and the solitude of the room took on an intensity. I peered around, seeing nothing, but my heart felt him with perfect clarity.

"Show yourself, Husband."

"Husband, is it?"

I inhaled quietly at the magnificent sight of him on my win-dow ledge, leaning back against his massive wings. The moon glinted silver off his locks of icy-platinum hair. His eyes shone like the deep lagoon in summer. One knee was up in his short toga, only a shadow hiding what lie beneath, and his chest was bare, muscles tense. Realizing I'd been holding my breath, I let it out with a shudder.

"Yes. *Husband*. I have not forsaken you. Have you brought my pets?"

He snapped his fingers and Mino and Sphinx appeared on my rug. I clambered to the floor, laughing as I took them in my arms, running my hands over them, dodging kisses on the mouth from the pup, who was nearly at his full height now.

"I am glad to see there is something about my home you miss and intend to keep," Cupid said.

I stood to face him, and the animals began to explore their new room. "Can you blame me for needing time? Your mother's account of the events leading up to our marriage were... troublesome to my heart."

He stood, and once again I found myself holding my breath as he came closer. What a marvel it was to watch the movements of his body, such grace, after being denied the sight during our time together. But his nearness clouded my head. I turned from him and climbed onto the bed, sitting cross-legged in the center.

Cupid came forward and stopped at the edge of the bed, leaning down on his palms, arms rigid, capturing me with those eyes.

"I do not blame you for needing space to think. However, for the first time in my existence, I find myself understanding the drive of humans. The fear that embraces one with the passage of time. Every minute that passes, Psyche, I am filled with an acute awareness of loss, for that minute could have been spent with you."

My heart seized. I took several cleansing breaths. "Pretty words."

"I have many such pretty words I have wanted to say but could not." He began a slow prowl around the end of the bed, never taking his eyes off mine. With every step closer to me, my heart beat faster. I edged away.

"Do you realize how many lives you upended in your goal

to keep me from marrying another? All of those men and their families?"

"I gave them love," he said with a shrug.

"You caused scandal!"

"Because the women were beneath their stations? Psyche…" He clicked his tongue. "Some would say the same for you and me. Such notions are nonsense. Self-important labels humans inflict on their kind to make those in power feel important."

I sighed and crossed my arms. "You are impossible. I'm not sure I can be with a man who does not take responsibility for his past mistakes."

Cupid stiffened, rearing back a fraction. Fear shot through me, certain nobody had ever told the god he'd been mistaken in his life. Except his mother, when it came to me.

"I never punished a soul who did not deserve it."

"My point is that you seem to do more punishing than blessing. And you seem to…enjoy it."

It was his turn to cross his arms. He turned toward the window.

"I admit it. I did enjoy punishing humans. And it has been nearly a century since I flitted about gaily and pierced young people with my arrows of love." He raised a hand in the air as if such notions were childish.

"Why do you sound jaded?"

"Because I am!" He turned to me again. "Humans fall in love so easily, and then they squander it."

"Not all." I thought of my parents.

"Far too many," he said. "And yet, I am a god and could not find anyone to love. I searched every curve of Earth and corner of Olympus, yet not one of the souls I encountered affected me until I saw yours."

I blinked, dropping my face as jealousy scratched my insides with her ugly claws. "You had many women."

Cupid shot to my side in a blink, making me cry out in surprise as he took my face and a wash of warm honey coated my senses. "I cannot recall a single one of their faces, Psyche. Hear what I am saying!"

The jealousy fell away, shattering, because I believed him, and I wanted to drag him down onto the bed with me.

I shifted past him, standing and walking several steps away. Mino began to jump at my legs, but Cupid snapped a finger and the puppy immediately curled up on the rug, asleep. When he began to move toward me, I held up a hand.

"I cannot think straight when you are so near."

"Why must you always think straight? I enjoy your crooked thoughts."

I covered my mouth as a quick laugh jumped out, and our eyes met. Everything inside me softened, but I still held back, needing something more from him that I couldn't name.

Cupid took a tentative step toward me, his palms up. "Jupiter has given his blessing. That means no one, including my meddling mother, will dare to impede us." He took another step. "I wish you could see your soul right now as I see it. How bright you are in your righteousness."

My chin rose as my breathing came faster. He stepped closer, near enough to smell, and I dizzied.

"Your beauty will never fade in my eyes, Psyche." His words and voice rolled over me, sweet and heady. "My wife. My princess. The one who shot me with her love."

My thoughts clarified, and as he stepped closer, I held up my palms to stop him. His brow drew together in worry.

"It is not only about me," I explained. "There is so much pain in the world. So many broken hearts. So much suffering." My eyes welled just thinking about it—about the power Cupid held.

His whisper was fervent. "And I shall never again raise my bow to add to the chaos of man. I swear it to you. Only the elixir of love will adorn my arrows."

A flutter of dove's wings soared through me at the assurance I needed.

I hesitantly brought up my hand, and he stilled as my palm hovered over his cheek. The corners of his full lips lifted.

"Yes, my love. You can touch me now. *Please* touch me."

My hand sank against his warm cheek and he brought his hand up to cover mine, closing his eyes. A fierce protective instinct overtook me as my heart fully claimed him.

"Husband," I said, my voice going husky. "You have seen all of me. It is time I saw you."

In a flash, without moving a muscle, the elegant wrapping around his waist disappeared, leaving him standing before me in all his naked glory, a look of amused pride on his face. And why shouldn't he be proud? Gods above. The full sight of him was almost too much for this pregnant mortal to take. All my bravado dissipated as my body lit up in a thousand sparks of heat.

I stepped back, overcome with nervousness and lust, and he walked forward until my back was at the wall.

"Or, if you prefer—" In a flash, he was Leodes, naked as the day before me.

"I…" I clammed up like a bumbling fool, which made him chuckle, his smile turning roguish. I forced lame words from my lips. "You will spoil me, giving in to my every whim so quickly. The both of you."

"I am not sorry." He took my face, moving forward so that our bodies were flush, a soft moan passing my lips. He flashed back into his true form. My eyes fluttered closed, overwhelmed. "Will you be shy now that your eyes can behold me? Perhaps if I disappeared for a moment…"

To my shock, he lowered to his knees and lifted the hem of my gown, pulling it over his head. Disappear, indeed! I held onto his head through the sheer layers as his mouth found my center, and my head flew back, hitting the wall with a satisfying *thump*. Cupid's hands held my backside, not letting me fall, though my legs seemed to lose their bones.

A brisk knock on my door made us go still.

"Princess?" called Boldar. "Are you quite all right?"

"My husband is here!" I blurted, then bit my lip. "Everything is fine!"

"Uh…all right, then." He cleared his throat and I heard his steps quickly retreating down the hall. I giggled briefly before Cupid's magical tongue erased all remaining thoughts.

I could scarcely move the next morning. My body was as exhausted as it had been upon returning from the underworld. That was saying a lot. When the sounds of seabirds made me open my eyes, I found Cupid leaning on his elbow next to me, smelling of honey. My blood thrummed at the serious look in his eyes. And then sickness pushed its way upward and I sprung from the bed.

Cupid was at my heels, rubbing my back as I retched. "Psyche, my love, let me take this ailing from you."

"No," I said, wiping my mouth, breathing hard. I did not want any godly magic. "I will tell you if it becomes unbearable, but I want to feel every bit of this pregnancy. If it is not harming me, or the child, I want it."

Cupid led me to a settee, and I lay back as he dabbed my face with a cool cloth. Mino jumped up beside me, laying the length of my hip and resting his head on my thigh, peering up at me with worry. I petted him and gave a weary smile to Cupid before closing my eyes.

"You are an attentive husband," I whispered. When he remained quiet, I opened my eyes to find him staring up at me from where he kneeled on the floor.

"So, you will remain my wife?"

After last night, I would have thought it was quite obvious, but I smiled and felt his cheek with my fingers. It gave me a thrill to touch him, to see him.

"If you will have me, I will remain your wife until my dying breath. You, me, our child, even Mino and Sphinx while they live. I want us together."

His bow-shaped lips turned up. "Come." He stood, already dressed, and took me by the hand. "Ready yourself. If you are well enough, we must see Jupiter at once."

"Jupiter?" My head spun as he urged me toward my clothing. I grabbed a green stola and pulled it over my head, fluffing my hair with tired arms.

Cupid tugged me forward, his face near mine. "He will make our marriage official for all of Olympus to know. And then we have much to decide. Will we live on Earth? Or will you join me at my palace? Every choice is yours, Psyche. You need only tell me."

Joy and disbelief filled me, and I took his smiling face into my hands. "Perhaps, we could travel?"

He lifted me, spinning us and laughing as I held on to his shoulders.

"I will show you all there is to see, Wife. Places in the world so scenic in their primitiveness that only a soul such as yours could look upon them and appreciate the differences of culture without feeling the need to change or conquer."

My eyes widened at his seriousness. In his eyes I saw a thrill of anticipation for our life together that matched my own. I slid down and wrapped my arms tightly around his neck. "I love you, Cupid."

He nearly squeezed the air from me. "And I love you, Psyche. I cannot wait to spend the rest of your life showing you just how much you mean to me."

I pulled back to see his face. "To Jupiter," I said.

"Hold on tight."

CHAPTER FORTY-FOUR

THE GIFT

Psyche

JUPITER'S PALACE PUT CUPID'S TO SHAME. IT WASN'T JUST A palace—it was a glittering city with every manner of immortal creature that one could imagine. Satyrs and centaurs stared at our joined hands as we walked the gold-stoned path through fantastical gardens with flowers as large as my head. A Pegasus walked on the high rooftop, its white coat shining as it stretched its wings as it shook its head.

My ears filled with song and I froze in place. The tune filled my ears and soaked into my soul. The source called to me. I needed to find the musicians. When I attempted to pull away from Cupid, he tugged me back and clicked his tongue, turning his head away from me to shout something. All became quiet and I turned to see three girls with slick, long, black hair draped in seaweed gowns, giggling at me.

"Sirens," Cupid muttered. A sickening realization slid through me. They'd been singing to me, trying to lure me in like some sad sailor, and I had completely succumbed! These immortals had a way of making mortals feel violated with their easy power over us. I glared at the three, and Cupid moved us quickly past them.

At the entrance to Jupiter's palace were two stone gargoyles like ones who guarded the entrance of the underworld, but these were clean and shiny. As we neared, they grew to life, softening and enlarging, their spears glinting in the sun.

"Lord god of love," one of the gargoyles said thickly through massive teeth that curved upward. "You have brought a mortal to Jupiter's home?"

"I have," Cupid said, clutching my hand. "This is Princess Psyche, my wife. Jupiter knows of her. He will grant us entrance."

The gargoyle lifted a hand to signal a younger beastly thing behind him. The creature ran up the alabaster steps faster than my eye could trail and was back just as quickly. He nodded his furry head and spoke with a squeak.

"The king says welcome!"

Cupid smiled at me, and we continued ahead as the gargoyles stepped from our path. I held tight to my husband, nervous about Jupiter's so-called "gift." It was hard to trust the immortals. After today, I would be glad not to step foot in Olympus ever again unless it was Cupid's property.

We were led by a sharply dressed, bearded satyr into a throne room that overwhelmed my senses. So large, so bright, so ornate—I had no idea where to look. My eyes flitted about, one hand on my chest, the other squeezing Cupid's hand hard enough to numb his fingers. It soon became clear where to look as Jupiter rose to his feet at his throne in the center of the room. Cupid bowed at the waist and I dropped to my knees in reverence, never letting go of my husband's hand.

"Stand, please, and come forward."

I couldn't control my nervous reaction, and I was never more grateful to have someone at my side who loved me. My head bowed again to Jupiter as we stood directly before him, and then I peered up into his eyes, like jewels that held the skies inside them. His beard and hair were utter perfection. But it was the way he stood, his imposing height and confidence, that cowed me. Even as he smiled down at me, I felt shy.

"I see you have made amends?" He grinned back and forth between the two of us.

Cupid and I shared a timid smile.

"Yes, Lord King," Cupid said. "We will remain husband and wife...for all of Psyche's days."

I brought a hand to my chest to cover the pang inside.

Jupiter studied us, gripping his thunderbolt. I stared at the thing, not able to wrap my mind around the power it held. All he had to do was point and command, and he could tumble whole mountains. I shivered and moved closer to Cupid.

"As I said, I have a gift." Jupiter walked to the high table nearby, beckoning us over. We followed. On the table were two golden goblets filled with shimmery nectar like the kind my husband had once shown me at his palace, though one appeared darker, like a star-filled night sky.

Cupid squeezed my hand. "What is this?" he asked in a hoarse voice.

"A toast," explained Jupiter. "To your lives together...if you so choose."

I gave Cupid a confused look, but he was staring at Jupiter with wide eyes.

"You don't mean...?"

"I do." Jupiter looked directly at me, and I had to fight the urge to fall to my knees. "I offer you eternal life, Princess Psyche. To be immortal. To live forever with your husband and the babe within you."

I blinked rapidly and swayed before righting myself. "I—what?"

The god chuckled, and Cupid's breathing quickened. "Truly, Lord King? But this...this is beyond..." My husband was beside himself, unable to finish a sentence. He turned to me and grasped me around the waist, lifting me and spinning me, making me scream with dizzy laughter as I gripped his shoulders.

"Immortality, Psyche!" Cupid set me down, his smile radiant. "You, me, our child!"

"Verily," I whispered, at a loss, because this was bigger than anything I could understand. The room spun, and I had to rest my forehead against his chest.

Jupiter's voice filled the silence. "I will leave you to decide."

I wanted to lift my face, to thank him, but bewilderment had struck me dumb. Cupid had to gently pry me back from his chest to tilt my face up to his. He must have seen the terror in my eyes because his own filled with disappointment.

"You do not want to be with me forever?"

"Of course, I do!" I whispered. "I just...it is so...permanent."

His shoulders drooped, but he managed a reassuring smile. "You are right. It is permanent. Perhaps I should give you a moment."

I held tightly to his waist when he tried to pull away. "Don't leave me. I need to process this, but I want you right here." I went into his arms and he wrapped them securely around me as my mind raced through the information.

Immortality. Why was I hesitant? I loved Cupid with all of my heart, but in that moment of absolute clarity, I was able to see my fear for the ugly thing it was. I feared Cupid would stop loving me, and I would be stuck living forever without him, long after my family was gone. The ultimate loneliness.

If I chose not to accept this gift, I would age and eventually make my way to the Underworld again. Without Cupid. He would live, unable to get to my soul, wherever it ended up. Would he find another to love? Would I spend eternity in the afterlife longing for the only soul who truly accepted and understood me? And who would take on the role of mother for my child?

My eyes squeezed shut. Cupid was not human. He'd had

many lovers in his lifetime, but had never loved until me. He was not an indecisive man of Earth, who allowed his sentiments to change on a whim. What did my instincts tell me? That he loved me. That his love for me would endure. So, would I allow my fears to steal the future from both of us?

No. I would never again let my fears lead me into regret.

I choose love.

I pulled back from my husband, letting our fingers slip away. The look of worry on his face nearly broke me. My lips rose into a nervous smile and I turned to the table, taking the darker goblet in my shaking hand.

"Is this one mine?"

Again, that smile of radiance filled his face, making my heart jump. He leaned down and took my lips with his, a firm profession without words.

"Are you certain?" he whispered against my mouth, our foreheads touching.

"I am," I whispered back.

"I will spend eternity making sure you never regret it." He took up his goblet, and we touched the rims together. "Forever, my love."

"Forever," I said.

And together, we drank.

EPILOGUE

Psyche

I THOUGHT I KNEW WHAT LOVE MEANT, BUT THE MOMENT I LAID eyes on the tiny person whom my body had wrought, a new type of love coursed through me, stronger than any instinct before it. She was mine to care for. Mine to teach. Mine to protect.

I peered up at Cupid, who stared down at our daughter with awestruck adoration, and I knew he felt the same. I had to amend my thoughts.

Ours to care for, teach, and protect. Ours to love.

"We shall call her Voluptus," Cupid whispered, meaning *Hedone: Pleasure.*

"Beautiful," I agreed. Together we lay there, admiring every detail of her being, from her tiny toes with miniscule nails to her silken ringlets of glistening tawny. Each mewl she made, every stretch, had us laughing and fawning. Even Mino kept trying to edge his way between us to lick whatever portion of the babe he could reach.

Sphinx could not have been less interested.

Renae bustled back into the room with a fresh basin of steaming water and clean cloths. She'd been my midwife, coaching me through the entire delivery. The woman could do it all. Cupid had wanted to place his hands on my body and remove every vestige of pain, but I would not allow it. Well, I allowed him to relieve my back when I thought it would crack in half. But I had wanted to feel as much as possible, to have the experience so many women had endured before me.

"Your soul right now," Cupid said, his eyes roaming me warmly. He shook his head as if there were no words, and my cheeks heated. I reached for his hand.

"I love you, Husband. I love our little family. I could want nothing more."

His fingers entwined with mine. "Your words echo my own heart."

We stared for a long moment before I knew I had to breach a delicate subject. "I would like my family to meet her. Mother, Papa, and Miracle. Will you bring them?"

His jaw was set, but he nodded, and my heart softened further. Since becoming immortal, visiting Earth was frowned upon, and in truth I had no urge to go there. But I did miss my family, and if they were willing to visit, we would bring them. Dawn wanted nothing to do with me. Miracle had said she was horrified to hear I'd given up my mortality. Her exact words had been, "Am I expected to bow down and worship her now?"

Nothing I did would be found pleasing to Dawn, and though it hurt deeply, I had to let her go. As for the rest of my family, their lives would be snuffed faster than I could blink. I would cherish every moment spent with them. Knowing their mortality was so fleeting caused me to hold my daughter tighter.

From outside the windows came a *whooshing* sound. Both Cupid and Renae rushed to the windows, their faces darkening.

"It is my mother," Cupid said. "I will send her away, Psyche. I will not have you upset."

"No," I said, sitting up to bundle the baby in a tight swaddle. "She should meet her granddaughter. Renae, send her in."

The servant gave a nod and left us. Cupid paced at the end of the bed.

"Worry not," I told him, but he glared at the door anyhow.

Inside, I was nervous too. I'd only seen Venus once since

Jupiter had gifted me with immortality. She had been silent on the matter. I had no idea how she felt and if she still harbored the abhorrence toward me that led to my near death. But I trusted her not to try anything now, and not to hurt the baby.

Venus swept into the room, her regal posture still affecting me as it always did. I wondered if the effect of the goddess would ever lessen.

Her eyes bypassed Cupid and me, going straight to the baby, and I watched as a transformation took place in her being.

She softened. Her eyes. Her stance.

"A girl?" she said. "And what shall you name her?"

"Voluptus." Cupid moved forward to stand at the edge of the bed.

A true smile formed on her radiant face, making me catch my breath. Her eyes never left the babe.

"Venus," I said. "Please, come meet your granddaughter. She will want to know you."

I never thought it was possible to see the goddess out of control of her emotions, but as I held the small bundle out, she came forward with haste, working her lips and swallowing back whatever sensations overcame her. She stopped short, looking at me as if I might pull the child back at the last moment.

My arms remained outstretched, although I was not able to spare a smile for the goddess. I would not keep her from her grandchild, but she would have to earn her way into my good graces.

Venus took Voluptus into her arms and immediately began rocking from side to side in a gentle sway. "Her eyes are like gems, lips like petals." She lifted the child to her face and breathed deeply of her hair, closing her eyes. "The scent of innocence. Oh, Cupid! There is nothing sweeter."

Even with his arms crossed and his stiff demeanor, he

managed a small smile at his mother's behavior. "This is true," he said.

Without looking away from the child, Venus whispered, "Thank you. I can only hope you will come to see how being a parent can cause fierce protectiveness. Some might say irrationalities. You will want the best for her, and at some point in time, she will want what you do not think is best."

My eyes burned, realizing this was as close as we would probably ever come to an apology from Venus.

"When that day comes," I said. "We will do our best to remain...rational."

"I promise nothing." Cupid's declaration caused Venus and I to stare at his serious face, and then his mother let out a burst of laughter that tickled my ears, making Cupid's chest shake with a deep chuckle of his own. I gave him a mock glare and shook my head, smiling despite myself.

When Voluptus let out a small cry, Venus shushed and rocked her. I felt my breasts tighten and tingle in a strange, nonsexual way.

"I think she is hungry," I said.

Without question, Venus came forward and placed the bundle of preciousness back into my arms. She and Cupid watched with rapt attention as I nestled our daughter to my chest, her skin against mine, and she latched on to feed. I let out a small gasp at the sensation of my body nourishing hers, and I looked up at Cupid with a smile of wonder. His own eyes were filled with all the things he felt, overwhelming me in his intensity. All for me. For our daughter. Even for his mother. Our family.

All for us.

THE END.

ACKNOWLEDGEMENTS

In the spring of 2018 on a thread in my Facebook group (Wendy Higgins Book Chat) Heather Young-Nichols mentioned her infatuation with the story of Cupid and Psyche and said I should write it. Not familiar with their tale, I ran to Google and immediately fell in love. Thank you for believing in me, Heather. I have all the heart-eyes and heart-hands for you, babe. Also, I just want to say HI AND I LOVE YOU to all my Sweeties in that group!

Massive gratitude to my beta readers for their priceless feedback and encouragement: Heather Young-Nichols, Katie McGarry, Amalie Howard, Jamie Shaw, Jen Fisher, Kelley Vitollo (Nyrae Dawn), Virginia Pepe, Jennifer Kline, Jill Wilson, Hilary Mahalchick, Laura Thalassa, Holly Klatt, and Malissa Coy.

Thank you to the incredible, magician artist, Jennifer Munswami for my cover. I still get that faraway, dreamy feeling when I stare at it.

To my agent, Hannah Ekren, I am thrilled for our new partnership and excited to see where this road of imagination and literary adventure will take us.

Thanks to Stacey Blake of Champagne Book Design for her detailed formatting. And Laura Wehr for her keen editorial eye.

As always, much love to my friends and family, especially my mama (Nancy Parry), and my kids Autumn, and Cayden, for continuing to be excited for me in all things and dealing with my writerly eccentricities. I love spending this life with you.

Isaiah 43:2.